A CUT ABOVE

The four goons seemed to materialize in front of him out of the gloom. Mike Assad sized them up as the local tough guys; a quartet of miserable buffoons who shared the same qualities and quantities of meanness and stupidity, and would happily kill him to strip his corpse to get a few rupees for his clothing. They pulled knives from beneath their *chadors,* and grinned.

They didn't waste time. The leader led his buddies into the fray. Mike sidestepped, and the guy was sent sprawling with a wicked *wakite* punch to the kidneys. A quick *yubi* punch to the second dropped him straight down in the dirt, while a vicious *marui* kick knocked the third over on his back. The fourth, who had been bringing up the rear, wisely jumped over his prostrate buddies and ran away down the alley into the darkness.

Mike stopped long enough to take a calming breath and then picked up the three knives. He chose the best to keep, and tossed the rest onto the top of the nearby mud huts.

SEALS
BATTLECRAFT

JACK TERRAL

JOVE BOOKS, NEW YORK

THE BERKLEY PUBLISHING GROUP
Published by the Penguin Group
Penguin Group (USA) Inc.
375 Hudson Street, New York, New York 10014, USA
Penguin Group (Canada), 90 Eglinton Avenue East, Suite 700, Toronto, Ontario M4P 2Y3, Canada
(a division of Pearson Penguin Canada Inc.)
Penguin Books Ltd., 80 Strand, London WC2R 0RL, England
Penguin Group Ireland, 25 St. Stephen's Green, Dublin 2, Ireland (a division of Penguin Books Ltd.)
Penguin Group (Australia), 250 Camberwell Road, Camberwell, Victoria 3124, Australia (a division of
Pearson Australia Group Pty. Ltd.)
Penguin Books India Pvt. Ltd., 11 Community Centre, Panchsheel Park, New Delhi—110 017, India
Penguin Group (NZ), Cnr. Airborne and Rosedale Roads, Albany, Auckland 1310, New Zealand
(a division of Pearson New Zealand Ltd.)
Penguin Books (South Africa) (Pty.) Ltd., 24 Sturdee Avenue, Rosebank, Johannesburg 2196, South Africa

Penguin Books Ltd., Registered Offices: 80 Strand, London WC2R 0RL, England

This is a work of fiction. Names, characters, places, and incidents either are the product of the author's
imagination or are used fictitiously, and any resemblance to actual persons, living or dead, business
establishments, events, or locales is entirely coincidental. The publisher does not have any control over
and does not assume any responsibility for author or third-party websites or their content.

SEALS: BATTLECRAFT

A Jove Book / published by arrangement with the author.

PRINTING HISTORY
Jove mass-market edition / August 2006

Copyright © 2006 by The Berkley Publishing Group.
Cover design by George Long.
Cover illustration by Larry Ronstadt.
Text design by Kristin del Rosario.

ISBN: 0-515-14172-0

JOVE®
Jove Books are published by The Berkley Publishing Group,
a division of Penguin Group (USA) Inc.,
375 Hudson Street, New York, New York 10014.
JOVE is a registered trademark of Penguin Group (USA) Inc.
The "J" design is a trademark belonging to Penguin Group (USA) Inc.

PRINTED IN THE UNITED STATES OF AMERICA

10   9   8   7   6   5   4   3   2   1

Special Acknowledgment to
Patrick E. Andrews
82nd Airborne Division and 12th Special Forces Group
(Airborne)

NOTE: Enlisted personnel in this book are identified by their ranks (petty officer third class, chief petty officer, master chief petty officer, etc.) rather than their ratings (boatswain's mate, yeoman, etc.) for clarification of status and position within the chain of command.

TABLE OF ORGANIZATION
BRANNIGAN'S BRIGANDS

COMMAND ELEMENT

Lieutenant William "Wild Bill" Brannigan
(Commanding Officer)

PO2C Francisco "Frank" Gomez
(Rifleman/Commo Chief)

PO3C James "Doc" Bradley
(Rifleman/Hospital Corpsman)

FIRST ASSAULT SECTION

Lieutenant (JG) James Cruiser
(Section Commander)

PO2C Bruno Puglisi
(SAW Gunner)

ALPHA FIRE TEAM

CPO Matthew "Matt" Gunnarson
(Fire Team Leader)

PO2C Garth Redhawk
(Rifleman)

PO3C Chadwick "Chad" Murchison
(Rifleman)

BRAVO FIRE TEAM

PO1C Michael "Connie" Concord
(Fire Team Leader)

PO2C David "Dave" Leibowitz
(Rifleman)

PO3C Arnold "Arnie" Bernardi
(Rifleman)

2ND ASSAULT SECTION

SCPO Buford Dawkins
(Section Commander)

PO2C Josef "Joe" Miskoski
(SAW Gunner)

CHARLIE FIRE TEAM

PO1C Michael "Milly" Mills
(Fire Team Leader)

PO2C Reynauld "Pech" Pecheur
(Rifleman)

PO2C Peter "Pete" Dawson
(Rifleman)

DELTA FIRE TEAM

PO1C Guttorm "Gutsy" Olson
(Fire Team Leader)

PO2C Andrei "Andy" Malachenko
(Rifleman)

PO3C Guy Devereaux
(Rifleman)

ATTACHED

Lieutenant (JG) Veronica Rivers
(Navigation/Weapons Systems Officer)

PO1C Paul Watkins
(Helmsman)

PO2C Bobby Lee Atwill
(Turbine System Technician)

Excerpt from Sun Tzu's *The Art of War* as paraphrased by Petty Officer 2nd Class Bruno Puglisi of Brannigan's Brigands:

It don't matter so much if you outnumber the enemy as long as the son of a bitches got no idea how many guys you really got. In a case like that, it's the way you deploy your troops that'll determine whose ass gets kicked.

Reprint of an article that appeared in a recent edition of *Advanced Technological and Scientific Design Magazine*.

THE *WATERFLYER*

By Eduard Andiwaczeski

Two Florida brothers have produced a prototype of an ACV that could revolutionize commercial traffic on United States rivers

The *Waterflyer* is an ACV (Air-Cushion Vehicle) but is not designed to carry passengers as are other similar craft. Instead, its unique function is to serve as a pusher-vessel in barge operations moving cargo via river transportation systems. The craft was created and built by brothers John and Harry DuBose at their workshop facilities along the Indian River in Brevard County, Florida. This river is part of the Intracoastal Waterway, which allows boat travel from Key West, Florida, all the way north to Boston on the Atlantic coast. On the Gulf of Mexico, the waterway connects Apalachee Bay, Florida, with Brownsville, Texas. The DuBose brothers—John, the older, is forty-two and Harry is thirty-eight—got the idea for their ACV from watching barge traffic passing by their Pine Island home.

"The barges were slow and ponderous," John explained. "Harry and I figured the transport of their loads would turn a better profit if the deliveries were faster. The biggest challenge of the concept was to have pusher-vessels that would be powerful drivers, yet could maintain high speeds at the same time."

"Technical projects are a hobby of ours," Harry added. "We've been coming up with ideas and

inventions since we were kids. At first we thought that
a propulsion system that combined both underwater
and air propellers might do the trick."

"But when we considered the drag on the pusher-
vessel going through the water, we knew that wasn't a
practical approach," John said. "So we had to try a
completely different methodology."

Although neither brother has had any scientific or
technical schooling, their innate ability to solve physical and abstract problems has amazed even the quintes-
sential rocket scientists at nearby Cape Canaveral. The
brothers admit they have consulted with several of
their aerospace friends on questions involving certain
disciplines and scientific difficulties that stymied their
progress now and then. One NASA engineer who
wished to remain anonymous described them as 21st-
century Wright Brothers who have the ability to absorb
technical knowledge, then turn it into reality. It also
helps that their private funding is practically unlimited.
John and Harry are heirs to the long-established Du-
Bose Citrus Farms in Orange County, Florida.

"We eventually turned to an air-cushion-vehicle
concept," John explained. "That eliminated the drag
problem, but there wasn't much of a possibility for it
to be a powerful pusher."

"Right," Harry interjected in their characteristic
way of speaking in turn. "The problem was the power
plant. We had to have something really strong to
move that hummer along while shoving tons of
weight ahead of it."

"We got on the internet and started making inquiries until we found out about this outfit in Argentina," John said. "They had developed a real
ass-kicking engine for moving sled-type equipment
vehicles down in Antarctica. We flew down and took a
look at it."

"The problem was that it was too small," Harry

added. "So we sat down with their chief design engineer and came up with some solid ideas. The company boss was so impressed that he retooled one section of his factory to accommodate the concept."

This company, Poder-Ventaja, S.A. of Cabo Blanco, offered a part ownership in the resultant product, but the brothers settled for a free engine with the options of claiming two more in the future. Four months after their return to Florida, their power plant arrived from Argentina and was installed aboard the newly christened *Waterflyer*.

"Things worked out better than expected," John stated happily. "My brother and I have ended up with an excellent product. We made a couple of short runs for a local barge outfit with great results."

"We just have to find somebody who'll buy it," Harry pointed out. "So far, none of the barge companies we've contacted are interested. They don't seem to be overly concerned about speeding up their operations."

"They simply don't have a 'hurry-up' frame of mind," John said.

The vessel is forty feet long, twenty feet wide, and propelled by a pair of eight-foot, six-bladed variable-pitch airscrews mounted on the stern. These and oversize rudders provide a fantastic turning radius that whips the ACV around on the proverbial dime. The lift comes from a ten-foot, twelve-bladed fan located on the bottom of the craft. The engine is a 1,000-horsepower Poder-Ventaja Marine Gas Turbine from Argentina. It has moved the vessel at a speed of ninety miles per hour over open ocean without a load. The brothers estimate that they could push forty tons of barges along at half that speed. Needless to say, it is *not* fuel-efficient!

The cabin offers excellent all-around vision and has such amenities as a head, a triple-tiered bunk, and a small but functional galley that contains a microwave oven and small refrigerator. The engine room is located in the aft portion of the cabin. Two semi-rigid dinghies are mounted on the sides of the hull for extracurricular maritime activities.

As of this writing, the prototype sits at the Du-Bose workshop dock, except for the times when the brothers take it out for tune-up runs between Titusville and Melbourne. It is an excellent vessel waiting for the right outfit to come along and take advantage of its features.

CHAPTER 1

PETTY Officer Second Class Mike Assad had disappeared.

The Arab-American member of Brannigan's Brigands wasn't AWOL, assigned on a TDy detail, on furlough, or transferred to a different outfit. He had simply vanished. Even though this extraordinary situation caused reactions from mere curiosity to outright anxiety, the United States Navy didn't seem particularly worried about this absence from his duty station. And this perplexed his SEAL buddies to distraction.

Mike's non-presence was discussed in much detail one evening at the Fouled Anchor Tavern in Coronado. This was the favorite bar of Brannigan's Brigands, and was owned by a retired SEAL by the name of Salty Donovan and his wife Dixie.

Salty had joined the Brigands at their table to partake in the near-ceremonial downing of pitchers of beer as well as discuss the discombobulating circumstances regarding Mike Assad.

"He wouldn't quit the SEALs, would he?" Salty asked. "I don't mean to suggest he turned chicken or candy-ass, but maybe he's figured he wants a change in his Navy career."

Dave Leibowitz, Mike's best buddy, violently shook his head at the suggestion. "Mike would rather die than not be a SEAL."

"Oh, shit!" Bruno Puglisi suddenly exclaimed. "You don't suppose—?" He stopped speaking as if what he was about to say was so horrible it shouldn't be spoken aloud.

"Go on with the theorem you were going to asseverate," Chad Murchison, ex-preppy and best-educated Brigand, urged.

Puglisi frowned in puzzlement. "I never understand a fucking word you say, Chad."

"I'm merely asking you to express your opinion on why Mike is no longer among us."

Puglisi hesitated, then blurted out, "Maybe he's gone to OCS."

"Oh, no!" Leibowitz said. "Mike would never want to be a fucking officer."

A murmuring of agreement followed, and Garth Redhawk, a taciturn Kiowa-Comanche from Oklahoma, sighed loudly. "It's just a deep dark mystery that may never be solved."

"I suppose we should just accept the fact he will no longer be with us," Joe Miskoski said.

"Oh, God!" Dave Leibowitz moaned.

THIS disappearance occurred after Mike been awakened from a sound sleep during a Standards of Conduct class being given by a droning female officer from the Naval District Human Relations Department. A shadowy figure in officer's attire had come quietly into the classroom and shaken Mike by the shoulder. The SEAL woke up instantly and was quietly ordered to follow the man outside. When the rest of the detachment returned to their quarters at the end of the duty day, they found Mike's rack stripped and his locker sealed up. The situation smacked of criminal activity, and everyone in the detachment tried to think of some felonious deed that Mike might have committed. But since his best buddy, Dave Leibowitz, was still present and accounted for, it didn't seem any wrongdoing was involved. After all, the two were inseparable.

Even the ever-knowing Senior Chief Petty Officer Buford Dawkins was at a complete loss as to the wandering lad's fate. His appeals to numerous contacts and friends had been futile.

6 SEPTEMBER

LIEUTENANT Wild Bill Brannigan, the skipper of the special SEAL detachment known unofficially as Brannigan's Brigands, had been summoned to the office of Commander Thomas Carey, the N3 of the base. Brannigan's mandatory invitation included instructions to bring along his 2IC, Lieutenant (JG) Jim Cruiser, and Senior Chief Petty Officer Buford Dawkins. The trio, still having misgivings about the mysterious circumstances surrounding Mike Assad, was not in a good mood when they reported in. The orders passed on to them by Carey did very little to improve their grumpy dispositions.

The commander glanced across his desk at them, grinning happily at their discomfiture. "How are you gentlemen today?" He slid three paper-clipped documents over to them. "These are xeroxes of a short article that recently appeared in *Advanced Technological and Scientific Design Magazine*. Are you familiar with the publication?"

"Never heard of it," Brannigan said.

"I'm not surprised," Carey said. "It deals with unusual and far-out scientific and technical matters. At any rate, I'd like you all to read it. Don't worry. It's not long."

The three SEALs quickly scanned the article concerning an ACV called the *Waterflyer*. When they finished, they looked up at the commander without further comment, waiting for him to get into the purpose behind the session.

"A special assignment has come down for you gentlemen," Carey said. "It involves this particular hovercraft or air-cushion vehicle or whatever it is. You'll be doing a bit of travel."

"Our assignments always involve *a bit* of travel," Brannigan grumbled. "Where're we going this time?" Since the detachment's activation, they had been to Afghanistan and South America where P.P.P.P. had all but gotten them wiped out on each mission.

"You'll be visiting the Sunshine State, i.e., Florida," Carey replied. "The Navy wants you to check out the potential of that newly designed ACV for SPECOPS."

"Us?" Jim Cruiser remarked. "We're not technocrats."

"The Navy realizes that," Carey said. "In fact, I don't think you guys would be qualified to pass judgment on potential wheelbarrows for the Seabees. There'll be a qualified engineer joining you later. All you have to do is see if you can fight with the damn thing. Take a ride on it with the inventors. That would be"—he glanced at the article—"John and Harry DuBose. As you just read, they built a prototype for the purpose of having it push barge traffic up and down the Intracoastal Waterway, but couldn't sell the idea. They contacted the government and the ball started rolling until it came to a stop right here in front of my desk."

"At least it'll be change of scenery for a while," Brannigan said. "When do we leave?"

Carey reached in a desk drawer and pulled out three packets. "Here're your plane tickets. You'll travel in civvies on a commercial flight out of San Diego International to Orlando

International. You can rent a car there and drive over to Merritt Island. Enjoy."

"Thank you, sir," Brannigan said, taking the papers. "I take it we'll have to make a written report."

Carey shook his head. "Let the engineer type take care of that, Lieutenant. You'll be grilled back here in Coronado in a combination discussion and critique on how all this will fit into your lives as SEALs."

Brannigan gave Cruiser and the senior chief their tickets, then looked back at Carey. "By the way—"

"I don't know a damn thing about Mike Assad," Carey interrupted. "It has nothing to do with this headquarters."

Senior Chief Dawkins screwed his face into what he considered a polite smile. "Maybe you could ask around for us, sir."

"There are certain situations in which inquiries are not made," Carey said. "Mike Assad is one of those. Sorry. See you when you get back from Florida."

The three Brigands left the office.

KUPANG, TIMOR ISLAND
7 SEPTEMBER
1030 HOURS LOCAL

THE Greater Sunda Shipping Line that operated out of Timor Island had been grandly conceived and named by its Indonesian owner, Abduruddin Suhanto. When he started the business with an inheritance from his grandfather, he entertained himself with fantasies of becoming a rival to the famous shipping magnate Aristotle Onassis. And, like the Greek tycoon, he would have hundreds of romances with beautiful women, then marry a stunning and famous American lady of high class. Maybe even a film star.

Unfortunately, his dreams deteriorated rather quickly and he never developed the contacts needed for lucrative shipping transactions. Politicking and socializing were not Suhanto's fortes. He ultimately ended up with a list of shady clients who operated in the darkest shadows of legal commerce. These customers did not pay well, if at all, and his fleet ended up as a quartet of fifth- and sixth-hand cargo vessels with documentation that had been changed, counterfeited, and transferred so many times that it was impossible to trace the rust-streaked tubs' original ownerships.

After a bit more than twenty-five years, Suhanto was now in as bad a physical condition as his ships. He was a fifty-year-old bloated wretch with a multitude of illnesses that had been brought on by shocking excesses of rich foods, alcohol, and sex. His feet were so swollen that he could wear nothing but flip-flops, and he walked with a heavy shuffle. His round face, which should have shown a healthy swarthy complexion, was faded and patched with a network of capillaries that ran through his cheeks and nose.

Suhanto's home life was as miserable as his business. The woman he'd drawn in an arranged marriage by his parents had been overweight, whining, and homely. This was a far cry from the comely svelte women he'd dreamed of in his youth.

Over the years of misery, the wife grew even worse. He had taken a second bride of sorts by purchasing a twelve-year-old girl in Thailand fifteen years ago. She was now moving into middle age and had adopted the first wife's love of chocolate candy and indolence. The two fat women now conspired together to make their husband's existence a living hell. Suhanto had lost all interest in having sex at home. He sought release for his infrequent passions between the legs of his favorite sexual partners: adolescent girls available in the city's brothels.

The shipowner's commercial life, however, did improve a bit after years of struggle. Suhanto began to realize a profit when his main business evolved into a busy smuggling operation. He turned out to be excellent at organizing such activities and his ship's captains were skilled at putting those plans into actual practice. The Greater Sunda Shipping Line made most of its profits in the drug trade, hauling heroin from Southeast Asia to rendezvous points where it was further transferred to the profitable markets in the West. While Suhanto made great sums of money in the business, he also lost a great deal of it through the payment of bribes and kickbacks. Also, a lot of his cargo was stolen away when crooked law enforcement caught him at sea. They simply took over the ship and made the delivery themselves. After collecting all the money, they released the captain to take the vessel back to Suhanto. Those corrupt officials knew that sooner or later they would catch the same ships yet again for more financial gain. After a few such scores, these clandestine pirates were smart enough to let a few vessels complete their runs. After all, if Suhanto made no profit at all, he would abandon the drug trade.

But this particular day was one that might bring a permanent and advantageous change to Suhanto's shipping activities. An Arab gentleman had sent an emissary to arrange for a meeting. The stranger had a smuggling proposition that would not involve narcotics. Suhanto knew it would mean arms shipments, and to him the change would be a step-up in life.

The shipper reached into his bottom desk drawer and pulled out a bottle of scotch whiskey. After taking a deep drink, he replaced the liquor and belched. The warmth from the alcohol spread slowly through his bloated body in a soothing way. He felt encouraged from this preliminary stimulation of alcohol. A knock on the door interrupted his reverie. His clerk, a spindly old man named Bachaman, stuck his head into the room.

"The gentleman you are expecting has arrived," the old man said.

"Show him in."

A moment later a slim Arab man with sharp features and a scraggly beard stepped into the office. He wore an ill-fitting Western business suit, and his hair was pulled back into a sort of ponytail arrangement. He nodded politely to Suhanto. *"Sabahil kher, Assayid Suhanto.* My name is Hafez Sabah."

"Good morning," Suhanto said, returning the greeting in the same language. "You know I speak Arabic, hey?"

"I know many things about you, Mr. Suhanto."

"Please sit down, sir," Suhanto said, not too pleased about that particular revelation.

"Thank you," the visitor said, taking a chair on the other side of the desk. "It was most accommodating of you to see me on such short notice."

Suhanto, who did not like idle chatter, got to the point. "What can I do for you?"

Sabah, taking the hint, cut to the chase. "My organization would like to make use of your four ships."

Suhanto shrugged. "I am involved in an especially profitable association at this moment, Mr. Sabah. You would have to offer me a most attractive proposition to lure me away from my present activities."

"I am well aware of your true situation," Sabah said. "You have a business that is either feast or famine. My proposition will even things out for you."

Suhanto ignored the affront. "What is it you would require of me and my fleet?"

"My organization wishes you to pick up goods at certain locations at sea near the Philippines, and make delivery to our people along the Pakistani coast."

"And what organization might this be?" Suhanto inquired.

"We are known as al-Mimkhalif," Sabah explained. "That is an acronym that stands for al-Mujahideen Katal."

"The Warriors of Fury?" Suhanto commented. "I've heard much about you on television and in the newspapers."

"I am sure you have. We are organized under the blessings of Allah to deal with the misguided brothers of Pakistan and Afghanistan," Sabah explained. "We have many connections around the world."

"Am I to understand that this will involve weaponry?"

"Of course," Sabah replied.

"Very well!" Suhanto said. "Payments for such enterprises is traditionally made in American dollars."

"We will pay you in Saudi rials."

Suhanto was thoughtful for a moment. "Mmm. That is acceptable. The currency of Saudi Arabia is steady and dependable. What terms are you offering?"

"You will be paid all expenses; including your crew's salary," Sabah said. "Additionally, a daily total of three hundred rials will be added to that amount."

"I should think a thousand rials would be more convenient."

"I am not going to bargain with you," Sabah said calmly. "Allow me to reiterate. You will be paid your costs plus three hundred rials daily while you actually work in our service."

"Unacceptable!" Suhanto exclaimed pulling out his calculator. He punched in some numbers. "That is only one thousand one hundred twenty-five American dollars."

"You have no choice, Mr. Suhanto," Sabah informed him.

"I refuse!"

"You are going to Hell, Mr. Suhanto," Sabah said. "You are a Muslim, yet you are not a faithful follower of Islam. I can smell liquor on your breath now. What other laws of Allah do you outrage? Perhaps eat pork? No daily prayers?" He paused. "By serving us, you have a chance of being forgiven for your transgressions and allowed to enter Paradise rather than spend eternity burning in flames tended by Satan and his demons."

"I am not a religious man," Suhanto said. "Such talk means nothing to me."

"Then, if you choose not to serve Allah, our spiritual leader will issue a death sentence against you."

Suhanto's pasty complexion blanched even more. If a member of the Islamic clergy condemned him to be slain, the man who committed the act would do so in the belief it was the way to eternal rewards. There would be countless applicants to perform the deed.

"I accept your terms."

"I am pleased, Mr. Suhanto," Sabah said, standing up. "You will be contacted within the week for your first assignment."

"I shall give you a list of the normal expenses of running my ships."

"We have already figured that out," Sabah said. He turned and walked to the door. When he opened it, he looked back at his host. "*Ilal lika*—I shall see you later."

Suhanto sat pensively for several minutes. He was not a fool. The fact that al-Mimkhalif had bullied him into being their shipper meant they were in trouble. The terrorists' former supply routes had undoubtedly been hit hard and possibly destroyed. Perhaps their ranks were rife with betrayers.

This was a situation where a prudent yet daring man of intelligence could profit greatly. Suhanto happily poured himself another scotch.

FLORIDA STATE ROAD 528
8 SEPTEMBER
0830 HOURS LOCAL

JIM Cruiser drove the rental Pontiac with Senior Chief Buford Dawkins sitting in the passenger seat. Wild Bill Brannigan dozed in the backseat as they rolled eastward on the highway called the Beach Line toward Merritt Island.

Cruiser noted the sign informing them they had entered Brevard County. But his mind wasn't on their location or even the purpose of their visit to Florida. "Everybody at the naval base is still talking about nothing but Mike Assad," the lieutenant remarked.

"It's obvious as hell that he's been sent down deep into some highly classified operations," Dawkins responded.

"I've heard of that happening," Cruiser said. "But I thought it was all bullshit."

"No, sir," Dawkins said. "Now and then an individual guy

gets tapped for a special assignment. We'll probably never find out the full story even if he comes back alive."

The conversation between the two woke up Brannigan. He looked around, then yawned and stretched. "Are we there yet?"

"We're getting closer," Dawkins answered, pointing at an exit. "That's State Route Three."

Brannigan took a quick look at the directions provided them back at the Naval Amphibious Base. "Go north to Pine Island Road."

"North to Pine Island Road. Aye, sir!" Cruiser said with a grin.

"Knock off that Navy shit," Brannigan growled.

Fifteen minutes later they arrived at the junction, and Cruiser made a left. He drove slowly down Pine Island Road past several orange groves as he headed for the combination home and factory of John and Harry DuBose.

This was an area known as Old Florida where the tourist spots, high-rise condos, and other features of the twenty-first century had not penetrated. Most of the residents were the home-grown variety of Floridians who dwelt happily in cleared areas amid the tangled vegetation, canals, insects, snakes, and alligators in bucolic isolation. The majority of these good people worked for modest salaries, getting by on limited income since their lifestyles did not demand much money. They supplemented their earnings with fishing, crabbing, hunting, and home-grown fruits and vegetables.

Cruiser left the main road to follow a narrow track that led toward the DuBose compound. Within five minutes they came to a wide area where a rambling house was situated. It was a two-story structure, well built from good architectural plans, and would easily fit into any exclusive neighborhood. In contrast to the upscale abode, the yard was messy with various types of technical junk that represented either failed or abandoned projects of the brothers. A large frame building on the riverbank was behind the house, and Cruiser pulled up to the structure. He had no sooner parked, then the back door opened and the DuBoses stepped out to greet the SEALs as they got out of the car.

"You're right on time," John DuBose said. "Just what we expected from the United States Navy."

The brothers were dressed in the local uniform of tank tops, shorts, and sandals. The family resemblance was strong, both being tall, slender, and balding. John, the older, was completely gray, while his younger brother Harry was still going through the process of having the original black color of his hair fade from age. John led the way with his hand outstretched as he introduced himself and his brother.

Brannigan shook with him. "I'm Bill. This is Jim and Buford." The skipper was in no mood for a period of aimless chatter. "It's obvious you're aware the United States Navy is interested in that ACV of yours."

"Oh, yeah!" Harry said. "We've been talking to lots of you folks."

"All right!" Jim Cruiser said enthusiastically. He had developed an interest in the vehicle. "Let's have a look."

"C'mon then!" John invited. "We'll show her to you guys." He turned and walked toward the large frame building with the SEALs following.

"Y'know," Harry remarked to himself as much as to the visitors. "We really ought to develop a sales pitch or something. Know what I mean?"

"I suppose," Brannigan said. "But a few words of explanation will be enough for us today."

They went inside the building, which was fully air-conditioned. This wasn't for reasons of comfort; the steaminess of the local summers could spoil a lot of machinery and chemicals that were left exposed. The interior was also as littered with projects as the yard, but these seemed to be getting some attention. Brannigan surmised the brothers worked on whatever their moods dictated on any particular day.

They stepped out another door and onto a dock. The ACV *Waterflyer* was tied up to their direct front. The three SEALs gave the craft a quick look, then glanced meaningfully at each other. There was no doubt this was a well-designed and well-built piece of water-going machinery. The brothers led the way aboard and the Navy men stepped from the dock onto the vehicle. The *Waterflyer* was immaculate, and still damp from a recent hosing-down. Brannigan walked to the stern to take a look at the twin airscrews situated on pylons in front of a pair of rudders.

"Those rudders might be overkill," John remarked. "The airscrews alone are enough to turn the vessel. As a matter of fact, you can slow the speed down on one and speed the other up for a gradual maneuver in case you don't want to mess with the rudders."

"You can also reverse both the same way," Harry interjected.

"Right," John acknowledged. "Or you can do it faster by turning them as a pair, and the rudders can be used to sharpen the maneuver. That wouldn't be necessary when pushing barges."

Jim Cruiser explained, "In this case, the Navy is looking for maximum maneuverability."

Harry asked, "Aren't they going to push barges or other vessels with it?"

Senior Chief Dawkins shrugged. "We was told they wanted a vehicle that could zip around and change directions quickly."

"Well," Harry said, "the *Waterflyer* can sure as hell do that. Do you want to see the cabin?"

When the Brigands stepped inside, they found an empty area of five hundred square feet with only the barest of steering gear. An open door on the aft side revealed the engine room. Brannigan frowned. "We read an article that said there were some bunks and a galley in here."

"That writer put that in to make it more interesting," John explained.

"Yeah," Harry said. "We told him how the cabin could be configured, and he wrote it up like we had already done it."

"Do you want to take it out for a run?" John asked.

"Yeah," Brannigan said. "That'd be a good idea."

"Yeah," Dawkins agreed. "Let's see her go with a wide-open throttle."

Jim Cruiser asked, "Can you do that on the river?"

Harry shook his head. "We got in trouble for that. Not only the police but the Wildlife Management issued us citations. But we can go out through the locks at Port Canaveral and let her rip on the ocean."

"Let's do it," Brannigan said.

Harry leaped on the dock to untie the bow and stern lines, then jumped back aboard. "All set, John."

John went to the controls, opened the throttle, and punched the starter button. The engine immediately roared into life, then settled back into a steady rumble as the throttle was brought back to a rearward position. Harry picked up an old ten-foot oar that lay on the deck. "We're thinking about adding thrusters to the hull configuration, but I'll have to use this in the meantime."

He set the blade of the oar against the dock and pushed, causing the craft to move out into the waterway. At that point, John took off the clutch to activate the lift fan and the ACV shook a bit as it rose off the water's surface. When the airscrews were powered up, the vehicle moved slowly forward toward the outlet that led to the Indian River. The old salt Senior Chief Dawkins noted that the ride was smooth and gentle, giving evidence of an incredible amount of control.

When they reached the river, John eased out into a position between the channel markers, then turned south. He sped up at the end of the maneuver and began traveling at thirty miles an hour.

Brannigan looked at the bare area where the instrumentation should have been. "Don't you have a speedometer?"

"We haven't bothered with that yet," Harry explained. "We estimated our top speed by running from a condo we know in Cape Canaveral down to the Doubletree Hotel in Cocoa Beach. It's a distance of one and a half miles. We made it in a little less than sixty seconds."

"That's ninety miles an hour or a bit more," Cruiser remarked.

"Right," John said. "When we get some serious offers, we'll install the correct instrumentation to get accurate, scientific measurements."

They continued on the route, being careful to stay in the channel. After ten minutes, John turned the *Waterflyer* toward the Barge Canal, which connected the Indian and Banana Rivers. He had to slow down considerably because of the manatee warning signs that limited both speed and wake in an effort to keep boats from colliding with the large, slow mammals. They went under the Christa McAuliffe Memorial Bridge, continuing on past Sykes Creek and down the canal until they reached the Banana River.

As they drew closer to the locks, Harry pulled a handheld radio out of a backpack hanging on the bulkhead. He raised the lock authority to make arrangements to pass through. The SEALs had a little trouble figuring out what sort of communication device it was. Harry noticed their curiosity. "John and I designed and built the radio," Harry said. "It works fine."

"But still another goddamn project we couldn't sell," John said with a laugh.

The trip took them past Port Canaveral and out into the Atlantic Ocean. Now John eased the course to ninety degrees to go due east off the Space Coast. He pushed the speed up for a quarter of an hour before wheeling starboard to face 180 degrees.

"Open it up, John!" Harry yelled happily.

"Wait a minute!" Dawkins interjected. "Isn't there anything to hang onto?"

"You won't need it," John said as he pushed the throttle to a wide-open position.

The *Waterflyer* eased into the run, quickly and steadily gaining forward momentum. Within moments it was at flank speed as Harry grinned proudly at their passengers. "Isn't it beautiful, gentlemen?"

"My God!" Brannigan said. They stood as steady as if they were still tied up to the dock. "This thing is fantastic."

The ACV roared across the choppy waves without a waver. John made some turning maneuvers, including a figure-eight, then zigged and zagged both gently and violently. After a few minutes he eased back on the throttle. "Any of you want to try it?"

"I'm pulling rank," Brannigan announced. "I'll go first."

"That's pretty chickenshit, sir," Dawkins complained.

"I agree!" Cruiser said.

"RHIP!" Brannigan crowed as he hit the throttle.

Harry leaned close to his brother's ear. "I think we got a sale!"

CHAPTER 2

INDIAN OCEAN
VICINITY OF 15° NORTH AND 70° EAST
9 SEPTEMBER
1800 HOURS LOCAL

THE freighter SS *Jakarta* of the Greater Sunda Shipping Line was hove to in the undulating waves as the Pakistani dhow *Nijm Zarik* pulled up alongside. The deep metallic popping of the smaller ship's engine was reversed for an instant, then cut off. Her scantily clad crewmen, stripped down in the merciless heat, threw lines up to waiting hands on the cargo vessel.

Captain Bacharahman Muharno of the *Jakarta* hollered down to the dhow's captain. "Peace be with you, brother."

"And with you," Captain Bashar Bashir called back. He was an incredibly thin old man with a long pointed beard. "I am Bashir."

"And I am Muharno," came the reply from the other, who was a heavyset man wearing a greasy merchant marine khaki uniform. "I bring you French mortars." Then he added, "At least that is what they tell me."

"Have you inspected the cargo?" Bashir asked in a worried tone.

"I have not," Muharno answered. "The customer was very explicit about that. You will notice that the sealing wax around the crates is unbroken."

"That is good for both of us, brother," Bashir said in relief. "I fear I could not accept anything that had been opened."

"There are twelve crates," Muharno said. "Everything is proper and in order."

During the conversation between the two captains, the crew of the *Jakarta* had opened the forward hatch and lowered a cargo net into it. The crewmen below muscled two oblong crates into the device, then signaled for it to be hauled up.

Muharno turned as the crane motor came to life. The cables creaked through the pulleys and within moments the net appeared from the hold. The crane swung the load over the dhow and gently lowered it to the smaller vessel. The crewmen removed the crates and stacked them into place on the deck. The unobtrusive figure of Hafez Sabah, special agent of al-Mimkhalif, stood in front of the dhow's wheelhouse watching the operation. He was there to observe the first delivery he had arranged with Abduruddin Suhanto of the Greater Sunda Shipping Line. Sabah carefully noted the condition of each crate as it was lifted from the net.

Within a half hour, all twelve crates of mortars were placed in such a way as to evenly distribute their collective weight of half a ton. The two captains once again turned their attention to each other. "Our hold is now empty," Muharno reported.

"The shipment tallies correctly," Bashir said. "All is well."

"We will see you on the next trip."

"I look forward to it, brother," Bashir said. "May Allah watch over you."

"And over you. Farewell."

The lines were cast off the *Jakarta,* and the *Nijm Zark*'s helmsman kicked his small ship's ancient engine into life, maneuvering away from the freighter. When the dhow was clear, he hit the throttle and turned onto the course for their next rendezvous, which would be off the coast of Pakistan.

Bashir joined Sabah by the starboard rail. The captain showed a wide-gapped, toothy grin. "I think this new system will work well for us, brother."

"We shall see," Sabah said. "The Indonesian shipper is worse than an infidel. He has fallen from Islam."

"May Allah cast him into Hell to be roasted by Satan!"

"Such a fate is written for those who turn their backs on the merciful and benevolent Allah," Sabah said. "Now I want to inspect the cargo."

The wooden vessel, its sails furled, continued under engine power toward its destination.

MERRITT ISLAND, FLORIDA
11 SEPTEMBER
1000 HOURS LOCAL

THE three Brigands had gone to their reserved rooms at the Radisson Hotel in Cape Canaveral to wait for the arrival of the engineer who would make a detail technical inspection of the ACV.

They had to endure almost seventy-two hours with nothing to do before the phone call they had been waiting for came through. It was Harry DuBose passing on a message to them.

"That Navy engineer is here with a crew," the inventor told Lieutenant Bill Brannigan. "They got in day before yesterday and really crawled all over the ol' *Waterflyer.*"

"Why wasn't I notified of their arrival?" Brannigan asked angrily.

"The engineer said there was a lot to do before you'd be needed," Harry explained. "They didn't even go to a hotel. They've been with the *Waterflyer* since they got here."

"I see," Brannigan said, thinking the engineer and his crew were among those dedicated nerds who sucked up nourishment from technical manuals and circuit boards.

"Anyhow, they seem to like the ACV, and they went right to work making alterations. They say they're ready for y'all to come on out here for another ride."

"Why are they making alterations?" Brannigan asked. "As far as I know, the vehicle hasn't been approved for government purchase."

"I don't know," DuBose said. "But they want to see you."

"Right. We'll be there in twenty minutes."

Brannigan hung up, then dialed up Cruiser's and Dawkins's rooms to roust them out.

1030 HOURS LOCAL

AFTER arriving at the DuBose compound, the SEALs parked and went around the house to the dock. Brannigan and his two companions were surprised to see that a dozen people were crawling all over the ACV installing instrumentation and other equipment. But they were particularly unnerved by the sight of a beautiful young lady clad in the khaki uniform of a lieutenant junior grade. She was slim with honey-blond hair and blue eyes that had a slight Oriental cast to them.

"Good morning!" she said brightly to the arrivals who were dressed in civilian clothing. "I'm Lieutenant Rivers, the engineering officer assigned to this project."

Jim Cruiser had a silly grin on his face. "I'm Jim. Jim Cruiser, that is. Also a lieutenant JG."

"Veronica Rivers," the young woman said, giving her first name.

"I'm Lieutenant Brannigan," the skipper interjected. "And this is Senior Chief Dawkins."

"I understand you are SEALs," Veronica said. "And that this ACV will be going on a mission."

"You're a few steps ahead of us at this moment," Brannigan said. "We haven't made our report yet."

"I called mine in last night with my complete approval,"
Veronica said. "I was told to inform you that you wouldn't
be going back to Coronado. Orders are being cut assigning
you to this ACV. Your whole detachment is included."

Senior Chief Dawkins glanced at Brannigan. "They must
have a mission lined up for us, sir."

"That's a fact," Veronica said. "When I came into the
Navy I never thought I'd be going on a real live SEAL operation."

The senior chief scowled. "What do you mean, *going* on
a SEAL operation?"

"I've been assigned as the navigations and weapons systems officer," Veronica said.

Cruiser's grin grew slightly sillier. "Well! Welcome
aboard!"

"Thank you," she replied.

Brannigan nodded toward the other people working on the
vehicle. "I didn't think the crew was going to be this large.
And it doesn't look there's room for that many people. Especially if a SEAL detachment has to be aboard too."

"Don't worry, sir," Veronica Rivers said. "Only two of
them—the helmsman and the turbine technician—will stay
as crewmen. The others were sent down to take care of their
particular equipment. The two DuBose brothers are also
lending a hand."

"I see," Brannigan said. "Let's go over to the ACV and
you can give us the Cook's tour so we can see what you've
done so far."

They crossed the dock and stepped onto the *Waterflyer*.
The busy people paid them no mind as Veronica led the
SEALs into the cabin. They saw a cramped but efficient design that included four bunks and one head for nature's calls.
However, it was obviously not designed to be lived aboard
for any great length of time. A small refrigerator and microwave oven were situated on the port side that served as a

tiny galley. Just to the front of that was a table with benches bolted to the deck.

"That would be our wardroom, would it not?" Jim Cruiser asked.

"Yes," Veronica answered. "Such as it is. That door on the stern bulkhead leads to the engine room. It's a very tight, compact space."

Brannigan turned his attention forward. He noted three leather chairs located in front of the instruments on the small bridge forward of the galley and bunks. One, a leather swivel model, was to the rear and slightly higher than the others. Veronica walked over and patted it. "This is your position, Captain," she informed him, following the custom that the skipper of a vessel always be addressed in that manner even if he actually ranked lower. She next touched the starboard seat. "This is where I sit to do my navigational-and-weapons-officer duties. I also man the chain gun during combat operations. The weapon is aimed by radar and fires 30-millimeter rounds at six hundred twenty-five rounds a minute."

Brannigan nodded. "It's obvious the port chair is for the helmsman." He noted the pair of control yokes for manipulating the variable-pitch airscrews, as well as the foot pedals used for the rudders. The throttle was to the right of the sticks. "What about the rest of the ordnance? Who's the designer?"

"That'd be me, sir," Veronica said. "It's all installed and the technicians have returned to their home stations. I'll operate it all from my position at the chain gun." She took them out to the deck and pointed to two weapons wings that had been added to the sides of the cabin. Each held three pods. "The first is a Penguin antiship missile," Veronica explained. "An AIM-9L antiaircraft missile is mounted on the second, and the third sports a seven-round 2.75-inch rocket launcher. All this is aimed inside by me from my station. I have combination radar and laser target-acquisition systems. I also spew out chaff and flares to throw off incoming enemy ordnance when appropriate."

"This was all done pretty fast," Brannigan remarked. "When we arrived here on the eighth, this was pretty much an empty shell."

"We've been working around the clock, sir," Veronica explained. "And a lot of this weaponry and equipment comes in kit form."

"I'd like to meet the two crewmen," Brannigan said.

"Aye, aye, sir."

The two sailors left their tasks when summoned and formed up as directed by the female JG. Brannigan walked up to them, stopping in front of the first. "Name and duties."

The sailor, a short blond man with intelligent eyes, presented himself. "Petty Officer First Class Paul Watkins, sir. I'll act as the helmsman as well as assist Lieutenant Rivers to navigate, maintain charts, and plot courses."

"Very well, Watkins." As Watkins stepped back, Brannigan turned his eyes on the second sailor, who was a kid with a happy-go-lucky expression on his face. "And you?"

"Sir, I am Petty Officer Second Class Bobby Lee Atwill," he responded in a marked Southern accent. He was covered with grease and oil, and was as short as Watkins but darker and more easygoing in appearance. "I'm the turbine system technician. I run and fix our engine."

"Have you developed a rapport with it as of yet?" Brannigan asked.

"Yes, sir," Atwill answered. "I sure have. What we have here is the Argentine Poder-Ventaja system. The DuBose guys helped design it, so they got with me and we took her apart and slapped her back together." He shrugged. "Well, not *completely* apart, but enough that I got to know her really good."

"What's your opinion of the power plant?" Brannigan asked.

"Cap'n, I'd marry her if I could," Atwill said.

Brannigan grinned at the kid's obvious enthusiasm. "I don't think Navy regulations permit that, Atwill, but you can go steady with her if you want. Is she ready for a trial run?"

"Gimme a couple of hours more, sir," Atwill said. "There's some last-minute tuning to do."

Brannigan checked his watch and glanced over at Veronica Rivers. "Let's take her out at fourteen hundred hours. Will we be able to play war with her?"

"Can do, Captain," she answered.

1400 HOURS LOCAL

BRANNIGAN, Cruiser, and Lieutenant Veronica Rivers situated themselves in the cabin, each taking their respective positions, while Atwill went aft into the small engine compartment. Veronica prepared herself for a simulated fire mission with the weapons system. Brannigan settled into his chair directly behind Watkins, who sat eagerly in the helmsman position.

"Let's take her out," Brannigan said. He picked up the intercom. "Engine room, what's your status."

"Everything is a go, sir," Atwill replied.

"All right then," Brannigan said. "Watkins, show us your stuff."

"Aye, aye, sir!" The helmsman hit the starter, and the strong vibrations from the gas-turbine engine could be felt as it kicked to life.

"Left full rudder," Brannigan said. "Ahead one third."

"Left full rudder," Watkins said. "Ahead one third, aye, sir." He manipulated the transmission and clutch levers to engage the airscrew and lift fan. He turned rudder and airscrews for a port turn and pushed the throttle forward from STOP to ONE-THIRD SPEED AHEAD. The ACV moved smoothly in the direction indicated, easing away from the dock.

"Steady on course," Brannigan ordered.

"Steady on course, aye, sir," Watkins replied straightening up with some deft manipulation of the controls. They moved over the water and to the inlet that allowed access to the Indian River. A trio of sailboats was to their direct front, and was allowed to move out of the way before the *Water-flyer* went to the channel in the river.

"I've been told we can't really open her up here," Brannigan said. "Too bad. Left full rudder and follow the channel markers."

Watkins eased them into the channel marked by the square red and round green markers. He played with the controls a bit to familiar himself with them.

"Half speed."

"Half speed, aye, sir."

It took only moments before the *Waterflyer* moved down the river, spewing out a spreading cloud of mist around her. The rate of travel was a steady forty miles per hour according to Watkins's electronic speed indicator. Rivers began running a drill with her system, picking out various targets on both the river and land. Her lock-ons registered quickly and exactly, and she turned to Brannigan with a thumbs-up signal.

The skipper felt confident and optimistic as they continued down Merritt Island and past the town of Cocoa.

THE short shakedown cruise had proven a success. The *Waterflyer* needed no more than some minor tuning from Bobby Lee Atwill's skilled hands to have the Poder-Ventaja gas turbine humming at top efficiency. All other navigational, observational, and weaponry systems checked out to Veronica Rivers's satisfaction.

As soon as the vehicle was tied up at the dock, Brannigan led his crew into the shop for a briefing. After getting sodas out of the refrigerator, they settled down around the electronic work bench.

"Okay, people," the skipper began. "The first thing I'm going to do is change the name of this ACV. *Waterflyer* is too candy-ass to suit me. It sounds like some kind of bug."

Senior Chief Buford Dawkins sighed in relief. "Thank God, sir! Have you thought of another name?"

"I sure as hell have," Brannigan replied. "From now on the name of our sturdy vessel will be the ACV *Battlecraft*. Get used to it. We're all in this together."

Lieutenant Veronica Rivers took a swallow of her Diet Coke. "Do you remember that last line in the movie *Casablanca* when Claude Raines and Humphrey Bogart were walking off together in the fog? 'This looks like the start of a beautiful friendship.'"

"That does seem apropos at the moment," Brannigan commented. "At any rate, I want Lieutenant Rivers, Atwill, and Watkins to go back aboard and button down their equipment. Make sure it'll be ready for the next run. We'll be taking the ACV *Battlecraft* out on the Atlantic Ocean."

"Aye, sir," Veronica said.

The helmsman and turbine technician followed her back to the dock while the SEALs stayed behind. Brannigan summed up their collective mood. "This is going to be a hell of a lot different than anything the detachment has done so far."

Cruiser shrugged. "As long as Lieutenant Rivers and those two guys do their job, we'll be all right."

"I don't have a problem with that," Dawkins said. "The *Battlecraft* is basically our transportation to and from missions. We jump off, kick some ass, and jump back aboard again."

"It's a bit more than that," Brannigan said. "If we're caught at sea, we may have to use the weaponry to save our asses." He finished his can of soda. "I hope Lieutenant Rivers understands that."

"It wouldn't hurt to have a word with her, sir," Dawkins suggested.

Brannigan walked from the building to the ACV, stepped aboard, and joined Veronica in the cabin. He nodded to her. "You seem satisfied with your systems."

"I am, sir," she replied. "They responded to today's testing with flying colors."

"Keep 'em that way, Lieutenant," he said. "There's a good

chance we might need 'em for something as fundamental as pulling ourselves out of some real deep shit."

Veronica turned and looked up at him. "I fully realize that, sir." She hesitated, "I hope you don't have any misgivings about having a female weapons officer."

"My wife is in the Navy, Lieutenant," Brannigan said. "She's a pilot stationed at North Island." He walked to the door. "See you later."

"Later, sir."

PAKISTAN
BALUCHISTAN PROVINCE
12 SEPTEMBER

MIKAEL Assad was the most popular man in al-Mimkhalif's Camp Talata. His aggressive attitude and good-natured personality made him likable to his comrades in the terrorist organization. He was eager to please, hard-working, and considerate of others. Assad was short but powerfully built, demonstrating extraordinary physical strength. On the other hand, one significant impression he gave was that he was not very bright. However, he seemed to recognize this shortcoming and showed a determination to make the best of things. He always sought the advice and guidance of the older mujahideen, and never argued about misunderstandings that arose from time to time in the demanding camp routine.

He was also an American.

Assad could speak only a stumbling brand of Arabic due to his home environment. He was the second generation of his family born in the United States, and he had grown up speaking mostly English. But he tried hard to acquire Arabic in his own bungling way, and he struggled faithfully to learn to read the scrawling written version of the idiom under the tutelage of his camp mates. There were many who considered this latter attempt a lost cause, but he labored so diligently over his lessons that they encouraged him to continue.

As one older mujahideen said; "Perhaps Allah in his wisdom and mercy will reward our brother Assad with a flash of intelligence and comprehension. If he is not brought deeper into the faith, he will not be martyred when he dies in battle."

0930 HOURS LOCAL

WHEN the overloaded Toyota pickup truck arrived at the camp with a load of crates, Mikael Assad dropped his Arabic lesson book and rushed over to help unload the vehicle. It was tough work, since each of the crates weighed in excess of forty-five kilos. Most of the men teamed up with another and made only one trip from the truck to the supply shack. But Assad took a total of three muscle-cramping turns toting the weapons by himself. When he put the final one on the stack, he went back to the truck and spoke to the driver.

"What in crates?" he asked in his stumbling Arabic.

"French mortars, Mikael," the driver replied. "Now we'll be able to rain shells down on the infidels and blow them to Hell."

"That good," Assad commented. "Where you get mortars?"

"They came by dhow from a ship it met at sea," the driver explained. "This is a new method we have for getting supplies to use here and in Afghanistan."

"Awa!" Assad exclaimed. "Yes! That very good! Infidels find our old way to bring in guns, and ruin everything, right?"

"Right," the driver said. "And may Allah punish them for three eternities."

"Yes. That a long time," Assad said.

He went back to his lessons, grabbing up his books and notebook to stride out of the camp to his favorite study place.

This was in the open country on the side of a hill where a lone tree grew in the scrub brush.

WHAT the other terrorists in Camp Talata didn't know was that Mike Assad was a U.S. Navy SEAL. He had been secretly assigned to a CIA mission called Operation Deep Thrust in which specially chosen operatives were sent to infiltrate various terrorist groups throughout the Middle East.

His buddies in Brannigan's Brigands wouldn't recognize him now. His hair had grown out and he sported a beard that was well on its way to becoming heavy and full. He also wore the traditional Afghanistan pakol wool cap along with baggy peasant jackets and trousers. With ammunition bandolier and an AK-47 assault rifle, he looked like a typical mujahideen fighter.

This new adventure started after Mike had been plucked out of that human resources class at the Naval Amphibious Base in Coronado, California. From there he was whisked off to a short but intense special orientation and training at the CIA center in Langley, Virginia. This was an accelerated class for specially qualified personnel like Petty Officer Mike Assad, who had unknowingly been given a complete security evaluation far beyond the norm due to his ethnicity. When he successfully completed the course, and impressed his mentors and instructors enough with his intelligence, physical conditioning, and raw guts, they had a doozy of a job waiting for him. He was assigned to penetrate the Islamic terrorist organization al-Mimkhalif; not in America, but over in a hot spot in Pakistan.

He went to Buffalo, New York, in the guise of being an underachieving, angry young Arab-American with little education. He began attending services at a mosque known to be a recruiting center for al-Mimkhalif. A Saudi clergyman invited Mike and other young men to attend some special classes at the mosque. It was at these so-called sessions in Middle Eastern culture and philosophy that he was recruited into the fanatical organization and sent to Camp Talata in Pakistan.

NOW, out in the open country around the terrorist center, Mike Assad sat feigning study of the Arabic lessons under the tree. After an hour passed, he stood up and casually stretched. He took a steady but subtle look around to make sure he was unobserved. After sitting back down, he pulled a sheet of paper from his notebook. He wrote a quick note regarding the new method of delivering arms and supplies, then wrapped it up tightly and stuck it into an empty aluminum tube. Mike stood up again for another survey of the nearby countryside before placing the tube into a hollowed-out area beneath the tree roots.

With that done, he gathered up his lessons and walked back to the camp.

CHAPTER 3

THE ZAUBA FAST ATTACK SQUADRON

THE most elite unit of the Oman Navy was the crack
Zauba Fast Attack Squadron stationed at the clandestine
Taimur Naval Base along a lonely part of the coast between
the city of Salalah and the Yemen border. This outfit, whose
name meant "Storm" in Arabic, was operating far outside
normal SOPs of the Oman armed forces. Outwardly, it
seemed to be a run-of-the-mill antismuggling unit, but in reality its sole purpose was to conduct quick-reaction missions. The squadron was bullied through its duties by its
egotistical and hard-driving commanding officer, Commodore Muhammad Mahamat.

The officers and sailors were handpicked, superbly trained,
and blindly loyal to Islam and Mahamat in that order. All officers were required to be fluent in the English language
before assignment to the squadron. The enlisted sailors had
to pass I.Q. tests and have superlative service records. They
were immediately put into English classes to develop a

strong working knowledge of the language. All personnel were sent to facilities of the United States Navy or Britain's Royal Navy for advanced studies in technical and tactical subjects.

Because of these special qualifications, all personnel received extra pay, rations, and perks not enjoyed by the rest of the Navy; earning all this through a demanding and continuing program of training exercises that kept them away from their homes most of the time. Morale was high among the men and their families due to their excellent living conditions and opportunities to purchase and enjoy luxury goods from the West.

The commodore ran his squadron using a *Province*-class British fast-missile vessel as his flagship. She was named the *Harbi-min-Islam,* which translated into English as "Spear of Islam." She carried a generous supply of French-built Exocet MM-40 missiles loosed from two quadruple launchers situated amidships. The main gun located on the bow was an Italian OTO compact gun that could kick out 6.3-kilogram shells at a rate of eighty-five rounds a minute. A Swedish Bofors twin-barrel 40-millimeter cannon on the stern was capable of delivering a combined rate of six hundred rounds per minute at enemy targets. The *Harbi-min-Islam* moved at a maximum speed of forty-five miles an hour with a range of three thousand miles when fully fueled. It was not a warship to be trifled with.

The remainder of this deadly squadron consisted of a half-dozen Swedish *Spica*-class attack boats well equipped with a mix of antiship and antiaircraft guns, torpedoes, and missiles. These boats, with lengths of 143 feet, could skim across the waves at seventy-five miles an hour.

The most surprising aspect of the Zauba Squadron was the fact that the perks, specialized training, and pay were not furnished by the Sultanate of Oman. The official naval budget did not indicate these extra expenses. In fact, the national government was unaware of all this power that Commodore Mahamat had at his fingertips. If anyone bothered to investigate the situation, they would find that most Oman officials did not know the Zauba Fast Attack Squadron even existed. This ignorance was shared with the world's intelligence agencies, who blissfully paid no attention at all to what was assumed to be an unremarkable, poorly equipped coastal patrol operation.

According to Oman's naval organization charts and logistic records, the squadron was operating with some aged surplus British *Ton*-class coastal patrol boats doing routine duties looking for miserable smugglers using old wooden dhows. The extra pay received by the officers and sailors, all the additional finances, equipment, and vessels were provided to Mahamat's outfit through the courtesy of Saudi Sheikh Omar Jambarah.

Another unusual practice followed by Commodore Mahamat was that the vessels of his squadron did not display Oman's national colors. Instead, they openly flew ensigns bearing a white scimitar and crescent moon on a solid scarlet field. This was the flag of the al-Mimkhalif terrorist group that was led by the sheikh, who used his nom de guerre Husan as he directed the far-flung operations of the fanatical band.

If any naval vessels made serious attempt to thwart al-Mimkhalif's oceangoing activities, they would eventually be drawn into battle with the Zauba Squadron without knowing it was out there to attack them.

GULF OF ADEN
VICINITY OF 13° NORTH AND 48° EAST
13 SEPTEMBER
1400 HOURS LOCAL

THE *Harbi-min-Islam* was hove to less than fifty meters from the Royal Saudi Yacht *Sayih,* and Commodore Muhammad Mahamat waited while his gig was lowered to the water. After the coxswain and boat hook were situated, Mahamat went nimbly down the netting and took a seat. "*Tanruh*—go!"

he commanded, and the boat hook pushed the craft away from the hull as the coxswain eased the throttle forward.

During the short minutes it took to reach the yacht, Mahamat surveyed the vessel appreciatively. Although he had seen her many times, he was always impressed with her striking beauty. The *Sayih* was a specially designed luxury ship thirty meters in length with a short forward deck, a longer stern deck, and a sleek state-of-the-art superstructure. The latest in radar, navigational, and communication equipment was evidenced by the various antennae showing above the bridge. The numerous portholes belowdecks were the cabins where specially invited passengers stayed. Sheikh Omar Jambarah of Saudi Arabia had private quarters that would rival any deluxe hotel suite in the world. All this on an oceangoing vessel.

This penchant for hedonism displayed by the sheikh confused Commodore Mahamat. Although the sheikh was closely associated with the Saudi royal family, he indulged in many decadent traits of the infidel West. The commodore excused this conduct, assuming that the sheikh was using this misbehavior as a cover. After all, he was the supreme commander of al-Mimkhalif—the Warriors of Fury—and such a lifestyle would confuse outsiders and infidels.

When the gig reached the accommodation ladder, the boat hook deftly tossed a line to the sailor waiting there. The coxswain slowed the engine, hit reverse, then moved into neutral as he came to a stop at just the right spot for the commodore to step easily onto the platform. Mahamat hurried up to the main deck, where he was met by a trio of tough, professional bodyguards. These were large muscular men totally dedicated to the sheikh's well-being. They were never addressed by their real names, instead being called Alif, Baa, and Taa, the first three letters of the Arabic alphabet.

Even the august person of Commodore Mahamat was not above a search by the three hard-core thugs. He submitted to the indignity, then was escorted toward the stern deck, where his host awaited his arrival.

The stern had a canvas cover rigged across that entire section of deck to keep off the sun. In actuality, the area was an outdoor drinking and eating patio lounge. A trio of waiters was available to attend to the guests, while a wet bar complete with an attendant was situated forward by the companionway. Numerous tables and chairs occupied the middle of the area, and a special place with comfortably padded chaise lounges was situated on the extreme stern. This latter area was where Sheikh Omar sat comfortably in bathing trunks and deck shoes.

Mahamat immediately noticed the number of thong-clad women with bare breasts who occupied the chairs. All were European and were either blondes or redheads. The commodore treated his eyes to the lovely, evil temptation for just a moment before he walked to the sheikh and bowed. "*Marhaba*—greetings, Sheikh Omar."

"And to you I offer *marhaba,* Commodore. Welcome aboard," the sheikh replied, pushing the leggy Russian blonde off his lap and dismissing her with a curt gesture. "I thank you for responding so quickly to my summons."

"It was my pleasure to obey, Sheikh Omar."

"Please sit down."

As Mahamat settled down on a lounge, a waiter appeared with a tray bearing a glass of pineapple juice. As Muslims, neither the sheikh nor the commodore would consume alcohol, though the women were freely tossing back various types of cocktails. The sheikh preferred them to be a bit tipsy when he wished to engage in his version of rough sex. It was easier for both him and whichever well-paid strumpet he had chosen for his playmate.

"Am I to understand al-Mimkhalif's new supply procedures have been put into place?" the commodore asked, taking a sip of his juice.

"Yes!" the sheikh said enthusiastically. "Thus, we will not be required to employ the Zauba Squadron to right the shipping situation at this time." He was a large, heavy man with a good deal of body hair. His beard was neatly trimmed and his thinning hair was skillfully barbered to make it look as thick as possible. "That is exactly why I had to speak with you. There remains the possibility you may eventually provide protection with your squadron as we establish the new routines and methods of delivery and pickup. There are always glitches—as the Americans say—in such activities."

"The Zauba Fast Attack Squadron is at your service," Commodore Mahamat assured him.

"*Nishkur Allah*—thank God!" the sheikh said. "Our main problem will be treachery from the owner of the miserable shipping line we have hired."

"What problem might we have with him?"

"The man is an immoral narcotics smuggler," the sheikh explained. "He is a fallen Muslim and exceedingly unreliable to the point we must control him with threats. We feel he will betray or deceive us at the first opportunity."

"Was there not a better choice?" the commodore asked.

"Unfortunately, there was not," the sheikh replied. "It would have been impossible to bring a legitimate firm under our influence if it were owned by a Muslim. However, he is not our only problem. The area he must ship our arms through is patrolled by the Philippine, Indonesian, Singaporean, Indian, and Pakistani navies. The United States also has a carrier force in the vicinity, but the battle group now on duty does not have the capability of coastal patrols." He chuckled. "One of my half brothers is good friends with an Undersecretary of the Navy in Washington. He always has useful tidbits of intelligence to pass on to me."

"That is indeed an advantage," Mahamat said. "If we have any encounters with war vessels, my squadron will be able to mount an instant devastating attack and destroy them, Allah willing." He paused. "The only essential thing, Sheikh Omar, is that we must be close by our transport vehicles to be able to effectively defend our interests."

"We have considered that," the sheikh said. "You will be apprised of the exact times and routes of each delivery so you can maintain an eye on the situation."

"My ships would have to be near enough to be in sight," Commodore Mahamat pointed out. "Would that not compromise security if we are seen by foreign warships?"

"We have taken that into consideration too," the sheikh said. "An agent from al-Mimkhalif will accompany each shipment. If there are any difficulties, he will be able to raise you by radio. Your speedy vessels may then make timely appearances and rectify any difficulties."

"Who is this agent?" Mahamat inquired.

"Someone you know," the sheikh said, smiling. "Hafez Sabah. He is a countryman of yours, *lae*?"

"An excellent man!" Mahamat commented.

The conversation was suddenly interrupted by the arrival of a tall blond German woman. She stood half-naked, wearing a thin bikini without shame in front of the two men whose own women were veiled and literally covered from head to toe with the traditional burka. The sheikh frowned angrily. "What is it you wish, Hildegard?"

"I cannot find my friend Franziska."

The sheikh shrugged. "She is not on board for this trip."

"Yes, she is!" Hildegard insisted. "I saw her come out on the boat with Olga and Adelaida."

"Then she must have gotten off before we sailed," the sheikh said.

"Olga and Adlaida said she did not get off," Hildegard insisted.

The sheikh stood up. "I told you Franziska is *not* on board. Now get back with the others! You have interrupted me in an important meeting."

Hildegard stood her ground. "What happened to her?"

"You infidel whore!" the sheikh yelled so loudly that everyone turned to look at him. He slapped Hildegard across the face with such violence that she staggered sideways against the deck railing. "If you bother me again I shall give you to Alif, Baa, and Taa. Do you want that? And after those big chaps have finished with you, they will pass you belowdecks to the crew. Those are some pretty crude fellows

down there. They would have a party with you that would
last three or four days before you succumbed."

Hildegard, rubbing her bruised face, fearfully stumbled
away. The sheikh sat back down, glancing over at Mahamat.
"I apologize for the slut's behavior."

"I understand," the commodore said.

"Her friend Franziska was pregnant with a child she said
was mine. An Arab child of the Faithful cannot be allowed to
grow in the godless body of a European slut." He chuckled.
"And I told Hildegard the truth. Franziska is not on board. At
least not anymore."

Mahamat grinned back at him. "Problem solved, *lae*?" He
eyed the other women, who now were subdued and nervous.

"Take your pick, Commodore," the Sheikh invited. "Rut
all you want in their unclean bodies. Allah does not consider
such fornication a sin when done to an infidel woman. They
are below sacred consideration."

"*Shokran*—thank you, Sheikh Omar," Mahamat replied.
He wondered if Allah really did not look upon sex with such
women as fornication. He decided to put the question to his
cleric. Meanwhile, he would take his host's word for it.

The sheikh took a final swallow of his fruit juice. "When
you've finished, I must see you before you return to your
flagship. I have the fourth-quarter funds for your squadron."

"Of course," Commodore Mahamat said. "*Shokran*, Sheikh
Omar."

He stood up and walked toward a plumpish redhead.

USS *DAN DALY*

THE USS *Dan Daly* LHX-1 was the newest vessel in the
United States Navy's amphibious assault inventory. The ship
and the concept that spawned her was so new and untried, the
Navy couldn't decide whether to put an "A" for general purpose or a "D" for multipurpose on her designation. Thus a temporary classification of "X" for test and evaluation was used.

Her homeport was Norfolk, Virginia, and she was a one of a kind in her job line; a compact, fully functional ship that, although limited in her ability to participate in large, complex operations because of her size, was better than her big sisters when it came to SPECOPS such as raids and other hit-and-run missions. She also had the significant potential of being a dandy flagship for a busy Naval admiral or Marine general in multiship amphibious situations.

The USS *Dan Daly*'s length was 390 feet, beam fifty-five feet, displacement twenty thousand tons, speed thirty knots, and the ship's company numbered five officers and 450 enlisted men. She boasted a floodable docking well that could accommodate one LCM-6 landing craft at a time—she carried a pair of these—and had parking space for eighty track and wheeled vehicles. A full battalion of Marines could be accommodated within her hull, though the environment would be rather crowded.

She protected herself and dealt out punishment with a radar-guided 20-millimeter cannon system to take on incoming enemy missiles. Additionally, the *Dan Daly* sported two eight-tube Sea Sparrow missile launchers, a pair of five-inch MK-45 guns, and lastly an impressive and devastating Phalanx Close-In Weapons system. Because of her petite configuration, she was not designed for fixed-wing takeoff and landing operations, but her flight deck could accommodate up to a dozen CH-46 Sea Knight helicopters. The USS *Dan Daly* was run from a CDC in her island structure with satellite communications gear and state-of-the-art command and control apparatus to direct all operations. She also had a dispensary of hundred and fifty beds for the treatment of casualties. Medical personnel beyond those normally allotted to a small crew were only available when the ship carried troops.

The ship was aptly named after another pint-sized warrior. Gunnery Sergeant Dan Daly was a five-foot-six-inch-tall United States Marine dynamo who won two Medals of Honor. The first during the Boxer Rebellion in Peking, China, and the second in operations in Haiti.

During the night of 15–16 July 1900, in the Boxer Rebellion, Private Daly and his commanding officer went on a reconnaissance patrol to pick a spot to erect an advanced fortified position to the front of the Tartar Wall of the Foreign Legation Quarter. The two Marines expected others to show up to build that barricade, but nobody appeared on the scene. Daly volunteered to remain in the dangerous area while the C.O. returned to see what had happened. Daly was alone in the area all through the night. He came under constant attack by the Chinese, and the little guy methodically shot them down, successfully holding the position until relieved the next morning. He was awarded the Medal of Honor for his bravery.

Fifteen years later, in October of 1915, Gunnery Sergeant Daly retrieved a machine gun lost during a hasty retrograde movement. He swam a river and took the weapon off a dead packhorse, swimming back to his patrol under intense enemy fire from hundreds of Caco rebel bandits. He received his second Medal of Honor in recognition of the deed.

Although he never received another Medal of Honor, he was awarded the Distinguished Service Cross for bravery in the Battle of Belleau Wood during World War I. The little gunny won this medal at a time when the Marines hit stiff resistance from well-entrenched Germans and the Americans' forward movement was stymied. Daly suddenly jumped to his feet, shouting to his men, "Come on, you sons of bitches! Do you want to live forever?"

**SPACE COAST, FLORIDA
VICINITY OF 28° NORTH AND 80° WEST
15 SEPTEMBER
1500 HOURS LOCAL**

THE *Battlecraft* emerged from the Canaveral Locks with Paul Watkins in firm control. As the vehicle skimmed across the Atlantic Ocean, the skipper, Lieutenant Bill Brannigan, sat in his slightly elevated position overlooking Watkins and Lieutenant Veronica Rivers on the weapons systems. Brannigan had already gotten into the habit of referring to the control area as "the office."

Bobby Lee Atwill sat with his beloved Poder-Ventaja gas-turbine engine in his small compartment just aft in the cabin. He monitored the instrumentation like a mother caring for her infant. The technician made minute adjustments when his ears picked up even the faintest out-of-tune sounds that betrayed rough spots in the power plant's operation.

Lieutenant Jim Cruiser and Senior Chief Petty Officer Buford Dawkins sat in the small space between the power plant and the space they jokingly referred to as the wardroom. Here were the refrigerator, microwave, table, and benches for eating and relaxing.

Veronica Rivers spoke into the intercom to the skipper. "Sir, I'm in contact with the *Dan Daly*. She's ready to receive us in her well. ETA is twenty minutes."

"All right, Lieutenant," Brannigan replied. "Helmsman, steady on course."

"Steady on course, aye, sir," Watkins replied.

The short voyage continued in silence as the Space Coast of Florida quickly faded from view off the stern. Watkins, holding to the course set by Veronica, had the throttle on TWO-THIRDS SPEED, and the ACV whipped along above the water at a steady sixty-two miles an hour. The ride was smooth with some gentle buffeting. During trials when the throttle was opened to FLANK SPEED, the *Battlecraft* hit a respectable ninety-four miles an hour. Bobby Lee Atwill swore he would be able to add another two or three mph within a couple of weeks.

"The *Dan Daly* is in sight, Captain," Veronica reported.

"All right, Watkins," Brannigan said, "take control and bring us into the well."

"Take control and bring us into the well, aye, sir."

Brannigan had realized that the custom of having the helmsman repeat every order was a thorny habit to follow during docking procedures. "I tell you what, Watkins. When you take over control of the vehicle to bring her into our mother ship or a dock, just do your thing without repeating what I say."

"Aye, aye, sir."

"If you do something wrong, I'll let you know," Brannigan said.

Senior Chief Dawkins added, "And I'll make a comment or two myself."

"I hear you both loud and clear," Watkins said with a grin.

When the throttle was cut back, Atwill came out of his engine compartment to join the crew. Watkins moved on a perpendicular course across the *Daly*'s stern, then made a sharp turn and brought the ACV into the ship's well in a smooth maneuver at ONE-THIRD SPEED, reversing the airscrews at just the right time to ease into the tight area at a slow crawl.

Chief Petty Officer Warren Donaldson of the *Daly*'s well-operations crew, whistled in admiration. "Damn nice job!" He looked into the cabin. "Hello, sir!" he called to Brannigan. "Welcome to the *Dan Daly*."

"Nice to be aboard," Brannigan said, stepping across the deck and jumping up on the well ramp. He pointed to the *Battlecraft*. "What do you think of our toy?"

"Jesus!" Donaldson said. "It looks like somebody took a helicopter fuselage and sat it on an ACV deck. Look at them weapons wings."

"It's pretty much the same idea."

Dawkins, Veronica Rivers, and Jim Cruiser joined them while Watkins and Atwill helped the ship's sailors secure the vehicle prior to the closing of the well. As soon as the task was finished, Brannigan introduced them to Donaldson. This was more than a formality. The chief petty officer would be sending them off on missions and greeting them when they returned.

"Sir, your detachment is up on deck waiting for you," Chief Donaldson said.

This unexpected linking up with the Brigands lightened Brannigan's mood. He motioned to the others to follow him, leading them to the ladder that would take them topside. The SEAL detachment, under the command of Chief Petty Officer Matt Gunnarson, had observed assault-section and fire-team integrity when they formed up to meet the skipper. Brannigan took Matt's salute, asking, "What about the gear for Lieutenant Cruiser, Senior Chief Dawkins, and me?"

"It's all waiting for you in your quarters, sir," Matt said. He caught sight of the attractive female officer. "Who's the hot chick?" he asked under his breath.

"That *hot chick* is Lieutenant Rivers, who is going to be our radar and weapons system officer aboard the ACV."

"You mean she's coming along on the mission with us?"

"Yeah," Brannigan said. He lowered his voice. "And tell the men to be extra nice to her. I'm beginning to think that Lieutenant Cruiser is developing a special interest in the lady."

"Aye, sir!"

Brannigan took over the formation and introduced Veronica, Paul Watkins, and Bobby Lee Atwill. He was about to give the SEALs a quick orientation on the *Battlecraft* when he was interrupted by the arrival of a young Marine lance corporal.

"Captain Gooding is waiting for you in the aft ready room, sir," the sharp kid said to Brannigan. "He told me he wanted you and your entire crew up there immediately if not sooner after you dock."

"Tell him we're on our way," Brannigan said. "And pass this on to your buddies. We're a detachment, not a crew."

"Understood, sir!"

Brannigan didn't bother with formalities as he ushered his people across the flight deck. The ship's crew eyed the strangers with friendly curiosity. The scuttlebutt had it that there were exciting times ahead for this mini-assault ship.

Brannigan hurried his people to the island and went up to the second deck and down a corridor. When they walked in, they didn't find the ship's skipper, as expected. However, the man waiting for them was not a stranger to the SEALs.

"Hello, Lieutenant," Commander Tom Carey said.

"You're a hell of a long way from home, sir," Brannigan remarked. "How did you manage to sneak out of Coronado?"

"I've been given the honor of acting as both your N2 and N3 from the *Dan Daly*," Carey said. "You and your people sit down and make yourselves comfortable. I'll give you a quick briefing and then you can settle in." Carey waited for Brannigan's detachment to situate themselves in the available seating before continuing. "Your mission will be to take your ACV out to designated patrol areas to look for vessels carrying arms shipments toward Pakistan. The terrorist group al-Mimkhalif has suffered grievous damage to their delivery program. Our intelligence tells us they have reorganized the system to a new methodology. We are going to discover what that is, and deal it a death blow—literally. As you've probably already figured out, we don't have a clue as to their supply sources, exact routes, or points of pickups and deliveries of weaponry under their latest SOP. So you and the intrepid Brigands are facing some real serious challenges."

"Will we be doing all our work at sea, sir?" Matt Gunnarson asked.

"Negative," Carey answered. "We expect raids on coastal areas too. That means fighting ashore. You'll develop your own SOPs for this activity as you go along, so I want you to all feel free to make suggestions. In other words, share all lessons learned. You'll be going up against a bunch of loonies who think that killing or being killed by those who they consider nonbelievers guarantees them an eternity in Paradise in luxurious surroundings with beautiful women."

"The same old shit we went through in Afghanistan," Bruno Puglisi said from the back.

"Right you are," Carey said. "We're going to be given a constant feed of the latest intelligence from several sources. This guarantees you the latest information that will throw some light in this dark tunnel you're going into. Any questions? No? All right then, get settled in. You'll go out as soon as we get the word to launch the operation."

Brannigan glanced at Dawkins. "Senior Chief, take over the detachment."

"Aye, sir!"

CHAPTER 4

THE seedy little waterfront bar had a name as did all such establishments, but in this case only the neighborhood inebriates knew it. The hand-painted plank that once identified the shabby establishment had blown off during the typhoon of 1998 and had not been replaced. The dinginess of the interior displayed even more careless attention to maintenance and housekeeping. A pair of handles to a broken beer tap remained mounted on the bar after becoming dysfunctional years earlier, the mirror on the wall to the rear was cracked and dirty, while an out-of-date pornographic calendar near the front door showed the faded likeness of a naked blonde lying back in a love seat with her legs invitingly spread open. A decade or so before, a Portuguese merchant seaman who fancied himself quite the artist had drawn a crude phallus entering the model's body.

Abduruddin Suhanto, chief operating officer of the Greater Sunda Shipping Line, sat at a corner table, nursing a cheap gin drink that had been served him in a dusty glass. He patiently awaited the arrival of an old antagonist who had intercepted dozens of his narcotics voyages over long years of smuggling. This bribable, focused opportunist was Commander Carlos Batanza of the Philippine Navy.

The barmaid, a faded corpulent veteran of a long-ago career spent entertaining sailors in dockside cribs, walked over to the table with another serving of gin. She brought a clean glass since Suhanto had tipped her a peso for the first drink. She scooped up some change from the table, including another tip, and went back to the bar, sitting down on a corner stool where she maintained watch over the drinkers. Two patrons, intoxicated almost to a state of unawareness, sat silently at the bar, staring down at their drinks. Another man was passed out under a table, lying in vomit and urine.

The barmaid's attention was diverted by the entrance of a short, muscular Filipino man who looked like a plainclothes policeman in his white suite and tie. He paused for a moment, surveying the interior. He spotted Suhanto and walked past the woman to join him at the table. The man smiled and nodded as he sat down. "Hello, my friend."

"Hello," Suhanto said.

The man, Commander Carlos Batanza, turned toward the bar. "A double shot of scotch," he ordered from the barman. "And don't shove any of that watered-down shit at me."

The drink was poured from a special bottle reserved for cops and other people who could make trouble for the bar owner. The woman brought the libation over and left abruptly after the delivery, knowing better than to expect any payment, much less a gratuity, from the customer.

Batanza tasted the drink, smacked his lips, and turned a heavy-lidded glare on Suhanto. "I am here. What is it you have to offer me?"

"I have come into a situation that has a great potential of producing much money for the two of us," Suhanto said softly. "I am speaking of a chance to become permanently wealthy. This is the sort of monetary reward that provides big investments, mansions, and villas in Europe."

"Really? I take it you mean more money than to simply buy an expensive car."

"Naturally, Commander. I have ventured into another area of surreptitious dealings. Arms." He was pleased to note that Batanza's eyes had opened wider. "Of course it all depends on how well—or bad—things go."

"Then what must I do for us to get our hands on this fortune you speak of?"

"You have the means to make deals in weapons sales, do you not?"

"I have certain contacts," Batanza replied. "But this is a very tricky state of affairs. Particularly if the weaponry has been stolen from government sources."

"These most definitely have not," Suhanto stated confidently, though he really hadn't the slightest idea where al-Mimkhalif obtained the goods. "These are untraceable and easy to resell."

"Then why do you not do it yourself?" Batanza wanted to know.

"I have no colleagues in that business," Suhanto admitted. "You, on the other hand, have displayed great efficiency in passing on many types of goods for a great profit."

"Mmm," Batanza mused. "And to whom are you supposed to deliver these weapons?"

"A Turkish arms dealer," Suhanto lied, knowing that even Batanza would not be greedy enough to steal from an Islamic terrorist organization. The corrupt naval officer was more used to the shadowy world of criminality with no political or religious agendas. Suhanto, on the other hand, would technically also be the one who was robbed as far as al-Mimkhalif was concerned. "I know the Turk only by the code name of Viski."

"Never mind him," Batanza said. "I shall not be having much to do with the fellow, eh?" He treated himself to another sip of scotch. "So what is your plan of operation?"

"I am now devoting all my ships to this new business," Suhanto explained. "In particular, I shall employ the *Jakarta*."

"Ah! Captain Muharno's vessel! An excellent man."

Suhanto smiled, thinking, *You've stolen enough off his ship, you greedy bastard!* But he said. "I know you find him trustworthy. At any rate, Muharno picks up the shipments off the island of Palawan at a predetermined location."

"I am not concerned with that," Batanza said impatiently, although he filed the information into his brain's memory banks.

"Of course not, Commander," Suhanto said. "From that point my vessels go to a specific location for delivery to other ships. Naturally, you are to intercept my cargo before the rendezvous."

"Of course!" Batanza exclaimed. "I think a seventy-five percent share is only fair for me."

Now Suhanto felt a surge of confidence. This time Batanza was not in the driver's seat. "In my opinion your share should be no more than a third."

"Ridiculous! I have the means of disposing of the arms."

"And *I* have the means of obtaining them," Suhanto said. "I will no longer bargain. It is sixty-forty in my favor." He leaned forward aggressively. "Take it or leave it."

Batanza's jaw tightened with anger for only a moment. This was a great opportunity to make what the Americans call "big bucks." "I acquiesce to your demands."

"Excellent," Suhanto said, knowing that the Filipino would not cheat him and spoil his chance at a continued source of big money. "I have a chart for you. It shows the routes from pickup to delivery. The first voyage will be early in the morning on a date yet to be determined. I shall dispatch the *Jakarta*." He handed the topographical rendering over to Batanza. "Choose where you wish to have the interception."

Batanza unrolled the chart and studied the course. "The best place would be in the South China Sea that same afternoon. I can give you the exact longitude and latitude later."

"I will inform Captain Muharno," Suhanto said.

Batanza grinned almost impishly. "Will you be returning to narcotics if these arms shipments cease?"

The question infuriated Suhanto, but he controlled his temper, keeping the expression on his face calm and inscrutable. "I thought perhaps we might work out a new deal in that instance since we are going to be colleagues."

"That will never happen," Batanza said. "It will be very rewarding for me to catch your vessels at sea with cargos of dope. I think I was getting at least a fifth of them, eh?"

"You were getting half," Suhanto said.

"You are a lying snake," Batanza snarled. "We will discuss this later."

"Let us concentrate all our efforts on that first arms shipment."

"Of course," Batanza said. He finished his scotch, then got to his feet. After a quick nod to his host, he left the bar.

Suhanto signaled to the old barmaid for another drink.

PAKISTAN-AFGHANISTAN BORDER
22 SEPTEMBER
0430 HOURS LOCAL

THE al-Mimkhalif raider group moved silently along the path that led from the foothills down to the plain where the mission objective—a police border guard station—was located some twenty-five meters inside Pakistan. The moonlight was intermittently blocked by clouds, but visibility was good enough that the mujahideen had no trouble in negotiating their way down the steep rocky terrain toward lower ground.

Mike Assad was toward the rear of the column of two dozen men. This superbly trained and experienced U.S. Navy SEAL had been playing the role of a not-too-bright amateur soldier since his insertion into the terrorist group. Consequently, he had been assigned the lowly position of ammunition bearer for the operation rather than being a member of the attack group. The rag-doll figures of mujahideen in their baggy clothes were barely visible to him in the semidarkness as he made his way within the column. Mike's strong physique easily supported the thirty-five kilograms of shells he carried in the ammo pack on his back.

Mike had already passed on the details of this raid through his dead-letter drop a few days earlier. At that time he was unaware that he would be a participant in the operation, and there was a good chance he had inadvertently put himself in a great deal of danger by revealing the raid. There was no doubt the Pakistani military would see this as an excellent opportunity to give al-Mimkhalif a very bloody nose.

Now his companions were at the end of the grueling twenty-kilometer march across rough mountain terrain, and the fatigue that dogged them was heavy and punishing. They were heartened, however, by the knowledge that at the end of this early morning attack, they would have police vehicles to carry them back most of the way to their base camp.

The leader called a halt at a signal from the two-man scout team ahead. The well-trained outfit immediately knelt down, each man facing toward his assigned firing area. Mike and the other ammo men squatted together in the middle of the formation.

The scouts came up and informed the leader that the target was close by. Orders were passed down to the subleaders to take their teams and position them in a semicircle formation that almost surrounded the police station. All this had already been worked out on an improvised sand table back at camp, and the mujahideen moved quickly and efficiently into position.

Mike followed his mortar squad to a predetermined location where they could fire their 51-millimeter shells to best advantage from the small French mortars. As they prepared the weapons, the others settled down to wait for the first sign of the rising sun over the eastern mountain ranges. After a passage of ten minutes, the only sounds were deep breaths now and then, though a snort of a snore erupted from time to time when a sleepy fighter dozed off. Such security infractions were followed by angry hissings and the smack of an open hand across the offender's face from his team leader. But mostly these warriors of Islam were silent, grateful for some rest after the exhausting hike.

0515 HOURS LOCAL

THE first pink showings of dawn brought a slight stirring to the crowd. Dozing men were shaken awake, and the mortar teams prepared for unleashing a short-range barrage that would blast the small police building to bits. This was not an important mission; its purpose was to do no more than harass the Pakistanis, who had sided with infidel Westerners to destroy true Islam. However, it would also give these men of al-Mimkhalif the practice and confidence that could be gained from a successful operation.

The top of the sun could now be seen on the horizon, and the orange of the early morning was being melted by ever-widening streaks of growing daylight. The loaders on the mortars laid out the shells that Mike Assad had borne on his back for many hours and kilometers. The squad, like the others, was now ready to begin firing at the leader's order.

Then all hell broke loose.

Automatic fire swept through the clusters of al-Mimkhalif fighters, knocking them into twisted bloody heaps. Skulls fractured and facial features imploded under the steel-jacketed onslaught along with ripped flesh and broken bones in body hits. Mike, his SEAL instincts now kicking in, went immediately to the ground. The spurts of earth around him indicated the mortar section was getting particular attention, and he low-crawled rapidly away from the emplacement. A quick glance brought him the sight of the dead and wounded mujahideen, and he continued on until reaching a stand of rocks.

He ignored potential snakes and scorpions and went into the cover as the firing continued.

Mike stayed hunched down until the flying bullets lessened noticeably, then stopped altogether. After taking a deep breath, he got to his feet and made a run for a distant patch of woods.

"Wakkif! Dur kawam!"

The command to halt and turn around was in Arabic with an Urdu accent. Mike complied immediately, finding himself facing a scowling Pakistani paratrooper. The man pointed back up the hill, and Mike walked in that direction with his hands high above his head. The two made their way through the scattered dead mujahideen to a spot where a quartet of dejected prisoners squatted in the midst of more paratroopers. The captured men's hands were tightly and painfully bound behind their backs.

Mike laughed inwardly at the irony of the situation in spite of almost being killed. Here he was a prisoner of war as a result of his own intel report. The guys back in Brannigan's Brigands would think the situation hilarious.

**ACV *BATTLECRAFT*
BAY OF BENGAL
VICINITY OF 10° NORTH AND 90° EAST
1100 HOURS LOCAL**

THE *Battlecraft* was into its first real patrol, skimming the waves at TWO-THIRDS speed, hitting exactly 61.99 miles per hour. They were not alone on the mission. A patrol of F/A-18 Super Hornets from a nearby carrier battle group shadowed them as aerial support.

Inside the ACV's office, Paul Watkins kept an eye on the direction indicated by the compass, making a few small corrections as the wind pressed unexpectedly from one or another direction. The next thing to get installed on the AVC would be an autopilot, but he enjoyed the hands-on experience. It made the veteran helmsman feel like a real sailor in the finest traditions of the United States Navy.

Lieutenant Veronica Rivers monitored the radar and kept a close eye on the electronic warning indicator. The First Assault Section had the duty that day, while Senior Chief Buford Dawkins's Second Section stayed behind on the *Dan Daly* doing PT and weapons PM. They were not in a good mood about being left behind on the first patrol, but when Lieutenant Bill Brannigan issued an order, it was his way or the highway. These administrative and/or tactical decisions were not open to discussion.

At that moment, Lieutenant Jim Cruiser and his two fire teams were topside, relaxing and taking in some sun with their weaponry close at hand, while Bobby Lee Atwill, the only crew member not at his station, lounged in the wardroom, slowly and happily consuming cold fried chicken from his box lunch prepared by the galley crew of the USS *Dan Daly.*

Lieutenant Bill Brannigan sat in the skipper's seat, glad to simply relax and enjoy the ride across the blue expanse of water while his crew concentrated on their duties. He noted Veronica Rivers getting up and going to the refrigerator for a Diet Coke. She glanced at Atwill and frowned at his oil-stained fingers. "You should wash your hands before you eat."

"Well, ma'am," the turbine technician replied, "engine grease is a nutrient to me. I've soaked up so much it's in my system and has to be replenished from time to time. I'm addicted, ma'am. I'm as much a grease-head as them NASCAR mechanics." He winked at her. "Except I ain't paid near as much."

Veronica laughed and got her soda. She went back to her console and sat down at the exact moment a blip appeared on the radar screen. She quickly called out, "Contact! One-one-niner. Distance ten miles."

"Go to course one-one-niner," Brannigan ordered.

"Go to course one-one-niner, aye, sir," responded Watkins.

Brannigan picked up the microphone on his command communications system and raised the F/A-18s, who were keeping far away enough not to alert any potential ships with contraband. "We've got a reading and turning to one-one-niner," Brannigan reported. "We'll be in visual contact within approximately six minutes. Over."

A pilot's voice came back immediately. "Roger, *Battlecraft*." The aircraft turned slightly to get on course.

Now, standing ready on the *Battlecraft*, the First Assault Section eagerly awaited a chance to jump aboard a bad guys' ship and do some real serious ass-kicking. Jim Cruiser scanned the horizon to their direct front through his binoculars.

Bruno Puglisi, holding his SAW, squinted his eyes in his eagerness to sight something ahead. "See anything yet, sir?"

"Affirmative!" the lieutenant answered. "One o'clock!"

Petty Officer First Class Connie Concord, leader of Bravo Fire Team, shifted his view to the right a degree or so. "Yeah!"

Paul Watkins, acting on orders from Brannigan, went to HALF-SPEED and then ONE-THIRD-SPEED. When they drew close enough, they could see it was a tanker heading on a course of two-two-five. She was riding high enough in the water to show she was empty.

"Probably headed for the Persian Gulf to make a pickup," Brannigan remarked. "Okay, Watkins. Bring her about."

"Bring her about, aye, sir."

"Lieutenant Rivers, give us a course back to the *Daly*."

"One-niner-two," Veronica reported.

"Got that, Watkins?" Brannigan asked.

"Course one-niner-two, aye, sir."

The *Battlecraft*, her first patrol now over, headed for hearth and home. Up on top, Petty Officer Garth Redhawk, a rifleman in Alpha Fire Team, was not happy. "I was hoping for a little more excitement."

His team leader, Chief Matt Gunnarson, glanced over at him. "I thought you Indian guys were the patient types."

Redhawk shook his head. "Not when it comes to fighting."

**POLICE HEADQUARTERS
DALBANDIN, PAKISTAN
23 SEPTEMBER
0830 HOURS LOCAL**

THE mud brick building was a typical provincial lockup with two large cells separated by a single corridor between them. Mike Assad and his four al-Mimkhalif companions rested uneasily in one of the confinement areas without the benefits of mats or blankets. The only thing they had plenty of since their capture had been beatings—the first within a half hour after they surrendered; the second before boarding the trucks for the trip to the jail; and the third when they arrived and got off the vehicles. Even the two men who were wounded received their share of physical punishment. Now the most seriously injured mujahideen seemed to have gone into shock. He had taken a belly wound when a paratrooper's submachine gun stitched him across the body. Mike and another man tried to help the poor fellow, who had lost a large amount of blood, but their rudimentary ministrations did him little good. The Pakistani police had grudgingly provided some dirty rags for bandaging the wounds, but it was obvious he was not going to survive long without proper medical treatment.

Now, sitting in the bare cell, Mike observed his companions rather dispassionately. They had been full of fervor during the sermons bellowed at them by the clerics in the camp, and danced around shouting pro-Islamic slogans that promised death and hellfire to Westerners and fallen Muslims. These demonstrations of outrage included the burning of crudely made American and Israeli flags that were then leaped on and trampled by the ferocious untried rookies.

This was something Mike hated to do, but he participated as was expected of him. He had learned during his SERE training that if the enemy wanted him to chant, "The American Flag is a dirty old rag," he was to go ahead and do it. His job was to stay healthy and maintain his cover. Any unwise demonstration of patriotism would accomplish nothing but compromise the mission.

The previously defiant mujahideen, after being caught in the murderous cross fire of a cleverly laid ambush, were crestfallen and frightened. They hadn't even had time to kill any of the enemy before the paratroop detachment opened up on them. What was supposed to have been a quick but bright victory had turned into a noisy scene of death as bursts of automatic-weapons fire plowed into them. They had been stunned into inaction by the unexpected onslaught.

No food or water was provided for the prisoners during the first twenty-four hours of confinement, and the police had begun to pull them out of the cell one by one for interrogation. Mike knew the reason behind this method; a comfortable prisoner can be a defiant prisoner under even rigorous interrogation. But someone who is stunned, hungry, and thirsty is aware of the power his captors have over him. It gives the captive a feeling of isolation and hopelessness.

Each of these periods of questioning had gone on for close to an hour, and when the captives were dragged back to the cell, they showed signs of additional mistreatment above and beyond that which they had already endured. Mike was the last, and when they pushed him out of the cell block, he fervently hoped the cops had expended most of their energy beating his predecessors.

He was wrong.

The two guards who had fetched him shoved him into the interrogation room, sat him down in a chair, tied him to it, then took turns punching him in the face. They didn't hit him hard enough to break his jaw or nose, but when they finished smacking him around, blood poured from his nostrils and his face was badly bruised. The initiation process didn't stop until an officer entered the room. He walked to a spot in front of the prisoner and glared at him with all the hatred he had for the foreign troublemakers in his country.

"Where are you from?" he asked in Arabic.

Mike knew he would never be able to pass as a citizen of an Arab country, so he quickly spoke up, saying, "I from America."

The Pakistani sneered. "*Hakkan*—truly?" Then he asked in English. "Where in America are you from?"

"New York," Mike replied, using his cover story. "I lived in Buffalo."

The Pakistani's eyes opened wide. "By Allah! You *are* an American!"

"Yes, sir."

The Pakistani laughed loudly. "So you are what they call a Johnny Jihad, eh? Well, my fine fellow, we have special instructions on what to do when we get our hands on a Johnny Jihad." He spoke over Mike's head to the two policemen. They also roared with laughter, and one slapped him hard across the back of his head.

"Is it really necessary to punch me so much?" Mike asked.

"Of course it is," the Pakistani said. "We will turn you over to the American Embassy and you can go home where they will coddle you and read you your rights, then put you in a nice comfortable American penitentiary with color television. We hear they even bring in whores for the convicts' enjoyment." He scowled. "But until you get there, we'll make your miserable life a hell on earth."

It took all of Mike Assad's inner strength and self-control to bear up under the beating that followed. He could tell they weren't hitting him hard enough to cause permanent damage, but it hurt worse than if they were trying to really kick his ass bad. He wasn't going to faint or pass out under open-handed slaps and kicks to his shins.

The three Pakistanis wore themselves out after twenty fun-filled minutes, and Mike was untied and dragged to another part of the jail to be thrown into solitary confinement.

CHAPTER 5

COMMANDER Carlos Batanza sat on the bridge of Patrol Boat 22 waiting patiently for the expected contact with the SS *Jakarta* and its arms shipment. He leisurely smoked a cigarette as his executive officer supervised the watch on duty.

Batanza was proud of his vessel even though she was a third-hand purchase by the Filipino government. She had begun her career as a minesweeper in the Royal Navy, where she proved her worth to the Queen's sailors during ten years of service done mostly in the North Sea. Eventually she was sold to Singapore, who converted her to a support ship for mine-countermeasures missions. After a short but useful career in that nation's navy, she was purchased by the Philippines and

redesignated a patrol boat to be used in antismuggling operations on the Philippine Sea, the South China Sea, the Pacific
Ocean, and the Celebes Sea.

Her only Filipino commander had been Batanza and during his five years as the skipper, he'd accomplished several
self-benefiting goals. His primary fait accompli had been developing a successful program of stopping and robbing various smugglers on the high seas. His father-in-law, a Manila
police inspector, had all the contacts necessary for the profitable disposal of goods and narcotics that the son-in-law
brought in from his patrols. The family fortune flourished
through these illegal enterprises, sending sons, daughters,
nieces, and nephews to college or setting them up in business.

Batanza had chosen a crew consisting of a trio of close
officer friends and fifteen ratings of long-service sailors
with whom he and his cohorts had established a close rapport. This comradeship had been developed through all that
mutual support and sharing of spoils. They knew Abduruddin Suhanto's Greater Sunda Shipping Line well, having re-
peatedly plundered his four ships over a period of a decade
and a half. There were other targets of opportunity as well,
and all members of the Patrol Boat 22 crew could realisti-
cally expect a much richer retirement when their personal
riches were combined with pensions from the Philippine
Navy. All drove big American cars and were able to provide
well for their families, as well as maintain attractive mis-
tresses on the side.

"Contact!" the radar operator called out. "Zero-one-one.
Five kilometers."

"That must be the *Jakarta*," the executive officer said.
This was Lieutenant Commander Ferdinand Aguinaldo,
Batanza's best friend.

"And right on schedule," Batanza said in happy satisfaction as he checked his watch. "Make the interception, Number One."

"Aye, aye, sir," Aguinaldo replied.

The distance between Patrol Boat 22 and the *Jakarta*

narrowed rapidly, and in less than a half hour visual contact was made. Aguinaldo got on the radio and ordered the merchant vessel to heave to and prepare to transfer cargo. Captain Bacharahman Muharno's voice came back with an affirmative reply. His good humor was evident over the radio speaker. This time there would be no piracy involved. This was a business deal that would benefit everyone on both ships.

The sea was calm and the maneuvering to bring the vessels close enough for the transfer of goods went smoothly and quickly. Batanza went out on the signal bridge with a bullhorn, waving to Muharno.

"Ahoy, the *Jakarta*!" the commander said, speaking through the device. "How are you this afternoon, Captain?"

Muharno, using his own bullhorn, waved back. "It is a beautiful day, is it not, Commander?"

"Indeed! What have you brought us?"

"An excellent shipment!" Muharno answered. "Stinger antiaircraft missile launchers. Sixty to be exact, along with one hundred missiles. That is two tons worth of cargo. Can your ship handle that much?"

"Easily! What we can't get in the hold, we can stack on the deck," Batanza assured him. "We have taken much larger loads in the past."

"I should have remembered," Muharno replied with a laugh. "This is not the first time cargo has been lifted from the *Jakarta* to your boat."

By then the cargo nets bearing crates of Stingers were being hoisted up from the hold of the civilian vessel. They were swung over the portion of the deck just aft of the patrol boat's bridge, and then gently lowered to the waiting Philippine sailors. These men quickly picked up the weapons to pass them to other hands formed up in a line that led down to the hold of the patrol vessel.

In less than a half hour the entire shipment was aboard Batanza's boat. Batanza waved the all-clear signal to Muharno that everything was aboard.

"See you next trip, my friend!" he said through the bull-horn.

"I shall look forward to it!" Muharno replied.

Connecting lines were cast off and the two craft carefully worked their way apart, before turning onto the proper courses that led to their next destinations.

POLICE HEADQUARTERS
DALBANDIN, PAKISTAN
27 SEPTEMBER
1045 HOURS LOCAL

MIKE Assad had lost track of how much time had passed since he was thrown into the solitary confinement cell. It was hard to tell if it was day or night since the only light came from a wall lamp in the corridor that shone through the small viewing port in the door. This provided a weak illumination, but it eventually improved somewhat as Mike's eyes got used to the dimness. There was nothing but a small straw mat on the floor, and his toilet consisted of a rusty bucket that leaked. But at least he had been provided with water and a glutinous meal of mutton and rice.

It was obvious the fact that he was an American had put him in a special category. It seemed his companions from al-Mimkhalif were going to suffer more deprivation and mistreatment. A lot of information would be given up on the terrorist organization before their ordeal ended. To make it worse for them, their future in the Pakistani penal system seemed to offer nothing but the bleakest of prospects.

Mike lay on the mat with his eyes closed, doing deep-breathing exercises to dispel the tension and nervousness that threatened his self-control. He missed Brannigan's Brigands and the comradeship he shared with them. He wasn't used to being off on his own. The company of those great guys gave him confidence and courage in the most dangerous of situations. He wondered what his best buddy,

Dave Leibowitz, was doing. Mike and Dave were called the "Odd Couple" by the other SEALs. They were the closest of friends even though one was Jewish-American and the other Arab-American. Both were Americans first, and fiercely loyal to the U.S.A. The fact they served together in the U.S. Navy's most elite unit reinforced that friendship and patriotism.

Mike turned his thoughts from Brannigan's Brigands to his life before enlistment. He remembered prom nights, winning the district wrestling championship in his junior year of high school, kissing Kathy Mubarak the first time, and eating his mother's specialty, *kabab samak,* a grilled-fish dish with tomatoes and green peppers.

"American!"

The sound of the jailer's voice out in the corridor jolted Mike out of his reverie. He sat up just as the door opened. The jailer motioned him to step out of the cell. Mike complied and was taken by the arm and walked down to the egress. From there they crossed a small exercise yard and went into another building. The enforced stroll ended up in an office, where he was unceremoniously pushed down onto a chair. Then he was left alone. Since he hadn't been tied up, Mike hoped it meant no more beatings.

Almost a half hour passed before the door to the room opened again. This time a Pakistani police lieutenant and two men in sports shirts and slacks came in. The casually dressed pair walked to the front of the prisoner and stared down at him. They were a real Mutt-and-Jeff pair. The white guy was a short, blond man with a stocky build, while the black guy was a tall, willowy African-American who looked like he should have been in the NBA.

"This isn't a Johnny Jihad," the white guy said. "He's a fucking towel-head."

"Yeah," the black guy agreed. He glared at Mike. "We figured you were one of those poor little Anglo rich boys who turned to Islam because you've lost your fucking faith in the local Episcopal church in Beverly Hills where you were born. Or maybe you're from the Hamptons in Long Island and grew disillusioned by your wealthy father's greed in making money. But you don't fit into those molds at all. So where are you from, ass-face?"

"Buffalo," Mike replied.

"Were you born in the States?" the white guy asked.

"Yeah," Mike replied. "Who are you guys?"

"Shut your fucking mouth, ass-face," the black guy said. "Where's your American passport?"

"My name ain't ass-face," Mike said defiantly.

The white guy leaned down, glaring straight into Mike's eyes. "Listen up good, ass-face. From this point on, you're in the gentle custody of the United States fucking Government. Got it? You're either going home for a trial where your rights will be observed, or you'll be on your fucking way to Guantanamo Bay in Cuba where your fucking rights *won't* be observed. It all depends on how cooperative and courteous you are."

"I'm an American citizen," Mike said, feigning fear and anger since he didn't feel it proper to reveal his true identification at that point in the proceedings. "You can't send me down to Cuba."

"Oh, ass-face, you're such a bad boy," the black guy said in pseudo-disappointment. "I guess we'll just hold you incognito since there'll be no records of your arrest. That will give us plenty of time to sweat what we want out of you."

"Yeah," the white guy said. "You're up that ol' shit creek without a paddle at this point. I personally hope you keep shooting off your mouth about your Constitutional rights. We've got some boys who'll give you a great big fucking attitude adjustment."

The Pakistani policeman laid a document down on the desk. "Please to sign here, gentlemen. Then you may take this scum and do what you wish with him."

The paperwork was quickly taken care of; then Mike was stood up and cuffed with his hands behind his back. They walked him from the building out to the street, where a van waited. The side door was opened and the prisoner was pushed inside. The rear area was bare, and Mike had to sit on the floor with his back up against the side of the vehicle. Within moments his escorts were in the front seat, ready to go.

They remained silent as they drove out of town, and turned onto a macadam highway, heading east. After a few minutes, the black guy, who sat in the passenger seat, turned to look at Mike. "How're you doing, ass-face?"

Mike declined to answer.

The black guy swung his hand up, holding a Beretta 9-millimeter automatic. He pointed it straight at Mike's head, saying, "Give me just one fucking excuse and I'll put a bullet straight into that thick traitorous skull of yours."

The white guy chuckled. "Let's stop somewhere along the way and shoot the son of a bitch. We can say he tried to escape."

Mike turned his face away to stare at the back door. This situation was something he'd never expected when he volunteered for the SEALs.

KUPANG, TIMOR ISLAND
29 SEPTEMBER
0900 HOURS LOCAL

ABDURUDDIN Suhanto sat in his office, smoking a cigar and taking nips from a pocket flask containing Johnny Walker Black scotch whiskey. His swollen feet were up on a padded stool as he gazed unseeing out of the window at the usual waterfront activity. One of his tubs, the SS *Surabaya,* sat in rusty squalor at a dock where its cargo of Taiwanese sewing machines was being offloaded. They were destined for a sweatshop in Bandung where a line of clothing bearing the name of a famous English actress was manufactured. It seemed that even Suhanto's occasional legitimate shipping activities were destined to be tainted by some sort of controversy.

The old clerk Bachaman rapped lightly on the door in his usual timid style.

"Come in!" Suhanto said loudly, irritated by the interruption.

The skinny little old man stepped into the office, his eyes opened wide in worry. "Mr. Sabah has arrived as per your invitation, sir."

"Send the gentleman in," Suhanto said. He quickly assumed what he considered a sad, regretful expression on his round face and waited for his guest to appear.

When Sabah entered, he walked directly to the front of the desk and glared down at the shipping company owner. "What is the bad news you have for me?"

"Oh, Mr. Sabah," Suhanto said, looking as if he were about to break out in cries of incalculable lamentation. "*Thasart k'tir*—I regret it very much! But your last shipment was stolen from us at sea."

"Do not tell me that!"

"Alas! I have no choice!" Suhanto wailed.

"How did such a thing happen? And who did it?"

"It was a warship," Suhanto said. "And my captain, Muharno, said it flew no flag. They simply came alongside and threatened to sink the *Jakarta* if they did not obey the order to heave to."

Sabah sat down in a nearby chair, looking suspiciously at Suhanto. "What language was this warship crew speaking?"

"Unfortunately, it was one Captain Muharno did not know," Suhanto said. "To my own thinking it might have been a Singaporean naval vessel. They speak many languages in that country. Malay, Chinese—"

"I know what languages are spoken in Singapore!" Sabah interrupted in a furious tone of voice. "There must be some way of identifying the thief!"

"Oh, I was very stern with Captain Muharno," Suhanto said. "I spoke to him in great anger, demanding that he remember more." He shrugged. "But I am afraid all he knows is that it was a warship."

"What sorts of uniforms and insignia was the crew wearing?" Sabah demanded to know.

"That is what is so strange," Suhanto said. "They were dressed in civilian clothing as is typical of merchant seamen. But their vessel was armed and well equipped as are those of navies."

Sabah's teeth were bared like those of a growling dog. "How did they know the *Jakarta* carried an arms shipment?"

Suhanto shrugged. "They probably did not know. They were after whatever cargo was aboard."

Sabah got angrily to his feet. "We shall look into this. Our organization has contacts in many places." He walked toward the door, jerking it open. Before leaving, he turned back toward Suhanto. "The loss of those weapons has been a hard blow to our antiaircraft capabilities. This is not the end of this incident!" Then he made an abrupt exit.

Suhanto smiled, speaking to himself under his breath. "That is right, you arrogant Arab bastard! This is just the beginning!" He reached for his flask and took another slug of the excellent scotch.

UNITED STATES EMBASSY
ISLAMABAD, PAKISTAN
1030 HOURS LOCAL

THE Marine guards on gate duty recognized the van as it turned off Embassy Road and onto Second Road. They waited alertly for the subtle all-clear signal to be flashed to them by the white driver, Mulvaney. He held the steering wheel with one hand at the top center. If there was a problem, both hands would have been in that position. If the situation was serious enough, such as being held hostage by a potential assassin or suicide bomber, the driver's hands would have been at ten o'clock and two o'clock. That would be the gesture to signal the sentries to stop the vehicle at all costs. Either way, the black guy, Wheatfall, in the passenger seat would have his arms crossed over his chest to indicate he concurred with the signal.

The vehicle slowed as the gate was opened, then sped through the opening and across the parking lot to continue around the building to an area that was blocked from view by a thick grove of chestnut trees. The van came to a stop at the same time that another pair of Marines stepped from the embassy building to meet them. Mulvaney and Wheatfall got out of the vehicle and walked around to open the sliding door on the side. They reached in and grabbed Mike Assad, dragging him bodily from the interior.

Mulvaney pulled a key from his pocket and unlocked the cuffs, removing them from Mike's wrists. He grabbed the prisoner by the collar and shoved him toward the Marines, who each took an arm. Mulvaney laughed. "Why don't you guys turn him loose? I've been wanting to kill the turncoat son of a bitch ever since we picked him up over in Delbandin."

One of the Marines grinned. "We'd love to, Mr. Mulvaney. But we've got orders to lock him up in the detention cell all safe and secure."

Mulvaney and Wheatfall waited until Mike was taken into the building before they entered through another door. The pair went down a corridor and upstairs to the office of their boss, the embassy's chief intelligence officer, Rod Barker. They rapped on the door and stepped inside.

Barker was a slim, clean-shaven man with longish hair. He looked up from the SITREP he was reading. "I take it you've brought in the prisoner as arranged."

"Right," Wheatfall replied. "And he's an American all right."

"The son of a bitch!" Mulvaney exclaimed. "God! I wanted to—"

"Never mind," Barker said. "What kind of shape was he in?"

"He'd gotten a few knocks from the Pakos," Wheatfall said. "But he's in fine fettle." '

"Yeah," Mulvaney said. "When do we start interrogating him? This guy should be able to cough up some great intel."

"I'm going to start with a friendly introduction," Barker said. "Y'know what I mean. Where's he from. What's his family like. All that kind of shit. I'll make friends with him."

"If you want to play good cop and bad cop, I'm volunteering for bad cop," Mulvaney said.

Wheatfall laughed. "And I'm volunteering for *worst* cop!"

"We'll get serious with him tomorrow," Barker said. "But, like I said, I'm going to be nice at first. I'll even let him have some lunch. I want to start with the impression that I'm more or less welcoming him home. Y'know what I mean? The old interrogation scam that the prodigal son returneth to understanding and forgiveness."

"Don't be too nice," Mulvaney said. "We can violate the hell out of his Constitutional rights over here. Once the bastard's back in the States, he'll have an attorney."

"Don't worry," Barker said. "I'm not going to be his butt boy."

1315 HOURS LOCAL

THE Marine guards walked Mike Assad ahead of them as they escorted him to Rod Barker's office. The prisoner was handcuffed and both men carried regulation billy clubs that any veteran of a Navy brig would have recognized. The pair of highly disciplined Marines displayed no animosity toward the prisoner other than a properly stern attitude. When they arrived at the door, one took Mike's arm while the other knocked.

"Come in."

Mike was taken inside to a spot in front of Barker's desk. "Here's the pris'ner as ordered, Mr. Barker," the senior Marine reported.

"Fine," Barker said. "You can leave us. We're just going to have a little chat." He smiled at Mike, then nodded to the Marines. "Let's take off those handcuffs. What do you say?"

"Yes, sir!" the Marine responded. He quickly removed the restraints. "Anything else, Mr. Barker?"

"I don't think so, guys," Barker said. He waited for the guards to exit the office before speaking to his unusual guest. "Sit down."

Instead of sitting, Mike smiled. "I'll stand, if you don't mind."

"Certainly. Suit yourself."

"What do you do around here?" Mike asked.

"I'm the embassy intelligence officer."

"All right then," Mike said. "I'm an operative in Operation Deep Thrust."

"Really?" Barker asked. "What's the weather like?"

"It's a cold day in Hell."

The words of the recognition phrase were so unexpected that Barker stood up. He started to speak, then went to his safe. It took him a few moments to open the security container, and he withdrew a red folder. He pulled a sheet of paper from it, giving the document a careful read for several moments. When he finished, he turned his attention back to Mike. "You're inserted into al-Mimkhalif?"

"Yep," Mike said, now feeling he was very close to getting back to the Brigands. "The name is Mikael Assad." Then he added, "United States Navy SEALs."

"*Good God!* This is a hell of a situation, isn't it?"

"Hey, no shit," Mike commented.

ACV *BATTLECRAFT*
USS *DAN DALY* DOCKING WELL
1500 HOURS LOCAL

LIEUTENANT Jim Cruiser sat in the skipper's chair watching Lieutenant Veronica Rivers run diagnostic tests on the *Battlecraft*'s communication, navigation, and weapons systems. She had been at it for over two hours, using various instruments that read impulses and other evidential data on

the condition of each piece of equipment. Although Lieutenant Bill Brannigan had assigned his 2IC additional duties
of maintaining the ACV's technical logs, he didn't really
have to be there since the results would be printed out. But
he was antsy on this day off from patrolling and didn't feel
like sitting around in his cabin.

"That's it," Veronica said, stepping back from the instruments. "It all checks out A-okay as the astronauts say."

"All right," Jim said.

"I'll tell you one thing for sure," Veronica said cheerfully.
"Those DuBose brothers put together one bad-ass machine
when they built this baby."

"I suppose so," Jim replied.

"Do you want to read the printouts?"

"Hell, no!" Jim snapped. "Put the info in the maintenance
log and I'll check it out when I sign off on all this shit."

"Sure," Veronica said, "if that's what you want." She was
surprised by her fellow officer's flash of temper. She gathered the printouts and put them in the maintenance folder.
"Is there anything else? If not, I'm going up to the wardroom."

"Suit yourself," Jim said grumpily.

He remained seated after she left, staring out the bridge
windshield at the activity in the well. They had accomplished nothing during a dozen patrols, but the lack of real
achievement in the mission wasn't the biggest thing bugging
Jim Cruiser. For the past couple of weeks he had begun feeling a downright boyish awkwardness when he was around
Veronica. This was nothing new for the young naval officer.
It was always the prelude of his developing an infatuation
for a member of the opposite sex. But the last thing he
wanted was to find himself in a romantic, sexual relationship
with the attractive young woman.

Jim Cruiser was a normal man with normal needs. He existed in a pattern of one-night stands dominated by the un-
spoken agreement that the coupling was only a temporary,
ships-that-pass-in-the-night thing. He even hired call girls

from time to time when the opportunity and his financial condition made it possible. All this left him physically satisfied, but emotionally pent up with normal desires for a meaningful relationship dammed like a river. He knew that a romance between him and Veronica Rivers would be a disaster for both of them. But the impelling drive of wanting someone was a hard desire to smother.

Jim abruptly stood up and walked outside, leaping from the deck onto the walkway around the docking well. There was a bottle of Smirnoff's Vodka in his cabin, and he could hear it calling to him.

CHAPTER 6

GREEN EMERALD RESORT AND SPA
SINGAPORE
30 SEPTEMBER
1030 HOURS LOCAL

HAFEZ Sabah, the agent for al-Mimkhalif, sat in the back of the cab paying no attention to the beautiful view as he rode across the causeway from the city to Sentora Island. The trip continued until the taxi arrived at the lobby entrance of the Green Emerald Resort and Spa. To casual observers, Sabah appeared to be a down-at-the-heels but respectable Middle Eastern businessman as he paid the fare and exited the vehicle. The doorman, a serious Malayan garbed in a gaudy uniform complete with aiguillettes, epaulets, and a high-peaked cap with a bill sporting an oak-leaf design, stepped forward looking like a comic-opera field marshal. He offered a salute, but the respectful gesture was dimmed by a glare of disapproval at the disheveled visitor.

"May I help you, sir?"

"I have an appointment with Mr. Harry Turpin," Sabah said. "I don't know his room number."

"Let me take care of that, sir," the doorman said. "May I have your name, please?"

"I am Sabah; a business associate of Mr. Turpin."

The doorman walked to a phone at an outside counter and punched a button that alerted security. "A gentleman by the name of Sabah wishes to visit Mr. Turpin."

"Wait," a voice responded. A few moments passed, then the man came back on the line. "You may send him over."

Now the doorman hung up and spoke to Sabah with genuine respect. "Mr. Turpin is in one of our cabanas, sir. I'll arrange transportation for you." He signaled down to a row of canopied golf carts. A driver immediately got into one and drove up. Sabah got onto the front seat next to the driver. The little vehicle whirred as it was driven away from the main building and out to a narrow street.

They wound around tennis courts, a golf course, driving ranges, and an Olympic-size swimming pool before arriving at a section of Siloso Beach where a long row of luxury cabanas sat along the sand. They came to a stop at the largest, which had a spacious veranda.

Sabah quickly slid off the seat and out of the cart, going straight to the door and knocking. A Chinese houseboy, obviously expecting the caller, opened the door and invited him to enter. The Arab was led across the living room to an outside patio.

"Mr. Turpin will be here presently, sir," the houseboy said. "May I get you a drink?"

"An orange juice," Sabah requested. "Will Mr. Turpin be long?"

"He should be able to join you within a half hour," the houseboy said as he went to the bar to pour a glass of the requested drink. "He sends his apologies for the delay, but an unexpected phone call of some importance has interrupted his daily schedule."

"Quite all right," Sabah mumbled in irritation.

"If you desire anything else of me, please press the
buzzer on the bar."

Sabah took a seat at one of the tables, appreciating the
outside panorama of beach and ocean as he sipped the drink
and waited for the arrival of his host.

HARRY Turpin was the type of scoundrel that only
London's East End could produce. He was now close to seventy years of age, and had begun a life of petty crime while
still in the knee pants of his generation. By the age of thir-
teen he had a rap sheet at Scotland Yard that rivaled that of
many older criminals. He spent more time in juvenile confinement than on the streets, but he learned the craft of the
Artful Dodger well, prospering between times in the lockup.
When National Service drafted him into the British Army in
the 1950s, he was running several profitable rackets and
cons, and had developed a craftiness that won the respect of
older gangsters.

As could be expected, his Army career was a total disaster. If ever a young man existed who could not adapt to military discipline, it was Private Harry Turpin. Even several
trips around to the back of the barracks where hard-fisted
corporals and sergeants treated him to punch-ups, did not
improve his attitude. After less than nine months' service,
the young hood was demobbed and sent back to Civvie
Street with a bad-conduct discharge.

Unfortunately for him, Turpin's attempts to restart his
former activities were seriously thwarted by upstarts who
had come on the scene during his absence. They displayed
an amazingly fierce dedication to territorialism. As far as
they were concerned, Turpin was an outsider trying to move
onto their turf, and they stopped him cold. The ex-soldier,
however, looked up an old friend—a loan shark and fencer
of stolen goods—who hired him as a debt collector. Unfortunately for the business arrangement, Turpin was a fellow
who succumbed to temptation like a Cockney drunkard to

cheap gin. After several months of making collections from his boss's debtors, temptations stimulated by the exposure to all that cash brought him to ruin. He made a clumsy attempt to abscond with a couple of thousand pounds sterling, and the end result was that a contract was issued on his life. This was a no-win situation and, ironically, Turpin had to turn to the military to escape from the threat. He fled the U.K. to join the French Foreign Legion.

The Legion did not care about Turpin's past. In that year of 1958, they were in the midst of a guerrilla insurrection in Algeria, and needed bodies to throw into the fray. They signed him up; gave him a new name—John Morris—and sent him out to fight the insurgents. This time Turpin's attitude toward military discipline was radically changed. Ninety percent of the noncommissioned officers in the Legion during the 1950s and 1960s were World War II veterans of the German armed forces. And this included the elite and deadly Waffen SS. It didn't take Turpin long to figure out they would do much more than give him a bloody nose if he misbehaved; those Teutonic bastards would continually send him out on near-suicidal patrols and raids until a burst of submachine gun fire from a rebel ambusher would rid the Legion of the troublemaker. Consequently, the English hoodlum began to tow the line, did his duty, and even earned a promotion to *caporal*. After three years of this enforced good soldiering, the situation turned more to his favor.

When the politicians in Paris decided to grant independence to Algeria in spite of the French Army crushing the revolution, the victorious officers, soldiers, and Legionnaires felt they had been betrayed. In April 1961 a mutiny broke out that spawned such organizations as the murderous OAS, the French acronym for the Secret Army Organization. The resultant bombings, assassinations, and other violence created a vacuum into which *Caporal* John Morris—né Harry Turpin—flourished. He joined the OAS, first as a gunman, then as a procurer of arms from military arsenals. Eventually, the OAS was brought to its knees through betrayals and attrition. At first this defeat looked bad for Turpin, but he figured out a way to turn the downfall into a private enterprise to benefit him personally. Wheeling and dealing his leftover weaponry wares to African revolutionaries and despots led to great profits, which eventually evolved into a full-scale, worldwide business that sold all sorts of arms to the highest bidders.

Now, over four decades later, Mr. Harry Turpin was a billionaire, still making the big bucks with his ever-expanding enterprise.

HAFEZ Sabah lounged on the patio, languidly smoking a cigarette as he enjoyed the peace and quiet of the upscale neighborhood. It felt good to be away from the sleaziness and hurly-burly of his job. The thing he disliked the most about his assignment in al-Mimkhalif was having to deal with infidels; but as soon as Allah permitted the great Islamic victory over the nonbelievers, that unpleasantness would be permanently eliminated. Such delightful environs as these would be enjoyed by the true followers.

"Ah! Good morning, Mr. Sabah."

Sabah turned to see Harry Turpin stride onto the patio. The Englishman had a bouncy step in spite of his heavy weight. His face was round and rosy and what was left of the hair on top of his head was combed straight back. He went to the bar and poured a double shot of whiskey into a glass, then joined the Arab at the table.

Sabah nodded to him. "How are you, Mr. Turpin?"

"Bluddy great," Turpin said in his Cockney accent. "And 'ow're you keeping?"

"I enjoy good health, thanks to Allah."

"I expected you to come by for a visit," Turpin said. "In fact, I've been waiting for you."

"What made you anticipate my calling on you?"

"A great big fucking coincidence," Turpin said, smiling. "I bought a cargo of Stingers some days back, and me warehouse man calls up and says they're the very ones I had sold to you not 'ardly a month ago. Blimey, says I, 'ow could that 'ave 'appened?"

"We paid for them, but they were never delivered into our possession," Sabah said carefully as he prepared for some verbal sparring.

"Sorry, mate," Turpin said. "But you see, I paid for the bluddy things again. So they're my property now, ain't they? Wot's the old saying? Possession is nine tenths of the law."

Sabah gave up any idea of broking a deal. "Who did you buy them from?"

"I'm afraid I can't divulge that information," Turpin said. "Business ethics and all that, wot?" He took a deep swallow of whiskey. "I take it you'll be wanting to purchase them again. Or do you 'ave some other type of weaponry in mind?"

"We need the Stingers," Sabah said. "I hope we shall not have any unpleasantness about an increase in the price."

"O'course not," Turpin said. "You Arabian blokes is good customers. I wouldn't want to take unfair advantage of you now, would I?"

"I wish you would tell me who sold them to you," Sabah asked again.

"Can't do it," Turpin said. "I keep me good name by being discreet. But you'll find out soon enough on your own, won't you?"

"It's just a matter of time."

Turpin laughed loudly. "Right! Just a matter o' time."

UNITED STATES EMBASSY
ISLAMABAD, PAKISTAN
1 OCTOBER

MIKE Assad enjoyed a special apartment in the embassy building in a secure section on the second floor. This was cut off from the rest of the structure and watched over by a twenty-four-hour interior guard. This was where the embassy staff quartered people like Mike and other incognito persons who were involved in risky and clandestine operations. At other times, contemptible but helpful scoundrels who were useful to American causes were also lodged in the area.

The first thing Mike did when he moved into the residence was take a hot, steamy shower and give his dirty, tangled locks a vigorous shampooing. Having to wear his hair mujahideen style was one part of his undercover assignment the SEAL found particularly distasteful. Next he turned his attention to his body, building up a thick lather of soap to wash away the smell of the al-Mimkhalif camp and the Pakistani jail.

After the grooming session, he sent down to the kitchen for a special meal: two cheeseburgers with onions, tomatoes, and lettuce; French fried potatoes; and a chocolate milk shake. After it was brought up to him, he ate slowly, savoring the taste of the American fare after months of consuming *mahshi* vegetables stuffed with chopped meat, *lubya* beans, and *bamya bil moza* okra.

The next order of business was a complete debriefing from a special CIA supervisor by the name of Sam Paulsen. He and his assistant, Mort Koenig, had mysteriously appeared from some secret location especially to take advantage of having a mole pop out of his hole who had the ability to dive back in. This verbal exchange gave Mike the opportunity to make a complete report since his messages left in the dead-letter drop were by necessity short and limited in number. He began his dissertation with a question. "Who picked up those messages I was sending?"

Paulsen only smiled. "Sorry. Now let's hear all you have to tell us."

Mike was able to give Paulsen a good layout of Camp Talata, names of various leaders and mujahideen, information about the operational status of al-Mimkhalif, and other valuable bits of information that could be shared with the FBI and military intelligence. The only thing lacking was a hard identity of the terrorist group's leadership. These individuals were completely unknown to the West, and it would be invaluable to learn their names, then work out some devious assassinations or kidnappings.

As Mike spoke, Koenig took notes. When the session was over, Koenig closed his notebook and gave Mike a meaningful look. "Your acceptance by al-Mimkhalif makes you one of the most important agents in the antiterrorist clandestine operations."

Mike shrugged. "They probably figured I was killed in that fucked-up raid."

Koenig shook his head. "You can be sure that the bad guys know exactly what happened to you and where you are. But they still don't know *who* you are."

"They think you're a prisoner here about to be sent back to the States," Paulsen said.

"Well, they're wrong, ain't they?" Mike remarked. "Except for being sent back to the States, I mean."

Paulsen checked his watch. "Koenig and I have a meeting scheduled with Rod Barker. We'll be seeing you later. If you recall anything else, jot it down for us."

"Will do."

After they left, Mike called down for another cheeseburger with fries.

1600 HOURS LOCAL

THE two embassy security men, Mulvaney and Wheatfall, took Paulsen and Koenig back to visit Mike Assad in his apartment once again. Mulvaney and Wheatfall had already made sincere apologies to Mike for their less-than-gentle treatment of him as a prisoner. He assured them he hadn't taken their conduct personally, but added that it might be unwise of them to ever show up at the Fouled Anchor Tavern in Coronado, California. Both men took the warning seriously.

When Mike answered the knock on his door, he was surprised to see the quartet of visitors. "Come on in, guys."

They all settled down in the living room and Paulsen gave Mike a careful look. "You seem fit and strong."

"I'm fine," he assured him.

"Are you ready to go back?" Koenig inquired.

"You mean to al-Mimkhalif?" Mike asked. "I was really hoping to be returned to duty with my SEAL detachment. That's what I am, y'know, a SEAL."

"It's understandable you would want to get back to your buddies," Koenig interjected, "and if that's what you want, it will be done. However, as I told you earlier, you're in a unique position that makes you a great asset in this operation. It would take months to replace you."

"A lot of innocent lives could be lost during that time," Paulsen pointed out.

Mike frowned. "I want to report back to my outfit."

"Your country really needs you, Mike," Paulsen said. "Can we ask you to take twenty-four hours to think things over?"

"Well," Mike said, "I suppose, but let me tell you—" He stopped speaking, then took a deep breath. "Aw, fuck it! All right. I'll go back."

Paulsen appreciated Mike's attitude. "You're invaluable to the antiterrorist cause, Mike. Koenig has worked out your escape with Mulvaney and Wheatfall."

"What escape?"

"From the embassy here," Paulsen said. He turned to the other CIA man. "Brief him."

"Right," Koenig said, leaning toward Mike. "You're going to leave here within a half hour with Mulvaney and Wheatfall for a ride in the van."

"I wasn't expecting to leave so soon," Mike said. "But what the hell? So brief me."

Koenig continued. "We're going to cuff you, but one of the bracelets has been jimmied so it won't lock. The pretext of the car ride is that you're going to go in front of a lineup at central police headquarters over in Rawalpindi. As a matter of fact, we've made arrangements for just that to keep things looking realistic."

"Understood," Mike said. "Am I to assume that is the time I'll be making an escape?"

"Assume away, my friend," Paulsen said with a laugh.

Wheatfall interjected, "We'll drive you to a city park. There's a political rally going on over there to protest against President Musharraf. So the people in the area are going to be anti-West. It'll be a safe place for you to make your initial run for freedom."

"Right," Mulvaney said. "Once you've entered the crowd, even the local cops won't follow you."

"After that," Paulsen said, "you're on your own. You'll have to make your way back to rejoin al-Mimkhalif. Do you think you can do it without a map?"

"I haven't got much choice," Mike said. "I can work myself west until I steal one."

"Be careful about stealing stuff," Koenig cautioned him. "This is an Islamic country. They cut off thieves' hands."

"I know the drill," Mike said. "I was brought up Muslim . . . sort of anyhow." He stood up. "Hell! Let's get going. I don't want to sit around here and think about what I'm getting into. Okay?"

"We're ready," Wheatfall said.

"Go," Paulsen uttered. "And good luck."

Mike followed Mulvaney and Wheatfall out of the apartment and downstairs to the rear parking area. Before they got into the van, the good side of the handcuff was attached to his wrist. When all was ready, Mulvaney drove them out of the embassy grounds and turned onto the highway for the fifteen-kilometer drive to Rawalpindi.

Within a half hour they rolled into the city and reached the park. The demonstration was going full blast with signs and the loud rhythmic chanting of anti-West political slogans. A couple of dozen nervous policemen stood on the perimeter of the activity, showing no inclination to get any closer.

"Okay, guys," Mike said. "I'm ready."

"Good luck, buddy," Mulvaney said.

Mike leaped from the car and raced across the street past two startled cops. In an instant he had plunged into the crowd. Mulvaney waited until the SEAL had completely disappeared, then turned the van around and headed back toward Islamabad. "I wonder what his chances are."

Wheatfall sadly shook his head. "He's got three hundred kilometers of unknown and hostile territory to travel through. I'd say slim to none."

MANILA, THE PHILIPPINES
2 OCTOBER
1730 HOURS LOCAL

THE traffic was heavy and the going slow, but Commander Carlos Batanza was in a good mood behind the wheel of his two-year-old Honda Accord. The CD player emitted the sounds of Dolly Parton—his favorite female vocalist; he admired her as much for her physical attributes as her musical talent—while the air conditioner fanned out a steady stream of cold air from each outlet.

Patrol Boat 22 had been in port for the previous couple of days undergoing routine maintenance and a minor overhaul of her engines. Mechanics from the base did all the work, so there wasn't much for the crew to do other than stand round-the-clock deck watches. Most of them had taken the week off to stay with their families or in the case of the bachelors, blow off some steam in bars and bordellos after a long period of intense patrolling. Batanza himself hadn't reported for duty that day until noon, and that was only to put his signature on the work authorizations. After that quick and easy task, he had gone to the officers club to play cards and have a few beers with his friends. He had hoped to see Ferdinand Aguilando, but the executive officer had gone to play golf at the exclusive Estrella Country Club outside Quezon City.

The traffic thinned out as Batanza approached the suburbs, and by the time he turned onto MacArthur Boulevard he was able to move along at a steady pace. The only thing that slowed him down was a stoplight, and he came to a halt when it turned red. A Vespa motor scooter came up beside him and halted. Batanza glanced disinterestedly at the two young men sitting on it, then turned his attention back to the light. He didn't see the guy on the backseat pull the MAC-10 from a gym bag.

The bullets streamed out in one long burst as the thirty-two 9-millimeter bullets in the magazine were fired into Batanza's car window. The naval officer was buffeted across the front seat as his flesh and bones were pulverized in the hail of heavy steel slugs. His foot slipped off the brake, and the Accord rolled into the intersection, where an oncoming bus slammed into it.

The Vespa made a quick U-turn, and sped away.

RAWALPINDI, PAKISTAN
2330 HOURS LOCAL

MIKE Assad wasn't sure where he was. He knew he was in Rawalpindi, but he had gotten turned around in futile attempts to find a way out of the city. He ended up in a run-down area where the locals were obviously hostile toward outsiders. These definitely were not the city's leading citizens. Many of the women were unveiled, and the men glared at Mike as if daring him to start something. He noted a few unfortunate individuals with notches cut in their ears. This was the police method of not only punishing petty criminals, but marking them for easy identification when making roundups of suspicious persons.

Now, instead of concentrating on getting out of the city, Mike was more concerned about getting out of that slum neighborhood to a safer area. He moved uneasily in the dim lights cast from windows onto the dirt street as he tried to find a route that would take him back to lighted surroundings. He caught himself passing a couple of places twice, which meant he had begun to wander in circles. Even the best orienteer in the world would start getting sloppy when in dark urban environs that had a sameness about them.

The four goons seemed to materialize in front of him out of the gloom.

He quickly sized them up as the local tough guys; a quartet of miserable buffoons who shared the same qualities and quantities of stupidity and meanness. They would happily kill him to strip his corpse to get a few rupees for his clothing. They had picked the spot for the murder and robbery with some skill. The street was narrow and long with no side outlets for at least fifty meters. Mike began walking slowly backward so that none could get behind him. They pulled knives from beneath their *chadors,* and grinned.

"*Ap khairiyat se hait?*" Mike greeted them in the only words he knew in the Urdu language. Next he tried Arabic. "*Kayfa halik?*"

They didn't waste time in launching their attack. The leader, a long stringbean, with lean whipping arms, led his buddies into the fray. Mike sidestepped, and the guy was sent sprawling with a wicked *wakite* karate punch to the kidneys as he went by. A quick *yubi* punch to the second dropped him straight down to the dirt, while a vicious *marui* kick knocked the third over on his back. The fourth, who had been bringing up the rear, wisely kept charging, jumping over his prostrate buddies and going down the street to disappear into the darkness.

Mike stopped long enough to take a long, calming breath, then gathered up the three knives. He chose the best to keep, then threw the others up on the top of the nearby mud huts.

He quickly left the scene in case there were backup robbers or the fourth guy returned with the rest of the gang. He walked rapidly and quietly away until discovering a street that led out into an open area that smelled like a garbage dump. He found the remnants of a mud wall to hide behind, and settled down to wait for daylight.

KUPANG, TIMOR ISLAND
3 OCTOBER
0315 HOURS LOCAL

THE car pulled off the main street and rolled into the ambulance entrance of the City Hospital. The man in the passenger seat quickly got out and opened the back door. He reached in and pulled Abduruddin Suhanto from the automobile, and shoved him toward the emergency room. The shipping line owner staggered backward a few steps as the man returned to the vehicle, which quickly sped back to the streets.

A tourniquet had been applied to Suhanto's right wrist where the hand had been severed. He sobbed aloud in shock and pain, almost fainting, but he gathered enough strength to lurch toward the medical help available in the building.

> In the name of Allah, the Beneficent, the
> Merciful: If a man or a woman steals, cut off
> their hands as a punishment for what they have done.
> They deserve this exemplary punishment from Allah,
> and Allah is Mighty and Wise.
>
> —as it is written in the Holy Qu'ran

Suhanto, like Batanza, had now paid for his part in the robbery of al-Mimkhalif's weapons. From that time on, he would have to eat with the same hand he wiped his rectum with after defecating. A supreme embarrassment in the Islamic world.

CHAPTER 7

THE *Battlecraft* skimmed over the placid surface of the ocean at a steady clip of forty-five miles an hour with the throttle set at HALF SPEED. Petty Officer First Class Paul Watkins had an easy time maintaining a course of zero-four-five, while to his right Lieutenant (JG) Veronica Rivers kept a constant vigil on her radar instrumentation, eagerly scanning the scope for contacts.

Lieutenant Bill Brannigan had now grown completely disenchanted with this assignment. Every day was the same. Get up early for chow, launch the ACV from the USS *Dan Daly*'s docking well, and spend some empty hours cruising the Indian Ocean finding absolutely nothing. Then return to the ship, pull any necessary maintenance, fill out the logs, report in to Commander Tom Carey, and end another dreary tour of duty that had accomplished absolutely nothing. Higher command echelons could not provide any leads on terrorist activities to investigate. Brannigan wished that some staff weenie would get at least an inkling of information to give them the impression there was something out there on the Indian Ocean or the Arabian Sea worth finding. Whatever the bad guys were doing was either out of sight or not happening on the *Battlecraft*'s watch.

The entire Second Assault Section was topside, taking in the sun and reading field and technical manuals in anticipation of MOS proficiency tests. Sometimes they broke the monotony by doing push-ups and deep knee bends to keep their muscles supple for any potential boarding of suspicious ships.

Down in the office, Veronica Rivers broke the silence. "I have a contact. Zero-one-niner at ten miles."

The announcement did not cause any excitement since there were always plenty of contacts during the reconnaissance tours. Merchant ships, oil tankers, and miscellaneous naval vessels of nearby nations constantly cruised to and fro as they went about their business in the area.

"Course zero-one-niner," Brannigan said to Watkins. He leaned toward Veronica. "What's it look like?"

"It's a weak contact, sir," Veronica answered. "Something out there is constructed of a minimum amount of metal."

"Great!" Brannigan said sarcastically. "From all indications it's probably a rowboat."

"It's under power," Veronica said. "Moving approximately seven to eight knots on an easterly course."

"Maybe it's the Pakistani rowing team going so fast they sped out into the open ocean," Watkins said, grinning.

"In that case," Veronica said, "they're a cinch to win a gold medal in the next Olympics."

Senior Chief Buford Dawkins had alerted his SAW gunner and two fire teams about the contact, and was using binoculars to scan the horizon in the direction of the target.

After a few moments, he climbed down the ladder to the office. "It's one of them towel-head dhows," Dawkins informed Brannigan. "A real antique, but obviously under power. The sails are furled."

Now Brannigan could see the antique vessel through his own binoculars. He retrieved the ensign-identification pamphlet and quickly scanned the contents, finding a green and white banner with a crescent moon and star. "She's flying the Pakistani flag. We'll check her out. The latest intelligence—such as it is—indicates the bad guys may be using a dhow in their operations." He took his pistol belt with the 9-millimeter Sig Sauer and strapped it around his waist. "Let's go topside, Senior Chief."

The skipper and Dawkins went up the ladder and the senior chief gestured to his two fire team leaders, Milly Mills and Gutsy Olson. "We're going to check out a dhow. Charlie Fire Team, stay here to cover us if things get hairy. That means you special, Miskoski. Keep that SAW ready. Delta Team will go aboard with me and the skipper."

"What the hell is a dhow, sir?" Gutsy asked as he and his men got to their feet.

"A traditional Arabian boat," Brannigan said. "Wooden. They go back centuries." The disappointment on the SEALs' faces was evident. This didn't seem to offer much potential in the way of meaningful excitement. Brannigan added, "There's an outside chance it's a terrorist craft."

"Now you're talking, sir!" Guy Devereaux, one of Delta's riflemen, remarked.

The *Battlecraft* closed in tight as Veronica attempted to contact the boat by radio to order them to heave to. It was a useless effort. "I don't think they speak English. All I get is that Arab gibberish in response to my command for them to break their voyage."

"They must get the drift of what you're saying," Watkins said, maneuvering the ACV into position to close in on the old ship. "The captain is slowing down."

Bobby Lee Atwill went out on the side deck to toss lines

to the crewmen of the dhow. Within moments, Brannigan led Dawkins and Delta Fire Team aboard, leaping over the railing into what seemed the tenth century.

Captain Bashar Bashir of the dhow *Nijm Zark* showed a toothy grin to the visitors. *"Asalam aleikum,"* he said.

The SEALs held their CAR-15 rifles ready, but the half-dozen Arab crewmen showed no unfriendly tendencies. They smiled and nodded silent greetings to the boarding party. Brannigan glanced around to make sure there were no more individuals lurking in any corners before he spoke to the captain. "Do you speak English?"

Bashir indicated a negative with a slight flip back of his head as is done in that part of the world.

"Papers?" Brannigan said. "Where are your papers?"

Bashir smiled with a blank look on his face. Brannigan turned to the SEALs. "Senior Chief, leave your men here. You come with me over to the hold." Brannigan and Dawkins walked to the hatch. Brannigan pointed to the dhow captain, then down to the hatch. Bashir said something to a couple of his crew, who walked over and pulled the entrance to the hold open. Another crewman fetched a ladder off the side of the cabin and courteously set it in position so the two Americans could go down to the cargo area.

Brannigan and Dawkins went below and found it completely empty. There was not one piece of cargo in the place. Brannigan sighed. "Here we go again. More or our time wasted."

Dawkins walked slowly around the hold. Suddenly he stopped and knelt down, touching an oily spot on the deck. "Sir."

Brannigan walked over to him. "Find something, Senior Chief?"

Dawkins raised his finger, which was soiled with some black gook. "Cosmoline, sir. The very stuff weapons are coated with for storage or shipment."

The pair searched around the hold finding other oily spots. There were enough to give ample evidence of numerous transports of weaponry on the old boat. Brannigan sank into thought for a few moments.

"Are we gonna tow her back, sir?" Dawkins asked.

"Nope," Brannigan said. "I'm going to check her papers and try to determine her name and home port. Then I'll turn the information over to Commander Carey and he can arrange for some sneaky folks to keep an eye on this tub. We'll catch her when she's got a full cargo."

They ascended the ladder to the main deck. Brannigan put a friendly expression on his face and indicated that the dhow captain was to follow him. They went into the cabin, and Brannigan said, "Papers."

Once again the Arab exhibited a look of incomprehension. Brannigan made a motion with his hands like he was leafing through some documents. Bashir caught on and went to a tin box. He opened it and took out a sheaf of papers, handing them to the American.

Most of the printing and writing seemed to be in Arabic script, but some Pakistani import and export licenses were in English, the nation's quasi-official language. Brannigan was able to determine that the name of the dhow was the *Nijm Zark* out of Karachi, Pakistan. The man identified as the captain was Bashar Bashir. The SEAL officer looked over at the old man and pointed to him. "You Captain Bashir?"

Bashir smiled and swelled his narrow old chest proudly. "*Raiyis* Bashir. I captain!"

Brannigan now pointed to himself. "I Captain Brannigan."

Bashir offered his hand and they shook enthusiastically. Brannigan entered the information off the licenses into his notebook, then went out on deck. "Senior Chief Dawkins, let's go back aboard the *Battlecraft*." He turned to Bashir. "Thank you, Captain Bashir. Thank you. Thank you. Good-bye."

Bashir grinned widely. "*Shokhran!* Thank you! Good-bye! Good-bye!"

Brannigan led the SEALs off the dhow, then went into the office as the dhow's crew threw the lines back to Atwill.

"Okay, Watkins. Set a course for the *Dan Daly*. We've actually accomplished something today."

Veronica Rivers looked at him. "Really? Were they carrying contraband?"

"Not a single piece, Lieutenant," Brannigan said. "But what we got was much more important. We picked up enough information to confirm some very valuable intelligence."

"The course to the *Dan Daly* is one-eight-seven, sir," Watkins reported.

"Go to one-eight-seven then," Brannigan said.

"Course one-eight-seven, aye, sir!" Watkins responded.

The *Battlecraft* kicked up its speed to TWO-THIRDS, heading homeward at a steady sixty-one miles per hour.

RAWALPINDI, PAKISTAN

THE people of Pakistan speak two dozen languages that are further divided into three hundred dialects. Unfortunately for Mike Assad, he didn't have as much as a working knowledge of any of them. The situation put him at a serious disadvantage as he moved deeper into the country. English is used in the government and the upper reaches of the nation's society, but the SEAL was deeply imbedded in the midst of lower social types, moving among them in an unavoidably conspicuous manner.

And he was still lost.

He could not find his way out of the city and was unable to ask directions. All attempts on his part to address anyone were met with scowls and insulting gestures that he figured either meant to move along or to go fuck a she-goat. A half-dozen instances occurred when he found himself face-to-face with one of the local toughs, unable to respond appropriately to a rough street inquisition. Most of the time he managed to stare them down, but on one occasion the guy pulled a knife and waved it menacingly at him with an

evil grin while onlookers ceased their normal activities to
urge the local hero on. Mike sneered back, knowing that if
he showed any fear at all he was a dead man since others in
the crowd would want a piece of him too. He pulled the
knife he'd gotten in the fight, and the potential assailant
noted that his own weapon was smaller than Mike's. He
backed off with a scowl, then made a quick turn and hurried away. When Mike glared at the spectators in a challenging manner, they suddenly discovered they had other
things to do.

An hour later, however, the odds caught up with him,
and Mike was in a situation where it looked like escape
would be impossible. At least two dozen merchants and
shoppers in one market place objected to his passing
through their neighborhood, and an impromptu mob situation quickly developed. They advanced in a disorganized
phalanx, encouraging each other through sheer weight of
numbers while shouting insults and threats. Once more
Mike went to the knife as he backed down the street. Several times one of them would prove to be a bit braver than
the others, and move toward him. In those instances, he
had little choice. If he was going to die, Mike was determined that he sure as hell was going to take a few with him,
and he made ready to fight with no intention of begging for
quarter or giving any. He stopped in his tracks, assumed an
aggressive fighting position, then lunged forward, bringing
his knife to bear. These counterattacks caused the bolder
individuals' courage to fail as they stumbled back to the
safety of their buddies. This gave Mike a chance to put a
bit more distance between him and the crowd, albeit by
walking backward. Eventually, the throng's numbers began
to lessen, and the threat slowly subsided as he moved out
of their turf.

At that point, Mike was close to abandoning his mission,
finding a taxi, and going back to the American Embassy in
Islamabad. A reunion with Brannigan's Brigands never
seemed so good.

1100 HOURS LOCAL

MIKE Assad wasn't hungry enough to consider the situation critical, but he knew that in another twenty-four hours, he would begin to experience a physical weakness and fatigue that would get worse before it got better if he didn't take in any nutrition.

He reached what seemed to be an active thoroughfare with both motorized and animal-drawn vehicular activity. He walked to an intersection that showed some promise. There were street signs in both English and Urdu that identified the site as the meeting of Adamjee and Kashmir Roads. Mike glanced down the street and sighted a mosque. He hurried toward it and entered through the gate, exploring the interior until he came to the *rassal* area. This was where the faithful washed before going into prayers. He went over to a bench and sat down. Here was a chance to catch his breath and organize his thoughts. He leaned forward and put his head in his hands and closed his eyes.

"Asalam aleikum."

The voice startled him, and Mike leaped to his feet and turned around. A young cleric with a pleasant smile regarded him in a friendly manner. Mike nodded and replied, *"Wa aleikum salam,"* as he had been taught in the al-Mimkhalif camp. *"Arabi?* English?" he asked.

"I speak English," the cleric said. "I am called Zaid."

"I am called Mikael."

"So your father named you after the archangel, did he?" the cleric asked. "Is there anything I can do for you, Mikael? You seem to be distressed."

"I seek *amniyi,"* Mike said, asking for sanctuary.

"From whom do you flee, Mikael?"

"I am an Arab-American," he explained, knowing that he had no choice but to turn to his cover story and hope for the best. "I have escaped from captivity in the American Embassy." He pulled back his sleeve and revealed the handcuff locked around his left wrist.

"This is extraordinary," Zaid the cleric said. "How did such an unusual event come about?"

"I left America to return to the lands and faith of my fore-fathers to offer up my life in a jihad," Mike said. "I am a mujahideen and fight with al-Mimkhalif. I was captured during an attack on a Pakistani police post. When they discovered I was an American, they sent for people from the United States Embassy to take me back to America for punishment. But I escaped and I am now lost."

"So you are in peril from infidels, *la*, Brother Mikael? In that case we will help you. What is it that you wish?"

"I desire to return to al-Mimkhalif to fight again," Mike said. "My band is in the mountains of Baluchistan Province." He shrugged apologetically. "And I am very hungry."

"Come with me," Zaid the cleric said. "We will give you food, and I shall send for a *hiddad*—a blacksmith—to remove the restraint from your wrist."

"Allah will reward you for your kindness," Mike replied properly.

He was taken into the interior of the mosque, where other clerics came to meet him. Zaid left to send for the blacksmith, and Mike was invited by the others to sit at a table where he was served with *gosht* and *ghobi*. This combination of mutton and cabbage took the wrinkles out of his stomach. He ate three large helpings, washing it all down with a milky tea called *dudh cha*. He had learned during his SERE training that if you are in a situation requiring long hours of tough physical exertion, you should eat and drink as much as you can to build strength for the ordeal ahead. Mike Assad followed that dictum to the letter.

By the time his appetite was appeased, a blacksmith with hammer, chisel, and hacksaw was brought in. It took the man only ten minutes to free him from the handcuffs. The smithy gathered up his tools and departed without a word, passing Zaid, who entered the room with an envelope.

"Here are bus tickets and a little money, Mikael," the cleric said. "You will be able to leave the bus station on Haider Road early tomorrow morning. It will take you to Baluchistan Province. After that you will be on your own."

"*Shukriya,*" Mike said.

The cleric laughed. "At least you can express your gratitude in Urdu, Brother Mikael."

"I have picked up a little in the camp."

"Perhaps you will know much more when we meet again, if Allah wills it," Zaid said. "We have something else for you." He handed Mike a chador. This was the wool blanket used by Pakistani men as shawls, coverings, and pillows as the situation might dictate. "This will keep you more comfortable during the cool nights."

"*Allah ikafik anni*—may Allah reward you for me," Mike said.

"Perhaps Allah shall," Zaid the cleric said. "Now we will find a place for you to sleep. Do not worry. You will be awakened early enough in the morning to catch your bus."

A wave of fatigue suddenly swept over Mike Assad at the mention of rest and relaxation. Now he could sleep undisturbed for a few hours. Between that and the food he had eaten, he would be in excellent condition for the ordeal ahead.

He felt like a SEAL again.

PATROL BOAT 22
INDIAN OCEAN
VICINITY OF 5° NORTH AND 100° EAST
1615 HOURS

THE Philippine Navy vessel cut through the waves with her throttle set at FULL SPEED. She was fast on an interception course with a slow-moving signal on the radarscope. The boat's new skipper, Lieutenant Commander Ferdinand Aguinaldo, knew exactly what vessel the blip on the screen represented. It was the SS *Yogyakarta* of the Greater Sunda Shipping Line on one of her regular runs across that part of the ocean.

This was more than just a routine mission as far as Aguinaldo was concerned; this was the day he would begin a concentrated program of harassment to avenge the death of his best friend, Commander Carlos Batanza.

"Closing in fast, sir," the radar operator reported. "Estimate visual contact in ten minutes."

Aguinaldo put his binoculars to his eyes and scanned the horizon to the direct front. The waves were placid that day, allowing the patrol boat to attain more than the usual speed. The new skipper spotted the smudge of the target within eight minutes. He considered that a good omen. He picked up the intercom to the radio operator. "Contact the ship on the international frequency and order her to heave to."

"Aye, aye, sir!" The radioman turned to his set and began broadcasting the demand.

The helmsman had plenty of experience in bringing the patrol boat alongside ships, and he gauged both the interception speed and angle accurately. By the time the old freighter was almost stopped, he had the naval craft in position at the accommodation ladder. Aguinaldo, with drawn pistol, led a team of a dozen armed sailors on board the target vessel. They scrambled upward to the main deck. When they arrived, the ship's crew was already opening the hatches in anticipation of a search and seizure. This generally meant the loss of a third to a half of the cargo.

The captain, an old seafarer named Wiranto, seemed confused. "I was not expecting this," he said to Aguinaldo. "Mr. Suhanto told me nothing of the delivery of this cargo being delayed."

"It is not being delayed, Captain," Aguinaldo said. "It is being confiscated."

"But there has been no arrangement for such a thing," Wiranto protested. "I am to deliver this to our customer. That's what Mr. Suhanto told me."

Aguinaldo turned to his senior petty officer. "Organize this tub's crew and begin transporting all cargo over to the patrol boat." He turned back to Wiranto. "Things have changed since Batanza's treacherous murder. We are going to continue to intercept all the arms shipments until Suhanto delivers twenty-five hundred kilos of cocaine to me. Then we will go back to the original agreement."

"I know nothing of Batanza," Wiranto protested. "Are you aware that Mr. Suhanto suffered the amputation of his right hand for betraying the Arabs?"

"I did not know," Aguinaldo said. "Nor do I care. You deliver the message to him. And tell him to inform his Arab colleagues that we are well prepared for any more crude murders. We will be looking out for them."

Wiranto took a deep breath and shuddered. "Sir, you are creating a situation that will cause much trouble for all of us."

"I am only starting to make trouble," Aguilando said.

Wiranto sighed, then turned to his boatswain to issue the necessary orders.

The crew of the *Yogyakarta* strained with the heavy crates containing various types of small arms and ammunition, passing them up from the hold, then carrying them down to the accommodation ladder to be lowered onto the patrol boat. The job took an hour and a half. When it was finished, the Indonesians were dripping wet with sweat and grimacing from strained back and shoulder muscles.

Aguinaldo and Wiranto looked over the side to see the cargo stacked neatly and properly on the boat's fore and stern decks. "Excellent," the Philippine officer said. "Now lower your lifeboats and man them."

"What?" Wiranto asked.

"I'm not going to give you a lot of time," Aguinaldo warned him. "I am about to send a party belowdecks to open your sea cocks."

"You are going to scuttle my ship?" Wiranto said. "I do not understand this."

"I wish to emphasize to Suhanto and his Arab friends that I mean business," Aguinaldo said. "Now do as I say or I shall further demonstrate my determination by shooting you dead this very moment!" He aimed the pistol between Wiranto's eyes.

The elderly captain turned to his crew. "Abandon ship!"

"Do not forget to mention that little matter of twenty-five hundred kilos of cocaine the next time you see Suhanto," Aguinaldo said with a smile. He gestured to the petty officer. "Send some men below to scuttle this rusty piece of shit."

CHAPTER 8

THE bus rumbled down the two-lane dirt highway, swaying badly, as Mike Assad sat hunched on the rear seat. The vehicle was crowded not only with people, but a pair of goats and a sheep were in the center of the aisle along with three cages of live chickens. All men with women were seated in the front seats, while males traveling alone had taken the rear accommodations.

Mike couldn't determine the make of the bus; it seemed to be assembled from two or perhaps three other vehicles. It was gaudily decorated on the outside with colorful swirl and scroll designs painted on in brilliant scarlets, yellows, and blues. Some of the windows were stuck shut, others stuck open, and a couple were missing altogether. The vehicle's shock absorbers were shot to hell, and each lurch and bounce was emphasized with jarring regularity. Mike had eaten a couple of *samosas* during a rest stop in Kohat, and now the potato-and-chickpea-filled pastries were sitting heavy in his stomach.

The tiresome journey continued with an annoying number of stops at which more people got on than got off, causing the crowding to increase markedly. The dusty, stifling heat inside the bus, combined with the smells of animals, humans, and the exhaust, caused Mike to seriously consider getting off and walking. But he had to travel far and fast if he was to get back to his mission in a timely manner. The sooner it was wrapped up, the sooner he could return to the Naval Amphibious Base in Coronado to renew his real career with Brannigan's Brigands.

NORTHWEST FRONTIER PROVINCE
1735 HOURS LOCAL

THE bus had passed through Bannu, moving closer toward the Afghanistan border, when the brakes suddenly squealed, snapping Mike out of a restless nap. He glanced through the dusty window glass, noting they were out in the open country. His attention was diverted to the front of the bus when a policeman suddenly got on board, shouting orders in Urdu. Mike didn't understand the words, but the quick evacuation of the vehicle was a strong indication the passengers had been ordered off.

He was one of the last to step down to the ground, and he did so with feelings of strong misgiving. The immediate area was encircled by a half-dozen uniformed officers, each holding an American M16 rifle. A man wearing the chevrons of a police sergeant went to the male passengers, speaking to them while ignoring the women. The men produced papers that he examined carefully and individually before moving on to the next person. Mike knew this was bad news. He had no papers and could not speak the language, which would lead the boss cop into assuming he was a refugee from

Afghanistan. The fact he was traveling made it appear as if he had made an unauthorized departure from his assigned camp. When the civil war across the border broke out, the Pakistanis had welcomed the unfortunate people who had been forced to flee for their lives across the international border. Camps were set up for the miserable refugees where food and shelter were furnished to them. But the situation soon grew uncomfortable for Pakistan when these heavily armed foreigners began competing for jobs and bringing about an alarming state of inflation. Clashes between the refugees and the native population led the Pakistani government to severely curtail the visitors' ability to move around the country.

Mike stood passively as the sergeant made his way down the line. The SEAL decided it was imperative that he not reveal his nationality. One more trip back to the American Embassy in Islamabad, and the effectiveness of Operation Deep Thrust would be seriously diminished. A full three quarters of an hour passed before the policeman reached him. The cop barked orders that Mike could only respond to with shrugs to show his inability to understand. After about three of these gestures of incomprehension, the sergeant signaled for a couple of men. Mike was unceremoniously grabbed, his hands tied behind his back, and he was frog-marched to a waiting van.

This was one type of vehicle he was beginning to hate with a vengeance.

THE police station was a rural setup with one room used as an office across from the cell on the other side of the building. The place was old, dilapidated, and dirty. It was obvious Mike was going to be held here for a spell, then possibly passed up to higher headquarters at the next opportunity. They pushed and pummeled him into the main office from the van, then untied him before locking him up in the cell. The wandering SEAL was relieved to discover he wasn't going to be punched around during this confinement.

These cops evidently weren't all that pissed off at him.

Mike still had the knife under his chador, and he was happy these members of the local gendarmerie were sloppy and ill-trained enough not to give him a thorough search. He looked out the bars at his captors, who were now filling out a report on his detainment. He studied the cell door, glancing down at the lock. Using skills acquired in his recent CIA training, Mike could see it was a worn ancient variety. The hole into which the bolt slid was enlarged through usage, and the bolt itself was badly worn. He reached down and pushed against the lock, shaking it. The policemen snapped their heads his way, and the sergeant growled something at him.

Mike smiled apologetically and stepped back. He walked to the rear of the cell and took off the chador, folded it neatly, and put it on the floor. He settled onto its softness, grinning inwardly to himself. The tumblers in the lock had rattled loosely when they were shaken. The lock had been used countless times over decades, and should have been replaced long before.

2010 HOURS LOCAL

MIKE Assad was given a cup of tepid water and a piece of bread made from unleavened wheat flour. He ate slowly to make the sparse meal last longer, then took the water in tiny sips. After the sun went down, a very corpulent policeman came on duty. The others took their leave while the new custodian lit a lantern. He walked up to the cell door and peered in at the prisoner. After a scowl of warning, he went back to the desk in the front and sat down.

2330 HOURS LOCAL

THE fat cop was asleep at the desk, his head down on his folded arms. His snoring was the blubbery sort common to fat people with sinus conditions. It made so much noise that Mike was amazed the guy could sleep at all. There was a marked advantage to it as far as the prisoner was concerned; it would mask any noise he might make.

Mike waited until it was obvious the fellow was deep in Morpheus's arms. Then he got slowly to his feet and pulled the chador around his shoulders after getting the knife from the lining. He tiptoed over to the cell door and carefully stuck the blade into the bolt hole. He applied some gentle pressure, working the blade deeper, then pried upward. The bolt moved hesitantly but steadily in the loose confinement, then came out. Now Mike put the blade between the end of the bolt and the bolt hole and pried yet again. It slid with a slight scraping sound until the door swung open on its own.

Mike stepped out of the cell and headed for the back door, but something caught his eye. A pistol harness complete with belt, shoulder straps, holster, weapon, ammo pouch, and two canteens hung next to the desk where Fatso snoozed in such deep contentment. Mike walked slowly over to the prize. He froze when the cop snorted loudly; but the guy drifted back to sleep after a couple of nasal whimpers.

The escapee took the belt and harness, then went to the door and looked out. The night was calm and empty, and he moved into the darkness, slipping his new treasure on under the chador.

GREEN EMERALD RESORT AND SPA
SINGAPORE
6 OCTOBER
1530 HOURS LOCAL

THE Philippine naval officer wore civilian clothing as he stood on Harry Turpin's veranda sipping a glass of Tetley's Bitter. The brew had been drawn by the houseboy from a keg behind the bar that had been sent directly from the English brewery to Turpin's home through a permanent arrangement. The Filipino would have preferred it cold, but the Brit Turpin, though far from his native shores for many decades, drank his beers and ales warm as he would have in a London pub.

Aguilando turned at the sound of footsteps as Turpin came out to join him. The Englishman's gaze was direct, betraying his curiosity. "I don't believe we've met. I'm Turpin. 'Arry Turpin."

"I am Ferdinand Aguilando," the visitor said. "I am the captain of the patrol boat once commanded by Carlos Batanza."

"What's 'appened to that bloke Batanza?" Turpin asked, though he knew the exact circumstances of the killing.

"He had an accident," Aguilando said. "A fatal one, unfortunately. I have been assigned to take over his boat."

"Right. So wot can I do for you, Captain?"

"I am taking up where Commander Batanza left off."

"Right. And?"

"I shall have more arms for sale quite soon," Aguilando said. "I would like to continue the same arrangement you had with Batanza."

"I 'ope there ain't no more orficers who know about this," Turpin said uneasily. "I always prefer to deal with one bloke at a time as I did with the late Mr. Batanza."

"I assure you that you will see only me," Aguilando said. "We will rendezvous with your people for the transfer of the cargo, but I shall be alone when we meet to discuss business and make the sales."

"Right," Turpin said. " 'Ow soon will you 'ave a delivery?"

"Within a week or so," Aguilando said. "I have some recently acquired arms stowed in a safe place for the time being. I shall contact you when I have an exact date and time."

"I'll be 'ere," Turpin promised.

Aguilando finished his beer, shook hands with his host, and went outside for the golf cart ride back to the hotel building. Turpin walked to the window and watched the officer leave. When the Filipino disappeared from view, the Englishman turned. "You can come out now, Mr. Sabah."

Hafez Sabah stepped out from an adjoining room. "My brothers and I appreciate the very helpful services you are providing us."

"I don't claim to be sodding ethical," Turpin said. "It would be bad for me business if word got round that I was making a bluddy 'abit of buying back cargoes I sold to somebody else after they was stole."

"Whatever the reason for your aid in solving this problem, we remain grateful."

"So wot 'appens to this bloke then?"

"He will be dealt with in the same manner as was done with Batanza," Sabah said.

Turpin shrugged. "Then some other orficer will take his place."

"This time there will be no more Aguilando, Patrol Boat 22, or any of its crew," Sabah said. "Again I thank you, Mr. Turpin. Good-bye."

"*Ma'al salama,*" Turpin said.

Sabah smiled. "Ah! You speak some Arabic, do you?"

"I picked up a bit during me Legion days in Algeria."

NORTHWEST FRONTIER PROVINCE
7 OCTOBER
1400 HOURS LOCAL

MIKE Assad was now avoiding all places where he might come into contact with people. He had fresh water, ammunition, an ancient Webley .455-caliber revolver, and some *chapattis,* a flat, round, unleavened wheat bread he had found in the pouch on the back of the harness and belt he had lifted at the police station. The SEAL moved at a slow but steady gait as he traveled through the scrub-brush boondocks toward the Afghan border to the west. Because of a complete CIA orientation and briefing about his OA, Mike knew and appreciated the adventurous history of the land he now trekked through.

This was where the British fought the warlike tribes of the area in the nineteenth century. A long string of forts were constructed across the territory to contain the native rebels as well as thwart any expansionist activities of Czarist Russia. The biggest problem the British soldiers faced was the fierce resistance of the Pathans. Things got so bad that when the Northwest Province was created, the Pathans were given control of a strip of land along the Afghan border to appease them. This didn't make the war-like people all that happy, and they rebelled in fury at various times, fighting skirmishes with British troops over many decades As late as 1937, the Pathans attacked and massacred an entire British column in one memorable battle.

Now Mike continued to move cautiously through Pathan territory, the pistol loaded and loosened in the holster. As he kept his vigilance at a high level, he caught sight of the plentiful wildlife. *Markhor* goats, gazelles, and foxes were in abundance, and he knew the place must be a hunter's paradise. He was well into a long afternoon of travel when he suddenly noticed the absence of animals. Obviously something had frightened them.

Then he sighted the horsemen.

Two riders were off to his left, close enough that Mike could see they were interested in him. He opened the holster flap and pulled the pistol out, sticking it in the belt. The thought flashed in his mind of saving one last bullet to put into his own brain like the British soldiers of old used to do if capture were imminent in that part of the world. A movement to his right caught his eye as another pair of riders came into view. Then a few more rode into sight. Mike knew that resistance with a pistol would be futile. The horsemen were all armed with rifles. They could leisurely pick him off without getting within range of the revolver.

Now they began to close in, and Mike put his hand on the weapon, deciding to sell his life dearly. Within ten minutes they had drawn up close to him, grinning with a menacing sort of amusement. One of them came forward. *"Chertha zey?"*

"Asalam aleikum," Mike said uttering the universal Islamic greeting. *"Arabi?* English?"

"How do you do? I am speaking English," the man said.

"Yes, you are," Mike said agreeably. "And very well too."

"Thank you for such kind words," the man said. "I attended a special school in Peshawar to be prepared for the diplomatic service. It is there that I learned to speak English and Urdu. I am called Sarleh Khey."

"I am called Mikael Assad."

"I have asked you *chertha zey* in my language," Khey asked. "It means where do you go."

"I am returning to friends near the coast," Mike replied. "I must confess that I am not sure of my exact location at this moment. All I know is that I am in the Northwest Frontier Province."

"It is so named by Englishmen," Khey said. "In actuality, you travel across the territory ruled by my people. We call ourselves Pashtuns, but in the West we are called Pathans."

Now Mike knew he was having an encounter with a tribe that boasted a long warrior tradition. "Since I have so impolitely intruded onto your land, I shall also refer to you as Pashtuns, if it so pleases you."

Khey laughed loudly, explaining to his friends what Mike had just said. Their former insolent grins immediately turned friendly. Khey said, "May I ask how it is that you speak English?"

"I am an American," Mike explained. "It is a long story."

Khey spoke again to his comrades, who did not mask their surprise. "We Pashtuns love long stories. Would you be so kind as to tell us yours?"

"My pleasure."

"Excellent! We invite you to come to our village as our guest. Hop up behind my saddle, Mikael."

Mike opened up his chador to reveal the pistol belt and accouterments. He smiled widely to appear as amicable as possible as he slowly and carefully pulled the weapon from the belt. He reset it into the holster and snapped the flap shut.

This made the Pashtuns laugh again and make remarks among themselves.

"My friends say you were prepared to defend yourself," Khey said. "That is most admirable. You showed no fear."

I was scared shitless, Mike's mind spoke silently, *and that would have been bad news for you fuckers!*

The Pashtun took his foot out of his left stirrup, and Mike stepped into it, swinging himself up on the horse. He settled behind his new friend as the group rode off, turning southwest.

1530 HOURS LOCAL

THE Pashtun village was unnamed, but well organized, with the mud buildings laid out in a zigzag pattern to create narrow streets that would suddenly turn ninety degrees, go a short distance, then turn back in the original direction. Mike Assad had seen this arrangement before during a mission to Afghanistan. Such streets would be easy to defend while attackers, unable to see ahead any great distance, would have to slow down at each intersection where ambushes would be waiting to be sprung on them.

Mike and his escorts went to a central building that was the largest structure in the small community. It appeared primitive on the outside in spite of having glass windows. The interior, however, was much more elaborate. Thick carpeting covered the floor from wall to wall, and several tables, standing no more than eighteen inches high, were arranged in a circular pattern. A raised platform, also carpeted, was at the head of the room. The table on it was twice as long as the others. Mike figured that was where the local board of directors sat during community meetings.

He and his new friends settled down around a table. Within moments three women appeared carrying an urn of *khawa* green tea, small cups, and a platter of deep-fried vegetables called *pakoras*. Mike knew enough not to look at the women, and he kept his eyes on Khey.

"I appreciate your hospitality," he said.

"This is a strong Pashtun custom called *melmastia*," Khey explained. "We are a people who believe in being especially courteous to our guests." He poured a cup of tea, passing it over to Mike. "Many outsiders think of us as murderous barbarians. In truth, we have a civilization unique unto ourselves."

The platter of *pakoras* was passed to Mike. Only after the guest had been served did the other men look after their own refreshments. Khey took a sip of the sweetened hot drink. "So, friend Mikael, we are most anxious to hear your story. It must be interesting because you are an Arab, yet an American too."

"I was born in America," Mike said. "My grandfather came there from Jordan. As an Arab and a follower of Islam, I felt an obligation to fight in the jihad against the West. I am a member of al-Mimkhalif. Have you heard of it?"

"Indeed," Khey said. He translated the words for his friends around the table, who nodded with approval, uttering words directed toward the American. "My countrymen wish martyrdom for you."

"Thank you," Mike said, thinking that only in Islam would someone wish death for you in such a way that you would thank him. "At any rate, I was captured by the Pakistani police during a battle." He went on to explain how he was sent to the American Embassy and escaped, then visited the mosque in Rawalpindi, where he was given help, then had to endure yet another arrest by the police during the bus trip. He told of the escape and how he stole the belt with pistol, pouches, and canteens.

Khey translated it all, and at the conclusion the Pashtuns all applauded and cheered Mike's resourcefulness. Khey clapped him on the shoulder. "Tonight we will take you to the elders. I am sure they will help you back to al-Mimkhalif.

Now let us finish the *khawa* and *pakoras,* then you may come to my house and rest."

With the guest's story now told, the group turned their full attention to the refreshments.

2030 HOURS LOCAL

AFTER a long restful nap and another meal, Mike Assad was taken back to the same building where he had been entertained that afternoon. But this time all the important men in the village were seated around the tables, and the exalted position at the front of the room was occupied by a quartet of very old males. The SEAL rightly assumed they were the village elders. He and Sarleh Khey were escorted to the table in front of the elderly men.

The windows were all opened and the faces of lower-ranking males and boys peered in to view the unusual sight of an American having an audience with the council of wise men. The opening ceremonies consisted of a man walking to the front of the elders and delivering a speech that Mike assumed was an announcement of the evening's agenda.

With this done, Khey stood up and addressed not only the council, but the entire room. He took three quarters of an hour explaining and describing Mike's adventures since the raid on the Pakistani police camp. This made Mike grin inwardly since he had been able to tell the whole tale in under fifteen minutes that afternoon. Khey gestured grandly, referring to Mike with sweeping arms. The words *al-Mimkhalif* and *jihad* were repeated within the jumble of Pashto. Mike was pleased to note the nods and smiles toward him. After his encounters in the slums of Rawalpindi, he found the friendliness quite comforting.

When Khey finished, he sat down. Now the elders spoke among themselves, gesturing as they all talked at once. It was hard for Mike to understand how they were to reach any conclusions in that disruptive manner, but they suddenly stopped speaking as if on cue.

The youngest of the elders stood up. He appeared to be in his seventies, and he made a half-hour address to the assemblage, also obviously discussing Mike. When he finished, there were murmurs of agreement in the crowd. Khey now took the floor again, speaking only a sentence to the assemblage. He looked down at Mike. "I have told them I shall speak to you in English to explain the decision of the council."

"Fine," Mike said, slightly worried. In truth, he really didn't know if he should be optimistic or pessimistic. "Thank you."

"In order for you to return to al-Mimkhalif, you will pass through dangerous territory with many bandits and bad people. They will kill you for the clothes on your back; your knife and pistol would be of great value to them also. Therefore, according to the dictates of our warrior code of *Pashtunwali,* our clan will provide an escort for you. This way you will be able to safely reach your comrades-in-arms and go to Paradise after you are martyred. We thank Allah he has sent you here to us so that we may serve the cause of your jihad."

Mike Assad almost felt guilty about fooling these generous people; but not quite.

CHAPTER 9

BACHAMAN, the old clerk at the Greater Sunda Shipping Line, was a nervous man even during the best of times. Now, with his employer having suffered a forced amputation of his right hand for misbehavior, the elderly man lived in a perpetual state of terror. He feared that even guilt by association could bring him a similar fate. The possibility that the wrath of those outraged clients might be extended to him caused the old fellow sleepless nights, nervous nausea, and a pessimistic outlook that bordered on near paranoiac schizophrenia. When the door to the outer office opened and the Arab Hafez Sabah stepped inside, all those mental disturbances roared up in a psychotic detonation.

Bachaman screamed and ran out that same door.

Abduruddin Suhanto rushed from his office to see what had happened. The sight of his hated client further spoiled what was already a terrible day. Not only did the wrist that used to have a hand attached to it throb, but the missing member also felt as if it were still there. He glared at Sabah, asking, "What happened to my clerk?"

"I do not know," Sabah replied. "I walked in and he screamed like a madman and ran out of the building."

Suhanto knew exactly how the old fellow felt. "What is it you want?"

"Let us go into your office for a more intimate chat," Sabah said.

Suhanto turned and led the way to his desk. He sat down, looking up at Sabah with an undisguised but futile fury in his eyes. "I ask again. What do you want?"

"I have instructions you are to pass to the Philippine officer Aguilando," Sabah said. "You are to tell him that a shipment of Russian machine guns will be aboard the SS *Jakarta* bound for al-Mimkhalif. Describe the cargo as very valuable PKM seven-point-six-two-millimeter models. And that is exactly what they will be."

"Where am I to pick up this shipment?"

"Follow established procedures," Sabah said. "Make sure those machine guns are aboard the *Jakarta*. Tell Aguilando that the ship will depart on October tenth at ten hundred hours following the usual course. Interception will be expected in the South China Sea. However, your captain is *not* to give the weapons to the Filipino when he rendezvous with him."

"And what happens when Aguilando shows up and Captain Muharno refused to turn over the cargo?" Suhanto asked.

"That is not your concern," Sabah said.

"It *is* my concern!" Suhanto angrily insisted. "I have already lost one ship."

"Believe me," Sabah said, "you will not lose the *Jakarta*. This I swear to you in the name of Allah."

"Very well," Suhanto said, knowing any further protests would be futile. "How much will I be paid for participating in this deception or whatever it is?"

"You will be allowed to keep your left hand."

"My God!" Suhanto cried. "How much more must I endure?"

"It was your greed that brought you to this sad state of affairs," Sabah reminded him. "Do you have any questions?"

Suhanto shook his head, wincing as his wrist throbbed again.

ROYAL YACHT *SAYIH*
GULF OF ADEN
VICINITY 48° EAST AND 13° NORTH
1200 HOURS LOCAL

SHEIKH Omar Jambarah was not a member of Saudi Arabia's royal family, but his clan enjoyed close relations with the rulers of the kingdom. One of the perks of this friendship was unlimited use of the Royal Yacht *Sayih.*

Sheikh Omar's forefathers were no more than country bumpkins from outward appearances; however, during several centuries of intrigues, rebellions, wars, and political infighting on the Arabian Peninsula, the elders of the family always managed to choose the sides and causes that were victorious. Even between 1915 and 1927, when the British claimed the area as a protectorate, the headmen of the Jambarah clan continued to stick with winners, giving them genuine devotion and loyalty. In 1932, when the Kingdom of Saudi Arabia emerged from the chaos, Jambarah's grandfather was granted a sheikdom by the grateful royal family. Eventually, oil was found on the land, and the Jambarah clan became incredibly wealthy. They established a city-state, sending their sons abroad to be educated at the world's finest universities. The latest of these male offspring was the present ruler, Sheikh Omar.

Jambarah went further than simply taking advantage of excellent schooling. He broke free of his strict Islamic upbringing and fell into the sins of the flesh offered in the

West. He dealt with this sinfulness with the rationalization that giving in to his base desires while not actually in a Muslim country meant he was not in conflict with Islamic law. He also used his abundant spare time and personal wealth to form the al-Mimkhalif Warriors of Fury to carry out a special jihad against the infidels. He did this not because of religious fervor, but to create a kingdom of his own that he would claw out of Saudi Arabia.

So much for loyal allegiance.

SHEIKH Omar Jambarah and his friend Commodore Muhammad Mahamat relaxed on deck chairs on the royal yacht's afterdeck. The naval officer and sheikh had been discussing the planned attack on the Philippine Patrol Boat 22 scheduled in two days. The imminent destruction of that point of irritation had put both men in a collective good mood. It was one less thing the sheikh had to worry about, and a grand opportunity for Mahamat to give his fast-attack boats a good workout the crews would enjoy.

The sheikh bit into a peach, chewing thoughtfully. "Is there anything else we should be considering at this time, Brother Mahamat?"

"Yes, Sheikh Omar," the commodore replied. "The Americans have deployed an air-cushion vehicle in the operational area of their carrier battle group. Its tender ship is a new amphibious attack vessel called the *Dan Daly*. As of this moment that is all I know, but after I meet with my friend from the American Embassy in Muscat, I shall have much more intelligence."

"Ah, yes!" the sheikh said. "Ply the infidel with liquor, hey?"

"It does tend to make them talkative," Mahamat said with a chuckle. "And speaking of the ACV, it actually stopped our dhow at sea, and dispatched a boarding party to make a search."

"*Shu halmsibi*—bad luck! What happened?"

"Not to worry, Sheikh Omar," Mahamat said reassuringly. "The old ship was empty and Captain Bashir's papers were all in order."

"Perhaps this is advantageous to our cause," the sheikh mused. "If the Americans see the *Nijm Zark* again, they will no doubt have no interest in her."

"I'm afraid the Americans are not all that convinced of Captain Bashir's innocence," Mahamat said. "My source tells me that orders have been issued to the carrier battle group that all ships sighting the dhow are to report the location and course it is following."

"Ah! They are suspicious then," the sheikh said. "But what if we used the dhow in the same manner we are going to use the *Jakarta*?"

"Do you mean to set a trap?"

"Of course," the Sheikh said. "If they are using that ACV as a patrol vehicle, we could draw it to the dhow at a predetermined location where your squadron could easily destroy and kill the infidel crew."

"Such a thing must be handled most carefully, Sheikh Omar."

"I am so happy that you appreciate the sensitivity of the situation," the sheikh said. "And there is another very important thing for you to consider. I have been entertaining the idea of having your fast-attack squadron take over the arms-delivery missions."

"It would be most feasible, Sheikh Omar," Mahamat said. "In fact, having us take a more active part in this program would present additional opportunities to destroy that ACV."

"You seem worried about that vessel."

"Captain Bashir told me it was well armed and moved extremely fast across the water."

"Then the sooner it is sunk, the better!"

"The Americans will replace it with another."

The sheikh laughed. "Then we shall sink that one too. And the next, and the next, and the next."

"We will be able to adapt to whatever situation the Americans create," Mahamat said. "I can guarantee that."

"*Allah biauwid alaik*—God will reward you!"

**PATROL BOAT 22
INDIAN OCEAN
VICINITY OF THE EQUATOR AND 90° EAST
10 OCTOBER
0800 HOURS LOCAL**

LIEUTENANT Commander Ferdinand Aguilando stood on the bridge as the vessel plowed through the slight choppiness of the sea. Four seamen—one each forward, port, starboard, and aft—scanned the horizon with their binoculars, looking for the arrival of the S.S. *Jakarta.* Aguilando was in a good mood. The cargo carried by the Greater Sunda Shipping Line vessel was made up of Russian PKM 7.62-millimeter machine guns. This had been confirmed by both Abduruddin Suhanto and Harry Turpin. Between that and the cocaine expected from Suhanto, Aguilando expected to purchase both a new motorcycle and automobile within a couple of weeks. It was only a question of the models and makes he desired. Additionally, he would move his mistress into a larger, more luxurious apartment. She showed her gratitude for special consideration in exceedingly pleasant ways.

The *Jakarta* was expected to arrive at the location sometime between 0730 and 1030 hours. It was difficult to be precise about the ocean rendezvous because of the vagaries of loading and transferring cargo in clandestine conditions. There also existed an outside chance that the law might interfere with the get-together as well. Patience and a certain amount of pessimism brought reality to such situations.

Aguilando went below to the radar station and checked the scope. Its circular sweeps revealed nothing but empty ocean surrounding the patrol boat.

FLAGSHIP *HARBI-MIN-ISLAM*
0830 HOURS LOCAL

COMMODORE Muhammad Mahamat relaxed in his
cabin, outwardly calm but inwardly excited about the morning's potential for excitement. The commanding officer of
Oman's crack fast-attack squadron had decided that he
needed no backup from any of the half-dozen attack boats
that made up the rest of his outfit. His personal flagship
could easily handle the day's mission.

A knock on the cabin door interrupted his reading of the
Masqat Nisr newspaper. "Come in!" he barked, slightly irritated at the interruption.

A sailor stepped into the cabin and handed him a sheet of
paper. "Radio message, *Amid.* The *Jakarta* reports she will
rendezvous with the Philippine patrol boat at approximately
0930 hours."

"Haida taiyib!" Mahamat exclaimed. He reached over
and turned on his intercom connection to the bridge. "Sound
general quarters!"

PATROL BOAT 22
0925 HOURS LOCAL

AGUILANDO stood by the helmsman as they slowed
to ONE-THIRD speed. The *Jakarta* was a hundred meters off
their starboard bow, moving at ten knots. The officer picked
up the microphone on the radio that was tuned to the international maritime frequency.

"Freighter *Jakarta,* this is Philippine Patrol Boat Twenty-
Two. We have spotted you and are ready to pick up the cargo.
Heave to and prepare for the transfer. Over."

The familiar voice of Captain Bacharahman Muharno
came back over the speaker. "This is the *Jakarta.* I will not
pass the cargo to you. Over."

Aguilando was confused. "Did you not pick up the machine guns?"

"I have them, but I refuse to give them to you. Out."

"Have you gone crazy?" Aguilando asked angrily. He could not believe the unexpected insolence. "Heave to or I'll send you to the bottom."

"If you do that," Muharno said, "the ship and machine guns will go down together."

"And also you and your crew!" Aguilando screamed into the microphone. "Now heave to, damn your lost Muslim soul! You pull that fucking tub over now, Muharno, or I'm going to put a cannon round through your hull! Over!"

"I say again," replied Muharno. "I am not going to comply with your order. Out!"

Aguilando started to press the transmit button again when the petty officer of the watch came up to the bridge. "Ship approaching off our stern, sir. A warship of unknown nationality."

Now a new voice came over the speaker. "*Jakarta*, this is the *Harbi-min-Islam*. Continue on your course."

Aguilando swung his eyes rearward. "This is Philippine Patrol Boat Twenty-Two, unknown warship. Identify yourself and your nationality."

A couple of seconds later, a French Exocet MM-40 missile whipped so low over the patrol boat that Aguilando's cap was whisked off his head as the rocket continued on toward the open ocean. A second shot came right after the first and slammed into the stern of the Philippine boat. The concussion of the resultant explosion blew forward, sending a thick shower of white-hot metal, sheets of flame, and roaring gases through the lower deck. In the unnoticeable passage of a millisecond, the crew in the area was reduced to minute specs of charred flesh and bone.

Aguilando and the other survivors above deck could feel the unbearable heat through their shoes, then saw clouds of steam rolling up from the sea as the boat began going beneath the waves. By that time the *Harbi-min-Islam* had come alongside and its Bofors twin-barrel cannon pumped bursts of 40-millimeter shells into the sinking hulk at a rate of six hundred rounds a minute. The Filipinos who had been topside joined their shipmates below in death.

Commodore Mahamat stood out on his signal bridge, watching as machine gun crews sent bursts of automatic fire into the debris of the patrol boat to ensure there would be no survivors. He looked up to see the *Jakarta* fading in the distance as it continued on to make its rendezvous with the dhow *Nijm Zark*.

ACV *BATTLECRAFT*
OFF THE PAKISTANI COAST
2200 HOURS LOCAL

THE *Battlecraft* was packed with people, weapons, and equipment. The entire Command Element along with the First and Second Assault Sections were all present and accounted for. Additionally, Lieutenant Veronica Rivers, Petty Officer Bill Watkins, and Petty Officer Bobby Lee Atwill were also present. This meant that a total of twenty-two warm bodies were crammed aboard. To make matters even more uncomfortable, two fifteen-foot CRRCs were strapped to both the port and starboard sides of the deck.

Veronica Rivers surveyed her radarscope, which displayed the nearby coastline. The location was in the direct center between the city of Karachi and numerous mouths of the Indus River that fed out into the Arabian Sea. The terrain in the area was wet and marshy, and although the ACV could have easily moved over it, the tactical situation dictated that the CRRCs be used to move the Brigands ashore. Noise was an important factor.

These raiding boats were normally propelled by outboard motors, but since silence was of the essence that evening, the men aboard would be paddling with oars. It would take them a while to reach their destination, do the job assigned them, then make the laborious return trip.

"We're in position, Captain," Veronica said to Brannigan, who sat in his chair above and behind her.

"All stop," Brannigan said.

"All stop," Paul Watkins, the helmsman, said. "Aye, sir."

Brannigan, outfitted for combat complete with web gear, weapon, and camouflage paint on his face, grabbed his CAR-15 and stood up. "Section Leaders! Take your men to your boats."

Lieutenant Jim Cruiser and Senior Chief Buford Dawkins immediately left their cups of coffee in the wardroom and went out on deck to get the mission rolling.

THE night's operation was almost an impromptu effort, except they had received a warning order three hours earlier. Intelligence from the Pakistani Army had been sent to Commander Tom Carey about a seaside camp of a small Islamic terrorist group that was sympathetic toward al-Mimkhalif. An informer had passed on the information that the local thugs were earning extra money by acting as errand boys for the bigger guys as well as reporting on police and military activities in the area. If the *Battlecraft* was to knock off al-Mimkhalif's transportation system, the camp would have to be taken out.

NOW the two CRRCs were launched into the water and the SEALs climbed aboard. The boats were designed to hold eight men, but each had an extra guy crammed aboard. The Number One Boat with the First Assault Section had Wild Bill Brannigan stuffed in between the two fire teams, while the Number Two Boat endured the presence of the detachment hospital corpsman, Doc Bradley. However, Doc elicited no complaints from the other SEALs. He had been instrumental in saving the lives of several Brigands in their previous two combat operations. A good chance existed he might be needed again on this raid.

Back on the ACV, Frank Gomez glowered with disappointment and anger at being left behind to monitor the AN/PRC-112 radio that was on the same frequencies with those of the assault sections. Veronica Rivers stood on the deck beside him, watching the rubber rafts disappear into the night's darkness. She had glanced in Jim Cruiser's direction as his two fire teams climbed into the raft, and she'd caught him looking back at her. They'd exchanged smiles. Jim had winked and waved, then turned his attention to the job at hand.

Frank didn't fail to notice the silent rapport between the two.

2356 HOURS LOCAL

COMMUNICATION between the fire teams was done by LASH radio headsets. The SEALs could whisper into the microphones and their voices would be transmitted through the earphones perfectly audible to the recipients. They were also supplied with night-vision goggles to make movement through the darkness of the swamp safe and easy.

Brannigan checked his GPS, noting they had come within a hundred meters of the target. He hoped the information he'd received about the water in the swamp was accurate. It was supposed to be no more than a meter deep and cover a firm bottom.

"Hold it," the skipper said over the LASH. "We're walking from here on in."

The paddling came to a stop, and the SEALs stepped out into the swamp, finding themselves in water just above their knees. A few tentative steps revealed they were in mud, but it wasn't deep or clinging.

Alpha Fire Team under Chief Matt Gunnarson moved out on the point in a skirmish line. Jim Cruiser and his SAW gunner Bruno Puglisi followed with Connie Concord's Bravo Fire Team behind them. Brannigan and Doc Bradley followed the Bravos.

Senior Chief Dawkins's Second Assault Section was in a similar formation, with Charlie Fire Team in the lead while he and his own SAW gunner, Joe Miskoski, were between them and Delta Fire Team.

Over on the far side of the enemy camp, a detachment of Pakistani paratroopers was supposed to be waiting to police up any enemy stragglers who might try to escape in that direction during or after the attack.

After a quarter of an hour of slogging through the dirty water, Garth Redhawk spotted the camp. He alerted Chad Murchison on his right and Matt Gunnarson on his left. All three SEALs slowed down, making sure they made no unnecessary splashing as they continued forward. The rest of the detachment had monitored Redhawk over the LASH system, and reacted accordingly.

The enemy camp was out of the swamp, up on a slight rise above the water. This dry land went all the way to a road a couple of hundred meters farther on. A few crude canvas-and-log structures were all the shelter the terrorists had. No fighting holes or bunkers had been built. The Brigands would have to strike fast and viciously to keep a minimum number of terrorists from fleeing the immediate area. If the paratroopers were not where they were supposed to be, those who reached the road had an easy run to safety.

Jim Cruiser swung the Bravos up on line with the Alphas while he and Puglisi moved between the two fire teams. When they stepped from the water and entered the edge of the bivouac, Cruiser ordered the attack. The CAR-15s blasted three-round automatic bursts while Puglisi played his SAW like an accordion, sweeping the barrel back and forth with four-to-six-round firebursts plowing into the huts and lean-tos of the terrorists.

Screams of wounded mujahideen filled the air for the first few seconds, then sporadic return fire answered the assault.

By then Brannigan and Bradley had joined the battle along with the Second Assault Section. The collective automatic fire became one long continuous burst, and a few fleeing terrorists could be seen running frantically toward the road.

"Cease fire," Brannigan ordered.

A sudden silence settled over the scene. The SEALs moved among the crude living quarters finding bullet-riddled bodies in and outside the shelters. The fire from the detachment had been so heavy and intense that there were no enemy survivors. Each sprawled corpse was bloodied with multiple wounds.

A search for documents or other intelligence items began at the same time that fresh firing broke out further inland. Cruiser glanced over at Brannigan. "It would seem the Pakistani paratroopers were right where they were supposed to be."

"Mission accomplished," Brannigan said. Then he repeated under his breath, "Mission accomplished." Those were his two favorite words.

Senior Chief Buford Dawkins reported to the detachment commander. "We didn't find any documents laying around, sir. I don't think them dumb bastards could read."

"Not even any Korans?"

"Negative, sir."

"This must have been just a temporary bivouac," Brannigan surmised. "But we broke up the operation." He took a deep, satisfying breath. "Okay, Senior Chief. Let's get back to the CRRCs."

FRANK Gomez had been raised on the AN/PRC-112 with the good news that the operation went off without a hitch. He made a report to Lieutenant (JG) Veronica Rivers since as senior ranking person aboard, she was in command of the *Battlecraft* until Brannigan returned.

"Were there any casualties?" she asked, looking intently at the RTO.

"The enemy caught it hot and heavy," Frank replied.

"What about the SEALs?"

Frank grinned. "No, ma'am. Lieutenant Cruiser is just fine."

Veronica's face reddened so much, it was apparent even in the dull glow of the illumination coming from the ACV's instruments.

CHAPTER 10

CAMP TALATA, PAKISTAN
11 OCTOBER

IMRAN and Ayyub were sixteen-year-old mujahideen who had just finished their elementary training and were now considered full-fledged though inexperienced fighters in al-Mimkhalif. They had not been present at the disastrous attack on the police station on the Afghanistan border because they were in the final phase of their battle instruction in the foothills.

The boys' entrance into the world of jihad had not come from a devout belief in the causes of Islam. They had been apprentice bakers in their home village in rural Yemen, working for a demanding and cruel master. Slowness in learning or inattention to detail by the neophytes meant solid painful blows across the back and buttocks from a heavy cudgel wielded with cruel abandon by their large muscular boss. Many times they were locked in the pantry overnight without supper for their transgressions. Unfortunately, Imran and Ayyub were not the brightest of the village youths, and they made more than their share of mistakes in not only preparing the shop's products, but in learning the skills of the trade at the pace demanded by the master baker.

Things came to a head early one morning when both overslept. Their first duty of the day was to be up at four A.M. to get the oven fires going so that when the master appeared at five, things would be ready to begin the day's demanding work. But that particular dawn began with the master's furious bellowing when he walked into a cold kitchen. The two apprentices sat straight up in their bed, looked at each other, and grimaced as they realized that this was the worst disaster of their short bungling careers. A prolonged brutal beating loomed in their immediate future.

Without exchanging a single word, they knew what they must do. The boys gathered up their few miserable belongings and went through the rear window of the bakery, and ran like hell toward the highway two kilometers away. This road led to the city of Sadah.

Luck was with them that day, and they were able to catch a ride on a truck that took them to the safety of the city where the brutal master would never be able to find them. Unfortunately, the pair of bunglers had no idea what they were going to do in the unknown metropolis, and after nearly starving for a week, they found a charity kitchen at one of the city's mosques located in the slums. More than physical sustenance was available in the dining hall. Clever clerics, looking for disenfranchised and frustrated youths to recruit into al-Mimkhalif, were waiting to preach to the boys prior to the serving of meals.

After several recruitment sermons—replete with messages of hate for the Great Satan America—Imran and Ayyub volunteered in the same unthinking manner they'd used when running away. It was a quick exit from a bad situation; better a dead martyr than be caught by the police and hauled back to face the master baker's rage and beatings.

1215 HOURS LOCAL

NOW Imran and Ayyub stood serious guard duty for the first time. They had been posted above the mountain pass that offered ingress to the camp. It was a narrow trail far below the bluffs that towered above it. A lot of their old careless ways had been driven out of them by hard-ass combat training along with cuffs and kicks in the military environment of al-Mimkhalif. They were also well indoctrinated, and they now tended to their assigned duty with discipline and determination.

"Look!" Ayyub exclaimed. "Someone is coming up the trail."

Imran looked in the direction his friend was pointing. "A lone man, hey?"

"Let's make sure he is alone," Ayyub said. "Remember what we were taught. Sometimes the enemy sends scouts ahead to draw fire to discover the locations of our positions. We must be patient. This could be an attack." After ten minutes passed, the rookie stood up. "The stranger is alone."

Imran cranked the field telephone kept at the lookout position, and raised the chief of the guard. "There is a solitary man approaching the camp through the pass. We have watched him for a quarter of an hour. He is by himself."

The chief of the guard put the receiver-transmitter back in its cradle, standing up and gesturing to the three riflemen relaxing at the midday cook fire. "Let's go, brothers. Someone is approaching the camp."

The chief took the trio with him as they hurried down to the spot among the boulders where they could safely intercept the interloper. Everyone was nervous since none of the camp's mujahideen was out on an operation. Somehow a stranger must have inadvertently wandered toward their camp. They took up their positions among the rocks and waited. When the stranger appeared, the chief called out.

"Wakkiff!"

The man obediently came to an instant halt, raising his hands.

"Walk slowly forward," the chief commanded. "Keep your hands raised high or we will shoot you." He watched carefully as the man approached deliberately and carefully. Suddenly the chief jumped up and joyfully shouted, "Mikael! It is you!"

Mike Assad grinned and lowered his hands, speaking in his crude Arabic. "I come home."

The chief and the riflemen ran out to exchange hugs and kisses with their comrade. This was another Middle Eastern custom that Mike had never gotten used to. Kissing a man did not measure up to making out with an affectionate girl.

The group hurried back through the camp as one of the riflemen ran ahead shouting the good news aloud. Others joined in the impromptu celebration, happy to see that a popular comrade they thought to be a prisoner had returned to them. By the time they reached the commander's tent, all the mujahideen not on duty had gathered around the canvas structure, chanting and clapping a welcome to Mikael. The chief went inside where the camp leader Kumandan, and Hafez Sabah sat consuming wheat loaves and rice.

"What is the disturbance outside?" Kumandan demanded to know.

"Mikael Assad has come back," the chief announced. "He is returned to us."

"Bring him in," Kumandan said.

Mike stepped into the tent. "*Marhaba*—greetings!"

Kumandan stood up and studied the man before him. "My God! We had heard you had been turned over to the Americans."

"I was," Mike said. "They take me to their embassy in Islamabad."

Sabah gave him a suspicious look. "You are armed, I see. It appears you have a government-issue Webley revolver and pistol belt."

"I steal it all in police station," Mike said. "It is a very old British weapon."

"Sit down," Kumandan invited. "Fill up a plate for your-self. You must be hungry."

"*Aywa!*" Mike said, going down into a cross-legged sitting position next to the food. "And tired. I come a long way."

Sabah was still not convinced. "Did you say they took you to the American Embassy, Brother Mikael?"

"Yes," Mike replied, reaching for the rice. "But I escape. They want take me someplace from there. I do not know where. I am in car and handcuff is loose on one hand. I take out my hand and open door and jump in street. Then I run like gazelle and get away in big crowd of peoples."

"*Haida taiyib!*" Kumandan said, congratulating him.

Sabah lost all interest in his food. He leaned forward, looking straight into Mike's face, speaking in the British English he'd perfected during his days at Oxford. "Let's you and I speak in your language for a while, Brother Assad. I am going to ask you some rather important questions about your adventurous escape."

"That will be fine, Brother Sabah," Mike replied. He wished he wasn't so damn tired, knowing he would have to be careful and not trip himself up under the questioning.

The interrogation was unfriendly at first, but after an hour Sabah was convinced of the truth in Mike's cover story. The episodes in the Rawalpindi slums, the mosque, the bus trip, and all the rest fell into place with some scattered incomplete intelligence they had received from the interior of Pakistan. The end of the session evolved into a friendly conversation between Sabah and Mike.

"You have been badly misjudged here in camp," Sabah said. "Many of your brother fighters think you are a bit on the slow side. I can see now that is because of your crude Arabic. This gives a mistaken impression of your intelligence."

"I was getting better," Mike said. "But since my capture I've been exposed more to Urdu than Arabic. I'll get back on track quick enough."

"Actually, I have a different assignment for you," Sabah said. "Our supply operations are going through some changes.

It has been quite difficult actually, and I could use a good chap to lend me a hand. Are you interested?"

Mike couldn't believe the opportunity that was being put before him. Any information gleaned on the supply methods and routes would be invaluable. He smiled and nodded. "I'm your man, Brother Sabah."

ACV *BATTLECRAFT*
INDIAN OCEAN
VICINITY OF THE EQUATOR AND 90° EAST
12 OCTOBER
1400 HOURS LOCAL

THE ACV had gone farther east than usual as Lieutenant Veronica Rivers monitored her radar screen. She was getting only the regular and easily identified signals of cargo ships that normally passed through the area. After directing Watkins to make a couple of changes of course, she noted spotty readings that had appeared in a corner of the tube.

"There's some stuff at zero-four-eight," she said. "About twenty miles out. I can't quite figure out what it is."

Lieutenant Bill Brannigan ordered Paul Watkins to steer to the azimuth, and walked over to check out what had gotten Veronica's attention. "It's not moving," Brannigan remarked.

"At this point I'm guessing it's debris," Veronica said. "I wonder if an airliner has gone down in that area."

"Negative," Brannigan said. "We would have been notified and changed over to a rescue mode. We'll check it out." He went back to his chair. "Watkins, maintain course and increase speed to two thirds."

"Maintain course and increase speed to two thirds, aye, sir."

The *Battlecraft* quickly attained the velocity, and the spray around her increased markedly as she continued toward the source of the signals. Lieutenant Jim Cruiser and his First Assault Section prepared for whatever situation awaited them in that part of the ocean. Bobby Lee Atwill took advantage of the increased RPM to run some quick diagnostics. When the power plant instrumentation indicated all was in order, he left the cramped engine room and joined the rest of the crew to see what Veronica had discovered.

Twenty minutes later the ACV arrived on the scene and the speed was cut to ALL STOP. Brannigan and Veronica went out on the bow and visually inspected the area. "Something crashed here," Veronica said. "Christ! Look at the mess."

Floating debris littered the area as it rolled with the waves. Pieces of wood, mattresses, and a fuel tank were easily identified. Then the first corpse came into view. Brannigan directed Watkins to move toward the body as Dave Leibowitz came down on deck with a bow hook. He snagged the clothing of the dead man, and pulled him out of the water and deposited him on the deck. Brannigan knelt down and rolled him over.

"A Philippine sailor," he said, examining the features. "From the blood coming out his eyes, ears, and nose, I'd say he was killed by a combination of concussion and drowning." He went through the pockets and pulled out a wallet. A Philippine naval ID card identified the man as a petty officer artificer.

"There's more that way," Leibowitz said, pointing.

Another three quarters of an hour was spent hauling dead crew members up on the *Battlecraft's* deck. A total of eight were discovered for examination. Veronica took pictures with the digital camera while Leibowitz and the other SEALs pulled the available documents and personal affects from the bodies. After each corpse was searched, it was gently rolled back into the water since there were no accommodations to transfer them to another location. The best that could be done would be to radio the position to the Philippine government from the *Daly* so they could come out and retrieve their dead; hopefully, before the sharks discovered the feast awaiting them.

When the grisly task was completed, Brannigan went back inside the cabin with Veronica following. "Okay, Rivers, set a course back to the *Dan Daly*. It appears we have a report to make. Too bad it has nothing to do with terrorists."

USS *DAN DALY*
1630 HOURS LOCAL

COMMANDER Tom Carey had the damp documents spread out on his desk along with the photographs of the dead crewmen. Bill Brannigan, Jim Cruiser, and Veronica Rivers sat in silence, watching him as he carefully perused the information they had brought back with them. Carey turned to his stand-alone computer and typed in some of the information he was able to glean from the paperwork.

"Okay," he said. "It's all substantiated here and cross-checked by the system. The vessel you discovered was from the Philippine Navy. That's pretty obvious from the dead guys. It is Patrol Boat 22, captained by a Commander Carlos Batanza until his murder. At that point, it was taken over by the exec, a Lieutenant Commander Ferdinand Aguilando."

"The captain was murdered?" Brannigan asked. "Does this have anything to do with our mission out here?"

"Batanza was known to be corrupt," Carey said. "His mission was interdiction of smugglers. For a couple of years he was a real straight arrow, but like many an underpaid public servant, the chance for bribes and outright thievery brought him to ruin. It is thought that his death was a payback for some drug deal gone bad."

"What about an arms deal gone bad?" Cruiser asked.

"Not likely," Carey remarked. "His exec, Aguilando, was also on the take, so he could have been also held responsible for whatever it was the pissed off the bad guys."

"That patrol boat was obviously destroyed by powerfully weaponry," Brannigan said. "I wouldn't think some drug smuggler would be carrying that sort of ordnance. It appears to me that only a terrorist group transporting a cargo of arms would have the capability of delivering that much punishment."

"We know of no terrorist group using warships, Lieutenant Brannigan," Carey said.

"Well," Brannigan conceded, "this probably doesn't have anything to do with us." He stood up and glanced at Cruiser and Veronica. "Going to chow?"

"Yeah," Cruiser said.

"Not me," Veronica replied. "I think dealing with those corpses took away my appetite."

"I'll go with you and Cruiser," Carey said. "I missed lunch."

"Enjoy you chow, guys," Veronica said. "I'm going to my cabin for a snooze."

LIEUTENANT Veronica Rivers's lack of appetite wasn't from the Philippine corpses. It was a much more personal condition that took away her desire for food. She was in love again. The object of her affections, Jim Cruiser, hadn't shown any interest in her. They had exchanged smiles when he left the ACV for the raid on the coastline, but he hadn't given any outward signs of interest in her since returning.

She lay down on her rack, staring at the overhead as she endured the sweet misery in silent thought. Most of the time it was futile for a female naval officer to expect a normal romance with a man on her ship. She wouldn't be the kind of woman male naval officers would seek out for romance or sexual pleasure. Too many official and unpleasant consequences could come out of such affairs. When it came to the opposite sex, those guys wanted to get as far away from women in uniform as possible. They'd pass up some attractive, intelligent young female officer to pick up a large-breasted, empty-headed floozy in the officers' club or a bar ashore for whatever sort of romantic or sexual adventure

they were looking for. And it didn't do servicewomen much
good to pursue civilian males either. Those guys might like
to take a military woman to bed once out of curiosity, but
they were too intimidated by females who held military rank
to seek a long-term relationship.

Petty Officer Frank Gomez had noticed her interest in
Jim Cruiser and made a couple of remarks on the ACV to
her. She wondered if Jim had become aware of her feelings
toward him. If he had, and wasn't responding, then she was
in for a long period of enduring unrequited love.

"If I were an aviator," Veronica said aloud to herself, "my
call sign would be 'Frustrated Female.' "

DHOW *NIJM ZARK*
15 OCTOBER
1100 HOURS LOCAL

CAPTAIN Bashar Bashir turned to Mike Assad and
Hafez Sabah standing on the small quarterdeck with him.
Down below, staying close to the railing, were the two ex-
baker apprentices Imran and Ayyub, who were in the final
agonies of a shared bout of seasickness that was beginning
to ebb away.

"See how the American planes only take a quick look at
us and fly away?" Bashir said.

Mike Assad felt homesick at the sight of the United
States Navy aircraft. "They do not seem interested."

Sabah nodded his agreement. "Not long ago an American
boat crew came aboard to inspect the dhow. They examined
Captain Bashir's papers and his cargo hold. They found
nothing."

Bashir laughed. "It was a good thing we were coming
back from delivering arms instead of carrying a cargo. At
any rate, they are under the impression we are no more than
an innocent merchant vessel."

"Most fortunate," Mike said.

"But our leadership is not going to take any chances," Sabah said. "Even at this moment a plan is being formed to lure the American boat into a trap and sink it."

"It was a strange boat," Bashir said. "It flew over the water at a very fast speed."

"No amount of speed will save it from the wrath Allah will impart on its infidel crew," Sabah said confidently.

"*Attamam*—excellent!" Mike said, thinking he had to get the word out on this very real danger to a U.S. Navy vessel. His first order of business when they returned to Camp Talata would be to get to his dead-letter drop.

MIKE Assad had become a celebrity of the al-Mimkhalif terrorist band after his escape from a supposed period of captivity at the American Embassy in Pakistan. The exploits of his cross-country adventures had been systematically exaggerated with each telling and retelling among the mujahideen. He was no longer thought of as the simple American with more bravado than good sense. Mikael Assad was now regarded as a cunning, clever fighter.

Kumandan, as al-Mimkhalif's field commander, had pulled him from the operational detachment and placed him directly under Hafez Sabah's authority. The American was to work closely with the agent in coordinating the finer details of the group's maritime and smuggling activities. The leader even assigned them the two former apprentice bakers Imran and Ayyub as their personal bodyguards. The two youngsters had been wild with happiness over the honor. When Imran and Ayyub reported to take up their new duties, they swore a solemn *mukaddas* oath on the Koran that they would willingly give up their lives for Mikael and Sabah.

NOW Mike and his companions continued the voyage aboard the old wooden vessel. This was an orientation trip for the American so that he could see firsthand how the arms were passed over to the dhow for delivery to the secret rendezvous point off the Pakistani coast.

1345 HOURS LOCAL

THE lookout clinging to the top of the main mast suddenly shouted out, "*Hai hi ahi!* The *Jakarta* dead ahead!"

Mike looked in the direction everyone else did and could see nothing for several moments. Then the shadowy figure of a ship could be sighted on the horizon. As the two vessels drew closer, Mike saw that the stranger was a small freighter. After a few more minutes, he could see the ship was not a particularly smart one. Streaks of rust coursed down from the deck to the waterline and the paint on the hull was faded and peeling.

Sabah walked up to stand beside him, speaking in English. "That is the ship we meet to pick up our arms shipments. She is the *Jakarta* from the Greater Sunda Shipping Company. The owner is a miserable sinner by the name of Suhanto. He tried to cheat us a while back. Since he was a thief, we cut off his right hand as dictated in the Koran."

Mike made a mental note of the names Suhanto and the Greater Sunda Shipping Company for his next dispatch. "How do you know when and where to meet this ship?"

"That is information you need not know at this point," Sabah said. "But not to worry. Much will be revealed to you when the time is right."

"I understand," Mike replied.

As the two ships maneuvered for the exchange, Imran and Ayyub took their AK-47s and positioned themselves to cover Mike and Sabah in case of treachery. It took three quarters of an hour before everything was in position and lines held the dhow and freighter close together. Captain Bacharahman Muharno of the *Jakarta* stood at the rail of his ship looking down at the Arabian vessel.

"*Marhaba!*" he called in greeting to Captain Bashir. "How do you fare, old friend?"

"I am well, *shukhar,*" Bashir yelled back. "What do you bring us today?"

"Automatic grenade launchers," Muharno said. "From Spain."

"Did the cowardly Spaniards give them to us out of fear more of their trains would be blown up?" Bashir asked with a cackle.

Muharno shook his head. "*La!* These were stolen from their garrison in Gibraltar. At least that is what I am told."

"They'll do nothing about this theft," Sabah yelled out as he joined in the conversation. "The Spanish government's fear of the mujahideen is now unlimited."

Mike was familiar with the weapons that were about to be turned over to the terrorist group. During his SEAL career, he'd been introduced to the LAG-40 automatic launchers that fired 40-millimeter high-velocity grenades at a rate of 215 per minute. The deadly missiles were pulled into the receiver for firing on linked belts that could hold up to thirty-two rounds. With a range of 1500 meters, they were a perfect ambush weapon. He glanced up at the freighter captain. "How many launchers you got?"

"A dozen, my friend," Muharno said. "Who are you? I do not believe I have seen you before."

Sabah interjected, "He is one of our greatest heroes who must remain nameless for the present. We do not wish his presence to be known."

"I understand," the captain said. He turned to check his crew's activity on the deck. "Ah! We are ready to transfer the cargo."

The net holding two crates was pulled from the hold by the crane, and swung over above the deck of the dhow. Mike watched as the transfer of the deadly cargo began.

CHAPTER 11

MIKE Assad had been surprised that their all-night voyage from the rendezvous site with the SS *Jakarta* back to Pakistan had not been discovered by U.S. Navy aircraft. He had mixed feelings about the possibility of being spotted; on the one hand it would keep the lethal automatic grenade launchers out of the hands of terrorists, but his effectiveness as a mole would be ended then and there. He still had plenty to learn about the new operational procedures al-Mimkhalif planned to use for supply deliveries. A second arrest would make any additional "escapes" incredulous to the enemy. That would be a disaster since it was vital that the SEAL find out who the real leaders were behind the organization. When that was discovered, the right people with the right attitudes could eliminate the rag-heads with extreme prejudice.

Now the crates of grenade launchers were being wrestled onto rafts by the dhow's crew. Several men from Camp Ta-lata had brought the floating devices through the gentle surf that washed up almost languidly on the Pakistani beach, rowing them to the side of the dhow. When the cargo was transferred, it would be taken back to the shore for the final trip to the al-Mimkhalif stronghold.

Mike was impressed with the skill of the mujahideen as they deftly handled even the heavy crates, putting them properly aboard the rafts to distribute the weight evenly across the plank decks. This was the first time he had wit-nessed this phase of the operation. As soon as the job was done, Mike and Hafez Sabah, along with the two former ap-prentice bakers, jumped aboard one of the rafts for the short voyage to the shoreline.

When the rafts were beached, the Toyota pickups arrived from concealment on a hill that looked down on the scene. Once more it took pure muscle as the weaponry was wrestled up onto the vehicles. When Mike turned to look outward from the beach, he could see that the dhow was already well on its way out to sea. The SEAL was fascinated by the an-cient vessel, realizing this type of ship had sailed that area of the world for centuries. It was possible that his own ancestors may have once used the vessels in their long-ago lifetimes.

The sound of shouts broke into his reverie, and he saw it was time to begin the trip up to the camp. He was honored to see that, like Sabah, they had left a place for him in one of the cabs. Imran and Ayyub jumped into the back of a truck with other mujahideen.

CAMP TALATA
1445 HOURS LOCAL

KUMANDAN sat cross-legged on the carpet in his tent, contentedly smoking his hookah water pipe. Mike Assad and

Hafez Sabah, similarly seated, faced him. The field commander took a drag and exhaled, then passed the mouthpiece over to Sabah. After his turn, Sabah gave the device to Mike, who treated himself to a shallow drag. As a nonsmoker, he did not inhale, merely taking a mouthful and blowing it out. Kumandan could tell that Mike was not enjoying the pipe, so he politely set the mouthpiece down when the American passed it over to him.

"I have called both of you here for a very pressing matter," Kumandan said. Since the politeness of greetings, a snack and the hookah water pipe had been observed, it was time to get down to business. "Important orders concerning you both have come down from al-Mimkhalif's high command."

"We are honored," Sabah said.

"As well you should be," Kumandan said. "It has been decided that you will be sent on a very special and dangerous assignment. This will involve you in the deepest secrecies of our brotherhood. You are going to visit the heart and soul of al-Mimkhalif."

"Our honor is tripled," Sabah said, deeply moved.

Mike leaned forward in anticipation. He hoped he would have enough time to send the information through his dead-letter drop before being shipped out.

"As of now we are going to place you and your bodyguards away from the others in camp," Kumandan informed them. "You are to move all your belongings into a tent that is even now being erected for your use. Guards will be placed around it on a twenty-four-hour basis, allowing no one but me to speak to you. Your food and water will be brought to you, and a portable latrine will be placed just behind your quarters. Do you have any questions?"

Mike felt a deep stab of disappointment. This situation was exactly like the premission isolation phase of SEAL operations. Now there was no way that he could get word out through the dead-letter drop. He cleared his throat and spoke in his crude Arabic. "Can you tell us where we go?"

"You will not know your destination until you arrive,"

Kumandan said. "Now you must get your things. Do not forget your bodyguards. I shall call upon you at the tent later with more instructions."

Mike and Sabah got to their feet, salaamed, and left the tent.

TAIMUR NAVAL BASE, OMAN
18 OCTOBER
1345 HOURS LOCAL

THE dusty limousine drew nearer to the distant front gate of the base after a monotonous but high-speed nine-hundred-kilometer trip down from the port city of Ras Al-had. The vehicle had been made available from them upon their midnight arrival at the port in the dhow. During the journey, the four passengers in the spacious back of the vehicle—Mike Assad and Hafez Sabah along with body-guards Imran and Ayyub—had enjoyed air-conditioned comfort. The scenery may have been no more than bleak desert terrain, but the refreshments provided the travelers more than made up for the wearisome countryside. Between restless napping, Mike and Sabah consumed fruit juices, sodas, candy, and pastries. Imran and Ayyub snacked too, but took their bodyguard duties serious enough for both to remain alert and awake at all times.

However, there was one disturbing aspect of the long ride. The quartet of travelers did not know their exact destination when the trip began, and this unexpected arrival at an Oman naval base unnerved Mike to a great extent. The thought occurred to him that he might have been compromised. Perhaps the mysterious entity who picked up his messages at the letter drop had rolled over for al-Mimkhalif. He glanced over at Imran and Ayyub, who sat with their AK-47 assault rifles nearby. Those weapons might end up being used to protect him; or perhaps kill him in a violent act of revenge. Mike turned to Sabah, speaking in English. "Have you been here before?"

"No," Sabah said. "But I know about this place and the man that is supposed to be in command." He suddenly pointed ahead over the driver's shoulder. "There is the entrance."

The two young naval sentries on duty gave the vehicle and passengers a careful scrutiny, then allowed the limo to continue onto the base. The driver went down a well-paved road for another ten minutes before buildings and dockside structures came into view through the hazy desert air. The ride ended in front of a two-story building where a petty officer opened the door to allow Mike and his companions to disembark.

"Min karib," the petty officer said, turning and walking toward the building.

The quartet of visitors followed closely, and Mike was more than a little relieved that their escort was not a firing squad. The two bodyguards slung their weapons over their shoulders as the group was led into the edifice and upstairs to an outer office. Evidently they were expected, for a door was being held open for them. Imran and Ayyub stayed outside while Mike and Sabah stepped into an office where an officer, bearing the large gold band of a commodore on his epaulets, stood up.

"Welcome to the Zauba Fast Attack Squadron," the officer said in perfect English, beaming a smile at Sabah. "It is good to see you again, brother."

"The feeling is mutual," Sabah replied. "I did not know whether it would be you greeting us or some other officer."

"You and your friend have been deemed important enough to be brought to me personally."

Sabah indicated Mike with a nod of his head. "Allow me to introduce my companion, Mikael Assad."

Mahamat smiled at Mike. "You seem uneasy, my friend."

"Indeed," Mike said. "I was not expecting to be brought to such a place as this."

"Sit down," Mahamat invited. "Brother Sabah and I met on a couple of occasions in the past. Thus, I shall explain the situation to you." He waited until his guests were comfortable before continuing. "We are an isolated unit, far from our higher headquarters. As far as everyone is concerned, we are conducting normal routine coastal patrols. That is an impression we work hard to maintain."

"I see," Mike said. "Am I to understand the impression is not entirely accurate?"

Mahamat laughed. "Of course it is not!"

Mike's thought processes were going full-speed as he assessed the meaning behind the commodore's words. He was not surprised by the officer's next utterance.

"We are part of al-Mimkhalif."

Sabah turned to Mike. "And what do you think of that, Mikael?"

"I am flabbergasted," Mike said, not having to feign shock and surprise. "How clever of our leaders."

"I have been informed of you, Mikael," Mahamat said. "You are a hero to our brotherhood. Imagine! An escape from the American Embassy in Islamabad, then making a lone journey of evasion across Pakistan to rejoin your comrades."

"It was our righteous cause that gave me the courage and skills I needed," Mike replied.

"And you, old comrade," Mahamat said, looking at Sabah, "are as appreciated as ever. Your efforts in organizing weapons and supply deliveries have also been noted by our esteemed leader."

"I am humbled by the honor," Sabah said.

"I never thought about a leader," Mike said. "I assumed we were commanded by a group of dedicated Islamic brothers."

"We have but one leader," Mahamat said. "And you will meet him soon. But first we have to prepare you for future operations that will be both dangerous and complicated."

"We are eager to participate in such a phase of our jihad," Sabah assured their host. "It sounds like decisive actions are going to be taken."

"Most assuredly," Mahamat said. "And the first thing we must do is have you outfitted as officers with complete uniforms. We will also see to it that your bodyguards are disguised as sailors. You will be going out very soon aboard my flagship to observe the first part of al-Mimkhalif's struggle to establish a destiny of victory dedicated to the glory of Islam. Because of the clandestine nature of these activities, you must not look like outsiders."

Mike was now eager for more information. "What will we be doing?"

"There is a troublesome small craft," Mahamat said. "An air-cushion vehicle, to be exact, that must be destroyed before we can continue. This must be taken care of before our strategy can be advanced toward its final phases. Even now, our decoy is out like a baited hook to draw our victim into a trap."

"It sounds as if this is all going to happen very quickly," Sabah said.

"We expect action in the next couple of days or so," Mahamat said. He pressed the buzzer on his desk and their petty officer escort stepped into the office. "*Raqib,* take these men and their servants to the tailor shop for uniforms as previously directed."

"*Aywa, Amid!*" the petty officer said with a salute. He gestured to Mike and Sabah to follow him as he walked toward the door.

DHOW *NIJM ZARK*
ARABIAN SEA
VICINITY OF 15° NORTH AND 70° EAST
19 OCTOBER
1200 HOURS LOCAL

CAPTAIN Bashar Bashir and his crew were bored into a state of numb lethargy. They had been tracking back and forth from east to west, then west to east since dropping off their passengers in Ras Alhad, Oman. To add to their frayed tempers, they were not being paid for the activity. But when one takes on jobs from al-Mimkhalif, one must expect certain disadvantages, such as unreasonable and unexplained demands. Once a vessel, even an old wooden one like the *Nijm Zark,* begins its association with a terrorist organization, she and the crew are at their client's mercy.

Bashir's mate, a surly individual named Bakhtiaar Ghanem, was standing wheel watch, working the spokes as he kept the compass as close to west as possible under the pressures of current and wind. Bashir stood beside him, glancing down at the quartet of crewmen dozing in the shade in front of the quarter deck. The fifth was up in the rigging on the mainmast, watching all points of the horizon.

Ghanem snarled. *"Shiyatin min jahannam*—the devils of hell! I hate being bait like this."

"Aywa," Bashir agreed. "But there is nothing we can do about it."

"What if those cursed American airplanes come around?" Ghanem said. "They'll make short work of us."

"I think if we are bait, there will be other planes nearby to attack the Americans," Bashir suggested.

"Are you crazy? What makes you think al-Mimkhalif has airplanes?"

"Then maybe a ship," Bashir said. "I don't think they would set us out here to be sunk."

"Maybe we are to keep the Americans away from somewhere else," Ghanem commented sourly. "What a cheap sacrifice for al-Mimkhalif, *la*?"

"You are forgetting the tracking mechanism they put aboard," Bashir said, pointing to the electronic instrument lashed to the after mast. "Our instructions are to turn it on if we see that funny boat that stopped us before."

"Ah!" Ghanem said hopefully. "Maybe nothing will happen. We have only enough fuel and provisions for another forty hours."

"Dir balak!" the lookout on the main mast called down. "The American boat is off the port side."

Bashir yelled back, "Are you sure it is the strange one that stopped us and its crew came aboard?"

"It is the same," the lookout assured him. "I can easily see the spray all around it, and it moves fast toward us."

"*Binnihay*—at last!" Bashir exclaimed. He walked over to the after mast and flipped on the tracking machine to broadcast its homing signal.

"Bait!" Ghanem said fearfully. "We are just bait!"

FLAGSHIP *HARBI-MIN-ISLAM*
ARABIAN SEA
VICINITY OF 17° NORTH AND 65° EAST

"**A** homing signal from the dhow has been picked up, *Amid*!" the excited young communication officer reported, looking over at Commodore Muhammad Mahamat.

Mahamat grinned with delight. "*Haida taiyib*—excellent! What is the course?"

"One-seven-seven, *Amid*. Approximately one hundred kilometers."

Mahamat turned to the helmsman. "Course one-seven-seven! Flank speed!"

Mike Assad and Hafez Sabah stood on the bridge with the commodore as the flagship began the maneuver, keeling with a quick response of rudder to wheel. Mike had been doing his best to make mental notes of actual locales and courses, but without access to navigational instruments, the more he observed the more confused he became about their location on the watery wilderness. Sabah, on the other hand, was content to merely make casual observations of what was going on.

"What is happening, Commodore?" he asked.

"A signal from our decoy has indicated that the American vessel we seek is approaching her," Mahamat said. He looked to the officer of deck standing nearby. "Sound general quarters!"

Mike felt a surge of nervous dread. "Are you speaking of the air-cushion vehicle, Commodore?"

"The same!" Mahamat replied. "She comes from an amphibious assault ship assigned to an American carrier battle group, and has been doing vigorous patrolling in this area for close to a month."

"Is she a threat, Commodore?" Sabah asked.

"Her potential to harm us must be neutralized at all costs," Mahamat replied. "Our contacts inform us she is called *Battlecraft* and is extremely fast and well armed. This day's task is to destroy her."

Mike turned away. The thought of watching American sailors being killed sickened him. For one wild, desperate moment he thought of getting the Webley revolver in his cabin and taking out key members of the flagship's crew. But he knew that would solve nothing except provide momentary relief before he was shot down himself. There was absolutely nothing he could do but observe the carnage to come. The worst part was that he was going to have to cheer when the American vessel was sunk by the super-fast missile attack vessel.

The *Harbi-min-Islam* sped across the Arabian Sea toward her objective.

ACV *BATTLECRAFT*
VICINITY OF 15° NORTH AND 65° EAST

THE flickering radar blip was a familiar signal to Lieutenant Veronica Rivers. She grinned, announcing, "The dhow is back, Captain. Three-five-zero at ten miles. She's heading due west."

"Right," Brannigan replied. "Okay, folks. Remember our orders when we caught her heading at two-seven-zero. General quarters! Did you get that course, Watkins?"

"Course three-five-zero, aye, sir!"

Lieutenant Veronica Rivers had her weapons system humming as per standing operational procedures even though they knew the dhow was unarmed. She checked her scopes for signs of aircraft. "Three aircraft off to the northeast at five miles."

"That would be the Hornet Escort," Brannigan said. He turned to the patrol frequency. "Hornet Escort, this is *Battlecraft*. Over."

The voice of the F/A-18 flight leader came back. "This is Hornet Escort. Over."

"We've got the dhow on our scope and are moving in," Brannigan said. "How about a security sweep around the area? Over."

"Roger, wilco."

HORNET ESCORT

"**DID** you monitor that transmission from the *Battlecraft*?" the flight leader radioed.

"Roger," his wingman replied. "Lead the way, Boss."

The wingman's RIO came on the air. "I've got a blip just about due east at maybe fourteen miles. Moving rapidly in a southern direction. She's got warship written all over her."

"Let check it out," the flight leader said. "It might be an awkward situation if some Middle East navy observes our activities up close."

The two F/A-18s moved toward the suspect blip, then went down from angels ten to angels two as they closed in. "We're almost there," the RIO reported.

"Okay," the flight leader said. "I've got a visual. She's a warship all right, but I can't make out the nationality. Let's make a close orbit around her."

The pair of aircraft began a flying a tight circle around the vessel that sped across the expanse of water below them.

FLAGSHIP *HARBI-MIN-ISLAM*

THE officer of the watch stepped in from the signal deck. "The two aircraft are American," he reported. "Super Hornets."

"Alert the Exocet crew," Commodore Mahamat ordered. "Lock and fire on the aircraft."

Mike Assad's knuckles turned white from his hard grip on the bulkhead railing. He trembled with impotent rage, taking deep breaths to keep his emotions under tight control.

HORNET ESCORT

"WE'RE locked on!" the RIO yelled. "Missile launch!"

Both the flight leader and his wingman reacted as quickly as possible, kicking out chaff and flares as the former broke left and the latter right in violent collective maneuvering.

It was too little too late.

The French MM-40 missiles had very little airspace to pass through and they found their targets easy marks. An American F/A-18E and F/A-18F were blown from the sky in instantaneous detonations of orange and red. Numerous pieces of the aircraft trailed smoke and flame, fluttering all the way down to the sea.

ACV *BATTLECRAFT*

"JESUS Christ!" Lieutenant Veronica Rivers yelled out. "Those Hornet Escort guys disappeared off the scope. They were locked on and hit."

"Where the hell did the ordnance come from?" Brannigan asked. "Nothing was fired from the dhow."

"Ship approaching from zero-zero-three at a high rate of speed!" Veronica reported. "They gotta be the bad guys."

Brannigan flipped to the inter-ship nautical channel. "Unknown vessel, this is United States Navy ACV *Battlecraft*. Identify yourself. Over."

"We're locked on," Veronica calmly informed the skipper. "Missile launch. Evade! I am launching chaff and flares!"

Paul Watkins, responding with instincts honed during their battle drills, went into a wide turn as he pushed the throttle to flank speed. Brannigan raised the *Dan Daly*'s CDC. "This is *Battlecraft*. We are under attack by an unknown naval vessel. Readings indicate this ship has blown away the two aircraft of the Hornet Escort. Over."

"Roger, *Battlecraft*," the tactical action officer responded. "Wait."

Brannigan yelled over at Watkins. "Continue to take evasion action!"

"Continue to take evasion action," Watkins replied in a businesslike tone. "Aye, sir." He abruptly steered the ACV onto another heading as Veronica kicked out more chaff and flares.

"Battlecraft," came the voice of the tactical action officer. "You are to immediately break off all contact and return to the home ship at flank speed. Over."

"This is *Battlecraft*," Brannigan said. "That vessel destroyed two American fighter aircraft. We have the capability of making a deadly response to that unprovoked action."

"I say again," the tactical action officer said firmly. "You are to immediately break off all contact and return to the home ship at flank speed. Over."

"Roger, wilco," Brannigan said through clenched teeth. "Rivers, what's the course back to the *Dan Daly*?"

"One-eight-seven," Veronica replied.

"Watkins," Brannigan said. "Steer to course one-eight-seven at flank speed."

"Course one-eight-seven at flank speed, aye, sir."

Veronica Rivers gave Brannigan a startled look. "What the hell is going on? I have a solid lock on that damn warship!"

"We're turning tail," he replied.

CHAPTER 12

THE ACV *Battlecraft* had been pulled from the water and hauled up into the loading bay of the ship for its first scheduled overhaul. Bobby Lee Atwill, the gas-turbine system technician, was able to handle the work on the Poder-Ventaja engine without help. He was very much aware that at that time, he was the only sailor in the entire United States Navy who knew the power plant inside and out. After spreading tarpaulins around the small wardroom, he began dismantling the engine to give each separate part a thorough inspection and cleaning. Within a quarter of an hour of beginning the task, he was happily lost in the greasy work, performing his version of exploratory surgery on the machine he loved more than any of his human shipmates.

The radar, weapons, and navigational systems were a different story. Lieutenant Veronica Rivers kept ahead of that game by a continuous self-imposed program of monitoring and adjustments. However, she and Jim Cruiser were both tasked with all the paperwork regarding the overhaul procedures and results. This consisted of two booklets of forms that had to be filled out and signed by them; countersigned by Lieutenant Bill Brannigan; then counter-countersigned by the skipper of the USS *Dan Daly*.

They also had to use all previous maintenance and repair procedures listed in the electronic, weapon, and engine logs as references. Not even a yeoman who could type a hundred words a minute would be able to lend a hand in this ponderous administrative procedure. It was a matter of filling out lengthy forms requiring signatures on each one. Jim and Veronica loaded all the documents into a couple of boxes, then lugged the weighty load of data from the docking well, across the flight deck to the island, and up three decks to an unused small wardroom on the aft end. After dumping it all on a table, they sat down next to each other to begin.

"Okay," Jim said, pulling a pen from his shirt pocket. "The first form is for the navigational system. Box one: name and number of vessel." He filled in USS DAN DALY, LHX-1, then went the rest of the way through the heading as Veronica laid out the maintenance sheets for reference.

"I hope we can get this done quickly," she said. "Everyone is anxious to revenge those Hornet guys who were blown out of the sky."

"You don't have to worry about that," Jim said. "The skipper says if anything big starts going down, the *Battlecraft* will charge straight into the fight even if we have to bolt it back together as we fly out of the docking well."

"Great!" Veronica said. "Now. What's the first thing on this rather complicated agenda?"

"The brand-new automatic pilot," Jim said. "Let's start with the first page of the AP maintenance log."

She pulled it out, and as he read the questions on the form

aloud, she carefully perused the dates and actions taken. As
they went through the routine, they looked up now and then,
their eyes locking. Both would avert their gazes, but at one
point when Jim asked her about the replacement of a
cathode-ray tube, they continued to gaze at each other without looking away. There are some things that adults of opposite genders can instinctively recognize in each other. And
the most remarkable is mutual attraction. He leaned over and
kissed her lightly on the lips, and she pressed back. They
embraced and exchanged a sexier, deeper lip-lock.

"Oh, God," J   aid as they reluctantly drew apart.
"What the hell are we doing?"

Veronica smiled. "That's kind of obvious, isn't it? I think
we both knew something was building up between us."

"That isn't what I mean exactly," he said, gently touching
her face with his hand. "I was thinking more along the lines
of where this romance is going to go."

"It's completely futile, of course," she said. "Hopeless,
really."

"And against regulations."

"Anything between us has the chance of that proverbial
snowball in hell," Veronica commented.

"Doomed from the start," Jim said, sighing sadly.

"Not a ghost of a chance."

"But from this point on we're going to pursue these feelings straight into a full-blown romance, aren't we?" Jim
asked.

"Damn right," Veronica said.

They kissed again, this time longer and with more feeling.

CARRIER BATTLE GROUP
1030 HOURS LOCAL

THE SH-60 Seahawk helicopter rose off the deck of
the carrier a little over two miles off the starboard beam of
the *Dan Daly*. The nose of the aircraft tipped downward with

the pilot's pressure on the cyclic, making it move forward toward its destination.

Within three minutes, the chopper reached the flight deck of the amphibious assault ship and went into another hover before lowering to a gentle landing. Immediately CIA field supervisor Sam Paulsen stepped from the aircraft followed by his assistant, Mort Koenig. They hurried over to the island, where Commander Tom Carey waited for them. After brisk greetings and handshakes, he led them into the interior of the structure and up three decks to the ready room assigned to the crew of the ACV *Battlecraft*.

The moment they entered the ready room, Lieutenant Bill Brannigan bellowed, "Atten-*HUT*!" He and Lieutenants Jim Cruiser and Veronica Rivers snapped into rigid positions of attention.

"Stand at ease!" Carey said, surprised at the military formality of the officers. He went to the front of the room while his visitors took seats off to the side. "Please sit down." He indicated the CIA men with a nod of his head. "This is Mr. Paulsen and Mr. Koenig. That's all you need to know about them right now. The first thing I want to do is take the rap for the order directing the *Battlecraft* to break off contact at the start of the confrontation yesterday. I know you are all anxious to avenge the loss of those three aviators, and I am also fully aware that Lieutenant Brannigan was getting ready to kick ass properly and effectively. But the fact the attacking vessel was obviously a warship belonging to a sovereign nation threw me for a loop. This could have been what might be classified as a friendly fire incident and I didn't want the foreign vessel blown out of the water even if her skipper was a stupid bastard sailing the seven seas with his head up his ass." He nodded to Brannigan. "Did you get a good look at her?"

"Yes, sir," Brannigan replied. "She was a fast-attack ship; British *Province*-Class to be exact. I looked her up in the *Jane's Warships of the World*."

"Well, shit," Paulsen said. "That could cover more than one navy in this part of the world. Did you see her ensign?"

"She showed no national colors," Brannigan said. "We caught a fleeting glimpse of a scarlet flag with a white device of some sort. It didn't look like any national colors that I recognized." He glanced at Veronica Rivers. "What about your observations, Lieutenant?"

"I just saw blips on my weapons scopes, sir," Veronica reported. "I read the launch against the Hornets; then they turned on us. They brought us under fire and we went into a quick evasion mode waiting for orders. However, I was locked on solid on the attacker when the order to disengage was received." She paused, almost glaring at Carey. "We could've blown the son of a bitch out of the water in less that a half minute, sir."

"I realize that, Lieutenant," Carey conceded. He turned his eyes on Paulsen. "Do you have any comments?"

"Well," Paulsen said, "only that we're keeping a tight lid on this until the State Department can sort through the mess. Meanwhile, we're not going to be sitting on our asses. I have official permission to inform you folks you're authorized to go out armed and angry. Therefore, in the future you are to retaliate against any hostile action with extreme prejudice— I say again—*extreme* prejudice no matter the attacker. Losses of American lives will not be tolerated no matter the circumstances."

The two SEAL officers and Veronica exchanged looks of grim satisfaction.

"All right then," Carey said. "Now I have some highly classified matters to discuss with Mr. Paulsen and Mr. Koenig. Since this a need-to-know situation at this point in time, you are all dismissed. Sorry if I don't give you more information on their backgrounds, but I'm sure you appreciate the situation as it now stands. My two colleagues and I are staying aboard the *Dan Daly* until this operation is brought to completion."

Brannigan gestured to his lieutenants. "Care to have some coffee in the wardroom before you go back to work?"

"Sounds like a winner, sir," Veronica commented.

Paulsen waited until the three left the room, then turned his attention to Carey and Koenig. "I haven't mentioned our secondary mission here to anyone yet. But I think you guys probably already know what it is."

"I would say finding out about Mike Assad's location and health," Carey said.

"That may be a real problem," Koenig said. "He's disappeared off the face of the earth."

Paulsen pulled a packet of papers from his briefcase. "Here's the latest poop we have on him, and it ain't much, guys. He made his so-called escape in Rawalpindi on sixteen October as planned. He must have been delayed somewhat, because he didn't turn up anywhere until twenty October, when he was picked up by the local cops in the Northwest Frontier Province."

"How did you get the word on that?" Carey asked.

"We've got informants scattered hither and thither within Pakistani police organizations," Paulsen explained. "Their reports filtered in from different points and the one from the Northwest Frontier rang a bell. The prisoner picked up from a routine bus inspection matched Mike's description."

"As I recall, Mike looked pretty nondescript in his duty costume," Koenig said. "That could have been just about anybody."

"Well, this prisoner managed to escape from the local lockup," Paulsen said. "And he took along some field gear, ammunition, and a pistol that belonged to the cops."

Carey laughed loudly. "Oh, man! That's Mike Assad all right! Only a SEAL could pull off that caper."

"The problem is that we don't know if he made it back to his al-Mimkhalif buddies or not," Paulsen said. "That Northwest Frontier is dangerous as hell. Along with all the natural perils of snakes, scorpions, and hyenas, there're bandits to boot. And let's take the Pathans or the Pashtuns or whatever the hell they call themselves into account. Those are some real bad asses. They'd slit a guy's throat just to listen to him gurgle."

"If he's dead, then Operation Deep Thrust is over and done," Carey remarked.

"I'm afraid so," Koenig agreed, "and I'll take that kind of personally."

"Koenig has been the guy picking up Mike's intel reports from the dead-letter drop," Paulsen explained. "He's been playing the role of a UN agricultural advisor in the area. But Mike hasn't been sending anything lately, so we pulled Koenig out. There was a lingering chance everyone and everything was compromised."

"I don't see that we can do a lot from where we sit," Koenig remarked.

"I've arranged it so that the instant he makes any kind of contact, we will be notified here on the *Dan Daly,*" Paulsen said. "If the circumstances warrant, I'm authorized to get him the hell out of any mess he might be in."

"How the hell are you going to do that?" Carey asked.

"Commander," Paulsen said with shrug, "I don't have the slightest fucking idea."

ROYAL YACHT *SAYIH*
GULF OF ADEN
VICINITY OF 13° NORTH AND 48° EAST
1345 HOURS

COMMODORE Muhammad Mahamat led the way as he stepped from his gig onto the platform of the yacht's accommodation ladder. He was closely followed by Hafez Sabah, Mike Assad, and their two young companions, Imran and Ayyub. The sheikh's trio of bodyguards—Alif, Baa, and Taa—stood at the apex, looking down at the visitors to the ship as they came aboard.

As soon as Imran and Ayyub were aboard, the bodyguards whipped out their pistols and aimed dead at the ex-baker apprentices who carried AK-47s. Alif growled, "*Haram*— forbidden! No one may bring weapons aboard the yacht!"

Sabah was angry about the discourtesy. "These two young men are mujahideen! As soldiers of Islam they are expected to be armed at all times. And they are *our* bodyguards."

Alif, with his eyes peering intently at the two armed boys, nodded his head toward Taa. "See Sheikh Omar about this." He scowled at Mike and Sabah as Taa hurried away. "Are you carrying weapons?"

"*La,*" Mahamat said, shaking his head. "We left our personal arms aboard the flagship."

Mike stepped off to one side and gave Alif and Baa a close professional scrutiny. Not too bright; highly dedicated; willing to die to protect the sheikh; fully trained; physically fit; and extremely aggressive with guard-dog personalities well imbedded within limited human intellects. To sum it up: They would be the deadliest of adversaries. That would be something to keep in mind.

Moments later Taa reappeared, going up to Alif and whispering in his ear. The head bodyguard lowered his weapon and Baa followed the example in a monkey-see-monkey-do reaction. Alif said, "The sheikh gives your bodyguards his kind permission to keep their weapons. Please come with us."

The four visitors followed their surly escorts aft to where the sheikh held court while ogling his consorts between periods of inflicting sexual battery on them. When the visitors stepped onto the stern deck, both Imran and Ayyub let out gasps of astonishment. The sight of bare-breasted European women wearing only thongs was almost more than the two country boys could endure. To them this was a situation expressly forbidden by the Holy Koran, and they looked away, then back, then away, back, and finally turned to stare across the water at the flagship *Harbi-min-Islam,* fearful that having gazed upon the naked temptresses, they would be banished to the fiery depths of Hell forever. Sabah, amused by their discomfiture, laughed at them.

"All right, boys," he said jokingly. "Go forward and take up posts on each side of the yacht. Make sure no submarines surface to fire at us."

The two apprentice bakers, both red-faced with shame and fear, rushed off to their posts.

The sheikh invited his guests to sit down after sending the women away. He lit a Turkish cigarette and expelled the smoke, as he looked at Mahamat. "Introduce your colleagues to me."

"Of course, Sheikh Omar," Mahamat said. "You already know Brother Hafez Sabah."

"Indeed I do," the sheikh said. "You are doing a superlative job as you continue to direct our program of transport and supply."

"I am most honored by your kind compliment, Sheikh Omar," Sabah said.

"And this," Mahamat said, pointing to Mike, "is Mikael Assad from America."

The sheikh laughed loudly. "So! You are the clever fellow who escaped from the Americans in Pakistan, are you?"

"I come back for to fight," Mike said.

Mahamat switched languages. "It might be better if we spoke in English. Brother Assad is still in the process of improving his grasp of Arabic."

"Of course," the sheikh said. "In what part of America did you live?"

"Buffalo, New York," Mike replied, falling back on his cover story. "I was not happy there."

Sabah interjected, "When Brother Mikael joined us, he knew very little Arabic and had no serious instruction in the tenets of Islam. However, he has proven to be an apt student and his growing faith inspires all of us as does his bravery and resourcefulness."

"*Ajib*—wonderful!" the sheikh exclaimed. "You have returned to the bosom of your culture and are now winning glory, Mikael."

"Yes, sir," Mike replied.

"You must address the exalted one as Sheikh Omar," Mahamat instructed.

"Yes, Sheikh Omar," Mike said, correcting himself.

"Now, Commodore," the sheikh said. "I understand that you had contact with the American air-cushion vehicle. How did it go?"

"In one way it was a glorious victory," Mahamat said. "We destroyed two American planes by blasting them from the sky."

"Mmm," the sheikh said. "And in what way was it disappointing?"

"The air-cushion vehicle was better armed than we anticipated," Mahamat admitted. "However, this is not an insurmountable problem. The next time I go out to do battle with the infidel vessel, I shall bring along all six of my fast-attack craft. They are heavily armed and capable of hitting speeds of one hundred twenty kilometers an hour."

"I see," said the sheikh. He reached down and picked up a folder on the table next to him. He opened it and studied a paper it contained. "According to Saudi intelligence, the American air-cushion vehicle can travel faster than one hundred forty kilometers an hour."

"From what I saw of it, I believe that to be true," Mahamat said. "But there is only one of them. When it meets with my squadron, it will cease to exist within a quarter of an hour. It cannot be in all places at once, in spite of how fast it skims the ocean."

"Do you have any special tactics in mind?" the sheikh asked.

As Mahamat began explaining his battle plans, Mike Assad's mind went into an analytical and evaluative mode. He now realized he was in the presence of the supreme leader of the al-Mimkhalif terrorist group. And the son of a bitch was a Saudi Arabian. Actually, that was no great surprise.

That vital information, combined with knowledge of the Zauba Fast Attack Squadron, had to be sent back to Paulsen, or the entire operation was doomed to a catastrophic failure that could affect the entire campaign against Middle Eastern terrorism.

Man! Mike mused in his mind. *This is some heavy shit*!

Mahamat finished his report, and the sheikh seemed pleased with his plans for confronting the ACV. He looked over at Hafez Sabah. "And how is our old friend Harry Turpin?"

"His cooperation is assured as long as he makes money off us," Sabah answered. "He betrayed Abduruddin Suhanto's treachery to us, but only because al-Mimkhalif is the better customer."

"Sometimes I feel a bit like the Communist Lenin," the sheikh said. "He took advantage of the capitalists' greed as much as we take advantage of the infidels' particularly materialistic tendencies."

Mike spoke up. "That is what I hated the most about America, Sheikh Omar."

The sheikh smiled. "You are a true son of Islam, Mikael."

"I pray your trust in me remains strong," Mike said sincerely since his mission success depended on the man's absolute confidence in him. *You smoke-blowing son of a bitch!*

USS *DAN DAILY*
INDIAN OCEAN
1900 HOURS

AN atmosphere of tension, crackling like electricity among the attendees, filled the briefing room. The late hour of the impromptu session added to the edginess of the four members of the ACV *Battlecraft*'s operational crew, Lieutenant Bill Brannigan, Lieutenant (JG) Veronica Rivers, Petty Officer First Class Paul Watkins, and Petty Officer Second Class Bobby Lee Atwill. The two assault sections were conspicuous by their absence from this meeting.

Commander Tom Carey opened the session with the terse announcement that this was a combat briefing plain and simple. "You are going into harm's way," he said. "This is strictly a sea attack, and your mission is to hunt and destroy that unknown warship that destroyed the two F/A-18s and fired at you."

Everyone instinctively sat up straighter, and glances were directed at Lieutenant Bill Brannigan, who had his notebook out and pen poised.

Carey continued. "You will not have air cover. The reason for this is that we want only one American blip showing up on radars whether they be friendly or hostile. This is not sound battle procedure; it is, instead, a political necessity because of pressures involving international diplomacy."

" 'Ours is but to do or die,' " Brannigan said, quoting from the poem "The Charge of the Light Brigade" by the Englishman Lord Tennyson.

"I'm afraid so," Carey said. "But don't think it means you are expendable. But as members of a volunteer professional military establishment, you must realize that from the first moment you put on that uniform, you volunteered to obey the orders of your superiors. That means first you follow those orders without hesitation, then bring forth your personal observations during debriefings afterward. And I emphasize that this session today is a briefing, *not* a *de*briefing. Thus, no expression of opinions is invited." He looked at Brannigan. "Poetic or not."

"In other words," Brannigan remarked dryly, "we lock our heels and follow orders."

"If a gust of wind blows those orders out a porthole, you follow after 'em right into the sea," Carey said, passing out charts to Brannigan and his crew. "Here is your operational area. Nothing new there. You've been out there dozens of times. Now, let's talk ordnance. Your missile load will be six AGM-one-nineteen-B Penguin missiles. These fire-and-forget goodies are usually launched from Seahawk helicopters, so now you know why weapons wings were placed on each side of *Battlecraft*'s cabin."

"*I* designed them that way, sir," Veronica emphatically stated.

"A point well taken, Lieutenant," Carey said with an apologetic smile. "At any rate, the Penguins' semi-armor-piercing, HE warheads are more than adequate to handle that warship. Of course Lieutenant Rivers will also have her thirty-millimeter chain gun. You will not have an antiaircraft capability for two reasons. The first is that our intelligence assessments conclude there will be no aerial attacks directed at you." He grinned wryly. "And the second is that you don't have room for all those Penguins and any sea-to-air weaponry too."

"Sir," Brannigan said. "Do we have *any* idea of the nationality of that warship?"

"Not the slightest, Lieutenant," Carey replied. "And here's the real hang-up for you. While I described this as a hunt-and-destroy mission, you are not to attack until you are fired on. Another disadvantage forced on you by the conditions out here."

Veronica asked, "Are you going to issue us an OPORD, sir?"

"I just have, Lieutenant," Carey said. "You will go immediately to the *Battlecraft* after this briefing for a final inspection of the ACV's condition. You will begin your mission tomorrow from the *Daly*'s docking well at 0530."

"Oh-dark-thirty," Brannigan remarked. "The regular ol' SOP."

"Right," Carey said. "Good luck and Godspeed, *Battlecraft*."

Everyone stood to attention as the commander left the room.

CHAPTER 13

PAUL Watkins had programmed the waypoint data into the automatic pilot, and the ACV ran the proper azimuths at a steady sixty-two miles per hour on TWO-THIRDS speed. Lieutenant Bill Brannigan, sitting in his captain's chair, ordered the fuel-consuming velocity for the dual purposes of attracting attention and making the ACV easy to identify by any unfriendlies who might be looking for her.

Over to Watkins's sight, Lieutenant Veronica Rivers maintained an electronic surveillance of their environment while keeping her weapons systems ready for a violent response to any aggressive actions directed toward the *Battlecraft*. Bobby Lee Atwill sat in the doorway to his engine room, sipping hot coffee from a grease-stained cup.

Lieutenant Rivers spoke tersely into the intercom. "I've got a target at three-two-one, twenty-miles. Estimate it's moving at forty-plus miles per hour. That's got to be our bad boy."

"I agree," Bannerman replied. "Helmsman, steer three-two-one. Maintain speed."

"Steer three-two-one, maintain speed, aye, sir!" Watkins said.

The autopilot automatically disengaged when Watkins manipulated sticks and rudder for the change in course. This was one of the times when the SOP and common sense called for manual control.

Veronica checked her instruments. "We're in their radar," she reported. "I'm locked onto it."

"Roger," Bannerman said.

"I've picked up six more signals, Captain," Veronica said. "Jesus! The little bastards are moving fast as hell. Seventy-plus miles per hour."

"Concentrate on the faster blips," Brannigan ordered.

"Aye, sir," Veronica replied. "They're spreading out now, getting into positions all around us."

"Roger," Bannerman acknowledged. He picked up the radio microphone and raised the Combat Direction Center on the USS *Dan Daly,* where Commander Tom Carey stood by with the two CIA men, Paulsen and Koenig. When Bannerman's initial contact was recognized by a reply from the CDC radioman, the SEAL delivered a short meaningful transmission:

"We are engaged. Out."

THE BATTLE
1140 HOURS LOCAL

THE half-dozen speedier enemy craft were the Zauba Squadron's *Spica*-Class fast-attack boats. Commodore Muhammad Mahamat knew that the ACV had an estimated speed advantage over the vessels of twenty kilometers per hour. He directed his battle plan from his flagship *Harbi-min-Islam,* and he ordered the smaller craft to spread out and come in at the ACV from various directions to neutralize that plus in the Americans' favor. Proper positioning would be the key to victory that day.

The Number One Attack Boat swung over to the outside, faking an envelopment maneuver, then quickly cut straight in at the ACV. This was the *Battlecraft*'s first target, and a fire-and-forget Penguin antiship missile kicked off the weapons wing. Its Mach-1.2 speed carried it with merciless swiftness to the target, and the warhead hit the attack boat less than a foot above the waterline. The hull split open as the upper structure bent and twisted in the blinding detonation. In less than five seconds there was no sign of the boat on the sea except for bits of debris and boiling water.

"Incoming!" Veronica reported.

"Evasive action!" Bannerman ordered.

Watkins kicked the ACV up to flank speed, quickly closing in on ninety miles an hour as he made several sharp turns, alternating port and starboard directions. Meanwhile, Veronica released chaff and flares to draw off the enemy missile. It sped straight to some flares floating down toward the ocean and went through them. Then, unable to match the ACV's erratic maneuvering, the deadly rocket continued harmlessly away until it hit the waves and exploded.

"Incoming neutralized," Veronica said.

Watkins was given a new course, and he slowed down to eighty miles an hour as Veronica chose the Number Two Attack Boat as the next target. The young skipper of the Oman boat took a couple of seconds too long to order a launch. *Battlecraft*'s second Penguin slammed into the small ship just aft of the bridge. Both the hull and stern whipped inward as the explosion violently split the port amidships frame.

"Incoming!" Veronica reported again.

"Evasive action!" Bannerman responded.

"Incoming!" Veronica repeated.

With two missiles streaking toward the *Battlecraft,* Watkins first threw the ACV into a series of powerful tacking maneuvers while kicking her back up to flank speed. The first missile was drawn off by the chaff while the second, coming in from a different angle, was not affected by it or the flares. Watkins made a sharp turn to starboard, waited a couple of beats, then whipped around again in the same direction. The second projectile was unable to match the swift maneuvering and flew toward the distant horizon.

Veronica was not distracted by the violent turns. She managed to get a solid lock on Number Three Attack Boat and kicked off the third Penguin. It hit the bow of the enemy vessel at a three-quarters angle, sending the force of the warhead's explosion down the entire length of the boat. In one terrifying millisecond, bolts popped, welds split, and flesh charred in the total destruction that was blown across two square miles of ocean.

Bannerman jumped down from his chair to stand behind the female weapons officer. He noted the blips of the remaining three attack boats. "Watkins," he yelled out leaning toward the helmsman. "One-quarter left rudder! Two-thirds speed."

"One-quarter left rudder, two-thirds speed, aye, sir," Watkins said as calmly as if he were making ready to move into the *Daly*'s docking well.

Veronica needed no orders. She picked out two of the remaining fast attack boats, locked on, and launched. In short seconds they disappeared from the screen. She glanced up toward Bannerman, her face lit with a fierce surge of happiness.

"Fish in a barrel."

FLAGSHIP *HARBI-MIN-ISLAM*
1155 HOURS LOCAL

COMMODORE Muhammad Mahamat's face was blanched with fear. His mighty Zauba Fast Attack Squadron was down to his flagship and a single, solitary surviving attack boat. He looked at his watch, shocked to note that in some fifteen minutes he had been roundly and solidly defeated by a cursed infidel air-cushion vehicle.

He jumped on his command frequency and raised the Number Six Attack Boat. "What is your situation? Over."

"I am fully armed," the young skipper answered. He tried to put a tone of bravado in his voice, but a slight tremble was detectable. He had seen his five sister ships disappear off the radar one by one.

"Then with the blessings of Allah," Mahamat said, speaking rapidly, "you will make an immediate attack on the enemy vessel. Over."

"I obey, *Amid*," the young skipper replied in the full realization that he and his crew were about to be martyred.

Mahamat turned toward the deck officer. "Set a course for Taimur Naval Base. Flank speed."

The deck officer turned away and breathed a surreptitious sigh of relief, then gave the orders to the helmsman.

USS *DAN DALY*
COMBAT DIRECTION CENTER
NOON

COMMANDER Tom Carey exchanged grins with the others in the center as Lieutenant Bill Brannigan's voice came over the commo speaker announcing the destruction of no less than six fast-attack boats.

"Well done, Lieutenant!" Carey exclaimed. "What about the big girl? Over."

"She didn't participate in the fight," Bannerman replied. "And she drew off while we were dealing with the final boat. We've expended our missiles. Request permission to pursue enemy vessel. Over."

"Permission denied," Carey said. "That's a fully armed attack ship and all you've got left is a chain gun. You'd never get close enough to her to put a single round into her hull. Over."

"Understood," Bannerman said. "We'll go about and search for survivors. Prisoners should be useful. Over."

"Roger. As soon as that task is done, set a course for the *Dan Daly*."

"Wilco. Out."

Carey put the microphone down and looked over at Paulsen and Koenig. "I would say that operation went rather well."

"I agree," Paulsen said. "It seemed they told us they were engaged and had destroyed the enemy in almost the same sentence."

Carey checked the printout of the commo log. "It was almost that fast. Bannerman said they were engaged at 1140 hours and reported the situation well in hand at noon. A victory in twenty minutes is sure as hell better than one in twenty hours or twenty days."

Koenig took a sip from his cup of coffee. "This is not the end of the incident, gentlemen."

"Certainly not," Paulsen agreed. "The diplomacy boys are going to be busy for the next few weeks. I hope the *Battlecraft* manages to pluck some prisoners out of the water. That would make it easier all around."

"I can tell you who's going to be working their asses off in the wake of this event," Koenig said. "The State Department's workday will be starting real early tomorrow morning."

Paulsen chuckled. "And that means our old pal Carl Joplin."

"Well, there's no better man for the job," Koenig opined.

TAIMUR NAVAL BASE, OMAN
1715 HOURS LOCAL

MIKE Assad stood on the second-floor balcony of the base officers' quarters looking out to sea. He had watched the entire Zauba Squadron sail out of the harbor the evening before, knowing they were on their way to attack a single American vessel. He wasn't familiar with air-cushion vehicles whether armed or unarmed, but the sight of the flagship and the six fast-attack boats was evidence enough that they would be a formidable task force. The impotent rage he'd felt kept him awake all that night, and he'd been unable to even enjoy brief naps as the day wore on.

Hafez Sabah stepped out of their shared room to join him. "We will have quite a celebration when the commodore returns with his victorious squadron." He checked his watch. "His estimated time of return is eight o'clock tonight."

Mike turned his face away from the Arab and only nodded at his remarks.

"Are you all right?" Sabah asked. "You seem ill."

Mike quickly turned to face him and smiled. "It is nothing, brother. I think the rich food in the officers' mess has upset my stomach. I have grown quite used to the simple fare of the mujahideen off in the mountains."

Sabah chuckled. "I too have felt as if my stomach is carrying a heavy load. Those thick sauces and all that meat! And the desserts! These Oman sailors live well, do they not?"

A siren suddenly sounded from the harbor area, the wail loud and steady. Mike and Sabah instinctively looked out to sea. A small dark smudge showed on the horizon.

"I wish we had some binoculars," Mike said, peering past the harbor at the distant open water.

The two continued to gaze into the distance for ten minutes before they were able to discern the shape of Commodore Mahamat's flagship. "Ah!" Sabah exclaimed. "They have returned from their victory. Praise Allah!"

"I don't see the other ships," Mike said. "I wonder where they are."

"Perhaps they cannot go as fast as the flagship," Sabah suggested.

"Actually, they are able to go much faster," Mike reminded him.

A staff car sped from headquarters toward the officers' quarters and pulled up just below the balcony. The passenger, a chief petty officer, waved up at them. "The commodore has sent a message that you are to await his arrival in his office. Come at once, if you please."

The two went into the room, grabbed the naval caps to match their uniforms, and went out into the hall. Their bodyguards, Imran and Ayyub, were startled when they appeared unexpectedly. Sabah told them where they were going and the two youngsters insisted on coming along. When the four got downstairs, it was a struggle for all of them to get into the back of the vehicle.

THE COMMODORE'S OFFICE
1800 HOURS LOCAL

A commotion in the hall marked Commodore Muhammad Mahamat's arrival in the headquarters building. Petty officers yelled and enlisted men scurried about as their commanding officer bellowed orders at them, his words tumbling and jumbling into unintelligible shouts. When he charged into his office, both Mike and Sabah were alarmed at his appearance.

"*Musibi*—a disaster!" Mahamat yelled. "All is lost!"

"What happened?" Sabah asked.

"There was more than one of those cursed ACVs!" Mahamat said, close to weeping. "There must have been a dozen! We were outnumbered and the infidels could go much faster than us. We were surrounded and the treacherous dogs loosed missiles at us from all sides! They would appear at one location and fire. Then another and fire! I think we must have destroyed eight or nine of them, but the remaining three or four were too much."

Mike glanced out the window at the undamaged flagship tied up at the dock. "How did you get away?"

"Only through the blessings of Allah and my skill as a

combat leader," Mahamat said. "But they sank all my fast-attack boats. Those poor lads did not have a chance."

Sabah, visibly shaken, sat down. Between this disaster and having to deal with the ship owner Suhanto's treachery, he had stood about as much as he could. "What do we do now, Commodore?"

"I have radioed from the flagship for a helicopter at a heliport just north of here," Mahamat said. "I will have them fly us to Sheikh Omar's yacht for a council of war. I fear we are finished."

Mike fought a desire to cheer, making his voice somber and low. "I think we should go pack our things for the trip."

"Yes!" Mahamat exclaimed, glad to have something to do. "We must be prepared to stay with the sheikh for a good long spell."

"We better tell Imran and Ayyub to get ready," Mike said.

"No!" Mahamat ordered. "There may not be room for them on the helicopter."

Sabah grabbed Mike's arm. "Let us go, Mikael!"

The pair, with their faithful bodyguards following, did not send for a car. Instead, they ran all the way back to the officers' quarters. By the time they managed to throw a few things together, the sound of rapid honking could be heard out in the street. Mike looked through the window and saw the limousine with a chief petty officer behind the wheel. It was the same vehicle that had brought them to the naval base. Mahamat stood beside it, gesturing for them to come down.

Imran and Ayyub had grown frightened in the atmosphere of panic and trepidation. When Mike and Sabah emerged from their room, the two former baker apprentices followed them to the large automobile. As soon as Mike and Sabah joined the commodore inside, the driver took off.

Mike turned and looked out the back window at the two forlorn kids, standing alone and abandoned.

CHAPTER 14

MIKE and his two traveling companions, Commodore
Muhammad Mahamat and Hafez Sabah, were driven across
the desert to a lackluster oil-survey station that been scarred
and marred by sun, sand, wind, and neglect. This was a far
cry from the sleek, well-maintained naval helicopter base
that Mike Assad expected to see.

The site was where a French geological survey team was
doing illegal work for the Saudis in Oman. The work crew
was a mix of unsavory French, Arab, and African workers
who looked as if they had been recruited from a den of
thieves on the Marseilles waterfront. After arriving at the dilapidated facility, Mike, Sabah, and Mahamat were met by a
corpulent, hairy, sweating supervisor who was not pleased to
see them. "My pilot will be veree cross," he said in a heavy

French accent. "He don' wan' get up from bed until midday."

As if on cue, the pilot shuffled out of the small dormitory in an unsteady manner. After giving the three passengers a scowl, he escorted them to a dirty, oil-streaked French Aérospatiale SA-360 chopper for the rest of their trip to the yacht. The pilot was a hungover, smelly Italian reprobate who stank of sweat and garlic to the extent his body odor filled the fuselage with an invisible rankness. The aircraft lifted off after a minimum warm-up run of the engine, heading toward the open sea for the relatively short flight to the royal yacht. Mike noticed the guy wore a badly faded military shirt, and the SEAL figured he had probably been cashiered from the Italian armed forces for drinking on duty. But at least he seemed a competent enough helicopter pilot.

A quick landing on the pad located on the *Sayih*'s superstructure lasted only long enough for the trio of passengers to leap off before the battered and ill-used aircraft coughed its way back up into the air for a return to its clandestine home field in Oman. The trio of Sheikh Omar Jambarah's bodyguards, Alif, Baa, and Taa, greeted Mike and his companions with their usual surliness as they searched the arrivals. After the less-than-gentle procedure, the searchees straightened out their ruffled clothing and followed the rude reception committee down to the bridge, where they were taken back past the officers' cabins to the area the sheikh used as his office.

Although Jambarah sat at his desk, he was attired in a bathing suit and sandals, showing he had come in from the stern deck to meet the unexpected visitors. The sheikh's face was glum and an unlit cigar was clenched between his teeth. "The message given me by the radio room indicated things did not go well in the confrontation with the American hovercraft. What happened?"

"We sailed into a trap, Sheikh Omar," Mahamat said. "There was more than one air-cushion vehicle. At least a half dozen sped around and among my ships, firing missiles while taking evasive action and jamming our electronics capabilities."

"We were told they only had one such boat," the sheikh said.

"It was all a great subterfuge, Sheikh Omar!" Mahamat cried. "The infidels cleverly made it appear they had only one by employing a single hovercraft until the battle. Then they brought out the rest along with other warships and even jet airplanes. Squadrons of F-14s raked across our squadron as my brave men were martyred. We stood no chance at all!"

The sheikh looked at Mike and Sabah, asking, "Were any of you wounded?"

Sabah shook his head. "We did not participate in the battle, Sheikh Omar."

"They would have been in the way," Mahamat explained.

"Very well," the sheikh said. "Continue telling me about the incident."

Mike stood back a short distance with Sabah, listening as the commodore described an attack force that would have served well in the great Normandy landings on D-Day in 1944. As Mahamat continued his verbal after-action report, it seemed that American missiles and bombs rained down from the sky as torpedoes snaked through the depths toward the Zauba Squadron like schools of crazed sharks smelling blood in the water. While Mike Assad had been a SEAL all his naval career, he had enough savvy to know that the type of naval assault being described was a logistical impossibility owing to the actual tactical situation in the Middle East. It seemed to him that even if the entire United States Navy was on site for the battle, they wouldn't have near the firepower that Mahamat was describing in such vivid detail. Mike was sure the commodore was covering his ass big-time; no doubt the defeat was completely his fault because of bonehead errors and the mismanagement of his command.

However, the sheikh's face showed an expression of shock

and surprise as Mahamat told of attack boats exploding in rows. When the erratic report came to its sputtering end, tears streaked down the commodore's face and he fell to his knees. He held out his arms in a beseeching manner. "Sheikh Omar! You must see that a new Zauba Squadron is created so that this great disaster can be avenged. Surely the Saudis with their unlimited wealth can finance such a crucial undertaking. Do what you can to convince them of this dire necessity. I beg you in Allah's name!"

The sheikh stood up and reached across the desk, grasping Mahamat's hands in his own. "Get to your feet, my brave friend! I will use all my influence and resources to see that replacement vessels are made available to you."

Mahamat wiped at the tears on his face. "I thank you with all my heart, Sheikh Omar. I would have martyred myself with my men, but I swear that Allah spoke to me in my heart of hearts to tell me it would better if I returned to you so that the great struggle of al-Mimkhalif can continue with al-Azeez—the Almighty, the Powerful—showering us with His most holy blessings." He sobbed loudly. "I fought the battle as best I could under the most dreadful of circumstances."

"Of course you did, my poor brave friend," Sheikh Omar said. "Nobody could have done better in the face of such overwhelming odds."

"You are most kind, Sheikh Omar," Mahamat said.

"You are exhausted," the sheikh said. "I will see to it that cabins are made available to you and your brave companions Mikael and Hafez." He picked up his phone and punched the button for the chief steward of the yacht. "I need two cabins prepared for my guests. One for Commodore Mahamat and another to be shared by his two companions."

Mike, though no trained actor, did his best to exude bitter disappointment and grief. In part, the emotions were genuine. It appeared there would be no way he could contact American intelligence. He was locked into a vacuum.

USS _DAN DALY_
INDIAN OCEAN
VICINITY OF 5° NORTH AND 65° EAST
1700 HOURS LOCAL

LIEUTENANT Veronica Rivers was so confused, she
was now irritated and more than just a little perplexed. Not
only were the SEALs off somewhere on their own, but from
the looks of things, they were purposely ignoring her. It
didn't make sense, and she was determined to find out what
was going on.

She made her way down into the docking well to see if
they had gone to work on the _Battlecraft_ for one reason or
another. Veronica noted that the ACV was tied at its place, and
a quick glance inside showed the helmsman Paul Watkins
running some checks on his steering equipment.

Veronica went aboard and joined him. "Have you seen
Lieutenant Brannigan or Lieutenant Cruiser around?"

"No, ma'am," Paul replied. "I haven't seen 'em since
early this morning."

She went over to the engine compartment to see Bobby
Lee Atwill. He was giving loving attention to his beloved
gas-turbine power plant as he changed oil with as much care
and affection as a mother preparing formula for her baby.
Veronica interrupted him. "I'm looking for the SEALs. Do
you have any idea where they went off to?"

"No, ma'am," Bobby Lee replied looking up from his
greasy chore. "I ain't seen any of 'em a'tall."

Veronica went back outside and walked over to Chief
Warren Donaldson, who was supervising maintenance on
the hydraulic system that opened and closed the well's
doors. "Have you seen anything of the _Battlecraft's_ crew,
Chief?"

"Lieutenant Brannigan don't like us to call 'em a _crew,_
ma'am," Donaldson reminded her. "He prefers the word _de-
tachment._"

Veronica's temper snapped. "I don't care if he wants

them referred to as the goddamned *New York Metropolitan Opera*! Have you seen them around?"

"No, ma'am," he replied. "Not since yesterday."

Veronica returned to the flight deck and took the trouble of walking the entire length of it, looking over the side in case her wandering comrades-in-arms had gotten together in one of the whaler boats. Maybe they'd decided to go off for a swim someplace. Or even go fishing. After a twenty-minute search, she figured there was nothing else to do but return to the wardroom and wait to find out what was going on. Her jaws were torqued tight with anger at being ignored. It seemed she would have to experience some male chauvinistic snobbery after all. It was a real shame. She had begun to almost feel like a SEAL herself, especially after going into battle with them. They owed her something for that, even if nothing more than polite consideration.

Veronica's mood didn't improve when she arrived back at the wardroom to find the coffeepot empty. Then there was nothing in the supply cabinet to brew a fresh batch. She was seriously considering throwing the empty container against the bulkhead when the door opened and Petty Officer Second Class Bruno Puglisi stepped inside.

"Oh!" he said. "There you are."

"Yes," Veronica growled. "Here I am."

"The skipper's really pissed off at you, ma'am," he said. "How's come you didn't come to the meeting he called up for'd in the pilots' ready room?"

"I didn't know a goddamn thing about any meeting in the pilots' ready room because nobody told me about it!"

"Well, you better come with me," Puglisi said. "And be careful what you say. Wild Bill's feathers is really ruffled. He don't like it when somebody misses one of his meetings. Fact is, he expects ever'body there fifteen minute before it even starts. And here you are—"

"I told you that nobody gave me the word on any godamn meetings, Puglisi, so back off!"

"Yes, ma'am!"

"Lead on, Puglisi," Veronica said in disgust. "Escort me to my doom. Does the firing squad have their weapons loaded?"

"I don't know, ma'am," Puglisi answered, missing the sarcasm. "Do you want me to check the ammo inventory?"

"Shut up!"

They made their way forward, going up a couple of decks in the island. The ready room for pilots was unused since no squadron was assigned to the *Daly* at that time. When they arrived at the door, Puglisi opened it and stepped aside to allow her to precede him into the interior.

Veronica took a deep breath and stepped inside, then stopped.

All the SEALs immediately got to their feet and broke into applause with wide smiles. She frowned in puzzlement now rather than anger, and was baffled by the silly grins they directed at her. Wild Bill Brannigan signaled for her to join him at the front of the room.

Senior Chief Petty Officer Buford Dawkins suddenly yelled, "Three cheers for Lieutenant Rivers!"

The three "hip-hip hurrahs" thundered out as she walked up to join the skipper. It was then she noticed the keg in the corner and the beer-filled paper cups everyone had at their seats. Petty Officer First Class Connie Concord handed her a cup. "It's light beer, ma'am," he said. "We know that's what you prefer."

"A toast to Lieutenant Rivers!" Chief Petty Officer Matt Gunnarson ordered.

"To Lieutenant Rivers!" the SEALs yelled out simultaneously as they raised their beers.

Veronica didn't know what the hell was going on, but whatever it was she liked it.

Suddenly Brannigan loudly commanded everyone to attention and they all snapped into the proper position. Then the skipper called, "Attention to orders!"

Lieutenant (JG) Jim Cruiser marched grandly to the front of the room. He turned to face the assemblage, holding a document in his hands. After clearing his throat, he began reading aloud from it.

"Ahem! Whereas Lieutenant Junior Grade Veronica Rivers, United States Navy, has been assigned to a mission with the United States Navy SEAL Detachment known as Brannigan's Brigands; and whereas the said Lieutenant Junior Grade Veronica Rivers, United States Navy, has participated in combat with the SEAL Detachment known as Brannigan's Brigands; then let it be known that the aforementioned Lieutenant Junior Grade Veronica Rivers conducted herself with courage and cool efficiency in a battle against an enemy naval force, firing weapons in anger while taking evasive actions to keep our ACV *Battlecraft* from being harmed. Therefore, the aforementioned United States Navy SEAL Detachment known as Brannigan's Brigands does hereby proudly, affectionately, and respectfully declare that the aforementioned Lieutenant Junior Grade Veronica Rivers is now and forever an honorary member of the United States Navy SEAL Detachment known as Brannigan's Brigands with all the rights and privileges that go with that honor. This, of course, includes permission to drink an unlimited amount of beer—regular or light as she prefers—in the Fouled Anchor Tavern in Coronado, California, in the company of United States Navy SEALs." He cleared his throat again. "Ahem! However, I must point out that her running up a tab in the joint depends on Salty and Dixie Donovan, the proprietors of the aforementioned Fouled Anchor Tavern."

Brannigan reached behind him to the podium, picking up a framed certificate. "By the authority of the proclamation just read, I am pleased to present this to Lieutenant Junior Grade Veronica Rivers, United States Navy, as a testimony to her new status."

Veronica took the certificate and looked at it. The SEAL trident insignia was displayed conspicuously at the top, and under it was her name. The other printing identified her as a full-fledged honorary Brigand.

Then Petty Officer First Class Milly Mills presented her with a neatly folded T-shirt and sweatshirt bearing the unofficial buccaneer insignia of the detachment. "You are also authorized to wear these whenever you choose, ma'am."

Veronica was close to crying, but she was determined it wasn't going to happen. She clenched her teeth long enough to bring her emotions under control, then glanced out at the assembled SEALs.

"You bastards! You wonderful bastards!"

ROYAL YACHT *SAYIH*
1800 HOURS LOCAL

MIKE Assad and Hafez Sabah lay on the bunks in their shared cabin. Sabah was morose and inconsolable, not speaking or acknowledging his companion as he stared up at the overhead. All the work he had done in building up a fool-proof transportation and smuggling system for al-Mimkhalif had gone completely to hell. Any further attempts to get arms to the terrorist group would be risky since the one sure oceangoing protection they once enjoyed had been blown away under the guns of the United States Navy.

Mike was in a well-concealed good mood about that particular situation. For all intents and purposes, al-Mimkhalif would slowly deteriorate like melting snow as their resources were used up. On the other hand, the SEAL was not exactly elated about his own situation. His mind churned with one unworkable idea after the other as he tried to figure out a way to get the hell off the yacht to find an opportunity to make contact with American intelligence. Unfortunately, Sheikh Omar Jambarah could bring the terrorist movement back to life within a year or so. Mike had to get the word out on the guy to knock out al-Mimkhalif once and for all. Once they knew who he was, the CIA could dispatch some real nasty types to kidnap him. Sweating the bastard out in Guantanamo Bay would produce a lot of useful information.

There was even a possibility that a large percentage of other terrorist programs could be eradicated permanently. That would be a giant leap forward in eliminating the worldwide threat.

Mike glanced over at Sabah, who continued to gaze forlornly at the overhead, a frown frozen on his features. One thing for sure; if the SEAL could make a clean break from the yacht, the last thing he would do before disembarking would be to cut the son of a bitch's throat.

The door suddenly came open and the large bulk of the bodyguard Alif filled the exit. He pointed directly at Mike. *"Inta! Ta'al mail!"*

Sabah turned his head to look at Mike. "He wants you to go with him."

Mike frowned. "What for?"

"I wouldn't ask," Sabah advised. "He is undoubtedly following orders from Sheikh Omar."

Mike got to his feet and joined the bodyguard. Alif turned and began walking down the passageway. Mike followed, noting that the Arab wasn't watching him closely. Evidently, this was not a summons involving anything too serious. They went up to the bridge deck and down to the sheikh's cabin. Alif knocked on the door, then opened it and peered inside. He turned back and nodded for Mike to enter.

The sheikh sat on a sofa, dressed in a tropical shirt, slacks, and sandals. For all intents and purposes, he looked like a wealthy Latin-American about to go out on a hot summer evening. "Come in, Mikael. Sit down."

"Thanks," Mike said, taking an indicated nearby chair.

"I wanted to have a chat with you," Sheikh Omar said. "I thought it might be beneficial for both of us if we became better acquainted."

"Sounds fine to me."

"Are you particularly religious?"

Mike thought that an odd question, and he responded in a manner that would not put him in an awkward position. "Not really, sir. My family, except for my grandfather, did not attend the mosque regularly. I haven't had a lot of religious education except for when I was at the training camp."

"That is interesting," the sheikh said. "I am not a devout person either. I suppose my lifestyle has made me more pragmatic and worldly than spiritual." He chuckled. "Well, since we are both fallen Muslims, could I offer you a drink?"

"You sure could," Mike said, grinning.

"Please go over to those panel doors. If you open them you will find a completely stocked wet bar. I would appreciate it very much if you would pour me a Grey Goose and tonic. Fix whatever you wish for yourself."

Mike went over and slid the doors open. A small but efficient bar was exposed, and he went around it. The shelf was fully stocked with the finest and most expensive of international liquor. He mixed a strong vodka tonic for the sheikh and grabbed a beer out of the small fridge for himself. He checked the label and noted it was a Spanish brand called Cristal.

Mike returned to the sheikh and gave him the mixed drink, then sat down. Mike raised his beer to display it. "I'm a bit of a lowbrow."

"There is nothing wrong with enjoying beer," the sheikh said, "though I prefer the European over those watery American brands." He took a sip of the drink. "Ah! You do know how to throw a good drink together."

"Glad you like it, Sheikh Omar."

The sheikh took a couple of sips, smacked his lips, and smiled. "By the way, you did say that you did not accompany Commodore Mahamat to the battle with the American Navy, correct?"

"Sabah and I both stayed behind at the naval base."

"I see," the sheikh said. "Tell me truthfully, Mike. What do you think of his version of the events?"

Mike had to be careful how he responded. If he were too glib and precise, it would reveal his own naval background. "Well, Sheikh Omar, I got to admit that it seemed kind of far-fetched. I ain't any kind of expert on this sort of thing, but I know from watching news on TV that the U.S. Navy ain't got near that kind of a force in this part of the world."

The sheikh chuckled. "My thoughts exactly. I believe the commodore is doing what you Americans refer to as covering his ass. Right?"

"Prob'ly."

"What do you know about the types of air-cushioned boats called hovercraft?"

"Well, they're real fast," Mike responded. "And can go just about anywhere since they raise above the water. I even seen pictures of Marines bringing them up on the beach. But I don't think there's a whole lot of 'em being used."

"You strike me as being particularly bright, Mikael. Perhaps if you had been raised in a part of the world where Muslims reign, you would have been given a chance to get a complete and advanced education."

Mike saw an opening. "As a matter of fact, I made good grades quite a lot when I was in school. But somehow, I just couldn't get along. It's hard to explain."

"I understand perfectly, my friend," the sheikh said. "I tell you what I would like to do, Mikael. I want you to become an advisor of sorts to me. I need a sharp fellow who is completely familiar with Americans and the ways they talk, think, and act. Do you think you could help me out?"

"Jesus! I'd be real happy to."

The sheikh chuckled. "You said 'Jesus!' Are you aware he is in the Koran? He is called Isa, and was not a messiah. He was a prophet according to Islam, and not the Son of God. Nor was he crucified and resurrected in Muslim beliefs."

"I have some vague knowledge of that," Mike responded.

The sheikh looked at his watch. "We shall be getting under way within a half hour. We are going to a place I use as a stronghold. It's a fortified port on the borders of Oman and Yemen. I call the place Mikhbayi. That name is Arabic for Hiding Place. We will figure out your job description when we get there. That's another American expression, is it not? Job description?"

"Yes, Sheikh Omar."

"I am going to move you into a cabin on this deck level. You will not have to share it with anybody else."

"That'd be nice," Mike said.

"And we shall get you some decent clothing and proper grooming at Mikhbayi," the sheikh added. "How does that sound?"

"Fantastic!"

Sheikh Omar pressed a button located in the arm of the sofa. An instant later, Alif stepped into the room. The sheikh spoke to him, then nodded to Mike. "Alif will take you to your new quarters. Make yourself comfortable and feel free to come out on the stern deck anytime you wish."

Mike recognized the dismissal, and he stood up. "Thank you, Sheikh Omar. I'm really happy you gave me this chance." He finished the beer and set the empty bottle on the bar. "Good evening."

"Good evening, Mikael. I shall see you tomorrow."

Mike followed Alif out the door.

2100 HOURS LOCAL

MIKE couldn't believe his good luck. He glanced around his new cabin with its own private head, a large bed, a wardrobe, a table suitable for intimate dining, a desk, and a settee and a couple of easy chairs. Twenty minutes after he arrived, two stewards showed up at the door. One had his suitcase from the quarters he had shared with Sabah, and the other carried a large silver bucket containing ice and a dozen bottles of Cristal beer.

Mike unpacked, noting that his attire looked drab and cheap in comparison to the plush surroundings. It would be nice to get some proper modern clothing when they arrived at that hiding place of the sheikh. The right garb would also help in any escape and evasion activities that might loom in the future.

The SEAL opened a bottle of beer, then settled on the settee to relax and think. The real plus side was that it appeared that a great opportunity for him to cut and run had just presented itself. However, over in the minus column of the situation was the time factor. Unless he could get back to American contacts quickly, the information he had to pass on could well be outdated. His thoughts were interrupted by a knock on the door. "Come in."

When the door opened, Mike's jaw dropped. A beautiful blond woman, carrying a liquor bottle and wearing a beach towel wrapped around her shapely body, stepped inside. She smiled, speaking English in a heavy German accent. "Hello. My name is Hildegard. Sheikh Omar sent me to see that bored you did not get tonight."

Mike Assad was a healthy young robust man with the appetites common to that breed of male humans. He had not seen his girlfriend in California since early September and here it was closing in on November. All his natural horniness surfaced in the first split second of Hildegard's appearance. His mouth was dry and it took him a moment to respond to the surprise. "Well . . . now . . . uh . . . hello . . . Hildegard."

"I brought a bottle of cognac," she said. "I do not know what is your favorite drink. But I always thought cognac well serving."

"Oh, yeah! Cognac is great."

She walked across the cabin, completely familiar with the interior, having entertained guests there many times. Some glasses were available in a cabinet next to the head, and she got a couple, then turned to give him a wink as she dropped the towel. After allowing him a moment to feast his eyes on her beauty, Hildegard walked over and joined him on the settee. She handed him the cognac to open, holding out the glasses. Mike quickly tended to the chore, pouring them each a generous serving.

Hildegard smiled and raised her libation. "Here is to a wonderful evening for the both of us."

"I'll drink to that," Mike said happily.

2330 HOURS LOCAL

MIKE Assad and Hildegard Keppler sat up in the bed leaning back against the padded headboard. Both were satiated from an intense period of sex that had carried the woman beyond her whore's immunity all the way to genuine passion as she experienced a trio of multiple orgasms. The physical release left her susceptible to both alcohol and emotion.

The original bottle of cognac Hildegard had brought with her to the cabin was long gone. More had been sent for, and now another had also been turned into a dead soldier and a third was being shared by the couple. This time they didn't bother with glasses, simply passing the bottle back and forth between them. Although Mike was tipsy, he was still under control. He needed information and here was a good source. "Have you ever been to Mikhbayi?"

"Sure, darling," she said. "Many times have I been there."

"What's it like?"

"It is like a castle near the water with guards," she said. "Inside is a little town. But we women on the yacht to go there are not allowed. We must stay aboard the yacht at the docks."

Mike had already figured the place boasted a waterfront since the sheikh was sailing the *Sayih* to the facility. "Are there lots of boats?"

"Oh, *ja*," Hildegard said. "The big freighter and passenger ships cannot come in close, so they are having boats that go out and get people and bring them to the dock."

Mike's mind was completely sober now. That meant good-sized harbor craft that would not only have to fetch in people, but cargo too. The German woman's mood began to ease down into a depression to the point where she suddenly burst out into tears.

Mike was alarmed. "What's the matter, Hildy?"

She snuffed and turned her face to his. "The sheikh—that *verdammen* sheikh—he killed my best friend Franziska."

Mike was impressed by the information and wanted to learn more, but it might be dangerous for the woman to speak aloud. He gently put his finger on her lips. "Shhh, sweetie," he whispered. He got up and went over to the CD player on the dresser, slipping in a French jazz disk. After going back to the bed, he got in beside her.

"Why are you doing this?" she asked, whispering because he was.

"We mustn't be overheard," he said, gently putting his fingers on her lips. "This place is prob'ly bugged. Microphones."

"Oh, yes," she said. "And cameras too. The rotter likes to look at tapes of his guests having sex."

"No shit?"

"All we women have watched them with him," Hildegard whispered. "So excited he gets."

"Strange dude," Mike said. He reached over and turned out the lights. "Listen to me. Why do you say the sheikh murdered your friend?"

"I know she got on this ship and then she is gone away," Hildegard said. "She did not go back to shore. She is dead and thrown into the ocean. No other thing could have happened to her."

"Can you prove this?"

"*Nein*—no, I cannot."

Mike thought a moment. "Would you like to get revenge on him?"

"*Rache*—revenge. Oh, yes!" Hildegard said, beginning to sob again.

"You got to listen very carefully," Mike said. "I can help you with this. But you must do everything I tell you."

Now it was Hildegard's turn to come out of the haze of alcohol. The words just uttered to her brought a sharp stab of angry satisfaction into her consciousness. "What do you want me to do?"

"At first nothing," Mike said, "except to not speak of this friend again. Make no reference to the incident, understand?"

"Yes!" she said enthusiastically. "Are you going to kill him, Mike?"

"What I can do could result in something he would consider much worse than death," Mike said.

She looked around the room. "We better do sex again so there will be no suspicion." She turned the lamp back on.

Mike did what he had to do.

CHAPTER 15

SHEIKH Omar Jambarah's al-Mimkhalif stronghold was a large walled garrison located some fifty meters inland from the sandy coast of the Arabian Sea. Millions of oil dollars from the Jambarah family's sheikdom and gifts from certain elements of the Saudi government had financed the construction of the fortress, and paid for its continuing maintenance. The place was built mostly of steel-reinforced concrete with sandbags along the top. Stations for recoilless rifles and heavy machine guns were spaced regularly along the walls, although they were not armed or manned. The interior was made up of a power plant, a water-purification facility, dispensary, living areas for the permanent staff and their families, and a headquarters building. Next to that was a special compound designed for the benefit of the sheikh's special friends, guests, and garrison officers. This latter structure consisted of quarters, dining facilities, and a recreation hall. Additionally, a small mosque complete with a minaret tower was located in the northeast corner. The local mullah ascended the minaret and called the faithful to prayer five times a day. This procedure was known as the *Adhan,* and began with the familiar *takbit,* which proclaimed, "*Allahu Akbarthis*—God is great!"

Even Jambarah could not flout the laws of Islam by bringing his pleasure women into the fortress for sexual playtimes. Consequently, Hildegard and her friends remained on the yacht and could not come out on the deck for fear of offending the sensibilities of the fortress inhabitants. Even if they changed from the thongs into Western-style dress, the sight of adult females not wearing burkas would be unacceptable to the general population. Islamic extremists among them would have caused a lot of bother, and they were in the majority within the population. The sheikh could have dealt with the fanatics, but it would have been a time-consuming struggle, causing bad feelings that would echo throughout all other terrorist organizations.

In truth, the presence of the concubines was an open secret, but nobody dared discuss the situation or call attention to it; not even the mullah. As long as the sheikh and his entourage did not flaunt their sinful activities by partying within the walls, everyone acted as if nothing was amiss.

The *Sayih* was moored at the docks that ran out from the beach to the natural harbor formed where the sea bottom dropped abruptly to a depth of some ten fathoms. Mike Assad had moved from the yacht to the officers' complex within the walls, but he visited Hildegard regularly during the ample spare time he enjoyed between meetings with the sheikh. It was more than lust and her usefulness in his mission that attracted the SEAL to the beautiful German woman. During times when their sexual appetites were satiated, they sipped cognac and talked, and Mike learned to like her. She spoke English, as did anybody receiving even a basic education in Europe, though her grammar and accent were far from perfect. The SEAL especially enjoyed hearing about her former life in Germany.

Hildegard Keppler had been born in East Germany before the wall came down. Her father had been an assembly-line worker in Dresden, employed at a washing machine factory that produced the typical shoddy products of a socialistic manufacturing system. Hildegard, like all her generation, joined the Young Communist League for activities and recreation that were punctuated with heavy political indoctrination. That part of the activities bored her, but she endured it, as she did the dreadful evening TV when government programs with such subjects as factory production records went on for hours.

It was at the local youth center that Hildegard met Franziska Diehm, a girl her age who became her best friend. Both were pretty and matured young, and when they were fourteen they caught the attention of the commissar who administered their chapter of the Young Communists. The lothario arranged to have them visit him at his retreat on Lake Ellbogen on weekends and during the vacation season.

The commissar's lakefront cabin was one of the typical places where the party elite enjoyed getting away from the pressure of administering a workers' paradise. These excursions were described as nature study to the girls' parents, who were under the impression that all the kids attended.

The first couple of visits were innocent fun with swimming, horseback riding, outdoor sports, and eating exotic foods brought in from West Germany. Eventually, the girls learned that there would be great advantages not only to themselves, but also their families, if they shared sexual favors with the commissar. They had already had some experiences with boys of their own age, and the older man seemed like a good sort, so they acquiesced to his request. At least his lovemaking was more than just a pimply faced adolescent rutting on top of them. The commissar kept his promises, and the girls's fathers were promoted to good jobs, and the families's lives improved as well as could be expected under the Communist regime.

After the Berlin Wall tumbled down, the two girls saw their personal lives spin out of kilter, but they had already learned the value of their bodies. After some futile attempts at finding well-paying jobs in the new united Germany, they decided that since using their sexual charms in a Communist country got them money and benefits, it would be even more rewarding under a capitalist system. After a few awkward months of streetwalking, the two girls met an enterprising middle-aged woman who ran an escort service. Hildegard and Franziska quickly entered her employ, eventually ending up as high-priced call girls in Berlin. As time passed, they eventually began servicing mostly wealthy Saudi Arabians in Germany on business. It was in these circumstances that they met Sheikh Omar Jambarah. He took an instant liking to the young women, and this led to the offer of more pay aboard the Royal Yacht *Sayih*.

Now, sure her friend had been murdered, Hildegard would go to any length to have revenge on the man who committed the crime. It seemed impossible at first, but this strange and likable Arab-American might be the answer to that great desire. He was a pleasant fellow, rather good-looking, and something about him made Hildegard feel there was some mysterious potency in Mike Assad. These qualities were clandestine but effective, and he seemed the type of man to latch on to, even if only temporarily.

0945 HOURS LOCAL

SHEIKH Omar Jambarah stood on the reviewing stand located atop the officers' quarters prior to a scheduled parade of the garrison mujahideen. Usually he had an entourage with him for such occasions, but this day he was accompanied by only one man, Mikael Assad.

Mike noticed that the other ranking officers and guests,

including Hafez Sabah, were located farther down out of earshot. Mike had been issued several sets of uniforms that were set aside for the al-Mimkhalif elite. These were specially fitted to him in the tailor shop, and were made of high-class olive-drab material woven in German mills. Like everyone else, Mike also sported an Afghanistan pakol cap. This headgear was considered a symbol of the successful resistance to the invasion by the Soviet Union of that country in the 1980s. Even the sheikh always had on one of these peasant caps when he went outside.

The garrison's small drum-and-bugle corps, consisting of three trumpeters, three snare drummers, and a bass drummer, opened the ceremonies. Mike didn't know the military march they played, but it was obviously Arabic and touched something deep within his psyche. Goose bumps broke out on him as the small musical group marched past, the exotic and ancient call to battle sounding across the parade ground.

The fortress guard force, except for those at their posts, next made an appearance. They filed past the reviewing stand in their platoon formations, properly dressed right and covered down. The British influence showed in their style of swinging their arms up to shoulder level, as hobnailed boots stomped in an even staccato across the hard-packed desert earth.

The sheikh glanced over at Mike, smiling. "What do you think of the garrison mujahideen, Mikael?"

"They look really sharp," he replied, remembering that he was not supposed to have any military experience other than the time he'd spent in al-Mimkhalif.

"British officers and soldiers of fortune moved into the Middle East after World War One," Jambarah said. "The type of drill we employ here—or 'bashing on the square'—is typical of the United Kingdom's armed forces. I received military training in Britain as a boy cadet in school."

"This is a smart-looking place," Mike said. As he watched the marching men, he thought they would have served their cause better up in the mountains under Kumandan's command.

"You are not aware of it," Jambarah said, "but you are in the supreme headquarters of al-Mimkhalif."

Mike forgot about the music and the marching as he saw the chance to pick up some excellent intelligence data without arousing suspicion. Any inquiries on his part now would seem no more than natural curiosity. "Does our great leader Husan stay here? I would like to meet him."

"You already have, Mikael," Jambarah said. "I am Husan. It is my nom de guerre. That is French for 'war name.'"

Mike was surprised in a way, but not completely. But he played the naïve-kid role and stared openmouthed at the sheikh. "Wow!"

"My family is tied in closely with the Saudi government," Jambarah said. "I will not discuss that with you now, but you will learn more about it later. You may be sure you are destined to hobnob with some very important people on the Arabian Peninsula."

Mike's mind swirled. *I gotta get the fuck out of here and back to American intelligence,* he told himself. He shook his head, showing an expression of wonder and surprise. "This is really big, Sheikh Omar!"

"Indeed," Jambarah said. "And you will be able to play an important part in our counterattack. This defeat suffered by that rascal Mahamat has not stopped us, though I admit we are slowed a bit." He chuckled. "And the final phase of that unhappy event is about to be played out. Look!" He pointed to a door in the wall across the way.

Commodore Muhammad Mahamat stepped into view from the portal. He was dressed in a simple cotton *tawilqamis*—the long nightshirt style of peasant dress—and his hands were tied behind his back. He was flanked by two guards and followed by a third man who carried a large sword as the group walked to a place in the middle of the parade ground.

Even from that distance Mike could see that the commodore was in a deep daze. "What's going on?"

"Mahamat is about to pay for both his defeat and lying

about it," Jambarah said. "I'm sure you've never seen anything like this."

Mahamat was brought to a halt, then his guards stepped
away. He swayed slightly as the man with the sword walked
up beside him. Mike peered carefully at the prisoner who
once commanded the all-powerful Zauba Squadron. "What's
wrong with him? Is he sick or drunk?"

"I have been merciful and seen that he was administered
a strong dose of *afyun*," Jambarah said. "He is barely aware
of what is going on."

Mike had seen men killed before and had taken others'
lives in battle, but what was about to happen to the drugged-
up commodore had an eerie quality about it. The man with
the sword raised the edged weapon and looked up at the reviewing stand. Sheikh Omar Jambarah nodded his head.

The sword whistled for no more than an instant before
slicing through the commodore's neck. The head rolled backward, falling toward the ground as the body took a jerky step
forward before collapsing.

"*Allahu Akbarthis,*" Jambarah said under his breath. "If
he does not deserve to die for his defeat, it matters not. Allah
will forgive him and take him into Paradise."

Damn, Mike thought, *wouldn't just busting the poor bastard down in rank have been enough?*

USS *DAN DALY*
INDIAN OCEAN
VICINITY OF 5° NORTH AND 65° EAST
NOON LOCAL

PETTY Officers Paul Watkins and Bobby Lee Atwill
had mixed feelings about Lieutenant Veronica Rivers's initiation as an honorary member of Brannigan's Brigands. Now,
heading up to the wardroom for a briefing on an upcoming
mission, Watkins expressed his resentment of the honor. "We
was in that sea battle. They ought to recognize us too."

"You're forgetting one thing, Paul," Bobby Lee said. "You and me don't have to be honorary SEALs. If we want it bad enough, we can volunteer for the training and become the genuine article."

"Are you crazy?" Paul exclaimed. "Haven't you heard of that Hell Week they go through?"

"Yep," Bobby Lee said. "And that's why I'm sticking to mending and maintaining turbine engines. Anyhow, I don't think I got what it takes to make it."

"Shit," Paul said resignedly. "I guess I don't either."

THEY walked into the wardroom, nodding greetings to the SEALs as they went to their customary places in the back of the room. None of the officers were present at the moment, and everyone was drinking coffee and talking among themselves. Suddenly Senior Chief Buford Dawkins called the room to attention, and everyone leaped to their feet.

Commander Tom Carey led the way as he, Brannigan, Jim Cruiser, and Veronica Rivers came in through the door. The three *Battlecraft* officers sat down in the first row while Carey went to the head of the room. Rather than having a manila folder with an OPORD, all he had were some notes.

"Good morning, people," he said. "Another operation is laid on for you, but a final date and time hasn't been established yet. I figure it'll go down in two or three days. The mission follows the KISS principle; that is, Keep It Simple, Sweetheart. It's no more than cruising around to look for trouble, and doesn't require a lot of finesse or fancy preparation. On the day of the event, you'll leave the docking well at oh-dark-hundred."

Veronica raised her hand. "What ordnance are we packing, sir?"

"Antiship and antiaircraft missiles," Carey replied. "By the way, congratulations on becoming an honorary Brigand."

"Thank you, sir," Veronica said, now more interested in the mission than the honor bestowed on her. "I suggest our AA weaponry be both heat-seeking and laser."

"I'll leave that to Lieutenant Brannigan," Carey said. "The only antiship stuff we have for you are Penguins, but they're reliable and worked well in this last outing."

Jim Cruiser asked, "Will there be anything for the assault sections to do?"

"We don't know," Carey replied. "And because of that, both should be ready to participate. It'll be crowded on the ACV, but you're used to that now." He turned back to Veronica. "You'll set a course up to be somewhere along six degrees north latitude and begin a sweep back and forth along that azimuth. It's been reported that there's a good chance that al-Mimkhalif sea operations are on hold because of the decisive defeat you all dealt them on the twenty-second. A rumor has surfaced that al-Mimkhalif has a seaside facility somewhere, and that can mean more warships. Although that's not been confirmed yet, I advise you to expect the worst."

Brannigan was confused. "Why are we taking both assault sections, sir? If we do any boarding of terrorist vessels, one will do. On the other hand, if we become involved in another fight at sea, those guys will be in the way, not to mention exposed to deadly fire."

"There is a chance that the need for a raid may pop up," Carey said. "Since you've got forty-eight hours minimum before going out, we can't be sure of anything. I want to emphasize that the situation is in a real fluid mode at this moment, so be ready for anything. As you were! I should have said, be ready for *everything*. As it is, you'll be out the maximum seventy-two hours. Gas, ammo, and vittles will be on loaded accordingly by the *Daly*'s crew." He folded up his notes and stuck them in his pocket. "That's it, folks. Consider yourselves on standby. I'll be calling you together a couple of more times before this thing goes down."

After Carey made his exit, the enlisted men were taken over by Senior Chief Dawkins, who took them out of the wardroom and down to the flight deck for a period of vigorous PT. Brannigan, Jim Cruiser, and Veronica stayed behind.

Jim looked at Veronica, then Brannigan. "Sir, we need to talk to you."

Brannigan, expecting some minor technical problem with the *Battlecraft,* took a sip of coffee. "What's up?"

"Veronica and I are getting married," Jim said.

"Well, I suspected—or I thought—maybe something might be going on," Brannigan said. He chuckled, "So you two have been fooling around?"

Veronica frowned. "What the hell do you mean *fooling around*?"

"I didn't mean that like it sounded," Brannigan said. "Sorry. I mean, I wasn't really aware of a serious romance going on among us."

"We've been real careful," Jim said. "But it's something that's bigger than both of us." He grinned and shrugged. "Isn't that what they say in the movies? Anyhow, a very sincere and lasting relationship has come out of the situation."

"Well," Brannigan said, "I'm in a service marriage, as you know. I don't want to throw cold water on your hot desires, but I have to tell you that there are times it can be rough. Lisa and I have gone through some touchy situations, and that includes coming close to breaking up."

"I'm not staying in the Navy," Veronica said. "My ETS is up just after the first of the year. I already have a job offer from an electronics firm in San Diego. Since I was going to take it anyway, it'll work out just fine for both of us. So, I'll just be a serviceman's wife."

"Okay," Brannigan said. "It seems you both have really looked into this thing." He shook hands with Jim and hugged Veronica. "Congratulations and best wishes."

"I want you to be my best man, Skipper," Jim said.

"You got it," Brannigan said. "But we're going to have to keep a lid on this until after the mission. Be careful where you . . . well . . . where you meet, okay?"

"We understand," Veronica said.

Jim laughed. "There's a lot of empty space around the ship since there's not a Marine battalion or a chopper squadron aboard."

Brannigan set his coffee cup down. "I'm happy for you both. Lisa and I'll have you over for dinner real soon."

"You see, darling," Veronica said to Jim. "Our social life is already starting."

FORTRESS MIKHBAYI
27 OCTOBER
1000 HOURS LOCAL

MIKE Assad, dressed in his al-Mimkhalif uniform complete with pakol and the stolen Webley revolver in a holster on his pistol belt, strode down the dock toward the Royal Yacht *Sayih*. He glanced over the wharves, where various types of small craft were tied up. The area was immaculate without oil spots, trash, or debris lying about. Mike chalked that up to Sheikh Omar Jambarah's time spent in a British military academy. If there were any folks that really knew spit and polish, it was the Brits.

He went up the gangplank of the yacht where the bodyguard Taa stood watch. Mike's new preferred status with the sheikh precluded any more rude searches of his person, and the pistol on his hip didn't get as much as a second look from the thug. Mike made his way to the stern deck, then turned to go down the passageway that led to the women's quarters. A small sitting room was located just aft of the cabins, and Mike found Hildegard reading a magazine while she waited for him. She stood up and they kissed.

"I wish we could for a walk go," Hildegard said. "Or at least on the deck to relax in lounge chairs."

Mike looked around. "Where are the other women?"

"They are where we eat up forward," she said.

Mike glanced through the viewing window on the port side and could see that Taa stood at his post by the gangplank.

Mike looked beyond and got a complete view of the wharf area. "Come here," he said. He waited for Hildegard to come up close, then he whispered in her ear. "We're gonna get out of here tonight. It will be dark and nobody will be able to see you."

"Where to do we go, Mike?"

"To some people who can help you get the justice you want for your friend Franziska," he explained.

"These people, who are they?"

"Never mind," he said. "They can help you, understand?"

"Yes!" she said, excited. "I will pack my things."

"No!" he hissed angrily. "The last thing you want to do is make people think you're leaving. It is important. Just dress comfortably for a trip over the ocean. Make sure you have a long-sleeve shirt and slacks, okay? And the wide-brimmed beach hat you have in your wardrobe. You don't want to get sunburned."

"How far do we go, Mike?"

"I got no idea, honeybunch," he said. "But I'll be back for you tonight. I'll have to take care of the guard at the gang-plank, then we'll be able to get down to the boats." He kissed her. "I'll see you later."

Mike left her and went back to the stern deck, going around to where Taa still stood watch. He nodded politely to the bodyguard, then went down the gangplank turning toward the wharf area. He walked along slowly, stopping now and then to give the impression he was wandering among the boats for no particular reason. It took nearly twenty minutes of seemingly aimless strolling, but he finally spotted something that interested him.

A naval whaler boat was tied up at a dock in the center of the waterfront. He hadn't been able to see it right away, but a closer inspection showed it was exactly what he was looking for. When he walked up, he noticed a couple of sailors refueling it while another was checking out the motor.

Mike nodded to them. "You take boat out?" he asked in his stumbling Arabic.

"No, brother," one answered. "We keep all boats prepared in case they are needed for emergencies."

That's real handy, Mike thought, *thanks a lot, you assholes.* He smiled at the guy. "May I get on boat for to look at it?"

"Of course, brother," the man replied.

Mike went aboard and gave the whaler a close inspection. He noted she was about twenty-five feet long and was powered by an inboard diesel engine. He also quickly caught sight of a radio that was available at the wheel console. From his own naval experience, Mike knew that normally there would be a crew of three, a coxswain, bowman, and radio operator. However, he would be able to handle her alone without any trouble.

Mike walked down to check out the radio, noting it was a standard marine model, quite easy to operate. There was also a GPS mounted just above the instrument panel. He made sure the sailors weren't watching him, then he switched it on. The device informed him that he was at sixteen degrees north latitude and fifty-three degrees east longitude. Now he had a starting place to navigate from.

He jumped back up on the dock, waved good-bye to the crewmen, then continued walking around so no one would get the impression he had any interest in that particular craft.

HILDEGARD'S CABIN
ROYAL YACHT *SAYIH*
2300 HOURS LOCAL

MIKE Assad turned off the cabin light, then went to the porthole and pushed the curtain aside. He peered out at the wharves, noting that there were no guard posts, either stationary or walking, within the area. He swung his gaze slightly forward and sighted the bodyguard Baa at the gangplank on the main deck. He closed the curtain, then looked over at Hildegard. "Are you ready to go?"

"*Ja,*" she said. "Ready I am." The woman was dressed in a long-sleeved blouse that buttoned up to the neck. She wore slacks and sandals with socks. The beach hat was looped around her neck. She would slip it on her head to keep the sun off during the hottest part of the day.

Mike picked up the tote bag from the bunk. It was heavily loaded with plastic bottles of Evian water taken from the women's lounge. Another lighter canvas container was filled with sandwiches that Hildegard had made in the galley. She was so excited about the coming adventure that the impetuous, reckless woman had unwisely told the Frenchwoman Blanche that she and Mike were going to sneak out for a picnic and not return until the next evening when it was dark. Hildegard knew all the women were jealous of her romance with Mike, and used the fib to rub it in.

"Now or never," Mike said, opening the door. "Let's go, baby!"

He carried the tote bag while Hildegard took responsibility for the sandwiches. They went slowly and silently down the passageway to the door leading out to the main deck. Mike slowly pulled the heavy metal portal open and peered out. He saw Baa, bored to distraction, leaning against the rail.

The bastard's evening was about to get more exciting.

Hildegard waited while Mike stepped out onto the deck. He staggered slightly as if drunk as he approached the gangplank. He hummed an out-of-tune rendition of the old rock standard "Getting Through the Night"—which he thought was an appropriate choice—as he drew closer to Baa. "*Kaefae haelik?*" he politely inquired.

"*Biher,*" Baa replied.

Mike drove the heel of his hand straight into Baa's chin with such force that he felt the jawbone break and slip out of joint as several teeth shattered. The Arab dropped to the deck without as much as a whimper. Mike turned back and motioned to Hildegard to join him. She hurried out, going to Mike's side while looking down at the unconscious bodyguard. All the women had been so intimidated by Alif, Baa, and Taa, they thought them invincible. Evidently, that was a mistaken assumption on their part. But witnessing violence against one of the men still unnerved her to some extent.

Mike took her hand and led her onto the gangplank and down to the dock. The couple stayed in the shadows as they made their way across the wharves to where the whaler boat sat. Hildegard got aboard as the SEAL loosed the bow and stern lines. He joined her, grabbing the boat hook and giving the vessel a push away from the dock. He winced at the whiny noise when he hit the starter. As soon as the engine caught, he throttled back to just enough power to get under way. Mike piloted the boat for open water, glancing back at the wharf area. He was relieved to note that no alarm had been raised. He looked over at Hildegard, who showed a nervous smile. Mike grinned at her, hoping to put the woman more at ease.

"Lovely evening for a boat ride, huh?"

CHAPTER 16

PETTY Officer Paul Watkins had slipped the stern fans into reverse, moving out of the docking well egress at BACK SLOW with water spraying up on the steel bulkheads of the *Dan Daly*. The lift fan's RPM was just enough to hold the *Battlecraft* a scant two feet above the water's surface as it eased out into the open ocean. The entire SEAL detachment was aboard along with the crew, and the vessel was as crowded as it had been on the night of the coastal raid.

The weapons wings bristled with Penguin antiship, and both laser and radar antiaircraft missiles. Extra ordnance for those sophisticated systems was stowed in the now unusable wardroom along with extra ammo for the SEALs' CAR-15 rifles and SAWs. Rather than pack along bulky foodstuffs for the microwave, MREs were kept above and inside the cabinetry of the small galley. In following the KISS principle, Lieutenant Bill Brannigan decided everyone would use FRHs to heat their meals. That meant the food could rapidly and easily be prepared anywhere on the ACV.

When the ACV cleared the mother ship, Brannigan took a final sip of coffee from his cup. "Due north at two-thirds speed."

"Due north at two-thirds speed, aye, sir," Watkins said, working the piloting instrumentation.

"Use the automatic pilot," Brannigan said to the helmsman. "We're going to be following this course for a while."

"Aye, sir," Watkins said, setting the instrument to read the preprogrammed waypoints. "On automatic pilot, sir."

Brannigan looked out the front windshield at the bleached sky blazing down on the deep blue of the Indian Ocean. "Those crazy DuBose brothers should have put air-conditioning in this vehicle."

"They did, sir," Lieutenant Veronica Rivers said. "I had it taken out to make room for the weapons systems."

"You are heartless," Brannigan said, half-joking.

Veronica smiled. "I'm just like Hard-Hearted Hannah the Vamp of Savannah in that old song. I'd throw water on a drowning man."

Brannigan chuckled. "I do believe you would, Lieutenant."

The First Assault Section was sprawled across the topside of the cabin, well coated with sunscreen and wearing wide-brimmed boonie hats to keep the sun off their faces. Normally, a canvas covering would have been rigged across the area to provide some shade, but the super speeds of the *Battlecraft* would have blown it off in an instant if Watkins kicked the throttle over to FLANK SPEED.

Down below in the crowded wardroom, Senior Chief Buford Dawkins's Second Assault Section had arranged themselves as comfortably as possible among the piles of ammo and other gear. They were not as comfortable as Jim

Cruiser's guys above, but at least they didn't have to worry about sunburn at the moment. That problem would have to be dealt with when it was their turn to move topside.

Bobby Lee Atwill baked in the engine compartment as he monitored the true love of his life; the gas-turbine power plant that kept the ACV flying over water, ground, swamp, beach, or any other reasonably flat surface. Bobby Lee didn't have to swelter in the company of the engine, but it was his habit of staying close beside her during the first few hours of a cruise. She might get nervous and develop hiccups, and he wanted to be there to calm her down for the job ahead.

A certain grimness gripped the mood of SEALs and crew alike. All sensed that the next few days would bring about the wrap-up of their mission, and that was always the most dangerous part.

FORTRESS MIKHBAYI
0600 HOURS LOCAL

THE mujahideen guard had just come on duty after relieving the man on the third watch, and he began his rounds slowly, still feeling the need for sleep after leaving his wife and bed less than a half hour before. He strolled up and down the wharves, gazing with disinterest at the boats, coming to a stop at an empty mooring place. One of the whaler boats used to fetch in passengers and cargo from freighters was usually docked there. He glanced out into the deepwater anchorage to see if a crew was tending to one of the merchant ships, but there was no activity out in that area. He yawned, then continued his circuit of the wharves.

Twenty minutes later he had worked his way back to the guardhouse up at the entrance gate, and stepped inside. He was happy to see a pot of coffee on the hot plate by the guard sergeant's desk. The guard poured himself a cup, sitting down beside the door. After a couple of swallows, he murmured, "Somebody has taken a whaler out."

The sergeant looked up from the roster he was updating. "Mmm? What did you say?"

"I said one of the whalers has been taken out from Wharf Three."

"It is probably being used to unload a freighter," the sergeant said.

"There is not a ship out at the anchorage."

The sergeant was thoughtful for a moment, then pulled out the previous day's journal. "No one signed it out for use. At least its departure has not been noted down."

"Some of the fellows are very careless about making entries into the journal," the guard remarked. "They get sleepy at night and miss things."

"Well, I don't want the guard captain to think it was us," the sergeant said. He reached for the ancient field telephone and cranked it. "This is Sergeant Aboud," he said when the call was answered. "Somebody has taken a whaler out and the guard sergeant last night did not make note of it. Yes. It is missing from Wharf Three. My man noticed it first thing this morning. Thank you. Good-bye."

The guard chuckled. "You just watch. There are a couple of careless fellows who are going to be sent out to a mujahideen camp to shape them up, eh?"

The sergeant grinned. "A bit of danger and hardship will serve them right."

THE bodyguards Alif and Taa walked down to the docks, turning toward the Royal Yacht *Sayih*. Since Baa had been on duty all night, he would have the whole day off, and the other two would split the watch until he came back at eight o'clock that evening. Alif glanced up toward the head of the gangplank.

"Where is he?"

Taa shrugged. "He must have gone to the toilet. I always dislike that all-night shift. All I think about is having to urinate. And as soon as I try, something interrupts me."

They reached the gangplank and hurried up, coming to an abrupt stop when they reached the deck. Their pal Baa was sprawled on his side, groaning softly. The two thugs rushed to him, kneeling down and roughly rolling him over on his back. Baa's jaw was at a peculiar angle, and his face was swollen all the way up to the bridge of his nose.

"What happened?" Taa asked.

Baa couldn't speak. He groaned, his eyes silently pleading for help. Alif got to his feet. "I'll go to the bridge and put in a call to the dispensary."

Taa stayed with Baa, looking impassively at the man, who was obviously in a great deal of pain.

SHEIKH Omar Jambarah toweled himself off after stepping from the large walk-in shower in his quarters. He had washed his thinning hair for the first time with a special brand of American shampoo that was supposed to thicken up fading locks of men suffering from male-pattern baldness. He stood in front of the mirror, running the drier from the front of his head all the way to back, wincing at the heat. After a couple of dozen swipes, he checked his reflection and noticed that his hair did look a bit thicker. Satisfied, he walked from the bathroom into his bedroom, where a valet had laid out a fresh tank top, shorts, briefs, and sandals. After changing, he took another door to reach his dining area, and settled at the table.

A steward poured his coffee, then prepared a plate of scrambled eggs, fried potatoes, and biscuits. After a decade and a half as a schoolboy in England, he swore he would never have another kipper for breakfast. The sheikh preferred the American style except for bacon and sausage. The meat of pigs was one prohibition of the Koran he believed in.

The steward set the plate in front of the sheikh, then stepped back to the serving table to await his master's next summons. Jambarah swept up some scrambled egg on his fork and shoved it in his mouth. He chewed thoughtfully, then said, "Go fetch Mikael Assad for me. I would like to have his company while I eat."

"I am sorry, Sheikh Omar," the steward said. "I went to his cabin earlier and he was not there. It appears the American brother did not sleep in his bed."

Jambarah laughed. "He was on the yacht, that's where he was! I think he has become quite infatuated with that German woman. Ah, well! I shall just have to speak to him later."

A knock on the door sounded, and the steward responded. Alif the bodyguard stepped into the room. "A thousand pardons, Sheikh Omar. A disturbing event has occurred."

The sheikh stopped eating, frowning at the bodyguard. "This had better be important."

"Somebody attacked Baa during the night on the yacht," Alif said. "He is badly injured and is in the dispensary being treated. Taa is staying with him."

The sheikh put his fork down. "Now how could such a thing happen? Is the ship damaged?"

"No," Alif said. "Everything is fine. I checked with the watch officer. The crew knew nothing of Baa's predicament."

Jambarah started to speak again, but was interrupted by yet another knock on the door. The chief of security came into the suite with the usual report he personally delivered to the sheikh each morning. The sheikh turned his attention to him. "Did you know one of my bodyguards was attacked on the yacht during the night?"

"No, Sheikh Omar," the man said, then quickly added, "The yacht is not included in our area of responsibility."

"I know it is not!" Jambarah snapped. "But perhaps one of your men heard a noise or something. Surely they are able to see and hear beyond that area of responsibility."

"Of course, Sheikh Omar," the security chief said. "But nothing was reported except that someone took a whaler boat out."

The sheikh leaned back in his chair. "Now why would anybody need a whaler boat?"

"I thought to tend to a freighter," the chief of security said. "But there has not been one here since the Liberian tanker a week ago."

The sheikh got to his feet. "Something strange is going on, and I intend to get to the bottom of it."

WHALER BOAT
INDIAN OCEAN
VICINITY OF 5° NORTH AND 55° EAST
0900 HOURS LOCAL

MIKE Assad stood at the wheel maintaining a course of due east on the compass. Three things were irritating the hell out of him. The first was that the radio in the boat was not hooked into the vessel's power. Instead, it ran on its own battery, which seemed to be quite low. That meant he could not maintain a continuous attempt to contact American warships. From the way things looked, the commo gear could possibly be completely dead within three or four hours.

The second vexing problem was navigation. Without a chart he could not plot a course to any particular point in the watery world he moved across. The GPS gave him accurate readings on his longitude and latitude, but he did not know the exact coordinates of the nearest landfall or where he might run into a U.S. carrier battle group. As it was, he hadn't seen so much as a single aircraft in the sky to give evidence of a nearby task force.

The third and most aggravating and exasperating part of this escape was his companion. Hildegard Keppler had begun the trip in a high frame of mind in spite of some preliminary nervousness. She'd thought it exciting to run away from the sheikh's fortress, but now her attitude had evolved into a petulant, demanding mood. Mike now realized she was an immature woman who demanded instant gratification for her wants and needs. The temperature was relatively temperate when the sun was on the other side of the world, but now it had been steadily climbing. The heat had increased markedly and without a bimini over the cockpit, the rays beat down on them in perceptible waves of stinging heat.

And it was only nine o'clock in the morning.

Hildegard reached into the tote bag for a bottle of the Evian water. Mike snapped at her. "Hey! Let's take it easy with that stuff, okay? We don't know how long it will have to last us."

She pouted. "But thirsty I am."

"I don't give a shit if thirsty you are," Mike said, mocking her in his anger. "If we drink up all our water in one day, then pretty damn quick it'll be dead we are. Understand?"

"Why you want to bring the water if drink it we are not?"

"We came with a case of that stuff, all right?" Mike said, forcing himself to calm down. "That's twenty-four half-liter bottles, see? Each of 'em is a little over a pint."

"A pint I don't know what it is."

"Look at the godamn bottles!" he growled. "You can see how big they are, right? Okay. Now we got to each drink no more than one of them a day, see? That gives us twelve frigging days. After that, we better find somebody within sixty to seventy hours or we're gonna die from thirst."

"Already I am dying of thirst," she protested.

"You just think you are," Mike said. "You ain't near thirsty yet."

"If a sandwich I eat, it is thirsty I get."

"That's another thing," Mike warned her. "If we eat a sandwich a day, we'll have food for five days. I figure we can go two or three weeks without eating anything at all after that."

"You did not anything say to me about this when you take me on this trip," Hildegard said.

"I took you because you wanted to go," Mike said. *God!* he thought. *You stupid broad. I guess you just want to keep being a punchboard for a goddamn Middle Eastern letch!* "When we get back to civilization, you'll forget all about this hardship. When the sheikh is nailed for your friend's murder, you'll be happy."

"But I am not being happy right now!"

"Please, God!" Mike said, looking up to the sky. "Just get me back to the Brigands! That's all I ask."

ROYAL YACHT *SAYIH*
FORTRESS MIKHBAYI
1030 HOURS LOCAL

THE five European women were terrified.

The Italian Lucia, Frenchwoman Blanche, the Portuguese Teresa, and the two Russians Olga and Adelaida had been herded into their lounge and now sat on the sofas and chairs. The Russians huddled close together. All the women were dressed relatively modestly, wearing halters, shorts, and sandals. The rules were that they were to never go bare-breasted with thongs when aboard the yacht at Mikhbayi. Even an accidental sighting of a woman's body was punishable according to the tenets of Islam, and Sheikh Omar Jambarah didn't want any morale problems with his mujahideen or their families.

The modern courtesans knew something was wrong, and expected to be blamed for it whether they were really at fault or not. It had to have something to with Hildegard Keppler. The German bitch had already caused trouble when she made a row over her stupid friend Franziska, and now both were gone. Hildegard had gotten uppity when she caught the attention of the American. The sheikh put her off-limits to other men, allowing her to have Mike as a lover while keeping her on the payroll. Hildegard continually boasted to the other women she didn't have to take battering and rape from the sheikh anymore or service any of his friends who came aboard.

The door burst open and Sheikh Jambarah stormed in, startling the women. He was followed closely by Hafez

Sabah and the two bodyguards Alif and Taa. The women feared the sheikh for his power, the bodyguards for their cruelty, and the Arab Sabah for his hatred of them as infidel whores. None of the women dared look up, and kept their gazes on the floor. Nothing happened for a few moments; then Alif suddenly grabbed the Portuguese woman and pulled her to her feet.

"Deixe-me só!" she begged. "Leave me alone!"

The sheikh approached her, putting his face close to hers. "Where is Hildegard?"

"I do not know," Teresa sobbed. "I am not a friend to her. I never talk to her. If she goes someplace, how am I to know?"

Alif slapped her hard, then looked over at the sheikh. Jambarah nodded his head, and the bodyguard pushed her roughly back to the sofa where she had been sitting. Taa reached down and hauled the Italian Lucia off the settee. He shook her hard, slapped her face, then shoved her toward the sheikh.

"Per favore!" she cried. "I know nothing."

"I think you are lying," the sheikh said. "I have noticed you being chummy with both Hildegard and her friend Franziska in the past. Where did she go?"

"I am not a friend to them," Lucia protested. "Nobody like those Germans. They are stuck up, both of them!"

Jambarah believed her and he nodded to Taa to let her go. The Italian ran to a spot behind the settee for safety. Blanche stood up, hoping to put off getting a hard slap. "I do not know where she go, but I see her in her cabin putting things in a bag. I say what are you doing? She say she go away with her *amant américain* Mike."

"Now we are getting somewhere," the sheikh said, smiling. "Where did she say she and Mike were going?"

Blanche cringed, her voice tinged with fear. "She did not tell me nothing except they go out on a picnic and come back when it is dark."

The sheikh suddenly laughed loudly. It seemed Mikael

had developed a very special sexual attraction for the German, and wanted to be alone with her in some intimate place outside the yacht and fortress. He looked over at Sabah and motioned for the al-Mimkhalif agent to follow him to the stern deck. When they were out under the canvas awning, Jambarah asked, "What do you think?"

"Mikael is not yet a complete Muslim, Sheikh Omar," Sabah said. "His morals have long been corrupted by exposure to Western culture in America. I fear he has sinful passions for the German whore." He started to say something about fornication, but stopped short as he remembered that the sheikh had regular sex with the foreign women.

"How much do you know of Mikael Assad?" the sheikh asked.

Sabah shrugged. "Not much," he admitted. "I met him after he had returned to Camp Talata after escaping from the Americans."

"We have been informed that a whaler boat is missing," the sheikh said. "I was wondering if Mikael would have been able to operate it. It would take some skill to handle such a vessel."

"As far as I know, there is nothing that indicates Mikael has any experience with boats."

"We must also consider the attack on Baa," the sheikh said. "Would Mikael be capable of such a thing? Baa is a very large and skillful fighter."

"I have learned nothing that indicates Mikael is an expert in hand-to-hand combat," Sabah said. "Perhaps he sneaked up behind your bodyguard."

"Baa was hit from the front in a most devastating way," the sheikh said. "The doctor in the dispensary has reported that the fellow remembers nothing of being attacked." He fell into a few moments of silence before speaking again. "How did Mikael enter al-Mimkhalif?"

"What I learned from Kumandan was that Mikael was sent to al-Mimkhalif from a mosque in America. The cleric who recruited him has been involved in obtaining mujahideen for a long time."

"All right," the sheikh said, "but I am beginning to feel that there is more to Mikael Assad than we figured."

WHALER BOAT
VICINITY OF 5° NORTH AND 57° EAST
1800 HOURS LOCAL

MIKE Assad throttled the motor of the whaler back to SLOW AHEAD. He had picked up a rapid current, and the GPS indicated he was making extremely fast progress; hence there was no reason to use up fuel unnecessarily. The afternoon had been an unrelenting hell of baking heat as the sun flared down on the boat, making all the metal parts too hot to touch. Mike had taken a rag from the toolbox and put it on the wheel so that he could handle it with a minimum of pain. A flicker of movement behind him was reflected in the windshield, and he whipped around to see Hildegard chugalugging a bottle of the precious water.

"What the fuck are you doing?" he bellowed.

"I am thirsty!" she said defiantly. "And something else I tell you. I eat a sandwich too."

"Do you really want to die out here?" he asked. "Some controlled, temporary discomfort is a hell of a lot better than dying of thirst. Because that's what will kill you. You'll dry out like a mummy before you manage to starve to death."

"Too much you worry," Hildegard said. "Ships will we soon see and plenty too."

He reached back and grabbed her arm, jerking her up beside him at the wheel. "Take a look at the fucking horizon! What the fuck do you see?"

Hildegard obediently looked around, noting nothing within sight. "Talk to somebody on your radio again."

"I haven't *talked* to anybody yet," Mike said, "because I haven't been able to *raise* anybody." He reached over and clicked the set on, then grabbed the microphone and pressed the transmit button. "Any ship at sea. Any ship at sea. Mayday.

Mayday. Position five degrees, six minutes north and fifty-four degrees, twelve minutes east. Mayday. Over." He repeated the transmission twice more and waited a few minutes for a reply. None came.

"*Ach, Himmel!*" she said, jerking her arm free. "You did not tell me it would be hot."

"You've been sailing around in these waters for weeks," Mike said. "Didn't you notice it was hot?"

"The deck we did not come out on when it was hot," she said. "I think better it is if back to the yacht we go where the air conditioner runs."

"What about your friend Franciska? Don't you want to avenge her murder?"

"Maybe not," Hildegard said, shrugging. "Franciska was a *torichist*—silly and always getting into trouble."

"Silly or not," Mike said, "we're not going back to that fucking yacht."

"But, Mike, out here we will die!"

He grinned without humor, speaking to himself under his breath. "That's one thing you're probably right about."

CHAPTER 17

KUMANDAN, the field commander of al-Mimkhalif, stood in the empty field of what had once been a thriving terrorist camp. Orders had come to destroy any equipment, ammunition, weapons, and other material that could not be carried away. The task had kept the entire group busy for a full two days of round-the-clock labor. When the job was finally finished, the mujahideen were divided up into three groups and sent by separate routes to the coast for pickup by the dhow *Nijm Zarik*. This was to happen at the exact location where the arms shipments arrived in the past. The reason behind splitting them was supposedly to assure that most would be able to reach the destination on the beach after sneaking through Pakistani police and military areas. From there, the lucky ones would be going to Mikhbayi to join the supreme leader, Husan.

The last column sent out was now wending its way down the mountain to the lowlands before turning west toward the Arabian Sea. In spite of their optimism and trust in their leader, the mujahideen stood no chance of making it safely to the objective. Kumandan had carefully mapped out the routes of the withdrawal so that the men were certain to run into military and police posts where death or capture would result. In actuality, he was using the operation as a way to rid of himself of the less desirable elements of his command. The only people left with him were the dozen members of his immediate staff. The unfortunates now heading out would be the decoys to draw the Pakistani authorities away from the trails he and his entourage would be following while making their own escape. The twelve men who accompanied him were his best and brightest. They had to be saved if al-Mimkhalif's field campaign was going to reestablish its jihad.

The last few weeks had been especially difficult for the terrorist group. The supplies of arms and weaponry had dried up to the point that they were unable to conduct meaningful operations. Rather than raid police and army outposts, the mujahideen of al-Mimkhalif had been reduced to no more than reconnaissance activities to keep track of their enemies. A shortage of food that had at first been no more than an inconvenience quickly became critical to the point that many of the men were visibly weakening from malnourishment. By then, all outside activities had been canceled and the camp routine was reduced to the most basic guard and sanitation duties to keep the weakening men from wasting away. It was expected that at least a quarter of them would not be able to make it all the way to the coast even if they were not harassed by the authorities. Kumandan and his chosen elite, however, were in fine fettle. They had hidden away rations for their own escape, and were strong and fit for the ordeal ahead.

KUMANDAN'S real name was Azam Marbuk. This leader of mujahideen had the slim muscularity of a naturally good physique, and intelligent dark eyes that betrayed a superior intellect. His beard was trimmed neatly and his hair wasn't overly longish, giving him a decidedly conventional appearance. He had been an officer in the Royal Jordanian Army with a bright future back in the early 1990s. He was the first of his military academy class to make the rank of captain, and he seemed destined for command and staff responsibilities at the highest echelons of King Hussein's army. His many career successes had made the young officer a bold and headstrong braggart; reticence was not a part of his personality. He was not hesitant about giving his opinions, and considered anything he had to say not only interesting to others, but most enlightening as well. It never occurred to him that anyone would disagree with his views.

One evening in the regimental officers' mess, Marbuk's inflated ego got the best of him. He stated that King Hussein's expulsion of the Palestinians from Jordan was unwise and against the best interests of Arabs. By turning against the fighters for Palestine liberation, the king was helping to maintain the state of Israel. That was bad enough to say in the company of six other officers, but things got worse when he also opined that it was a shame that the king's wife, Queen Noor, was an American. "She may be of Arab ancestry," the brash captain said, "but only a woman born and raised in the Middle East has the right to be the queen in an Arab monarchy." Then he brazenly added, "I do not consider her any more cultured and refined than a fishwife shopping for food in the markets."

This treasonous conduct was dully reported by a couple of other junior officers jealous of Marbuk's quick rise within the commissioned cadre. The regimental commander hated to lose an excellent officer, but unless he took drastic steps against Marbuk, he would be guilty by association. This could not only end his career, but possibly his life. He went directly to the brigadier, who went to the chief of staff.

In less than a week Captain Marbuk had been broken in rank and tossed out of the Army. To add more shame to the dishonor, he was also exiled after being stripped of all his property. Even his family suffered when some lucrative government contracts with his father's shoe factory were abruptly canceled.

The ex-captain, bitter and infuriated, turned to the lodge in his hometown's mosque for help. They too had been unhappy with the king. The best they could do under the circumstances was arrange for Marbuk to go to Syria, where another chapter of their religious brotherhood was located in the city of Hims. The Syrians and Jordanians had been on opposite sides of several issues due to King Hussein's policy of minimal commitment to Arab causes, and the Syrian brothers were happy to welcome Marbuk into their midst.

The lodge was filled with activists who hated Israel and the West with a zealous fervor. Several members of the chapter were well placed in the Syrian government and were most effective in directing those passions. The membership had developed close ties with a burgeoning terrorist organization called al-Mimkhalif that was in the midst of organizing a fighting force to strike against the foes of Islam. When the well-trained, proficient officer with command and staff experience settled in, he was contacted by an operative named Hafez Sabah, who was an agent of al-Mimkhalif. The two became fast friends, and it was Sabah who recruited Marbuk into the group. They went directly to Mikhbayi to meet with Sheikh Omar Jambarah aka Husan, who assigned the Jordanian officer as his field commander. It was at that time that the Jordanian adopted the nom de guerre Kumandan. He was dispatched to set up a training and operation camp in Pakistan. Marbuk and Sabah worked well together, organizing training, logistics, and combat missions. Most of their operations were successful, the one big exception the disastrous raid on the police border guard station. No one had been able to figure out how the Pakistanis learned of the planned attack.

Other operations, while minor, were all successful, and with the arms smuggling running smoothly, the future of al-Mimkhalif's field campaign looked bright. Then things began to fall apart after the defeat of the Zauba Squadron, and the situation rolled back to square one.

NOW Kumandan checked his watch, then turned to the twelve men gathered around him. "It is time to go, brothers," he said. "I do not want you to think of this as a defeat. It is no more than a setback that can be put right."

One of the men shouted, "*Allah akbar*—God is great!"

"That is true," Kumandan said emotionally. "Al-Sahara— the Great Provider and Sustainer—shall guide us through this difficult time all the way to the golden victory that awaits Islam." He picked up his rucksack and slung it on his back, then grabbed his AK-47. "Let us go, brothers!"

They formed into a single column, walking toward the trail that would take them down to the lowlands.

WHALER BOAT
INDIAN OCEAN
VICINITY OF 6° NORTH AND 63° EAST
NOON LOCAL

MIKE Assad had heard his grandfather speak of "the anvil of the sun," a place in the Middle East where the heat and fury of the fiery orb slammed down on the earth like a blacksmith's hammer. Mike was sure he was right in the middle of that proverbial anvil. The only advantage he enjoyed was the strong current, and he was able to run the engine at SLOW SPEED while making excellent headway.

The heat was so intense that taking a breath was like sucking in air from a blast furnace. His exposed hands on the boat's wheel were burned as dark as prunes and were about as wrinkled. The SEAL, able to tough it out, felt a genuine sympathy for Hildegard Keppler. The blond woman was actually getting sunburned through her light cotton clothing. Her lips were chapped and swollen and she sat on the deck of the cockpit, her wide-brimmed straw hat turned down to cover her face.

"Please, Mike," she said in a weak, hoarse voice. "Water I must have. I die for the thirst."

Mike checked his watch, then went to the locker on the port side. He had a padlock on it that had been in a tin box with the boat's maintenance paperwork. He unlocked it and reached in for one of the plastic bottles of water and a cup. He poured a small amount of water in it, and handed it to her.

Hildegard quickly swallowed it, then held the cup out. "Give me more, Mike. Please. I think dead I will be soon."

Mike sincerely wished he could do more for her. "Sweetheart, we have to make this water last. You won't die from thirst at this rate, but if you drink it all up, you'll sweat it out and there'll be nothing left to sustain you. At least you can replenish your body fluids a little at a time."

"You are bad like the sheikh!" she said. "If you don't give me water, over into the sea I shall jump." She reached up and grabbed his trousers, pulling herself to her feet. She staggered over to the gunwale. "I prefer to drown than die so slow."

"You won't drown, Hildy," Mike said, applying a bit of crude psychology. "The sharks will eat you before that."

"Ach, mein Gott!" she cried, sitting back down. "Now horrible fishes to eat me!" She crawled over to the small bit of shade in one corner of the cockpit and began weeping. She sobbed bitterly, her body shaking with the effort.

Mike knew the woman wouldn't last much longer. His conscience bothered him a bit since he had lied outright about her being able to get revenge for her murdered friend Franziska. It would be virtually impossible to prove that Sheikh Omar Jambarah had killed her. Mike's real reason for getting Hildegard to come with him was as an intelligence asset. She undoubtedly had a lot of information regarding the sheikh's operations, ports of calls, visitors, and other subjects that could be fed into the intelligence files.

He glanced at her huddled in the shade. If she got steadily worse, he would give her the rest of the water and sacrifice himself, leaving a note revealing her usefulness to the antiterrorist cause. Maybe that way she could last until a ship turned up. He looked around at the unforgiving environment, then turned to the radio.

"All the ships as sea," he said. "Mayday. Mayday. Mayday. I am at six degrees five minutes north and sixty-three degrees twenty minutes east. I say again. Mayday. Mayday. Mayday. Position six degrees five minutes north and sixty-three degrees twenty minutes east. Over."

He switched off the radio to save the battery, then gave the throttle a little push to get the boat a bit of momentum in the rapid current.

DHOW *NIJM ZARK*
OFF THE PAKISTANI COAST
30 OCTOBER
0445 HOURS LOCAL

CAPTAIN Bashar Bashir and his first mate, Bakhtiaar Ghanem, stood at the wheel of the dhow, staring into the light to the east. They had been silently sipping hot tea as the old boat strained against its anchor cable. Ghanem, as usual, was fidgety and cranky. "I hope they are not late."

"Whatever happens will happen because Allah wills it," Bashir said.

"I am not as complacent as you," Ghanem said. "Things do not always happen through Allah's will. If we are caught by the Pakistani Navy this close to shore, it will be because the people who are to meet us are delayed."

"Either way, it does one no good to worry," Bashir counseled him. He looked upward and raised his voice just enough to be heard by the man standing watch up on the main mast. "Badr! Do you see anything yet?"

"La, Raiyis!" Badr answered. "Nothing."

"I tell you, brother," Ghanem said. "Something has gone wrong with al-Mimkhalif. We have not been called to pick up arms or supplies for them for a long time, eh? Hafez Sabah and that American fellow have dropped out of sight. This bodes ill for us all. Perhaps they are dead. Or worse! Captured!"

"If there had been a serious reversal of their fortunes, we would not have been called to serve them tonight," Bashir said. "You seem to know so much. Have you been speaking with their leaders?"

"Of course not," Ghanem said, "but I am not a stupid man, only an uneducated one. Most of them could be rotting in Pakistani jails this very moment, and if things go wrong today we may well join them."

"I admit that I am not optimistic about the situation," Bashir said. "We were supposed to have warships we could call if we got into trouble. Now nobody has spoken of that for a while. To tell you the truth, I would not be sad about going back to hauling cargo between Alula and Bombay."

"Nor I!" Ghanem exclaimed. "We did not make much money, but we knew we could return home safely unless a storm caught us at sea."

"Ah, well, if al-Mimkhalif is truly destroyed, we will be free of them," Bashir said.

"I told you we should have turned them down when they first approached us with their offer."

"You did no such thing, Bakhtiaar Ghanem!" Bashir said. "You were already making plans to build a big house in Alula when we took on the first job for the mujahideen."

Ghanem shrugged. "Perhaps, but—"

"People on the beach!" Badr, the lookout, called down.

Bashir pulled his ancient telescope off the binnacle and focused it shoreward. He could see some shadowy figures pulling rafts from hiding places in the brush. These were the same floating platforms used to come out to the dhow and pick up cargo, then ferry it back to the beach. They were divided into two groups, each taking one raft and dragging it across the sandy expanse to the water's edge. It took some hard work, but they got the things into the water in about ten minutes, then began muscling them through the gentle surf that lapped in from seaward. As soon as the water was waist deep, everyone jumped aboard and began paddling.

"Sloppy!" Ghanem snorted.

"I agree," Bashir said. "They are not as good as the men who normally pick up the cargo. This appears to be their first time at the task."

"Ha!" Ghanem laughed. "That means these fellows were the big shots in the camp. They sat on their arses while their underlings came to do the hard work. So this is the first time for them to come out to the *Nijm Zark*."

One of the rafts began to broach. As it turned, the riders on it went into a frantic effort of uncoordinated paddling to try to face it back toward the dhow. But the incoming waves, though slow and shallow, were persistent and within only moments, the raft was pushed back to the sand.

Ghanem laughed again, this time with more derision. "Those buffoons could not cross a lake properly."

Bashir grinned and shook his head in amusement. "We may be here for a while."

The leading raft drew alongside the wooden ship and the crew helped the seven men climb over the railing and onto the deck of the *Nijm Zark*. One of them was Kumandan, who looked around. "Where is the captain?"

"Here I am, *effendi*," Bashir said, recognizing the man's authority by his well-tailored uniform. "Bashar Bashir at your service, if it pleases you."

"How do you do," Kumandan said. He glanced toward the beach. "What happened to them?"

"They broached, *effendi*," Bashir said.

Once again the crew of the second raft pushed their vehicle into the sea, then leaped into it to begin paddling. They bobbed awkwardly, not making much headway as they struggled across the undulating waters.

Kumandan growled in his throat, then turned to Bashir. "If they broach again, we leave them."

"As you command, *effendi,*" Bashir said with a slight bow.

The raft began to lag and list a bit, but the riders worked hard until it suddenly straightened up and began moving straight toward the dhow. It took them twenty minutes, but they finally reached the old boat. As soon as they were hauled aboard, Kumandan nodded to Bashir. "Sail to Mikhbayi."

Bashir salaamed. "As you order, so I obey, *effendi.*"

ACV BATTLECRAFT
INDIAN OCEAN
VICINITY OF 6° NORTH AND 63° EAST
1400 HOURS LOCAL

THE collective mood aboard the ACV was one of irritability. There had been a couple of flare-ups between the two assault sections involving Bruno Puglisi and Dave Leibowitz versus Joe Miskoski and Guy Devereaux. It involved some inadvertent bumping when they were changing places between topside and the cabin. Puglisi gave Devereaux a hard shove with a snarl of warning, setting off a spontaneous clash. The situation didn't have a chance to escalate into a brawl, however, because Senior Chief Buford Dawkins and Chief Matt Gunnarson each grabbed their respective men by the collars and pulled them apart with threats of throwing them to the sharks. Lieutenant Bill Brannigan jumped up and locked some heels, delivering an ass-chewing that seemed hot enough to scorch the paint off the overhead and bulkheads. Everything quickly settled down, though Puglisi muttered under his breath for the next quarter of an hour before finally becoming quiet.

Now they were back into the routine, moving at ONE-THIRD speed as Veronica Rivers monitored her scopes. Brannigan checked the fuel gauges and began to ponder about radioing back to the *Dan Daly* for instructions. There was a choice of returning for more fuel or meeting with the combat-support ship attached to the local carrier battle group. After deciding to let a couple of hours drift by before making inquiries, he settled back into his chair and stared out the windshield at the wet nothingness that lay before them.

"I've got a reading, sir," Veronica announced. "It seems to indicate a small craft moving on a heading of zero-niner-zero. Really slow."

"Roger," Brannigan said wearily. "Set an interception course, Lieutenant. Then give it to Watkins."

"Aye, sir," Veronica replied. A couple of beats passed, then she announced, "Change course to one-six-seven."

"Change course to one-six-seven," Watkins repeated. "Aye, ma'am."

The speed remained the same as they moved toward the dot on the scope. Twenty minutes passed, then a smudge appeared on the horizon. As they drew closer, the target shimmered into view. Senior Chief Dawkins, standing topside with his binoculars, shouted, "It's a whaler boat!"

"A whaler boat?" Brannigan said. "The damn thing either belongs in a harbor or to a nearby ship."

"There is no indication of other vessels in the immediate area, sir," Veronica informed him.

Bobby Lee Atkins, standing just behind the skipper, grinned. "I've heard of people getting lost, but this guy's got to be the lostest son of a bitch in the world. I bet he couldn't find his ass with both hands."

Brannigan had just reached for his microphone to raise the stranger when a static-filled broadcast came over the speaker. The voice was distorted by a weak transmitter as it said, "Unknown ship. Mayday. Mayday. Mayday. I am just off your port bow. Over."

"We've spotted you," Brannigan said. "Are you alone?"

The voice began breaking up. "I have one other . . . with . . . we're . . . in . . . shape—" Then the signal faded out altogether.

"The guy must not have paid his electric bill," Brannigan said. "Take us over there, Watkins."

Doc Bradley came forward with his medical kit. "Those folks may be in bad shape."

"Yeah," Brannigan agreed. "Or this could be some kind of trick."

Now Jim Cruiser joined them. "I've heard of suicide bombers going to the extreme, but I doubt if someone would send one out on the open ocean in a whaler."

"Maybe not," Brannigan said. "But get your men out there and put Puglisi to the front with the SAW."

"Aye, sir!" Jim replied.

Within short moments the First Assault Section was on the port side of the ACV, ready for whatever might happen. As Watkins maneuvered alongside, Puglisi aimed the SAW at the man behind the wheel. "Put your hands up, you mujahideen motherfucker!"

"Hey, there's a woman on board with him," Connie Concord said.

"And quite comely," Chad Murchison remarked. "Though rather sunburned."

Jim Cruiser ordered Garth Redhawk and Arnie Bernardi into the whaler to help the two people up onto the *Battlecraft*'s bow. The woman was weak and could barely stand, but the man was able to get aboard without help. He was heavily bearded and wore one of the pakol caps the SEALs had learned to hate from their experiences on their first mission together in Afghanistan. The SEALs also did not fail to notice the man's uniform.

Brannigan came out on the bow, and approached the mujahideen, looking closer at him. "Who the hell are you?"

The man's eyes opened wide as he stared into Brannigan's face. Then he looked at the others in the First Assault Section. Suddenly he snapped to attention and saluted.

"Sir!" he said sharply. "Petty Officer Second Class Mike Assad reporting for duty!"

CHAPTER 18

MIKE Assad sat in the middle of the front row of seats in the ready room. He wore a brand-new uniform that showed the creases of storage. An entire new outfit complete with web equipment and a CAR-15 rifle had been sent over for him from the nearby carrier battle group. The combination of conventional U.S. Navy garb and his long hair and beard gave the wandering Brigand an appearance that was both startling and ludicrous to his old buddies.

Directly across from the newly outfitted SEAL, Commander Tom Carey, Sam Paulsen, and Mort Koenig sat mesmerized as he made a complete oral report of what he had been through since the contrived escape from the American Embassy in Rawalpindi, Pakistan. He took them through the confrontations with hostile slum residents; the help from the mosque; the bus trip; another escape, this particular one from the rural police lockup where he lifted a revolver; meeting the Pashtuns; and finally reaching Camp Talata to rejoin the al-Mimkhalif terrorist group.

Koenig, who was taking notes, kept grinning as he jotted down the discourse in his shorthand. "Damn! Goddamn!" he whispered under his breath from time to time.

Mike's dissertation continued on through the special assignment with Hafez Sabah, the Zauba Squadron, and on up to his escape with Hildegard Keppler from Fortress Mikhbayi and the subsequent meeting with the ACV *Battlecraft*.

"You had quite an adventure," Carey remarked. "And put in a damn good job in the bargain."

"That's for sure," Paulsen agreed. "How about giving us some names and descriptions?"

"Okay," Mike said. "I'll start small and work up to the bigwigs. They are using a dhow for bringing arms to the Pakistani coast. I know the exact location they used, and I'll point it out on the map. The captain of the dhow is an old guy by the name of Bashar Bashir."

"We already know about him," Carey said. "The *Battlecraft* intercepted them at sea. Even though the ship was empty, Senior Chief Dawkins discovered numerous spots of Cosmoline on the deck of the hold when he and Lieutenant Brannigan went aboard to take a look around."

"Jesus!" Mike exclaimed. "You guys haven't exactly been on vacation either. Okay. So here's another name. Commodore Muhammad Mahamat. Does that ring any bells?"

Paulsen looked at Koenig, then back to Mike, shaking his head. "It doesn't do anything for me."

"Well, the poor bastard is dead anyway," Mike said. "He was publicly beheaded for losing a big sea battle."

"Aha!" Carey exclaimed. "That has to be the one where the *Battlecraft* really kicked ass. Can you tell us the origin of the enemy force?"

"It's part of the Oman Navy," Mike answered. "But I better explain some things before you get ready to declare war on that country. The outfit gets extra funds and other goodies through Saudi Arabian sources. The name was the Zauba Fast Attack Squadron. Even the government there has no idea just how strong the outfit is. They thought it was just a small half-ass coastal patrol outfit. But instead of second-hand Brit hand-me-down vessels, the Saudi financiers were able to arrange some modern Swedish fast-attack boats and a missile boat used as a flagship."

Paulsen's eyes opened wide. "Now there's some news. Nobody in the intelligence community had any idea of that situation."

"It don't matter now," Mike said. "It was completely de-stroyed except for the flagship. It is still at the naval base with some of the surviving personnel who are waiting to be resupplied and refinanced."

"That will *not* happen!" Paulsen said forcibly.

"Right," Koenig agreed. "We'll work on that straight-away."

"Sounds like a job for the special section of the State De-partment," Paulsen said. "Dr. Joplin is the man to handle that."

Mike got up to pour himself another cup of coffee, then came back to his chair. "The number-one agent for al-Mimkhalif is a guy named Hafez Sabah. I got to tell you, he's one hell of an organizer. He took over the arms-delivery activities of the group and it's still going like a well-oiled machine. He was educated in Britain and speaks fluent En-glish."

"We have him on a list," Paulsen said. "Any more names?"

"Just two," Mike said. "The field commander for the al-Mimkhalif is a pretty savvy guy called Kumandan. It's not his real name—it actually means 'commandant' in Arabic—but he knows how to organize and direct combat, recon, and security operations. I wasn't able to find out his real identity; they're real careful about that."

"Who's the other guy?" Koenig asked.

"Here's a big one," Mike said. "And I got in good with the son of a bitch. Sheikh Omar Jambarah. He's a Saudi who rules a small but wealthy sheikdom within the kingdom. His clan is in good with the Saudi government for past support, and they ended up in an area that's practically floating on oil."

"The name is familiar," Paulsen said.

"I know about him," Koenig interjected. "He's just one of a list of potential assholes, but now we know to upgrade him."

"Well, he uses the war name Husan," Mike said. "He is the supreme leader of al-Mimkhalif."

"Holy shit!" Carey exclaimed.

"He operates out of two places," Mike continued. "One is the royal yacht *Sayih* that the Saudi government has more or less given him as a gift. It's sort of a permanent loan without a lease. He has a coastal fortress that's nestled along the border of Yemen and Oman," Mike said. "It's at sixteen degrees, fifteen minutes north and fifty-three degrees, five minutes west. I checked the GPS in the whaler boat before I took off."

Carey laughed. "I think that should be sufficient enough for us to locate it."

"Anything else?" Paulsen asked.

"I think that's it, but I'm sure I'll remember other stuff eventually," Mike said.

"Okay then," Koenig said. "You've given us some good intelligence, so we now have some for you." He paused with a grin. "Al-Mimkhalif's field operations are wiped out—at least for the moment. Three different groups of mujahideen made a run for safety, but were intercepted by the Pakistani Army and shot up bad. The prisoners' morale was low and they rolled over quickly under some vigorous interrogation. The result of what they gave up resulted in a raid on Camp Talata by Pakistani paratroopers. They found the place deserted."

"Did they get Kumandan?" Mike asked.

Paulsen shook his head. "No. We figure he got away with the best men after sacrificing the sad sacks."

"Now let's get to another matter," Carey said to Mike. "Give us the scoop on that German broad you've been out boating with."

"Her name is Hildegard Keppler and she was one of the call girls Sheikh Omar kept on that yacht," Mike said. "I showed an interest in her and he gave her to me as a play-mate."

"What did you do?" Koenig asked. "Fall in love with her or something? Is that why you brought her out with you?"

"No," Mike said. "I brought her along as an asset. She's prob'ly fucked half the terrorist leadership in the Middle East. Not all of them guys are devout Muslims, know what I mean?"

"Way to go," Carey said. "She's staying with Lieutenant Rivers right now."

"Let's get her down here," Paulsen said. He glanced at Mike. "Take a break, guy. You've done a great job."

"All in a day's work."

1000 HOURS LOCAL

CAREY, Paulsen and Koenig looked up as Lieutenant Rivers came into the ready room with Hildegard Keppler. Veronica introduced the men to the German woman and they shook hands with her in a friendly, respectful manner, invit-ing her to take a seat. Veronica had no need-to-know regard-ing the interview, and made a hasty exit so they could settle down for an intimate tête-à-tête with the woman.

Hildegard, sunburned and haggard from exhaustion and exposure, did not look her best, but she was still attractive. The trio of intelligence men appreciated what they saw in her femininity. Paulsen began the proceedings with a simple question. "Would you tell us your name, please, and where you're from?"

"I am Hildegard Keppler and from Germany I am," she said. "I was born in the East in the city of Dresden."

"And you were in the employ of Sheikh Omar Jambarah?" Paulsen inquired diplomatically.

"Ja," Hildegard said, her sunburn hiding the blush that crept across her face.

"You performed your duties aboard a yacht called the *Sayih,* I believe."

"Ja."

"Do you know who owned the ship?" Koenig asked.

"Somebody told me the Saudi government."

"I understand from Mike that you had the opportunity to meet a lot of Arab men aboard the yacht," Carey said. "Is that true?"

"Ja."

Koenig took a folder off the desk and handed it to her. "Here are some photographs of some Middle Eastern gentlemen. Would you look at them, please, and tell us if you recognize any?"

Hildegard took the photos and started to look at them; then she glanced up at the three Americans. "A good woman I am! After united was Germany, we had no work in the East. I did what must I do to get by."

"Of course you did, Ms. Keppler," Paulsen said in a kindly tone. "We understand perfectly. We are all men of the world, do you understand?"

"Ja, danke—thank you," Hildegard said. She began going through the photographs, carefully studying each one. When she finished, she had separated a half dozen from the group. "On the yacht come these men."

Paulsen tried not to grin at the Freudian slip. "Thank you, Ms. Keppler. What do you know of the gentlemen?"

"They with the sheikh had many dealings," Hildegard said. "Always big meetings they had with much talk. Arrangements of many kinds, but the things they planned I do not know."

Koenig was extremely happy with the six identified photos. Four of them were Saudis who were suspected of working closely with terrorists while putting on a façade of friendliness toward the United States. Diplomacy and sensitivity in certain areas had made outright accusations imprudent. That situation was now changed. "You have been most helpful, Ms. Keppler."

"I am happy," she said. She hesitated, then said, "My friend Franziska Diehm murdered by the sheikh. Will you arrest him, please?"

Carey leaned forward. "Why would the sheikh murder her?"

"Certain I am not," Hildegard said. "I know that pregnant she was."

"Actually," Paulsen said, "we're planning on doing much more than simply arrest Sheikh Omar Jambarah."

Hildegard smiled through her chapped lips.

WHEN Mike left the ready room, he went directly to the wardroom, where Lieutenant Bill Brannigan and Lieutenant Jim Cruiser were drinking coffee as they went over some of the scheduled maintenance that had to be done on the ACV. The rest of the detachment was out on the flight deck getting the kinks worked out by double-timing up and down the length of the ship. Senior Chief Buford Dawkins ushered them through the activity with rude remarks punctuated by loud shouts of criticism.

Mike snapped to in front of the skipper. "It looks like I'm officially back with the detachment, sir."

"Right," Brannigan said. "How're you feeling, Assad? It must have been pretty rough out on that whaler boat."

"It wasn't so bad, sir," Mike said. "I'm ready and raring to go."

"Good," Brannigan said. "I'm going to put you with the Command Element as a rifleman. That way you'll be handy to fill in when needed."

"Great, sir," Mike said. "I'm anxious for some recon with Leibowitz. I really missed that son of a bitch when I was an acting mujahideen."

"You seemed to have done all right in that outfit," Cruiser said with a wink. "Did you make much rank?"

Mike thought a moment, then a devious thought flashed through his mind. "Oh, yes, sir! As a matter of fact I was a general. I assume the Navy will pay me in that rank for the time I spent in al-Mimkhalif. Actually, I was in command of an infantry division, what with all those tanks and cannons. Twenty thousand men. Oh, yes, sir! A lot of responsibility being a general. I should be compensated accordingly, right?"

Brannigan scowled good-naturedly. "If you keep that shit up, you'll be lucky to get paid in your regular grade of E-five, Assad."

"I understand, sir," Mike said. "How about per diem pay? I had to eat, y'know."

"No problem," Brannigan said. "Put the paperwork in and I'll sign it. Of course, DJMS will forward it to al-Mimkhalif for the funding. Any more questions?"

"Shit, sir!"

"I didn't ask for *comments,* Assad, I asked for *questions*!"

"No questions, sir."

"Dismissed!"

"Aye, sir!"

"And get rid of that long hair and beard, goddamn it!" Brannigan growled, "You look like one of those fucking hippies from the nineteen-sixties."

"Aye, sir!"

Mike wasted no time in heading belowdecks to the area where the detachment was billeted. He had had only sporadic contact with those guys who meant more to him than his own life. Now he wanted to settle back into the Brigands as quickly as possible.

With no USMC personnel aboard the *Dan Daly,* the SEALs had more than enough room to make themselves comfortable. By the time Mike reached the area, the Brigands were back in after the long period of PT administered by Senior Chief Dawkins.

His best buddy, Dave Leibowitz, like the others, was stripping down for a shower, and spotted him coming into the compartment. "Hey, Mike, are you completely debriefed yet?"

"Yeah," Mike replied. "They wrung me dry. By the way, where's the ship's barber on this tub? The skipper told me to get a haircut and get rid of the beard."

"There ain't one," Dave said. "If there was Marines aboard, they'd have a full ship's complement, but the *Dan Daly* is understaffed right now."

Chief Petty Officer Matt Gunnarson walked by, overhearing the exchange. "We've got a field barber kit."

"Yeah," Dave said. "Arnie Bernardi has been doing a pretty good job with it. He gave us all haircuts last week." He looked down the row of racks. "Hey, Arnie. You got time to give Mike a haircut?"

"You bet," came back the call.

Within five minutes, Mike was seated on an empty ammo crate while Bernardi took the hand clippers and began running them down through his beard. Arnie asked, "How you want your hair? Long enough to comb?"

"Naw," Mike said. "Take her down to the scalp. Believe me, after weeks and weeks of this shit, it'll feel good to be a cue ball."

"You got it, buddy," Arnie said, applying the squeaky instrument to the task.

Chad Murchison, with a towel wrapped around his waist and a soap dish in his hand, walked up. "Tell me something, Mike. How does one manage to go off on a recondite mission into the ferity of the Middle East, then return with a pulchritudinous woman?"

"Damn it, Chad!" Mike snapped. "Will you fucking speak fucking English?"

Dave laughed. "I think he wants to know how you managed to go off on an undercover operation and come back with a good-looking woman."

"Oh, her," Mike said. "I met her on the yacht."

"On the yacht!" Dave bellowed. "What the fuck were you doing on a *yacht*?"

"Oh, God!" Mike moaned. "It's obvious I'm back among the peasantry, so let me explain. I'll speak in simple terms so you poor bastards can understand me. I was on a luxury yacht complete with stewards and beautiful women."

"You son of a bitch!" Dave growled. "Here we were all worried about you being off on a dangerous mission, and you were in the lap of luxury."

"Mmm," Mike mused. "I suppose you would really get pissed off if I mentioned my harem, huh?"

"Hey, Arnie," Dave said. "How about cutting off his head with them clippers?"

FORTRESS MIKHBAYI
NOON LOCAL

SHEIKH Omar Jambarah, Kumandan, and Hafez Sabah had just finished a Western-style lunch of grilled-cheese sandwiches, potato chips, and Coca-Cola in the sheikh's office. An air of seriousness hung over the trio, who had been busy formulating the preliminary plans to get al-Mimkhalif back on its feet.

"I do not wish to change the subject, but there has been something in the back of my mind for several days now," the sheikh said. "What has happened to Mikael Assad?"

Hafez Sabah had a view on the subject. "To tell you the truth, I am not sure exactly how smart or dull-witted Mikael really is."

"I am wondering about that too," Kumandan said. "I recall that when he first came to Camp Talata, he appeared to be quite slow. He stumbled with his Arabic lessons and did not impress anybody with any great show of intelligence."

"Perhaps he appeared to be not too bright because of the way he spoke our language," the sheikh suggested. "I conversed with him in English, and while he did not give the impression of having a university education, he seemed to be a clever fellow."

"I will concede him that," Kumandan said. "It was very cunning the way he escaped from the American Embassy. We know that as a fact."

"Mmm," Sabah said with a nod of his head. "Could it be that he was a spy for the CIA?"

"We have irrefutable evidence that he was recruited in a mosque in Buffalo, New York," Kumandan said. "He arrived in camp with several other men who had been there with him. And the letter from the cleric had his name in it."

"There is another thing," Sabah said. "If he were a spy and wanted to escape from here, why would he take the German woman? She would be a burden to him."

"He was a young man raised in America," the sheikh said. "His physical wants got the best of him. One of the women on the yacht said the German told her they were going to sneak away on a picnic. Odds are that after they took the boat, something untoward occurred since he could not handle it properly. They may have drowned."

"Well," Kumandan remarked, "we'll have to forget Mikael Assad for the time being."

"I agree," the sheikh said. "I do have some good news at last. I received word via the communications center that fifteen million dollars from my sheikhdom treasury is being laundered through Saudi banks even as we sit here. The high price of oil is providing great benefits to our cause."

"*Ajib!*" Sabah exclaimed. "Things are not so bad! Fortress Mikhbayi is a strong place with a force of loyal and well-armed men. This is the perfect haven while we reorganize and restart al-Mimkhalif."

"However, we are at risk," Kumandan said. "The women on the yacht are a threat." His outspokenness came to the fore and he glared at the sheikh. "You are a fornicator! It is written in the Holy Koran that one must not go into fornication. It is an indecency and an evil way. Al-Mimkhalif might be punished for your sins. It is also written that the fornicator should receive a hundred stripes of the whip. This is found in the Holy Koran."

Sheikh Omar was only barely able to contain his fury at the bold insolence. "And who will scourge me with a hundred stripes?"

"Renounce your ways and Allah will forgive you," Kumandan said. "And He will bless our jihad for Islam. The women on the yacht must die."

Sabah summoned the courage to say, "I agree, Sheikh Omar. You must atone for you sins. I asked my cleric if I sinned when I took one of the women. He said I could go to Hell, but since I was not sure if it was a sin with an infidel woman and was truly sorry, that Allah would grant me pardon."

The sheikh took a deep breath and was thoughtful for several moments before speaking. "Very well. I will see to it that they are poisoned. Their corpses shall be taken out and fed to the sharks of the Indian Ocean."

WASHINGTON, D.C.
THE STATE DEPARTMENT
1 NOVEMBER
0900 HOURS LOCAL

HUSAAM Sakit, a special envoy from the Sultanate of Oman, glared incredulously over the desk at his host, Carl Joplin, Ph.D. This American Undersecretary of State had just given him some information that was completely illogical and unbelievable. Such a thing could not possible be true!

"All the money for the Zauba Fast Attack Squadron was funneled through the Wusikh Marahid Bank in Riyadh," Joplin had said. The African-American career diplomat referred to his notes as he continued. "The flagship called the *Harbi-min-Islam* and the Swedish attack boats were financed through that same account."

"This cannot be!" Sakit insisted. "The Oman Navy has no

such units. The naval squadron at the Taimur Naval Base is no more than a few secondhand British coastal patrol boats. Their objective is to stop smugglers. Modern attack boats are not needed when one's adversaries are no more than wooden dhows propelled by wind and old engines."

"I suggest you investigate Taimur," Joplin said coldly. "You will find a modern naval base and as I mentioned, a flagship which is a British *Province*-class missile vessel." He cleared his throat. "Ahem! And you'll also discover a few overpaid officers and sailors as well. They and their families enjoy an excellent standard of living far beyond that of the rest of your nation's armed forces."

"If what you tell me is true, then Captain Mahamat, who commands, will be in serious trouble."

"Captain Mahamat evidently promoted himself to the rank of commodore sometime ago," Joplin informed him. "But you will not find him there. He was executed at the headquarters of al-Mimkhalif for losing a battle with an American vessel. A beheading, I have been informed. At any rate, they did shoot down two American F/A-18 Hornet aircraft and attacked a hovercraft of the United States Navy. All our protests will be kept under wraps and the President of the United States will not call in the Oman ambassador. But please inform His Excellency that we expect the situation at the Taimur Naval Base to be rectified. You should also let him know that all this information has now been supplied to other international intelligence agencies. Thank you."

Still confused and mentally reeling, the Oman envoy got unsteadily to his feet and walked slowly to the door.

1030 HOURS LOCAL

DR. CARL JOPLIN slowly drank a cup of coffee as he waited for his next caller. He had made notes of his meeting with Husaam Sakit from the Sultanate of Oman, organizing them into a file on the Zauba Fast Attack Squadron. This was now an official document of the State Department.

A slight rapping on the door caught his attention, and his aide, Durwood Cooper, stepped into the office. "The Saudi envoy is in the outer officer, Dr. Joplin."

"Did they send Hasidi as I requested, Dur?"

"Yes, sir," Cooper answered.

"Great!" Joplin said. "I'm looking forward to a chat with him."

Cooper went to the door, opening it to admit Jaabit Hasidi. The Saudi was a large, corpulent man with a short-cropped beard. His bald head reflected the overhead fluorescent lights as he walked into the office. He showed a half smile, saying, "What can I do for you today, Dr. Joplin?"

Joplin didn't bother going through a useless shaking of hands. "Sit down, Mr. Hasidi." He waited until the large man had wiggled himself in between the arms of the chair designed for normal-sized people. Joplin had chosen the piece of furniture so his caller would be physically uncomfortable. This was one of those times when it didn't pay to be a congenial host. Joplin began his presentation, stating, "I am representing the President of the United States on a grave matter. It is so serious that you may consider this a protest, although the details of it will not be released to the public nor sent through international channels."

Hasidi sighed. "We are not going to discuss the exaggerated subject of teaching hate of the West in our schools, are we? I believe we have already—"

Joplin interrupted in a most undiplomatic manner. "I am not offering you a game of three guesses, Mr. Hasidi. I have a statement. May I continue? Thank you. The government of the United States objects to the overt aggression brought against our armed forces through the direction of a Saudi citizen. The gentleman of whom I speak is Sheikh Omar Jambarah, who is heading up the al-Mimkhalif terrorists using the nom de guerre Husan."

"This is preposterous," Hasidi said. "I personally know

Sheikh Omar. He is from an old desert clan that has shown great loyalty and respect to our royal family."

"He is financing an Oman naval squadron to carry out war at sea for al-Mimkhalif. The sheikh is also brazenly maintaining a headquarters base and various camps for al-Mimkhalif. He has suffered a setback and now he sits in a fortress on the border between Yemen and Oman, licking his wounds."

Hasidi held up his hands in a gesture of astonishment. "Why do you Americans insist we Saudis are your enemies? The kingdom is among the staunchest and truest friends your great republic has."

Joplin continued to ignore the protests. "The President of the United States expects King Fahd to take appropriate action to put an end to this outrageous activity."

"How can His Majesty take action against a phantom program that does not exist?" Hasidi asked.

"I shall report to the President that the Saudi government rejects his protests and warnings," Joplin said. "This leaves him no alternative but to see that appropriate actions are taken. Thank you, Mr. Hasidi. Good day."

"Good day to you, Dr. Joplin," Hasidi said struggling from the chair to his feet. "My fervent hope is that the President of the United States acts prudently and cautiously, lest this situation gets out of hand. That is my advice to him."

"The President wouldn't be interested in your counsel," Joplin said.

USS *DAN DALY*
2 NOVEMBER
1000 HOURS LOCAL

BRANNIGAN'S Brigands and the two crewmen, Paul Watkins and Bobby Lee Atwill, stood at attention as the skipper, Commander Tom Carey, and Lieutenants (JG) Jim Cruiser and Veronica Rivers came into the ready room.

"At ease!" Brannigan commanded. "Take your seats." He waited until everyone had settled down. "All right, here's the skinny for this morning's pleasant little get-together. We're going out to commit some felonies on a mission called Operation Whup Ass."

"Haw!" Bruno Puglisi laughed. "Who named it *that*?"

"*I* did!" Brannigan snapped. "What's the matter? Don't you like it?"

"I love it, sir," Puglisi said, grinning weakly. "Whup Ass is a beautiful name. It sort of tugs at my heartstrings."

"I'm glad you're so crazy about the name, Puglisi," Brannigan said, shifting his attention back to the others in the room. "Now as I was saying, we're going to commit outrageous atrocities and numerous unmentionable acts."

Chad Murchison raised his hand. "What flagitious deeds are we going to perpetrate, sir?"

"Mainly kidnapping," Brannigan said. "Our mission will be to break into a terrorist stronghold called Fortress Mikhbayi and kidnap three individuals; namely, a sheikh, his field commander, and a crafty agent at large. Last night we acquired some satellite photographs of the installation. These are pics that have been around a while. No one took any special notice of them, thinking they showed no more than an unremarkable naval facility."

Mike Assad looked at his buddies. "It's a hell of a lot more than that, guys."

"Right," Brannigan said. "Petty Officer Assad has brought back intelligence that reveals this is no less than the supreme headquarters of al-Mimkhalif. He has given us enough information to get in and out of the place with the least amount of fuss and bother. Therefore, we are able to draw up a rock-solid OPORD. Everything fits so well that we're not going to bother with a preliminary OPLAN. The infiltration and exfiltration phases are the responsibility of Commander Carey. I'll let him explain those parts of the action before we get into the execution portion of the evening's activities."

Commander Carey stepped up to the podium. "It will be a parachute infiltration with T-10s by the raiding party. They will go into the AO in a V-22 Osprey we're borrowing from the nearby carrier battle group."

"Sir," Senior Chief Dawkins said, "who of us is going to be in the raider party?"

"The First Assault Section and Fire Team Charlie along with the Second Assault Section's SAW gunner," Carey replied.

The senior chief glowered. "Does that include me?"

"Negative, Chief," Carey answered. "You will be acting as Lieutenant Rivers' Two-I-C aboard the *Battlecraft*."

"Aye, sir," Dawkins growled in acute disappointment.

"Now," Carey said, "back to the raider party. Petty Officer Frank Gomez will be going in with Lieutenant Brannigan as the RTO. We've acquired an excellent AN/PRC-148 radio with handset so the raider party will have commo with both the *Dan Daly* and the *Battlecraft*. It's been decided to pull Petty Officer Leibowitz from Bravo Fire Team and put him with Petty Officer Assad. They will be the raider party recon."

"Ah!" Chad Murchison said. "The Odd Couple sallies forth yet again."

Doc Bradley stood up. "Sir! Where do I fit into the picture?"

"You'll be with Lieutenant Rivers and the two crewmen of the ACV along with Fire Team Delta on the ACV," Carey answered. "You people will handle the exfiltration. I'll get to that later." He went to the wall, where two large sheets of paper were pinned up. He pulled one down, revealing a satellite photo of the operational area. "Your drop zone will be five kilometers to the west of the fortress. Here. The raiding party will then move to the target area, sneak over the wall, and go to the officers' compound to search out and capture the 'persons of interest' as the cops back home say. Petty Officer Assad knows the place like the back of his hand and will be in the forefront with his buddy Leibowitz."

Bruno Puglisi grinned. "Hey, Mike. Don't forget to take us to that harem you told us about."

"*Knock it off!*" Senior Chief Dawkins roared.

Commander Carey chuckled. "Do not—I say again—*do not* exit the target area with any female captives. This is *not* authorized."

A collective groan went up among the assembled SEALs.

"All right," Carey said. "Once you have those persons of interest in hand, you will proceed to the docking area, where the ACV will appear. This is going to be the hairiest part of the whole evening, gentlemen. The *Battlecraft* is a beautiful vessel, but she's louder than a grizzly bear with a toothache. Although you're going to be heavily outnumbered, you'll have both surprise and the total unpreparedness of the garrison working in your favor. Be fast, be efficient, and be at the right place at the right time. When you're aboard the *Battlecraft,* you'll be able to haul ass at ninety per."

"What are the times of all these different phases, sir?" Chief Matt Gunnarson asked.

"That's going to be worked out later," Carey answered. "In fact, it's something you guys are going to figure out together. And that includes the exact date of when this event goes down."

Brannigan took over. "Okay. Save any further questions for when we're brainstorming together to bring everything into focus. We've got a lot of work to do while Commander Carey is making his final coordination for transport and logistics. Assad has drawn a diagram of the interior of the officers' quarters of the fortress. We'll use that to work out a plan of action to get the main players."

Garth Redhawk raised his hand. "Is ever'body we're after in the same place?"

"Affirmative," Brannigan answered. He looked over at Dawkins. "Senior Chief! Take over and move the detachment down to the pilots' wardroom. We'll have more room to work up there."

"Aye, sir!" Dawkins responded. "All right, me hearties, you know where you're going. Get there!"

The SEALs got to their feet and filed out, their minds already filled with all the possibilities, probabilities, and potential catastrophes and/or glories of their immediate future.

INDIAN OCEAN
VICINITY OF 16° NORTH AND 53° EAST
2300 HOURS

THE waves were not too steep, but the small motorized skiff rocked on top of them enough to make the two men in it uncomfortable. They had to struggle to maintain their balance after the motor had been cut. Five sewn canvas bags lay in the forward sheets of the boat, and the men were anxious to be rid of them. The sooner the loads were in the sea, the sooner the little boat could be turned around to get the bouncy ride back to port over with.

One by one, they picked up the long weighted containers and rolled them over the gunwales into the water. Each sank immediately, slipping into the depths. When the final one hit the sea, the senior boatman went back to the motor and kicked it to life. He sat down and grabbed the tiller, aiming the bow back toward Fortress Mikhbayi.

> *Adlaida from Russia*
> *Blanche from France*
> *Lucia from Italy*
> *Olga from Russia*
> *Teresa from Portugal*
>
> *Requiescant In Pace*

CHAPTER 19

THE fifteen men of the raider party were chuted up, going through a jumpmaster inspection by Senior Chief Buford Dawkins as part of the prejump routine. Although he wasn't going in with them, it had become a detachment custom for him to do all the parachute inspections prior to missions and training exercises. The gruff old salt worked in the light coming off the island on the starboard side of the deck as he went through canopy-release assemblies, quick-release boxes, reserve parachutes, static lines, webbing, and other parts of the proud and proven T-10 main parachutes and reserve parachutes the Brigands had strapped around themselves.

The men were going in lean and mean. Aside from the CAR-15s, ammo bandoliers, and the SAWs for Puglisi and

Miskoski, they would be bringing only night-vision goggles, LASH radio headsets, one canteen each, first-aid kits, personal knives, and holstered Sig Sauer 9-millimeter pistols with one fifteen-round magazine loaded and inserted. There would be no hand grenades or other pyrotechnics. Some communal equipment made up of grappling hooks and nylon line for climbing walls was divided among the group. Frank Gomez had the AN/PRC-148 radio to lug around in addition to the other goodies. That way, if things went wrong, Frank could call in air support for what would be politely termed a strategic withdrawal. Lieutenant Bill Brannigan, pragmatic and outspoken as always, referred to it as hauling their butts out of deep shit. As it was, the skipper had received strict orders not to request air cover unless the situation had deteriorated to almost hopeless. Once again Brannigan recalled the dramatic line from "The Charge of the Light Brigade": *Ours is but to do or die*.

As the preparations continued, Lieutenant Veronica Rivers stood with Delta Fire Team watching the proceedings out on the deck. Her eyes were on Jim Cruiser, whose parachute had already been checked. He was next to Brannigan and the two fire team leaders, Chief Matt Gunnarson and Petty Officer Connie Concord, watching the senior chief as he attended to his tasks quickly and efficiently.

Veronica marveled at the calmness of the SEALs. They were not going into a controlled situation with consoles and cathode-ray tubes to fight with laser- and radar-guided missiles, and it didn't faze them a bit. They were completely blasé about the fact they would be on the ground sneaking bodily into a heavily armed enemy stronghold, having to rely on skill, stealth, and trigger fingers to get the job done. From the look of them, one would think they were in the midst of preparing for a family barbecue.

An engine sound eased out of the distant darkness over the ocean, steadily growing louder until the Osprey appeared in the distance with blinking lights. This unique aircraft could fly either as a helicopter or a fixed-wing aircraft; depending on the angle at which its engine/rotor assemblies were tilted. It was capable of carrying up to twenty-four fully equipped troops and had a range of over 2400 miles. With a maximum speed of 345 miles an hour, it could get its various loads to their destinations in a timely fashion.

The aircraft came in toward the *Dan Daly,* and the ship's LSO went to his station to direct it in. The engine/rotors tilted smoothly, slowing it down, before coming in for a smooth vertical landing on the deck. The pilot throttled back the engines while the crew chief opened the rear ramp to allow the parachutists to enter the fuselage when they were ready to enplane.

Dawkins double-timed across the deck to the aircraft and went aboard to check the preparations for the jump. As soon as he got aboard he came face-to-face with a Force Recon Marine gunnery sergeant. Dawkins looked at him intently, speaking out of the side of his mouth. "What can I do for you, Gunny?"

"Nothing, Senior Chief," the Marine NCO said. "Ever'thing is well in hand."

"Oh, yeah?" Dawkins said. "I'm assigned as jumpmaster for this operation."

"Oh, yeah? Well as it just so happens, *I'm* assigned as jumpmaster for this operation."

"Oh, yeah?"

"Yeah!" the Marine retorted. "This here's a United States Marine fucking aircraft, see? Tonight I'm the guy what's re- ·sponsible to see that it's properly rigged for T-10 exits. And that includes the guys unassing the aircraft. I'm in charge back here from start to finish. Understood?"

Dawkins knew the guy was right. He looked around the interior of the Osprey, quickly eyeballing the anchor line and seating arrangements, then said, "All right. It seems to be shipshape." He turned and stepped back on the deck, taking a couple of strides before stopping to make an impromptu about-face. "Hey, Gunny. Take care of my guys, huh?"

The gunnery sergeant gave him a thumbs-up. "I promise you that, Senior Chief."

Dawkins hurried over to Brannigan, stopping and snapping a salute. "Sir, the aircraft is prepared proper for the jump. A jarhead is aboard as jumpmaster."

"It's their airplane, Senior Chief," Brannigan said. He turned to the men. "All right! Board the aircraft in reverse stick order! Snap it up!"

The men formed up and headed for the Osprey.

OVER THE YEMEN-OMAN DESERT
500 FEET ALTITUDE
0200 HOURS

LIEUTENANT Bill Brannigan stood at the head of the fifteen-man stick, looking down at the dark desert floor below. It was a hot cloudless night and the illumination of moon and stars was bright enough that he could pick out terrain features in the short distance between the aircraft and the ground. Over to his left, the Marine gunnery sergeant, wearing an intercom headset, was speaking to the pilot. He raised his hand, and Brannigan nodded to him. When the arm dropped, the SEAL skipper jumped off the ramp into empty space.

He could feel the static line playing out of the stowage loops; then the deployment bag whipped off his back as the skirt of the canopy played out. The wind filled the air channel and the parachute blossomed and Brannigan's feet hit the ground. He twisted into a perfect PLF, hitting calf, thigh, and push-up muscles before letting his legs go over his head as he twisted onto the opposite push-up muscle.

It was that quick.

He was on his feet in an instant, pulling the safety fork out of the quick-release box and hitting it. The harness slipped off, falling to the ground, and he pulled the CAR-15 off his shoulder. He turned to see the others also on their feet, ready to rock and roll. Mike Assad and Dave Leibowitz trotted up grinning.

Brannigan nodded them a greeting. "How'd it go, guys?"

"I gotta tell you something, sir," Mike said. "We really have to use more altitude."

"Yeah," Dave agreed. "I just started my count and I was on the ground."

Lieutenant Jim Cruiser joined them. "What'll we do with the chutes, sir?"

"Mmm," Brannigan mused. "Roll 'em up and put 'em in the kit bags. They belong to the Marines, so they'll probably come out here to retrieve everything after all this is said and done."

Chief Matt Gunnarson heard the exchange and turned to the men. "Roll up the chutes and put 'em in the kit bags. Bring 'em over here and we'll stack 'em neatly to be picked up."

"Right," Bruno Puglisi said. "Make sure they're dressed right and covered down. The gyrenes are real sticklers about that shit."

Garth Redhawk reached down and grabbed the apex of his chute, whipping the canopy around for daisy-chaining. "Maybe we oughta spit-shine the zippers on the kit bags before we move out."

"Just do what the chief says," Connie Concord, leader of Bravo Fire Team, ordered testily. "And be damn quick about it!"

Within five minutes all the kit bags were stacked in one spot. Brannigan turned to the men. "Column of twos! Assad and Leibowitz, take the point. The line of march will be the Odd Couple, Alpha Fire Team, then Gomez, Miskoski, and me. After us comes the Bravo Fire Team, Lieutenant Cruiser and Puglisi, then Charlie Fire Team. Move out!"

Mike and Dave trotted to a point twenty meters ahead of the others. They had been known as the Odd Couple ever

since the activation of Brannigan's Brigands. The idea of an
Arab-American and a Jewish-American ending up as best
buddies struck the other SEALs as a peculiar arrangement,
thus the appellation.

The column began moving through the night, heading toward Fortress Mikhbayi.

USS *DAN DALY*
DOCKING WELL

THE ACV *Battlecraft*, under the skilled hands of Petty
Officer Paul Watkins, eased sternward from the well out into
the expanse of the Indian Ocean. It seemed strange that not
only was Lieutenant Bill Brannigan not aboard, but Senior
Chief Buford Dawkins was in the skipper's seat. He was not
there to command since the acting captain was Lieutenant
(JG) Veronica Rivers. Dawkins was in the position to be able
to use the radio. Veronica was the only one capable of operating the ACV's weapons and navigation systems, so she
was wearing two hats for the mission.

Delta Fire Team—Gutsy Olson, Andy Malachenko, and
Guy Devereaux—were glumly sitting in the small wardroom area drinking coffee. When the Osprey took off with
the raiding party, the Deltas had looked on in frustration
from the flight deck. It was a hard thing to bear, watching
the majority of the detachment head off to a combat parachute jump while they were assigned to be Johnny-Come-
Latelies, riding onto the scene after the real fighting was
done.

Veronica spoke to Watkins after plotting the course.
"Two-eight-seven, half-speed."

"Two-eight-seven, half-speed, aye, ma'am," Watkins
replied as he worked throttle and steering levers.

The *Battlecraft* turned away from the *Dan Daly,* rising up
on her lift fan to head for the operational area.

FORTRESS MIKHBAYI
OFFICERS' COMPOUND

AZAM Marbuk aka Kumandan sat in his quarters with the lights out, staring across the compound at the eastern wall as he leisurely smoked some of the Turkish cigarettes that Sheikh Omar Jambarah had given him. He rarely slept more than three hours a night, and knew this restless energy had been the driving force of all his life's successes. A lot of that inner strength came from a devotion to celibacy. The ex-Jordanian Army officer could focus a hundred percent on his life's goals without the distraction of lusting after women. Only an occasional involuntary wet dream distracted him.

Not long after arriving at Fortress Mikhbayi, he had informed the sheikh that he no longer wanted to be known by the nom de guerre of Kumandan. It goaded his large ego that his real name wasn't out there to be recognized. Of course, this temporary setback for al-Mimkhalif was something he didn't want to be linked to, so perhaps he was the beneficiary of timing. That could have been something arranged by Allah to recognize his faith and devotion to Islam.

Marbuk particularly wanted his former fellow officers of the old regiment to hear about him directing a large insurgency that was bringing down the infidels' invasion of the Middle East. After a few smashing victories, the jealous wretches would forget their pettiness and demand that he be brought back into the Royal Army at a high rank. Marbuk saw himself toppling the young King Abdullah II's monarchy and being crowned to rule in his place. But before that happened, he would have to see that the sheikh was incapacitated somehow so that he could take over the whole show. A field commander could be easily shunted aside by an ungrateful leader, as had happened to him in his old regimental officers' mess. At the present time, however, eliminating the sheikh was completely out of the question since without the money from the sheikhdom and wealthy Saudi supporters, al-Mimkhalif would be as crippled as a Baghdad beggar.

Allah's blessings on his ambitions were something Marbuk truly expected. His bold chastisement of the sheikh for his wanton fornicating must have been noted in the Great Benefactor's Book of Behavior and Deeds, as was his criticism of the late King Hussein and Queen Noor. Marbuk fully expected the sheikh to go back to his evil ways at the first opportunity, and this would ensure that the Jordanian would be the real leader of al-Mimkhalif. After his death and the two angels examined him as he lay freshly buried in his grave, Marbuk would ascend to Paradise to exist for an eternity with seventy beautiful houris. This holy reward would make his time on earth seem less than a snap of one's fingers.

Contented and optimistic, Marbuk enjoyed the cigarette as he contemplated the moon above the desert.

OPERATIONAL AREA
0315 HOURS

THE west wall of Fortress Mikhbayi loomed just on the horizon, looking shadowy in the dull light of moon and stars. The Odd Couple slowed their pace as Mike Assad contacted Brannigan via the LASH headset. "Objective in sight! Hold up while we check it out. Over."

"Roger, out," said Brannigan's voice.

Mike and Dave Leibowitz felt safe enough to continue forward in upright positions, but at a slow pace. They carefully scanned the terrain around them through their night-vision goggles. Mike had determined that security was lax on that side of the facility from having spent time there, but it was wise to always expect the unexpected. Especially with Kumandan in the vicinity. Mike recalled the al-Mimkhalif field commander had a penchant for suddenly changing routines and procedures. The guy was as restless as a prowling leopard.

The pair instinctively spread out a bit more as they drew

within fifty meters of the fortress. When they reached the base of the wall, they stopped to spend five minutes listening for sounds in the immediate area.

"Silent as the grave," Dave observed.

"You could've used a pleasanter comparison," Mike complained. He turned to let Dave remove the grappling hook and line from his harness. They had already decided that it would be best for Mike to make the first climb for a look-see since he was familiar with the area. He would be able to quickly spot anything unusual.

"Okay," Dave said. "Do it!" He stepped back with his CAR-15 ready as he looked upward for any interlopers who might make a sudden appearance while Mike was hefting himself upward.

Mike swung the hook, then sent it flying upward over the wall. It landed with a clink, and both waited to see if there would be a reaction. When nothing happened, Mike grabbed the line and tugged to make sure it was anchored securely. Then he began going up to the top of the six-meter-high wall. When he climbed over the parapet, he knelt down to observe the interior. The parade ground to his front was empty. His eyes roamed to the spot where Commodore Muhammad Mahamat had gotten his head lopped off. He shuddered involuntarily, remembering the grisly sight. He quickly got back to business, noting that no guards or nightly wanderers were present in the area.

"Skipper, I'm on the wall," he whispered in the LASH. "Looks good."

Back in the column, Brannigan gave the word to resume the march. It took the main group less than five minutes to join Dave Leibowitz. The grappling hooks began flying, then were checked by Mike above to make sure they could support the weight of the climbers.

"C'mon up," he invited them. "The celebration will begin shortly."

Immediately a half-dozen SEALs began the ascent of the wall.

AZAM MARBUK'S QUARTERS

THE field commander formerly known as Kumandan liked sitting in the dark during night hours when he was unable to sleep. There was something restful about the solitude that eased his mind into deep contemplation. Many people with insomnia complained about the condition, but as far as Marbuk was concerned it gave him an advantage over those who required eight hours of slumber a night. That was the time when he mulled over past events and made himself ready for future activities. Thus, when he emerged into the waking world in the morning, the Jordanian knew exactly when, where, and how he would take action on the coming day.

Marbuk stood up and stretched, then ambled toward the window. He glanced out, and suddenly his instincts kicked his psyche into an even higher state of alertness. He grabbed his German light-enhancing binoculars, focusing them on the wall opposite the compound. He could see uniformed, armed men climbing silently and steadily over the parapet, dropping into kneeling positions as each arrived. Marbuk's first instinct was to call out the guard, but he quickly changed his mind. The security force at the fortress wasn't all that sharp. When he took over al-Mimkhalif, there would be no full-time rear-echelon guard duty. Everyone would be a mujahideen, and such soft assignments would be rewards for enduring the dangers and hardships of active combat. Veterans of fighting would be given breaks from the grind by being rotated from operational status to safeguarding facilities when practical.

Marbuk grabbed his AK-47 and a bandolier of ammunition by his bedstead, rushing from the room and across the building to the sheikh's suite. If he could rouse up the bodyguards and catch the raiders in the open, he would receive full credit for saving not only the sheikh's life, but the al-Mimkhalif organization too.

When he reached the bodyguards' quarters, he burst in. "*Faiyak*—wake up!" he ordered.

Alif and Taa sat up in their bunks, coming instantly awake with their bodyguard instincts in high gear. "What do you require of us, *effendi*?" Alif asked, grabbing his Beretta pistol.

"Where is Baa?" Marbuk asked.

"He is standing watch at Sheikh Omar's suite," Alif explained. He and Taa were already getting dressed.

"Just as well," Marbuk said. "He is still in a daze from the attack on the yacht." He saw the trio's arsenal in a glass cabinet on the other side of the room. AK-47s, bandoliers, and even hand grenades were inside. "We are being attacked. Even now a force of infidels has snuck over the west wall. Get your AK-47s and some grenades. The three of us are going to give them a hot reception."

Alif went to the closet and grabbed a pair of combat vests. He tossed one to Taa and began putting on the other. With that done, they went to the cabinet, getting three bandoliers and two grenades each. The latter was stuffed into the vest pockets.

"Follow me!" Marbuk said, leading them from the room and out into the corridor.

INSIDE THE FORTRESS COMPOUND

THE SEALs stayed in the shadows of the wall, moving swiftly and silently with Mike Assad in the lead. When they reached a spot opposite the officers' quarters, he called a halt through the LASH.

Brannigan moved up to join him with Miskoski, the SAW gunner from the Second Assault Section. The skipper was ready to go. "Now's the time. Body snatchers move up."

Alpha Fire Team had been detailed to go into the building with Brannigan and the Odd Couple to make the kidnappings, and Chief Matt Gunnarson led Garth Redhawk and Chad Murchison up to join the skipper. "Ready, sir," the chief petty officer reported.

"Then let's do it," Brannigan said. "Assad and Leibowitz! Take us in."

The SEALs left the shadows to cross the short distance between the wall and the officers' quarters. They had gone no more than fifteen meters when bursts of automatic fire blasted at them from their direct front. The body-snatching detail dropped to the ground as bullets split the air and ploughed up the sandy soil around them.

Muzzle flashes made it easy to see that the incoming was directed at them from the right side of the building. The ambushers had concealed themselves in the palm plants near the entrance. With security no longer a matter of concern, the remainder of Brannigan's Brigands replied in kind to the attackers. A SAW and seven CAR-15s sent regulated automatic bursts of 5.56-millimeter rounds into the immediate area of the vegetation. The body-snatching detail, with their buddies' bullets flying inches above them, hugged the terra firma.

As soon as the unfriendly fire ceased, Brannigan leaped to his feet and led the body snatchers forward. When they arrived at the scene of the ambush, they could see three corpses sprawled alongside the building. Mike Assad took a quick look at them. "That guy there is Kumandan," he said, pointing to one of the corpses. "He was the field commander of al-Mimkhalif. He was supposed to be one of the guys we bring out with us."

"Who're those other two with him?" Brannigan asked.

"They're the sheikh's bodyguards," Mike explained. "There's three of 'em, so the other must still be inside."

"Jesus!" Brannigan said, already hearing shouts from around the fortress area. "We got to get this thing rolling fast. Murphy's Law is now in full operation." He looked back at Frank Gomez. "Raise the *Battlecraft*. Tell 'em we're compromised and step on it!" His attention was next flashed over to Jim Cruiser. "This place is going to be crawling with rag-heads in about a minute. Form a perimeter around here and hold it until we get back with those persons of interest.

If we haven't returned within fifteen minutes, get the detachment the hell out of here to the dock area." Now he switched his gaze to Mike Assad. "Well? What the fuck are you waiting for?"

Mike rushed toward the entrance with the others behind him. He led the way down the corridor, up a flight of stairs, then down to another entrance. Just as they drew up to the door, Baa the bodyguard stepped out. He took one look at Mike Assad, his eyes opened wide in astonishment and dread as the memory of the assault on the yacht leapt suddenly and unbidden into his mind.

"Ya la! Ma tani marra!" the thug moaned. "Oh, no! Not again!"

Mike delivered the heel of his hand into Baa's jaws just as he had done the last time. The ferocity and force of the punch undid all the setting and wiring done by both the doctor and oral surgeon in Salalah. The jaw broke afresh, patched teeth cracked, and Baa flipped over on his back, hitting the floor so hard he was knocked unconscious.

After doing in Baa, Mike continued down the hall toward the sheikh's suite with the rest of the SEALs behind him. Hafez Sabah suddenly appeared from his own room, carrying a Russian Tokarev automatic pistol. The Arab acted quickly, raising the weapon and pulling the trigger. His aim was high and the bullet flew over the Americans' heads into the ceiling. Mike, at the front, had no time to renew their friendship, and he went for the trigger on his own weapon. He forgot the CAR-15 was set for a three-round burst of automatic fire, and the trio of bullets formed a pattern only three inches apart as they simultaneously slammed into Sabah's torso. The terrorist, almost cut in half, flew backward as if a mule had kicked him, twisting in the air before crashing face-first to the hallway floor.

By then both Dave Leibowitz and Garth Redhawk had caught up with Mike, and the three burst into the sheikh's suite. They came to such an abrupt halt that Wild Bill Brannigan and Chief Matt Gunnarson bumped into them so hard, they were knocked forward a couple of steps. Now Chad Murchison, who was bringing up the rear, joined the others.

The place seemed empty.

Mike put his finger on his lips to signal the others to quiet down. He eased up to the door he knew led into the bedroom. "Sheikh Omar! It is me. Mikael Assad. Are you all right?"

A couple of moments passed; then the voice of an obviously shaken man came from the interior of the other room. "What is going on, Mikael?"

"American SEALs have attacked Fortress Mikhbayi, Sheikh Omar," Mike said. "I think you better surrender or you'll be martyred."

"Wait a moment, Mikael," the sheikh said. "I shall be right out."

When the sheikh stepped out into the room, he came to a halt with his eyes opened wide. He stared at Mike Assad, who stood wearing a camouflaged uniform that was exactly the same as those of the other men in the room. It took him a moment before he recognized the shorn appearance of the SEAL. Then the truth dawned on him. A smile slowly formed on his face.

"You had us all fooled, Mikael. Are you CIA or perhaps an employee of a PMC?"

Mike shook his head. "I'm a SEAL in the United States Navy."

Suddenly Dave Leibowitz and Garth Redhawk dove on the sheikh, forcing him to the ground. The fallen Arab did not struggle as they slipped the plastic restraints around his wrists. He was jerked back to his feet.

Mike turned to the skipper. "Sir, the guy I shot out in the hall was another one we wanted to bring out. Now we got only one, but he's the big fish."

"Good enough for me," Brannigan said. "Let's get back to the detachment."

The gunfire outside began increasing with such intensity that the concussion made the window panes rattle. The sheikh smiled. "I am curious as to how you are going to fight your way out of here."

Brannigan laughed loudly. "Hell! So am I!"

ACV BATTLECRAFT

SENIOR Chief Buford Dawkins pressed the transmit button on the ACV's radio. "Raider Party, this is *Battlecraft*. Over." As soon as Frank Gomez responded, Dawkins asked, "What's your situation? Over."

"We're still waiting for the body snatchers to emerge from the building," Frank reported. "We're holding a perimeter right now, but the pressure is building every fucking minute. Over."

"Understood," Dawkins said. He glanced down at Lieutenant (JG) Veronica Rivers, who was monitoring the radio through earphones. The look she gave the senior chief silently conveyed what she did not have to say aloud. The woman was an expert in electronic weapons and navigation, but she was woefully uneducated in handling ground-combat situations. Any decisions on the fighting were the senior chief's call. Dawkins nodded his understanding to her, then pressed the button again. "Raiding Party, we're going to close in on the dock area. I got the diagram Assad made of the facility. It looks like the wharf where that yacht is tied up is the best place to meet you. The ship offers some cover from a large portion of the wall. Y'all will make the decision when to withdraw. We'll be standing by to pick you up. Along with Delta Fire Team, we also got a chain gun to give you covering fire. Over."

"Roger," Frank said. "The First Section Commander wants to know if we can get air cover. Over."

"Negative," Dawkins said. "I've already tried. There's been a change made in the arrangement. Evidently, politics and diplomacy have stuck their ugly mugs into the operation. You'll be on your own until we have visual contact with you. Out."

Veronica concentrated on preparing the chain gun. The First Section Commander was the man she wanted to marry, and if he asked for air cover it meant the situation was deteriorating rapidly. She quickly squeezed off some test rounds and the chain gun spit out a sharp series of the heavy 30-milimeter rounds.

As Dawkins watched her, he suddenly remembered something his grandpa once told him as a boy back on the farm in Alabama. "They's two times you don't want to mess with a pissed-off woman, Buford. One is when she's defending her young'uns, and the other when the man she loves is in danger. She goes from human to female tiger in an instant."

The senior chief eyed the lieutenant, thinking, "Here we got a tigress."

THE FORTRESS

BRANNIGAN led the way downstairs to the first floor of the facility. When they reached the landing, the group almost stumbled over a pile of dead Arabs. Jim Cruiser was standing by, his relief at seeing them evident on his face. "We were starting to get worried about you guys."

Brannigan surveyed the corpses. At least a dozen dead men were sprawled the distance of the hallway. "Who the hell are they?"

"Evidently they live—*lived*—here," Jim explained. "They came from someplace farther back in the facility, armed to the teeth and looking for a fight. We gave it to 'em."

Mike Assad glanced over the bodies, recognizing them. "These guys are officers who have quarters in the building. They were unit leaders in al-Mimkhalif."

"Whatever," Brannigan said dismissing what was obviously no longer a problem. "What's the situation, Jim?"

"We're under heavy attack, sir, and pinned down pretty bad" the lieutenant reported. "I estimate a hundred or so have us under their gun sights."

"My kingdom for a mortar," Brannigan said to himself under his breath. He raised his voice, "We're going to have to fight through the bastards and reach the docks."

"Yes, sir," Jim said. "Gomez has been in contact with the *Battlecraft* and she's standing off the coast waiting for the word to move in and pick us up. The senior chief wants to meet us by that fancy yacht." He quickly added, "Forget about requesting air cover. It's not going to happen. The senior chief said something about politics and diplomacy."

Brannigan understood. "Right now we're invading the sovereign territory of both Yemen and Oman. I figure our CIA friends Paulsen and Koenig have gotten the word to make our presence here as minor a disturbance as possible."

Jim patted two grenades he had attached to his vest. "We found these with those three guys that sprung the ambush on us."

"Hang on to 'em," Brannigan said. "They may come in handy." He turned to the Odd Couple. "Leibowitz! Report back to your fire team. Assad! Stick by me. You're going to have to point out the best route to that fucking yacht."

Dave Leibowitz rushed off to join Connie Concord and Arnie Bernardi of Bravo Fire Team. When he reached his mates, he found them behind cover of some vehicles just outside the door. They were busy returning fire at a point on the rag-head perimeter that continued to sweep the area with hasty, unaimed fire that was dangerous just the same.

Brannigan and Mike eased out of the building, rushing over to a point between the Alphas and Bravos. Mike pointed toward a gate fifty meters to the east. "That leads to the docks, sir. Once you're through there, you're out at the wharves and it's a short dash to where the royal yacht is tied up."

Brannigan looked at the door, his mind going flank speed. "All right!" he said through his LASH. "Listen up! Both SAW gunners and Charlie Fire Team are going to lay down some heavy covering fire. Jim, I want you to stay with them. The rest of us will make a run for that door in the wall. When we get there, Lieutenant Cruiser and his guys will join us while we provide cover for them. When we all join up, we'll go through the door. Assad will be in the lead, and we'll go directly down the dock where that big yacht is tied up. Hopefully, the *Battlecraft* will be there waiting. Get ready!"

Garth Redhawk and Chad Murchison, with Sheikh Omar Jambarah between them, joined Brannigan. Frank Gomez also showed up, knowing that the skipper would be needing him. He hadn't caught his breath before Brannigan ordered him to raise the *Battlecraft*.

"Okay, Gomez, tell Lieutenant Rivers to come in for us." Gomez made the voice transmission as quickly as possible without waiting for a reply. Brannigan once again turned to his LASH. "Get ready! All right! Execute! Execute! Execute!"

The covering fire came on strong and heavy, the slugs from the weapons kicking up dust and slamming into the walls behind the garrison defenders. Mike Assad took off running with the Alphas behind him. Brannigan and Gomez along with Redhawk and Murchison, who were frog-marching the terrified sheikh, all headed for the gate at all possible speed. Because of the fire they attracted, not even the sheikh dragged his feet. His men would think that accidentally killing their leader would guarantee a spot for him in Paradise. Jambarah didn't have that much faith in the martyrdom principle.

The Bravos were the last of the desperately running men. Although it took only seconds to reach the door, it seemed like long minutes. As soon as Mike reached the portal and kicked it open, everyone stopped and began firing to provide cover for Jim Cruiser and his men.

Mike went through the door and immediately came under fire from a dozen guards. He jumped back inside the wall, rushing to Brannigan. "Sir, we're between a rock and a hard place. About a dozen of the garrison guard is out there, and they got us pinned in. We can't get through that fucking door more than one or two at a time."

Now the entire raider party was crowded around the door,

returning fire desperately as their precious ammo supply dwindled like water going through a sieve. Brannigan reached over and grabbed the handset of the AN/PRC-148 off Gomez's harness. He spoke tersely into the device. "*Battlecraft*, move up to the end of the dock. We're getting incoming from out there. Spray the whole fucking area with that fucking chain gun. Do it for sixty seconds on my mark. Wait." He checked the sweep hand on his watch. "Now!"

Suddenly the area outside the wall turned into a roaring hell as heavy 30-millimeter armor-piercing slugs swept through the docks at over six hundred rounds a minute. The SEALs were now slamming their last magazines into the SAWs and CAR-15s as Brannigan monitored his watch. When the sixty seconds had passed, he jumped up and ran over to the door, kicking it open. "Haul ass!"

The SEALs and their prisoner rapidly slipped through the opening to the other side of the wall. Jim Cruiser stopped long enough to pull the two grenades off his harness, and throw them as far as he could at the enemy troops who had quickly begun to pursue them. The two explosions made them hesitate an instant, and Jim rushed through the door. Brannigan sent his last rounds at the rag-heads. Then he turned and joined the others running down the dock toward the *Battlecraft*.

Veronica Rivers could see them coming, happy to spot Jim Cruiser among them. She had to be careful with the chain gun now to avoid hitting any of the SEALs. Delta Fire Team along with Senior Chief Dawkins was on top of the ACV's cabin, firing over the heads of their rapidly approaching mates. As Brannigan and the others jumped aboard the side deck of the ACV, rag-heads appeared at the door of the wall.

Veronica lowered her aim directly at the narrow portal, turning the mujahideen into hunks of bloody humanity that were shaken and pummeled by the searing hot slugs that kicked them sprawling to the ground. When she spoke over the intercom to Watkins, her voice was low and calm.

"Back at flank speed!"

"Back at flank speed, aye, ma'am."

"Full right rudder, forward at flank speed."

"Full right rudder, forward at flank speed, aye, ma'am."

The *Battlecraft* spun around and sped off across the Indian Ocean quickly working her speed up to a very respectable ninety-four miles an hour.

CHAPTER 20

THE facility was not a working farm. It was a three-hundred-acre government property that was far off the beaten track, surrounded by deep sections of forest and bog, and kept under rigid security. A two-lane dirt road that wound ten miles off the main county route was the only way to reach it overland. To discourage wandering tourists who might blunder onto the property, the two creeks on the acreage were not bridged. In order to cross them, it was necessary to enter up to two feet of water through what had been called "fords" back in the good old days of horse and buggies. However, a helicopter pad and a short airstrip capable of accommodating small aircraft were available in the center of the bucolic estate.

The farm's main building was a one-story, split-level rambling ranch house that looked as if belonged more in

California than in the hinterlands of a Southern state. When Undersecretary of State Carl Joplin, Ph.D., had been assigned an office in the place, he was both mortified and elated. He felt bad because the change obviously meant he was as high up in the State Department as he was going to ascend in his diplomatic career. However, he was also happily excited because this isolation was a strong indication that his duties would be channeled into the special clandestine situations he had mastered during his twenty years of public service. This was a career path he found challenging and stimulating.

At the moment, the African-American international relations specialist was taking a slow stroll out toward a wooded area in the company of the Saudi Arabian envoy Jaabit Hasidi. The extremely obese Arab gentleman was obviously not in the mood to go for a walk or take part in any other form of physical exertion. Getting him out of the building to do some unaccustomed exercise was more of the psychological pressure that Dr. Joplin was applying to the man. He did not want Hasidi to be comfortable and complacent; rather he desired him to be ill at ease both physically and emotionally. This would add to the distinct advantage the American diplomat had over him in the state of affairs they were currently discussing.

Joplin's facial expression was grim, close to angry, as he spoke in a firm voice. "We have learned much from Sheikh Omar Jambarah in these past two weeks. And I must emphasize that most of the information he has supplied is very embarrassing to the Kingdom of Saudi Arabia. The governments of both Yemen and Oman are even now taking over a facility he had erected without permission on their sovereign territories. A project, by the way, financed through certain Saudi channels. And I don't know if the two countries are willing to return the royal yacht to Saudi Arabia or not."

Hasidi, with sweat trickling down his wide face, tried to appear self-assured as he lit a cigar. "Any opinions the sheikh states are his own, and not that of the Saudi government, Dr. Joplin."

"He is not giving us *opinions,* Mr. Hasidi. He is providing us with *intelligence,*" Joplin said. "In other words, the sheikh is passing useful information, names, dates, and other most precise data, to the U.S.A."

"The Saudi government can make no comments on what the sheikh has told you until we appraise the contents of his discourse."

"Of course," Joplin said. "But allow me to point out to you that it is obvious to the United States government that Saudi Arabia will be very disturbed by what has been revealed."

"I think this matter must be taken up to a higher level than you or me," Hasidi said. He nervously puffed on his cigar. "My government will also take under consideration that he is under duress as a prisoner."

"All his information has been researched and found to be accurate," Joplin said. "And more importantly, all of it is provable. For those reasons, my government prefers to let you and me work out the details." He let the words sink in for a moment before he spoke again. "As you Saudis know, the American public is most distrustful of your nation. In spite of the TV spots you have run giving them many reasons to have confidence in your friendship, the U.S. public is not buying it. In short, they do not like your nation. They do not trust your nation. As a matter of fact, Mr. Hasidi, much of the correspondence sent to our senators and representatives from their constituencies indicates that angry Americans are suggesting that Saudi Arabia be turned into a glassed-over parking lot that glows in the dark."

"Irrational words from zealots," Hasidi said, dismissing the seriousness of the reactions. "Such people toss nuclear bombs around as jugglers do balls."

"It is true that these people express extreme views," Joplin said. "But it reflects a serious attitude toward your country. The extent of the participation of Saudis in 9/11 has infuriated even the more cool-headed of our population."

"Are you going to make war on us?" the Saudi asked with a snort of laughter.

"I don't think so, Mr. Hasidi," Joplin said. "At this juncture we wish to make *deals*. If we keep all this out of the press and take no overt actions, we would expect concessions from the Saudis."

"What sorts of concessions, Doctor?"

"A sincere and flourishing program of moving against terrorists within your sovereign territory would be the primary one."

"But we are—"

Joplin cut him off. "As I stated, Mr. Hasidi. A *sincere* and *flourishing* program of moving against terrorists. Not just useless efforts that are no more than eyewash. We want to see obvious and positive results."

Hasidi said nothing, looking off over the Virginia countryside, now perspiring more as he took nervous drags off the cigar.

"You seem uncomfortable, Mr. Hasidi," Joplin said in a friendlier tone. "Would you like to return to the house? We should really discuss the final disposition of Sheikh Omar Jambarah, should we not?"

The Saudi nodded silently, and the two men retraced their steps.

TAIMUR NAVAL BASE, OMAN
18 NOVEMBER
0530 HOURS LOCAL

THE bugler marched out to the front of the headquarters building and came to a halt. He raised his instrument in a sharp military manner to his lips and blew reveille. He made a right-face and repeated the call, then an about-face to send the blaring notes out in that direction. Afterward, he brought the bugle down, performed a left-face, and marched back toward the edifice, his morning duty done.

The sailors stationed in the barracks streamed out in their clean white uniforms, falling in formation to respond to the roll calls of their chief petty officers. The crews aboard the ships in the harbor were already doing the same; and that included the missile vessel *Shams-min-Oman—Sun of Oman*. This had once been the flagship of Commodore Muhammad Mahamat, but now had been claimed and renamed by the sultanate's navy. They had no record of the vessel ever being purchased by their government, but since it was in the possession of their armed forces, they made claim to it. So far no objection had been raised from any part of the international community.

The Zauba Squadron, which had once occupied the base, was disbanded. The remaining officers were arrested and charged with treason, but its remaining well-trained sailors were forgiven after placing their hands on the Holy Koran and swearing loyalty to the nation's government. Two young mujahideen named Imran and Ayuub had been discovered living and working in the kitchen of the officers' mess. They were arrested, questioned, and found to be bewildered and frightened. The pair of ex-baker apprentices were then driven to the city of Salalah and dumped out on the streets to fend for themselves.

Meanwhile, antismuggling operations along the Oman coast were brought back to normal—a half-ass program of patrolling the coast in a sporadic, careless manner, replete with bribes and other corruption.

MANILA, THE PHILIPPINES

THE national media had been filled with the news of the arrest of a respected police official on charges of selling contraband seized during raids on vessels at sea. A two-year investigation by a special anticorruption unit of the Federal Police had revealed that Inspector Francisco Reyes had been receiving goods his son-in-law, the late Commander Carlos

Batanza, took from ships hauling illegal cargo within his jurisdiction. The goods included narcotics, liquor, and tobacco. Evidence indicated the practice had gone on for almost five years.

The newspaper articles and television broadcasts noted that the son-in-law had been killed by persons unknown early the previous month. A few days after the murder, the wreckage of his previous ship along with bodies of the crew had been discovered by the United States Navy in the Indian Ocean. The cause of the disaster, which occurred under mysterious circumstances, had never been discovered.

KUPANG, TIMOR ISLAND

ABDURUDDIN Suhanto, owner of the Greater Sunda Shipping Line, sat at the desk in his office studying the new prosthesis on his right wrist. It wasn't a very realistic-looking hand, but a leather glove had come with it. With the covering on it, people would assume his hand was crippled or scarred, not missing. In the Muslim world, that saved him from the embarrassment of having people assume the missing member had been lopped off for thievery. It also made it more acceptable that he had to eat with the same hand he wiped himself with after going to the toilet.

With al-Mimkhalif collapsed and the loss of the SS *Yogyakarta,* Suhanto prepared himself for a long struggle to rebuild business dealings with his former clients. He was blissfully unaware that Western intelligence agencies knew all about him and his activities. They were keeping him under surveillance to see if he might lead them to other persons or organizations "of interest."

Within a few days after he began his comeback program, he was contacted by no less a personage than Captain Bashar Bashir of the dhow *Nijm Zarik.* Bashir, also under clandestine observation, was in the middle of getting back to his old life. Things quickly looked up when a brother-in-law

came to him with a job offer. This one did not involve terror
ists. A highly placed Afghanistan political figure needed an
unobtrusive way to ship opium poppy gum to the outside
world. This type of smuggling was normally done by air
craft, but lately the authorities were having no trouble in
locating the pilots and the airfields they used. Countless personnel, aircraft, and cargo were lost through raids by the po
lice and military. It occurred to the Afghan dealer that one of
the dilapidated old dhows that sailed that part of the world
would be a great way to get the product to market. Since the
range of such vessels would be limited, they needed an in-
conspicuous merchant ship of low value and performance to
take on the cargo at sea and transport it to the final debarka-
tion point in Saudi Arabia for Europe.

Bashir remembered the Greater Sunda Shipping Line's
SS *Jakarta* from the work done for al-Mimkhalif. He gave
the name to his brother-in-law, who came to Kupang, Timor
Island, to make a deal with Suhanto. A business arrangement
was quickly formed and within forty-eight hours no less
than three trips had been made to bring the politician's enterprise back up to speed.

Suhanto earned a big payoff and was able to purchase
the artificial hand. If things kept going as they were, he would
be able to afford one of the fancy models with moving fingers.

DRESDEN, GERMANY

HILDEGARD Keppler was returned to her native
country through the courtesy of the United States Government. Before departing for Europe, she was rewarded with a
payment of fifty thousand dollars, and she told Sam Paulsen
and Mort Koenig that she planned on getting out of prostitu-
tion and opening a beauty salon with the funds when she got
back home.

But before leaving, Hildegard spent a week at Langley,

Virginia, deep in the confines of the CIA. She provided them with an account of all she had seen and observed while working as a courtesan aboard the Royal Yacht *Sayih*. She dropped many names, mostly of Saudis, which gave American intelligence solid confirmation of which subjects of the kingdom could lead them deeper into terrorist groups.

She also told them about the other women on the yacht along with all the particulars she knew about them. This information was sent to their nations' intelligence services for further investigation. Unfortunately, the five had all disappeared. A thorough search of the royal yacht gave ample evidence of their having been aboard, but it was impossible to learn their fate from any members of the crew. It was assumed they had been killed to keep them from passing on any information on al-Mimkhalif. None of the survivors at Fortress Mikhbayi purported to have any knowledge of the harem.

When Hildegard first arrived home, she was closely watched by the German Nachrichtendienst intelligence service to see if she had any more Arab contacts in Europe. The agents noted that at the first chance, she leased a fancy apartment in the well-to-do Üppigschaft section of Berlin, then began advertising herself as an escort service in several local pornographic publications.

A month later she was broke, and looked up her former madam to go back to working ritzy hotels again.

EPILOGUE

SALTY and Dixie Donovan closed the bar for the holiday and hired a caterer to come in and serve traditional turkey dinners to their special guests, Brannigan's Brigands and their families and girlfriends. Thanksgiving was going to be observed in a very special way with great emotion that year; the detachment had returned without a single casualty during their operation ashore and aboard the ACV *Battlecraft*. There was no better reason for a sincere celebration of gratitude.

A total of forty adults and children attended the event, including the newlyweds Lieutenants (JG) Jim Cruiser and Veronica Rivers. Everyone at the dinner had also attended the small wedding in addition to the bride and groom's immediate families. It was a quietly happy occasion held in the base chapel. Lieutenant Bill Brannigan had been the best man and Veronica's sister had been the maid of honor. The new bride was already processing out of the United States Navy, and would be a civilian around the first of December. She was scheduled to start her job as an engineer with a San Diego electronics firm the first Monday after her discharge.

Another special couple was Chad Murchison and his girlfriend Penny Brubaker. She was stationed in Afghanistan with a UN relief team and was on furlough for the holidays. Both were from wealthy families and had grown up together in Boston amidst affluence, luxury, and privilege. But they were not in the least turned off by the plain surroundings of the Fouled Anchor. His SEAL service and her time in the wilderness had taken the edges off their inbred snobbery.

Mike Assad was there with his pal Dave Leibowitz. They were double-dating a couple of National City girls, but everyone kept asking Mike if he'd heard from Hildegard Keppler since he'd gotten back Stateside. His date was beginning to turn cold toward him and it looked like he might not get lucky that night. Dave started to worry because if Mike's girl became angry and wouldn't be in a romantic mood, then his date probably wouldn't either. Luckily, Mike came up with a story that Ms. Keppler was a middle-aged, unattractive missionary working in a refugee camp in Pakistan. He enhanced the falsehood by saying she was teaching girls who had been victimized by the Taliban. The poor children were illiterate, and old Ms. Keppler was preparing them for a life of fulfillment and independence.

Everyone had the holiday season to look forward to, and the only damper on the situation was the new orders that had come down. After the first of the year, the entire detachment would be shipped back to the USS *Dan Daly* in Middle Eastern waters as a permanent assignment. That would mean a minimum of a year's deployment overseas. Consequently, most of them would be taking furloughs to visit family and friends in their hometowns before reporting for their new duties.

Most of the wives would wait for their men in the San Diego area where their kids attended school. Frank Gomez's wife was the exception. She was already four months pregnant and wanted to go home to have their baby in the bosom of her family.

Before they went through the buffet line, everyone charged their glasses while Lieutenant Wild Bill Brannigan, with his arm around his wife Lisa, proposed a toast.

"Here's to the camaraderie we all enjoy as SEALs," he began. "We are honored that our country has called on us to serve her in this great cause of freedom. We don't fight for conquest, plunder, or empty glory. We fight to maintain our liberty and to bring it to others less fortunate than us." He raised his glass. "To the United States Navy SEALs and everything the trident badge represents."

"Hear! Hear!" came the yells as the drinks were downed.

Retired Chief Petty Officer Salty Donovan gave the crowd a look of stern fondness, then shouted, "The mess deck is open!"

The stampede toward the food was fierce, loud, and rowdy in a good-natured way.

GLOSSARY

2IC: Second in Command
AA: Anti-Aircraft
ACV: Air-Cushion Vehicle (hovercraft)
AFSOC: Air Force Special Operations Command
AGL: Above Ground Level
AKA: Also Known As
Angel: A thousand feet above ground level; i.e., Angels Two is two thousand feet.
ARG: Amphibious Ready Group
ASAP: As Soon As Possible
ASL: Above Sea Level
AT-4: Antiarmor rocket launchers
Attack Board (also Compass Board): A board with a compass, watch, and depth gauge used by subsurface swimmers
AWOL: Away Without Leave, i.e., absent from one's unit without permission, aka French leave.
BOQ: Bachelor Officers' Quarters
Briefback: A briefing given to staff by a SEAL platoon

regarding their assigned mission. This must be approved before it is implemented.

BDU: Battle Dress Uniform

BUD/S: Basic Underwater Demolition SEAL training course

C4: Plastic explosive

CAR-15: Compact model of the M-16 rifle

CATF: Commander, Amphibious Task Force

CDC: Combat Direction Center aboard a ship

CNO: Chief of Naval Operations

CO: Commanding Officer

Cover: Hat, headgear

CP: Command Post

CPU: Computer Processing Unit

CPX: Command Post Exercise

CRRC: Combat Rubber Raiding Craft

CS: Tear gas

CSAR: Combat Search and Rescue

CVBG: Carrier Battle Group

DPV: Desert Patrol Vehicle

Det Cord: Detonating cord

DJMS: Defense Joint Military Pay System

Draeger Mk V: Underwater air supply equipment

DZ: Drop Zone

E&E: Escape and Evasion

EPW: Enemy Prisoner of War

ESP: Extra-Sensory Perception

ETS: End of Term of Service

FLIR: Forward-Looking Infrared Radar

French Leave: See AWOL

FRH: Flameless Ration Heater

FTX: Field Training Exercise

GPS: Global Positioning System

Gunny: Marine Corps for the rank of Gunnery Sergeant E-7

H&K MP-5: Heckler & Koch MP-5 submachine gun

HAHO: High Altitude High Opening parachute jump

HALO: High Altitude Low Opening parachute jump

HE: High Explosive

Head: Navy and Marine Corps term for toilet; called a latrine in the Army

Hors de combat: Out of the battle (French expression)

HSB: High-Speed Boat

JSOC: Joint Special Operation Command

K-Bar: A brand of knives manufactured for military and camping purposes

KIA: Killed In Action

KISS: Keep It Simple, Stupid—or more politely, Keep It Simple, Sweetheart

LBE: Load-Bearing Equipment

LSSC: Light SEAL Support Craft

Light Sticks: Flexible plastic tubes that illuminate

Limpet Mine: An explosive mine that is attached to the hulls of vessels

Locked Heels: When a serviceman is getting a severe vocal reprimand, it is said he is having his "heels locked," i.e., standing at attention while someone is bellowing in his face.

LSO: Landing Signal Officer

LZ: Landing Zone

M-18 Claymore Mine: A mine fired electrically with a blasting cap

M-60 E3: A compact model of the M-60 machine gun

M-67: An antipersonnel grenade

M-203: A single-shot 40-millimeter grenade launcher

MATC: a fast river support craft

MCPO: Master Chief Petty Officer

Medevac: Medical Evacuation

Mk 138 Satchel Charge: Canvas container filled with explosive

MRE: Meal, Ready to Eat

MSSC: Medium SEAL Support Craft

Murphy's Law: An assumption that if something can go wrong, it most certainly will.

N2: Intelligence Staff

N3: Operations Staff

NAS: Naval Air Station

NAVSPECWAR: Naval Special Warfare

NCO: Noncommissioned Officers, i.e., corporals and sergeants

NCP: Navy College Program

NFL: National Football League

NVG: Night-Vision Goggles

OA: Operational Area

OCONUS: Outside the Continental United States

OCS: Officers' Candidate School

OER: Officer's Efficiency Report

OP: Observation Post

OPLAN: Operations Plan. This is the preliminary form of an OPORD.

OPORD: Operations Order. This is the directive derived from the OPLAN of how an operation is to be carried out. It's pretty much etched in stone.

PBL: Patrol Boat, Light

PC: Patrol Coastal vessel

PDQ: Pretty Damn Quick

PLF: Parachute Landing Fall

PM: Preventive Maintenance

PMC: Private Military Company. These are businesses that supply bodyguards, security personnel, and mercenary civilian fighting men to persons or organizations wanting to hire them.

PO: Petty Officer (e.g., PO1C is Petty Officer First Class)

POV: Privately Owned Vehicle

P.P.P.P.: Piss Poor Prior Planning

PT: Physical Training

RHIP: Rank Has Its Privileges

RIB: Rigid Inflatable Boat

RIO: Radar-Intercept Officer

RPG: Rocket-Propelled Grenade

RPM: Revolutions Per Minute

RTO: Radio Telephone Operator

SAW: Squad Automatic Weapon—M249 5.56 millimeter magazine or clip-fed machine gun

SCPO: Senior Chief Petty Officer

SDV: Seal Delivery Vehicle

SERE: Survival, Escape, Resistance and Evasion

SITREP: Situation Report

Snap-to: The act of quickly and sharply assuming the position of attention with chin up, shoulders back, thumbs along the seams of the trousers, and heels locked with toes at a 45° angle.

SOCOM: Special Operations Command

SOF: Special Operations Force

SOI: Signal Operating Instructions

SOLS: Special Operations Liaison Staff

SOP: Standard Operating Procedures

SPECOPS: Special Operations

Special Boat Squadrons: Units that participate in SEAL missions

SPECWARCOM: Special Warfare Command

T-10 Parachute: Basic static-line-activated personnel parachute of the United States Armed Forces. Primarily designed for mass tactical parachute jumps.

TDy: Temporary Duty

UN: United Nations

Unass: To jump out of or off of something

U.K.: The United Kingdom (England, Wales, Scotland, and Northern Ireland)

VTOL: Vertical Take Off and Landing

Watch Bill: A list of personnel and stations for the watch

Waypoint: A location programmed into navigational instrumentation that directs aircraft, vehicles, and/or vessels to a specific spot on the planet.

Whaler Boat: Small craft loosely based on the types of boats used in whaling. They are generally carried aboard naval and merchant vessels and are diesel-powered.

WIA: Wounded in Action